LEECHES

David Albahari

LEECHES

*Translated from the Serbian
by Ellen Elias-Bursać*

Houghton Mifflin Harcourt
BOSTON   NEW YORK
2011

F
ALb

For information about permission to reproduce selections from this book,
write to Permissions, Houghton Mifflin Harcourt Publishing Company,
215 Park Avenue South, New York, New York 10003.

www.hmhbooks.com

Library of Congress Cataloging-in-Publication Data
Albahari, David, date.
[Pijavice. English]
Leeches / David Albahari ; translated from the Serbian by Ellen Elias-Bursać.
p. cm.
ISBN 978-0-15-101502-3
I. Elias-Bursać, Ellen. II. Title.
PG1419.1.L335P5813 2011
891.8'235—dc22   2010042764

Printed in the United States of America

DOC 10 9 8 7 6 5 4 3 2 1

LEECHES

Now, SIX YEARS AFTER the fact, I realize things might have gone differently, but back then, on Sunday, March 8, 1998, when it all began, it was impossible to imagine any other way for events to unfold. Also perhaps I made no effort to imagine something different, believed I had no choice, no choice at all, but was instead looking at the inevitable, which I could not have influenced even if I had wanted to. It no longer matters, because what was happening, whether I chose it or not, became destiny, which nothing will ever be able to change. The apple drops from the tree, red and firm, and is nearly hidden in the dense grass, but the ants, snails, and wasps find their way to it, and in the end nothing is left of the apple; the grass will right itself in time. I must be mentioning an apple now because that Sunday, six years ago, I left the house holding an apple, not a red one, true, but yellow, which I later ate, all of it, even the seeds and the stem. To be fair, I didn't actually eat the stem, I held it between my teeth for a time, mashing and nibbling at it slowly, until it finally came apart. I always took a walk on Sundays along the Danube, no matter what the weather, in rain or the blustering *košava* winds. Not even the snow stopped me. It wasn't snowing that day though, nor was there much of a wind blowing: the clouds tumbled across the sky, the sun gleamed from time to time, then slipped again behind a cloud; all in all, it was an ordinary, though chilly, March day. I went out after lunch, at about two in the afternoon. I took the first bite of my apple when I crossed the square, and choosing the shortcut between the new high-rises, came out onto the quay. As I bit into it, the yellowish peel, dotted with golden freckles, resisted for a moment, then burst. Three drops of apple juice sprayed my face: one on the forehead, two on the left cheek. I moved my hand to brush them off, and between my fingers as I was touching my forehead I caught sight of a young man and woman standing at the water's edge. My eye wasn't drawn by their proximity to the river, which could be reached only by wading through the mud or hopping cautiously from stone to stone, no, it was something in their gestures that set them apart from their surroundings, as if they belonged to another world, a realm completely alien to the people strolling on the quay. Whatever it was, it stopped me in my tracks. I sat down on the nearest bench, pretending to stare off into the distance at the outlines of the buildings of Belgrade, at everything but those two people. All that was left of the apple at that point was the stem. I mashed it between my teeth, savored the bitterness, and just then, with no warning, the man slapped the woman. The slap may not have been hard; from where I was sitting it looked as if he had swung more from the elbow than the shoulder, but it might have only looked that way from where I was sitting, the angled trajectory of my gaze; the woman staggered, swayed to the right, as if she were combining the force of the blow with a lunge to evade it, then carried by inertia, sloshed back with her right foot into the river. One could clearly see how the water splashed at her ankle, how her sock soaked up the wetness, how her leg sank into the muck. The man raised his hand as if to slap her again, then dropped it, turned, and walked back to the riverbank. I too turned, but no one else seemed to have noticed anything. The man was soon on the path. He passed close by me on his way toward Hotel Yugoslavia. I watched him until he had disappeared in the crowd. Meanwhile the woman hadn't budged: her right foot was still in the water, her body twisted, her hands at her chest. I thought she might be in a state of shock and that I ought to help, and I was ready to start down the steep slope that ran from the edge of the promenade to the riverbank when I noticed a man in a black trench coat. He was standing next to a seesaw in a playground, staring straight at the woman. To this day I am not sure whether it was the same man I ran into later, but he was why I decided not to go down to the river's edge. Gnawing at the mashed apple stem, I knelt and pretended to be fiddling with my shoelaces. When I looked up again, the man in the black trench coat had gone. The woman had moved: she was wading through the mud, skirting the rocks, until she reached the steps that led to the promenade. She carefully made her way up, one step at a time, as if reluctant to get to the top. Between us was a small playground with a shabby little merry-go-round, seesaws, and a train tugged by a grinning caterpillar. I paused there for a moment, a group of fathers and mothers cheered on the children in the battered little green wagons and on peeling horses, and over their shoulders I watched the woman's progress. The train had made a full circle before her head appeared. She ascended a few more steps, turned to look behind her as if she were afraid of heights, and finally stepped onto the pavement. She glanced over at Hotel Yugoslavia, then looked the other way, toward Venezia Restaurant, and just as a child began to howl when his mother took him off a black-and-white horse, she started walking in that direction. I waited for her to get ahead, then set out after her. I wasn't thinking at all, I didn't pause to wonder what I was up to, I didn't say to myself that I should follow her, I simply put one foot in front of the other, and followed her. I don't know why. I was bothered by the way she had been slapped, though I had no right to be. I knew nothing about her, or about the man she had been standing with in the water, and countless possibilities might have led to that slap, though none, in my opinion, could justify it. She walked faster down the quay, and when she got to the restaurant she began to run. I saw her get beyond the building that used to house the Harbor-master's Office and then I too began to run, but along the other side of the building, certain that I would be shortening the distance between us. When I reached the farthest corner of the building, however, I could no longer see her. I went around to the front, peered into the gallery that had replaced the Harbormaster's Office, looked out over the boats. She was gone. I went back to the restaurant, from where she might have gone in any number of directions while I was circling the building and checking the gallery. I was furious at myself for having made that mistake, though meanwhile insisting that I shouldn't care one way or the other. It was not as if something consequential had happened: a slap, wet socks, silence, a chase. In the context of what was going on in the world, these were niggling details. Exactly, I thought to myself, and gave up. The next afternoon I was back at the corner of the Harbormaster's, ready to scour the streets down which she might have escaped, having persuaded myself that she had seen me following her and that she was not running away from the horror of the slap, but from me, and that I must find her and explain my role, which was not really a role so much as the position of an involuntary extra. I didn't run into her anywhere, of course. I glanced into two or three doorways, ventured into a yard, stopped by an open window, studied some crumbling façades: all of it pointless, I knew, but I couldn't stop myself. I had barely slept the night before. I'd lain in bed looking at the ceil-ing, and every time I closed my eyes, I saw the man's hand slapping the woman's face. I fell asleep just before dawn, and when I awoke, I was more tired than I was when I'd gone to bed. I drank my coffee and had a piece of bread spread with apricot jam. My hands felt heavy, my thighs wobbled, there was a buzz in my head, and it was clear that I would not be getting any writing done that day. I called my editor and told him not to worry, that he would get the piece in time for the coming issue. Fine, said the editor, and hung up. I lasted in my apartment until lunchtime, then went out to the quay. From the place where I'd been standing the evening before, there was nothing to see along the riverbank, at least not where the woman and man had been. I went over to the steps the woman had climbed, but found nothing there either. Several chunks of dried mud might possibly have come off her shoes, as well as a crumpled leaf resting on the highest step, however, the mud and the leaf could tell me nothing that I didn't already know. I went across the quay, all the way down to the Venezia, and then circled back to the Harbormaster's. If she had seen me, or if she had somehow figured out that I was following her, where might that have happened? I never came too close, and anyway there were lots of people walking along the quay and many going in the same direction as the two of us. Why would she think that I, of all people, was following her? Then I remembered the man in the black trench coat. Maybe he was the one who had drawn her attention to me? Nonsense, I thought, but the more I tried to forget the man, the more I thought of him. And later, as I walked the streets where she might have slipped by me, the man in the black trench coat was, so to speak, there with me. I went down Gospodska, Zmaj Jovina, and Karamatina streets, and the streets that crossed them. The only one left for me to explore was the street that ran parallel to the promenade, toward the Golden Oar café. Just then, as I was turning, I noticed a button on the sidewalk at the corner of Zmaj Jovina Street. Black, shiny, a winter coat kind of button, with wisps of thread still in the buttonholes, it lay by a crack that spread across the asphalt like a root. Both the woman and the man had been wearing dark navy blue or black jackets, of that I was sure, but I was also sure that the jackets had had zippers, and not buttons. Besides, the button on the sidewalk was too big for a jacket, so it couldn't have been hers. I started off for the Golden Oar. After a couple of steps, I stopped and spun around. The button was still there, in the exact same spot. I picked it up, then noticed a little sign under it, probably written with a felt-tip pen: a triangle inscribed in a circle, and inside it, another triangle pointing the other way. I put the button down and stood up. I was baffled, I admit. Maybe it was a sign, maybe it even had something to do with the woman, but the tricky part was that the triangle was pointing in three different directions at the same time, to Zmaj Jovina Street, to the Harbormaster's, and to the street that ran to the Golden Oar. The café, in fact, didn't mean the end of the woman's possible movements, even if she had gone that way, because the street ran on, by the power plant, all the way to a newly constructed apartment building. The kind of embarrassment she must have felt heals best in isolation, and if she lived there, she would have run straight across the street and into her building. It's possible of course that she might have turned right by the Golden Oar and come out on the square that is on the way to the open-air market and the Zemun city center, but that struck me as making her route unnecessarily long, since she would have reached the center of town more easily and quickly if she had gone along the streets that fanned out from the Harbormaster's. No one, however, was at the Golden Oar. The door was locked, the windows shrouded with curtains, the stoop littered with trash. For a moment I considered picking up each piece of trash to see if there was still another sign under it, but I soon gave up and started home. The day was drawing to a close, and I needed to work on the article I had promised the editor. These last few months I had been writing short essays and commentaries for the weekly paper *Minut,* and that, with the occasional literary translation, was my chief source of income. Several of my pieces had elicited quite a response from the readers, which led the editor to raise my fee, especially when the debate over my piece on the pillaging of the national museums had spilled into the rest of the press and onto television. Most of what I wrote, I should add, was not so sharply intoned, and that piece, which made my reputation, so to speak, had originated with a good friend of mine who worked at one of the ransacked galleries. The thieves, as I put it, were not criminals in the employ of some rich art lover or the black market, but rather public figures who used their connections to borrow paintings and art objects, then simply neglected to return them. I named a few names—some actors, directors of large companies and members of the Academy of Arts and Sciences, politicians and bureaucrats—and that seemed to draw attention to my column, which virtually no one had bothered to read before. Who cared about my angry tirades on ecological neglect, the lack of investment in culture, the knee-jerk predictability of juries in awarding the most prestigious literary prizes? The list of the people prepared to help themselves to things that belonged to others, things that, as I pointed out, belonged to us all, had far greater appeal. I was pleased, because the editor upped my rate, even if I hadn't produced another story along those lines since then. The obligation to write the articles remained, however, and, like all obligations, became increasingly arduous: it used to take me fifteen minutes to write a piece, and now I would labor over the opening paragraph for an hour. I spent most of the time staring at the flickering blank screen of my computer, miserable that I had to write at all. I yanked sentences out of myself as if I were extracting molars, then raged because I couldn't link them together; the piece wouldn't sound like a cohesive whole, but rather like a series of discordant, differing positions that often contradicted themselves. That evening, however, I wrote my article without a hitch. I sat down, turned on the computer, double-clicked on my word-processing program, and began to write. At first I wasn't sure what to write about, but then up came mud, then the river and the riverbank, the bridges, the quay, and in closing I lambasted our mindset, our traditional aversion to water, and the municipal authorities who have not embraced the fact that the Danube and the Sava rivers define our city. Not a particularly original argument, but there was a certain passion to the tone and rhythm of sentences, which gave me a special satisfaction. Also, that I wrote the piece as fast as I had written the early ones was cause for celebration. I thought about rolling a joint, but it was still early in the day for hashish, so I went into the kitchen and poured myself a little brandy. Outside it was dark. The light of the street lamps shone across the street, reflected off the traffic signs, melted into the passageways and dark entrances. Should I go back to the Harbormaster's? Sometimes one sees things better in the dark than in the light of day. I took a sheet of paper, an old compass and a plastic ruler, and started to draw the sign I had stumbled on under the button. I used the compass to draw the circle, and then marked six equidistant points along the periphery of the circle, and connected every other point, which gave me an equilateral triangle. I measured the sides of the triangle, marked the midpoint on each side, and when I connected those points, I got a new triangle, which was facing in the opposite direction, so that its apex intersected the base of the first triangle. I stared at the geometric figure, sipped the brandy, and shook my head. If there was any meaning in all this, I was not getting it. And besides, why would it end here? There was yet another new little triangle that could be inserted inside the inner one, or, indeed, another circle, and such additions could, at least theoretically, go on forever, and nothing would change, of that I was certain. Or should I, perhaps, have been less certain, should I have been more skeptical? Again I looked at the geometric figure on the piece of paper. By placing the smaller triangle inside the larger one I had actually created four like-sized small triangles, and when earlier I had inscribed the larger triangle inside the circle, I had made three pieces in the shape of apple slices. My grasp of mathematics had always been weak, but perhaps these combinations of geometric shapes, their surfaces, or the proportional ratios had some hidden meaning? The longer I chewed on this, the more convinced I became that the explanation for the events on the quay and

the woman's disappearance lay in these mathematical relation-
ships, and that if I were to penetrate their secret, they would
lead me straight to her door. I remembered that Dragan
Mišović, who had attended gymnasium with me, went on to
study math and, as I had heard at the most recent alumni gathering, he was working at a scientific institute. Dragan had not
come to the gathering himself, nor did he come to any of the
earlier ones, and the person who had mentioned him said that
no one had seen him and that apparently he lived in isolation,
a kind of hermit. Winter and spring, he wore the same coat
and the same shoes, though his shirt was always clean and
ironed and the cufflinks polished to a high sheen. If someone
came up to him, the person continued, they could never be
sure whether Dragan would respond or just stare at them in
silence, regardless of how long they had known each other.
Sometimes, out of the blue, Dragan would start screaming at
whoever he happened to be speaking with, insult them and
threaten to sue them or call the police, and then only a few
minutes later he would grin and offer them the mints he always carried in his pocket. I understood his passion for mints
because I shared it, I remember I said at the time, but as for the
rest of it, all I could do was tap an index finger to my temple
and shake my head sadly. I did precisely that, and the laughter
that erupted brought any further conversation about our old
schoolmate to an end. I slightly knew the person who had spoken of him; I looked up her phone number and gave her a call.
The darkness outside had thickened, it was night. The phone
rang once. At first she said she didn't know who I was, then
claimed she had never said anything about Dragan Mišović;
then, when she remembered what she had said, she said she
didn't know where he lived; when she realized I wasn't going
to go away, she suggested I look at the lists of tenants in the
New Belgrade high-rises located near where there used to be
an underpass. She said she ran into him there from time to
time, but not since she'd moved to Banovo Brdo a few months

before. This cannot be a good sign, I thought. I go looking for a person who is supposed to help me find someone, and then it turns out that, in a figurative sense, I am looking for that person, too. What kind of a world is this, in which so many people go missing? And if they are all lost, what guarantee do I have that I myself didn't get lost long ago? If I had smoked that joint I had in mind earlier, I would understand the questions that were assailing me, but after a little brandy the only thing I felt was my head aching. I got undressed and lay down. Amazingly, I fell asleep instantly and didn't open my eyes until nine the next morning. The sun was shining, and clouds were skittering across the sky, as if racing one another. I got up, and I looked for the piece I'd written the day before. Reading it first thing in the morning, when my mind was empty like a Zen priest's, was the best way for me to gauge whether I'd written a decent piece the day before. A fear of water, I read at the end of the text, is the beginning of all our other fears and a source of general malaise, and until we learn to control that fear, we will be forced, like Sisyphus, to keep going back to the beginning. This was not a particularly original insight, as I said before, but the piece roused the emotions, and when I read it out loud, to feel its rhythm, my voice trembled and some of the sentences crumbled and broke. I didn't know what to attribute such sensitivity to that morning: after all, if someone doesn't like the river, it is not the end of the world. It struck me then that in writing about the muddy riverbank, I was actually writing about the man and the woman, about his hand slowly lifting, then swinging down fast on her cheek, and about how when she came up the steps, she was like a diver rising from the river bottom, anxious about coming up to the surface. The piece of paper with the combined geometric figure on it lay on the table. Nothing had changed, the circle was still guarding the triangles, the triangles were still silent, the apple-slice pieces held their balance on the slippery sides, the peaks pointed in different directions. Had I been at all reasonable, I would have crumpled that piece of paper and tossed it in the basket. Instead I got dressed and decided to go look for my gymnasium friend among the high-rises in the periphery of New Belgrade. But first I had to go to the *Minut* editorial office to deliver my article, which meant heading the other way, since the *Minut* office was in the center of Belgrade, but I saw nothing wrong with that, in fact it seemed to be in sync with what the triangles were suggesting. You must be mad, I said to myself in the mirror as I was shaving, otherwise why would you believe in something that has no meaning? Because nothing can exist with no meaning, I shouted over the buzz of the electric shaver, and because everything speaks to us, it's just that we are not skilled enough to hear and understand. The face in the mirror shook its head but said nothing. I rubbed my face with lotion, combed my hair, licked my lips. I picked up the envelope with the article in it, slammed the door behind me, shoved my keys into my pocket, and dashed down the stairs. In the crowded bus I remembered that I had not given the piece a title, but pressed from all sides, surrounded by unpleasant smells and the stench of sweat, I couldn't come up with one. Fear of Water, said the editor after he'd read the piece, there's no better title. I didn't like it personally, but I kept my mouth shut. You're getting back into form, said the editor, keep this up, and feathers will fly. I had no idea what he meant, and I hoped he was not expecting me to write about a chicken farm. Of course the grim reality in which we were living didn't give me much leeway. Today a river and the river mud, tomorrow chickens and slippery chicken shit, the day after tomorrow who knew, but as long as it was possible to write about something, and as long as *Minut* was willing to print what I wrote, there could be no giving up or complaining. I left the editor and went over to the accounting office. Mirjana, in Payments, was waiting for me with cash. I signed for the money, kissed her on both cheeks to the giggles of her office mates, and hurried off to the Zeleni Venac bus stop and the buses that ran to New Belgrade. The railway line no longer ran between Zemun and New Belgrade, but I knew which high-rises the person who met Dragan Mišović from time to time had meant. The minute I got to the first building I had a problem: the light in the stairwell was out, and the tenant list was hung up high on the wall above the mailboxes, lit by a feeble light that shone wanly through the glass front door, impossible to read. I had to go to the nearest newspaper kiosk to buy a box of matches, then, striking match after match, I studied the handwritten list of names. There was not a single Mišović among them. In the next high-rise the light was working but there was no tenant list. I had to climb all the way up to the top floor, the sixteenth, if I counted them correctly, reading the names on all the doors. Some of the doors, on the third, fifth, and eleventh floors, had no nameplate, so I had to ring the doorbell and ask whether a Mr. Mišović lived there. He didn't live behind any of those doors, nor did he live in the makeshift apartment at the top of the building, adapted from rooms designed for communal use. There was a family by the name of Mišović in the third high-rise, but no Dragan among them. I rang their doorbell, just in case. A boy, about ten years old, opened the door, and when he heard my question, went to ask his mother, then returned with the news that Grandpa Dragoslav was away in Montenegro. Impossible, I said, but the boy had already shut the door. There was one more building that met the loose description offered to me, but after the possibility that Dragan Mišović might have moved to Montenegro, if he was indeed the grandfather the boy had referred to, I wondered whether there was any point in going into the third building. In I went, nevertheless, driven by the urge to be systematic in everything I did, which compels me to line up the books on my shelves in alphabetical order and arrange the plastic bags, cans, and glass jars by size. None of the other entranceways had been clean, but this last one was sickeningly filthy. Heaps of trash carpeted the floor, old newspapers were piled in the corner, cigarette butts strewn everywhere. The stench of urine hung over it all like a thick curtain. Despite the state of the entranceway, there was a framed list on the wall with the names of the people who lived there, and on it, as I struggled to hold my breath, I found the name I was looking for. Dragan Mišović lived on the eighth floor, in apartment number 42. I pushed the button to summon the elevator, but it didn't appear even after several minutes had gone by, so I started up the stairs. When I had made it to the sixth floor, I heard the clang of the metal elevator door slamming shut a floor or two above, and the lit elevator cabin shot by me, hurtling toward the ground floor. For an instant, through the translucent glass, I caught sight of a dark silhouette. I couldn't be sure whether the person was a woman or a man, but I was certain that he or she was wearing a cap. Not until I'd made it to the door of apartment number 42 did it occur to me that perhaps the person in the elevator had been Dragan Mišović. If he wore the same coat winter and summer, why wouldn't he be wearing a cap on this balmy March day? It was too late, of course, for me to race down after the elevator, though I could have called it and checked whether I could detect a lingering whiff of mint. I pressed the doorbell and it announced: *Ding-dong.* I rang again, waited a little longer, though I knew I was waiting in vain, and then slowly, gripping the banister, I headed downstairs. About halfway down, on the fourth or third floor, the elevator passed me on its way up, dark and empty. So it goes in life, I said to the person who had run into Dragan Mišović from time to time, while some are on their way down, others are on their way up. I was thinking of the woman clambering up the muddy bank to the paved promenade, but this I didn't say out loud. There are some things we can always rely on, the person said, adding she was especially gratified to hear that since she had moved to Banovo Brdo nothing had changed in the vicinity of the former underpass. Now at least she knew that she could go back there any time if it turned out she didn't like life in Banovo Brdo, because there was nothing worse than going off somewhere and then, once you had decided, for whatever reason, that you wanted to go back, finding that the place you had left behind was no longer the same place that you had, in symbolic terms, taken with you. Did Dragan Mišović, I asked the person, wear a cap, and if he did, exactly what kind of a cap was it? The person said nothing. Hello, I said. No, answered the person. She didn't remember a cap, though she might well have been wrong and his coat might have so distracted her that it prevented her from registering other details. But the cap, I said, you had to have seen it, unless it was an invisibility cap, in which case the whole person would have been invisible, the coat would have been walking by itself. But that is just how it looked, said the person, because the coat was so oversized it nearly reached the ground, and when Dragan turned up the collar and pulled his arms into the sleeves, it really looked as if the coat were walking by itself. One should keep in mind, said the person, that Zemun is a damp place, and dense fogs are not uncommon. And if Dragan Mišović was sensitive to the cold, and the person thought that he was, though she didn't say why, then he withdrew into that coat as a turtle did into its shell. Didn't I remember, the person asked, how Dragan was always closing the windows in our classroom, even after the teacher had opened them? As soon as the teacher turned around, the person went on, Dragan would sneak over to the window and close it, which would, of course, have all of us in stitches. I didn't remember that, the part about the windows or the part about the stitches, but I didn't let on, just as I didn't know why I'd called this person again and told her how my search for our schoolmate had turned out. My guess is that I simply wanted to talk to someone, and no one else came to mind. Should I ever run into Dragan Mišović, the person said, I must certainly give him her regards, though he might not remember her. Sure, I said, and then I wrote a letter in which I asked Dragan Mišović to take a look at the enclosed geometric figure and tell me if anything was hiding in that arrangement of a circle, triangles, and the pieces shaped like apple slices. I rang his doorbell at nine o'clock the next morning. No response. I leaned my ear against the door and listened. I couldn't hear anything. I rang again, knelt, and tried to slip my letter under the door. I couldn't. I had to toss it into his mailbox, downstairs, at the entranceway, though I'd wanted to avoid doing that not only because of the filth and nauseating stench of urine but also because I was afraid that someone might pull it out of the half-smashed mailbox, and that the letter might get into the hands of someone other than the person for whom it was intended. When we don't have much of a choice, I said in passing to a little boy who was calling to his mother in a squeaky voice, the choice we do have is a good one. The boy fell silent for a moment, then stuck his tongue out at me and fled into the building. His tongue was blue, as if he'd been sucking on a hard blue candy. I walked between several buildings and came out on Radoja Dakića Street, which ultimately led me to the Zemun park, and from there, walking by the high school and the Air Force Center, to the main street. I decided to retrace the streets I had walked the day before. I turned from the main street onto Karamatina. As had been the case earlier, I had no notion of what I was looking for, not counting the geometric figure under the button. I looked everywhere, scanned the walls, curtains, and shutters, wooden and glass doors, and carefully moved aside the crumpled sheets of newspaper or cigarette wrappings on the sidewalk. When I reached the quay, I turned right onto Zmaj Jovina. At the corner, where I had found, and left, the black button, I could see nothing, not even when I knelt close to the pavement. I went down the street and soon I could hear the noises of the market. There was more litter along this street, so I moved slowly, looking carefully around, yet it was by chance that I discovered a new lead. While I was preoccupied, head bowed, with a mess of cigarette butts, I bumped into a woman, who in the collision dropped her shopping bag, full of vegetables and fruit. Potatoes and bananas littered the sidewalk. I knelt to pick them up and, on a step leading to a building painted yellow, I saw the familiar sign. I handed the woman her bag, apologized once again, and when she moved down the street I crouched by the stairs. There could be no doubt. It was that same combination of a circle and triangles. The symbol was drawn on the first of three steps leading to a tall double door. I tried the knob: the door was locked. I knocked, the door didn't open. How many more doors were there going to be like this one? I stepped back and checked out the windows. There was nothing visible through the curtains, which didn't lessen the chance that someone inside might easily be able to see what was happening outside. I continued toward the market, the main street, and the theater, passed a hairdressing salon, a fabric store, a bookstore, and a display window full of souvenirs, and then, when I was least expecting it, I caught sight again of the geometric figure. I was standing for a minute, studying a poster on a large wooden gate, a poster advertising a beginner's course in tai chi, and when I came close to it, I saw that the circular sign, which from farther off I had taken to be the black-and-white Taoist symbol for yin and yang, was in fact the design of the circle and triangles. First mathematics, and now Eastern meditation through movement, who knew where this sign would take me next? The big gate was not locked, I pushed it and stepped into a dark passageway leading to a small courtyard with a bench, two flowerpots with barberry plants, and a water pump. I couldn't remember when I'd last seen an old-fashioned pump like this, with a long handle, and I stared at it as if I had just arrived in a spaceship from another planet. I circled around the pump cautiously, first in one direction, then in the other. Someone watching would probably have thought we looked like a hunter and his prey, though when I looked up, it turned out no one could have seen us. None of the walls facing the courtyard had windows. The courtyard was tucked in behind a building that faced the street. I went over to the bench and sat down, and silence instantly settled around me. I saw every inch of the barberry bush down to the finest detail, as if I were studying it through a microscope, and the gently curving line of the pump handle was so precise that it looked as if it were fashioned from pure radiance. I didn't breathe, or I thought I was not breathing, my heart was beating softly, as if not to disrupt the stillness. I looked up and the surrounding walls seemed to have suddenly lengthened, nor could I see where they ended, though the piece of sky arching over them was still recognizably blue. I shut my eyes. Someone was playing a musical instrument, not in one of the buildings but far away, yet the notes reached me, and somehow I knew they were intended for me alone. The moment I opened my eyes, the music stopped. The glow above the pump slowly faded, my heart began to pound again, my temples throbbed. When I stood up, my knees buckled. I don't know how that could have happened, I said to Marko that evening. We were sitting in his kitchen, listening to *Get Up with It,* a double album Miles Davis recorded between 1970 and 1974, and passing a joint back and forth, a joint of marijuana that Marko had grown the year before near his vacation house in Slankamen. Sounds to me, Marko said, as if you had dropped acid and tripped. Nonsense, I answered, and took a drag, it had nothing to do with earthly things, it felt like ascent and submersion at the same time, like being in two places at once. You're losing it, said Marko, maybe you should stop smoking. He passed me the joint, but I shook my head. There is something strange here, I said, I don't know what, but I'm getting a bad feeling. Like I said, Marko laughed, give it up. He stubbed the joint out in the ashtray. That's not what I meant, I went on, I meant everything that happened, the geometric figure, the way it kept cropping up, my search. Marko said nothing. You know, I asked, what I was thinking before I came to see you? How could I? Marko replied. You're the mystic here, not me. I was thinking, I said, that the man deliberately slapped the woman so I'd see it and go after her, follow her. How could he know that, Marko protested, I mean it's not as if you're famous for taking off after injured parties whenever you witness a violent act to, I don't know, I guess, hold their hand. Hey, tell me, he continued, how many times have you done anything like that in your life? This was a first, I answered. Exactly my point, said Marko, so, no matter what you thought, this didn't happen just so someone could lure you into something, and, by the way, you don't even know what that something is. Maybe this is for starters, I answered, maybe I'll only figure out later what's going on, but Marko didn't want to talk about it anymore. He rolled another joint, put the record on again, and talked about how Miles Davis had made the recording. I didn't listen, I was floating on the waves of the homegrown cannabis, and, somewhere inside me, I was back at the scene by the Danube. Something was not quite right: was it the impact of the blow, the movement of the hand delivering the slap and the woman's behavior afterward, the way she staggered and sloshed into the water? They were not in sync; it was as if something else had been agreed upon, as if the man was supposed to hit her harder, and when the moment came, he hit her differently, and the woman, not expecting it, hadn't had the time to adjust and instead reacted the way they had agreed she would react, as if she had genuinely lost her balance from the blow and nearly fallen into the shallows. What about the man in the black trench coat? Why would he disappear so quickly, unless something had gone wrong, different from what they had planned? I didn't mention the man in the black trench coat to Marko, or he would have been truly convinced I had lost my mind. People who buy into conspiracy theories, Marko had told me many times, have a void in their head they don't know what to do with, so they fill it with junk, and sooner or later, they become victims of sketchy plots, secret organizations with one goal only: to drag that person into something that promises to undermine the very foundations of the world. It was here that I caught on to the sound thread of Miles Davis's trumpet and stopped thinking. Had I been home, I would have fallen asleep, but here, at Marko's, I had to struggle to stay on the surface. I stood up and slowly, as if walking under water, got ready to leave. Marko offered me a bed, which I declined. A challenge is better than surrender, I said. Besides, he didn't live far from me, only three blocks of buildings between us and a small park behind the elementary school, but when I got home I was exhausted, as if I had walked fifteen miles. I will not fall asleep, I thought, massaging my calves, but when I woke up the next morning, it was no longer morning, but noon. I put on water for coffee and dashed out to buy fresh bread and a paper. When I came back from the store, I saw something white in the mailbox. I unlocked it and took out a letter with my name written on it in Cyrillic script on the front, and Dragan Mišović written in Latin script on the back. Only a few minutes earlier, when I came down the stairs, I could have sworn there'd been nothing in the mailbox, and so I raced out into the street, looked to the left, looked to the right, no pedestrians in long winter coats, just one kid wearing a baseball cap, but cap or no cap he was not the person I was looking for. I went back up to the apartment, poured the water into the coffeepot, and made my coffee. Though I was dying to know what was in the letter, I first leafed through the newspaper, perused the articles in the crime section, scanned the cultural listings, and tried to solve the chess problem off the top of my head, without the key. I didn't succeed, though it looked so easy at first glance, but whatever I tried, a solution that saved the black pieces kept coming up, and my bishop was more trouble than help. I put aside the paper and reached for the letter. Once again I inspected my name on the front of the envelope and the name of the sender on the back. The letters were obviously written by the same hand, but why one name, mine, was in Cyrillic, and the other in Latin, I will probably never know. I didn't have the patience to slice carefully through the top of the envelope, so I poked my finger in and ripped it open with a single motion. Unlike our two names, the letter was written on a computer, in Latin script, and printed out on a quality printer. I don't know what this is about, the letter began, but I hope I won't be getting caught up in any more nonsense. What could possibly be hiding in such a simple geometric figure, the letter went on, except the futile desire to make reality different from what it is? Reality is reality, and no path can bring one to its other side, where everything is supposed to be different, closer, I guess, to the truth. But that is something, the letter continued, of no interest to me, so I won't speak of it, for triangles and nothing but triangles are the order of the day; or, I should say, the order of the night, because it is night now. As far as the triangle is concerned there is no difference between day and night, of course, that should be obvious to anyone, but one never knows. People construe all sorts of things, even the possibility that within a triangle inscribed within a circle, or a triangle inserted into a triangle, there are answers to questions. A triangle is a triangle, and that's that. It is, however, true that triangular diagrams such as these, the letter continued, are connected to Möbius's barycentric coordinates, which play a role in the chemistry of color, but there is no additional meaning there that could enrich or facilitate an understanding of the figure (sloppily drawn, by the way). Far more interesting is that a very simple transformation of these coordinates gives what we call the Lamé coordinates. Lamé introduced them in his solution to the problem of the cooling of a prism with a base in the shape of an equilateral triangle, then he came upon the same problem in an analysis of the vibrations of an elastic membrane stretched taut over a triangle, and in the end he noticed that the same equation turned up in the description of an acoustic tunnel with soft walls. In brief, it is necessary to solve the eigenvalue problem

$$\Delta T\,(x,y) + k2\;T\,(x,y) = 0$$

where

$$\Delta T\,(x,y) = \frac{\partial 2\;T}{\partial x2}\;\frac{\partial 2\;T}{\partial y2}$$

is the Laplace differential operator, and the function T (x,y) satisfies a Dirichlet boundary condition: T (x,y) = o along the legs of the triangle. Lamé's solution to this problem, the letter went on, was based on a very broad discourse on the geometries that lead to characteristic functions expressed with the help of sines and cosines. The most incredible, and for me the most intriguing aspect of this figure, the letter continued, is that characteristic functions expressed using combinations of sines and cosines ordinarily appear in rectangular geometries, and not in the triangle. In fact Lamé, and here I'll finish, didn't prove his formula. Pinsky did, using the technique of functional analysis, and there still is no final proof, though it's a matter of days now. And that was it, no signature, no real explanation, at least not for someone who, like me, understands little of mathematics. I read it through once more just in case. I still didn't understand a thing, and I doubt that anything would have changed even if Lamé had been investigating acoustic tunnels with hard walls. I can't believe the letter is serious, I said to the person who had run into Dragan Mišović from time to time, because if it were serious, he would've at least made a stab at articulating things in a manner accessible to ordinary mortals. That's what he's like, the person said, adding that she was certain he was sincere in his response. He simply sees the world his own way and doesn't understand that no one else sees it as he does. In other words, I said, he genuinely believes what he wrote. Just that, said the person, just that. That was how he was, she added, before I moved up to Banovo Brdo and lost touch with him, though there is no reason to assume that anything has changed in his life. We're often inclined, she said, to assume, when we feel like changing, that everybody else is changing too, just as she was convinced, because she had moved to Banovo Brdo, that Dragan Mišović was no longer taking his regular walks near the former underpass, where she had run into him from time to time, or that her neighbor from the building where she used to live had stopped emptying ashtrays out the window, which was, of course, a delusion, because even when we have left a place, nothing changes there, the cigarette butts continue to fly from the fifth floor, the ashes waft through the air, and Dragan Mišović cautiously paces the streets, skirting the puddles, the litter, the cracks in the pavement. So what now, I thought when the conversation ended, what path should I take? The question was, in fact, the wrong one, because I saw no path ahead. I could have gone back and walked along the pathways I had abandoned, but that looked like a futile ritual with no value other than the very act of repetition. So I decided to stay at home for a few days. I got up early, had coffee and read the paper, worked on the translation of a Pinter play in the morning, wrote or at least tried to write stories in the afternoon, and in the evening I sat in the armchair, in the dark, and listened to recordings of John Martin, Tom Waits, and the bands Weather Report and Steely Dan. I smoked hashish and watched it get dark outside. The lights flicked on in apartments, in some places you could see people sitting at tables or in front of television sets, the streets emptied, there was a longer interval between buses coming and going. On Sunday I wrote a new piece for my *Minut* column. There was nothing specific in the text, it was more a description of a condition than of any one event: I started with gloomy sentences about our helplessness to grasp fully the horror of the times we were living in, and went on in even gloomier terms about the helplessness that swamps us when we can't find a way out of the nasty situation we're in, and finally in terse sentences I invoked the void that awaits us. The last word, which stood alone, was "nothing." The editor was doubtful. When spirits are low, he said, people need encouragement, and you're pouring salt on their wounds. Exactly, I replied, but sometimes flagging spirits and a total absence of will become the most alluring alternative, and a new shock, no matter how jarring, can jolt people into shedding the snakeskin of helplessness. The editor thought about this for a minute, then looked again at the text, nodded, and sent me off to Payments. As I left the building it was raining, one of those irritating light rains that you can't protect yourself from. I walked across the square, past the statue of Prince Mihajlo, and all the way to the Café Majestic. I sat at a table by the window and ordered tea. When the waiter brought the tea, I ordered a slice of fruit tart, and when he brought the tart, I ordered a double espresso. The rain picked up and at one point there was no one left on the street; people were huddled in entranceways. The tea tasted terrible, as if brewed from reused mint tea bags; the coffee was better. I turned to look for the waiter, so I didn't see who opened the door to the Graphics Collective Gallery across the street from the Majestic, but when, after vainly twisting and gesticulating, I turned to the window again, I caught sight in the gallery of a woman who, from a distance, looked a lot like the woman who had been slapped on the Danube riverbank and had staggered into the mud. The doors of the gallery swung shut and the reflections on the glass surfaces made it impossible to see what was happening inside. I got up, grabbed my jacket, found the waiter, and paid. The raindrops were ricocheting off the pavement, brimming rivulets coursed down the curbs, and the few steps required to cross the street were enough to get my feet completely wet. I pulled open the gallery door and went in. There was no one inside. Wet footprints led into the back, to a staircase leading to the next level of the gallery, which served as an office and portfolio storage. I studied the art, feigning a lively interest, but perked up my ears to hear if anything was happening upstairs. Only one voice was audible, a woman's, and she must have been on the phone, because she repeated patiently, several times, information about the price of paper, the cost of making calling cards and catalogs, and the stores where you could still buy good-quality pigments. I walked to the other part of the gallery to see who was up there, who was talking, but no matter how I stretched or stood on my toes I could not see over the edge of the railing. Finally I opened the door and started up the wooden staircase. When I reached the top, the woman sitting at the desk moved the receiver from her ear and asked what I wanted. A friend of mine, I said, came into the gallery not long ago, I spotted her from the Majestic, and now I can't find her anywhere. The woman covered the receiver with her hand as if she was about to tell me a secret. No one had come into the gallery, she said, for the past forty-five minutes, which surprised her, she went on, because the gallery was usually thronged with people when it rained, no matter what art was on display, but this time, though it really had been pouring, there was no one there, and even her sister wasn't there, the woman added, though she was supposed to be there an hour ago, way before the downpour. She waited for me to say something, but I said nothing, so she brought the receiver back to her ear. Sorry, she said, though I couldn't tell for whom this was intended. I turned and went down the stairs. I considered pointing out the wet footprints to her, but when I stepped into the gallery, I saw they had been overlaid by my own prints. I left and looked across the street at the illuminated window of the Majestic. Where I had sat, another man was sitting now. He was reading a newspaper, and as though he had felt I was looking at him, he lifted his head and turned toward me. If I couldn't see his eyes from where I was standing, how could I have been sure whom I had seen going into the gallery, provided somebody had gone in? Whatever I try, I said that evening to Marko, winds up being a dead end. I'm getting nowhere, I'm stuck, I added. Listen to this, said Marko, Miles Davis was never finer than in this recording. He didn't say which record he was referring to, and to be perfectly frank, at that moment I didn't care: I inhaled from the pipe he passed and hoped that by the time I opened my eyes I would have forgotten it all. I didn't, of course, forget a thing, and the next day I set out again for Zmaj Jovina Street, but no matter how hard I looked, I couldn't find a single sign. First I thought the rain might have washed them away, then I was alarmed by the idea that it was not the rain, but that someone was regularly, carefully wiping them away, removing any trace. Someone was drawing the signs, I thought, to warn someone of something or to alert someone to an event, and once the event had occurred, the signs are destroyed or concealed, thereby reducing the likelihood they would be misused. It is possible, I thought as I stood at one end of the Zemun market, that the same person was doing both, but more likely two different persons were involved, or perhaps more, and a third was coordinating, scheduling the time for the new signs to appear and to disappear. The air was humming with the bustle of the marketplace while my head spun with images of mystical gatherings of a secret society, where everyone wore masks or, at the very least, dark glasses, and conversed through the deft movement of their fingers. These visions, of course, were silly, but I could think of nothing else. I went through the section of the marketplace where dairy products were sold, and I tasted the farmer's cheese and sour cream at three or four stalls, then went back to Zmaj Jovina and bought a crescent roll at a bakery. The poster for the beginner's class in tai chi was still hanging on the old wooden gate, but now there was no symbol on it. I ate the roll, pushed open the heavy gate, walked through the passageway and into the courtyard. Everything was just as it had been before: the bench, the flowerpots with the barberry bushes, the water pump with the curved handle, and when I sat down and shut my eyes, the silence enveloped me again. This time, however, I heard no music, but someone, a man or a boy, singing. He sang in a soft voice, in a language I didn't know, and the voice faltered, as if at any moment he might sob. The song was not sad, but not happy either, and it spoke, I was sure, of some terrible event, an immeasurable loss, but one over which there was no point in grieving. I could have stayed there forever, eyes shut, given over to that voice, but someone coughed, the voice was gone, and when I opened my eyes I saw the woman from the riverbank. I saw her; she apparently had not seen me. She walked across the courtyard as if moving through some other space, separate from the space I inhabited. This fact, if someone's invisibility can be called a fact, struck me dumb, though everything in me was straining to speak. In several strides the woman crossed the paved courtyard and faded into the twilight of the passageway toward Zmaj Jovina Street, and when I finally pulled myself together and hurried after her, she had disappeared among the people on their way to the marketplace or returning with their arms laden. I went back to the stone courtyard. She probably came out of the building facing the courtyard, I later told Marko, though the roster of tenants listing ages and professions showed that pensioners or couples with small children lived in all the apartments. Marko took a drag on the joint and handed it to me. What would have happened if she had seen you, he said. I don't know, I said, and passed the joint back, maybe we would have talked, and maybe I would have finally learned her name. A name means nothing, said Marko. As far as that goes, call her what you like. No, I said, because it's one thing if her name is Violeta, and something quite different if her name is Marta. Her name cannot be Marta, Marko protested, who is called Marta these days? You would be surprised, I said, this spring I actually met three women called Marta. Marko stared at me, burst out laughing, then turned very serious. Life is short, he said, you know? I shook my head. We will live forever, I said, but I could see he didn't believe me. I didn't, in fact, believe myself. What had been happening around us the past few years convinced me that my life was, for all intents and purposes, over, that I was now living at a later time, in a life with no life. The war, inflation, poverty, political terror, hatred, all of that confirmed the berserk nature of the world that was supposed to be my home. Marko was right: you couldn't imagine living like that forever. Forever dead, possibly, but at its best life was an accumulation of fragments, a makeshift raft barely afloat. Am I sinking, I asked Marko, or does it just feel that way? Marko didn't answer. He closed his eyes, leaned his head against the wall, crossed his hands in his lap. With the tip of his tongue he touched his upper lip. All I want, I said, is to understand what's going on. Not the war, I hurried to add when I saw Marko's raised eyebrows, not the war, I will never be able to understand that, I gave up trying long ago, but the thing on the Danube, the reality or absurdity of the slap, the meaning of the circle around the triangle, the song I heard in the courtyard on Zmaj Jovina Street. Marko sat there, silent. Nothing exists alone, I said, everything is interconnected, everything is part of a larger or smaller web, which in turn is part of ever larger webs, and so it goes, until the whole world is woven together, and the one who weaves that last web knows the structure of all the others, but the ones who are creating the smaller webs know nothing about them and get snared in them, not realizing what they mean and where they are leading. In its own web, Marko said, a spider is a spider, but in someone else's web that same spider is just another fly. True, I said, except that I am not keen on being a fly or a spider, and the sticky web of our reality from which no one seems able to break loose is all I can handle. I'm with you totally, said Marko, and shut his eyes again. I wondered where the joint had gone to: had Marko swallowed it? The door opens for one who knocks, said Marko, and one who rends the webs will pass between them. He straightened up, turned toward me, and I saw the joint: stubbed out, squashed, slightly matted in hair, tucked behind Marko's right ear. Maybe, I said, just maybe it's wrong to say she went by *as if* she hadn't seen me, maybe she genuinely didn't see me, maybe back there in that corner I was invisible, hidden who knows how from the rest of the world? You're crazy, said Marko, though I understand the urge to become the invisible man. Better the invisible man than Batman, I replied, and slipped out the door to avoid Marko's tirade about comic book characters and their symbolic meaning. The chill darkness awaited me outside, or I would have gone straight to the courtyard at Zmaj Jovina. Early the next morning, it may have been before six, the phone rang, and continued to ring so insistently that I had to get up and stumble over to the side table in the living room, but when I finally lifted the receiver, there was no one there, and a few seconds later I heard the click of the connection being broken. I went back to bed but couldn't sleep. I tried to read; alas, that magical formula for falling asleep works only in the wee hours, not in the early morning. Actually, the book I had picked up to read, which described the system of German concentration camps during World War II, made me even more awake. I finally got up at seven with a grinding headache, dressed, put water on for coffee, went down to buy my paper. Hardly anyone bought the newspapers anymore because the news they carried and the accompanying commentary were so predictable, but the morning reading of the paper with a cup of black coffee was a ritual I could not relinquish. It was better than watching television, which never ceased to be a source of official propaganda, a parade of bizarre creatures often of stunted intellectual capacity. The newspapers were different: you could always skip the first pages and focus on the sections about life in the city, practical advice, and sports; on the other hand, even in the first section, there was the chance that a journalist might slip in a subversive twist, a tiny signal that reality was not what the government claimed it to be, and the search for those twists provided an appealing intellectual game, as long, of course, as the reader didn't have a headache. So I gave myself over to the pages with the obituaries, neutral enough for the pain assaulting my forehead and temples. Death, judging by the obits, was busy those days, as usual discriminating in no way among gender, age, or place of residence. The faces, old and young, male and female, even children, looked me straight in the eyes, as if it were my fault that they were there, offered briefly to a world that had never cared about them. I sipped my coffee and turned to the section with the personals and classifieds. The small number of readers meant a small number of ads, and under the heading Miscellaneous there were only two. The first offered a universal product for the cleaning and repair of scratched autobodies, which, it said, was not the only way this product could be used. The second ad read: Sometimes a slap can change the entire cosmos—Code Palm. I stared at the words, unable to believe my eyes, though I was certain they were written for me alone. Again I saw the woman stagger and the man say something savage, which, I sensed, had startled her. Something had been set in advance, had not gone according to plan, and at that moment the cosmos had begun to collapse for all of us, to shed the skin containing it. One question, however, still begged to be answered: Why was all this being played out before me? What could I possibly mean to the people who had devised the game? I was not caught up in any political shenanigans, I had no friends in high places in the government or cultural institutions, I had no ties to international humanitarian organizations, at times I didn't even know my own name. Perhaps this was all a mistake, it suddenly hit me, as I was still poring over the ads page, maybe they had confused me with someone else, an important writer or professor, someone they needed to communicate with or draw into a tangled game from which, in fact, it would be best to flee, and fast. I poured more coffee, sipped the cold liquid, and sat back in the chair. Even if it's a mistake, to whom should I report it? If I don't know who made the mistake, how can I tell that person to stop bothering me? I looked at the ad. My headache had meanwhile receded, leaving only a small knot on the right temple. I pressed my index finger to it, and the dull throb made me suck in my breath. Then I stood up and went over to the computer to write a message using the code word *Palm*. After thinking about it at length and after several dozen trial sentences, I wrote, I know what a slap that can destroy the entire cosmos looks like. I was there, and I heard the sound that the cosmos releases as it dies. I haven't told anyone, I lied, because some things must never be said out loud, but now I am convinced the time has come for the cosmos to be renewed. I gave my phone number, tucked the message into an envelope, and sealed it. My message, I had to admit, sounded ridiculously naive and immature, but that, I consoled myself, was how the ad had sounded too. It wouldn't surprise me, I thought, if in the end aging hippies, equipped with sticks of incense, showed up with stories about good vibes and disturbances to the equilibrium of the world. The slap from the ad suddenly sounded like the question about one hand clapping, one of those essential Zen questions that had a huge influence on the hippy movement. I lifted my hand and stared at the palm. Marko laughed when he heard my story. I stopped in to see him after I had dropped the envelope off at the *Politika* personal ad department. If he understood correctly what was going on, Marko said, I was obviously slowly sinking into madness. Either that woman, he continued, scrambled your brain, or you scrambled your own brain and are making up stories, which, no matter what happened, treat everything as if it were part of a big plot. Either everything is interconnected with everything else, I replied, or nothing is interconnected with anything; there's no third way, but if I had to choose I would choose the former, because even if it were plausible no one could keep the latter going, and faced with that level of chaos, I said, we would collapse. You just might think about not smoking, Marko said, and passed me the joint. Drunks see white mice, and people who get hooked on cannabis see conspiracies. Sometimes you talk too much, I said. Marko closed his eyes and stretched out on the couch. That's because, he said, I haven't found anyone to be silent with. Not long after I heard his deep breathing, I found a blanket, covered him, switched off the light, and left the apartment, pulling the door shut behind me. It was raining outside and I made my way slowly through the pedestrians with umbrellas, so it was much later—I'd nearly made it home—when I realized that as I'd left Marko's building I passed a man in a black trench coat. When I spun around there was no one behind me. If he was following me, the man in the black trench coat was exceptionally clever. I stood a while longer at the entranceway, surveyed the street, but saw no one wearing a black trench coat or taking an interest in me. The damp crept under my clothes, invaded my body, and robbed me of my warmth, but I waited patiently until my teeth were chattering. The next days I didn't venture out. The damp and cold did their work, and I had to surrender to aspirin and hot tea. Colds usually put me in a vile mood, but this time I was glad to stay home, because that way I could be sure not to miss the call of the person who had placed the ad in *Politika*. Three days later, with the cold letting up, I began to doubt the call would ever come, so I was all the more surprised when on Tuesday, I think it was, a man's voice at the other end of the line said he was calling in response to my response to the ad. He was curious, he said, about where I had heard the sound of the cosmos dying. On the riverbank, I said, where else could I have been? And the sound, he asked, what was the sound like? Unique, I answered. I understand, said the voice, which had suddenly gone still; then he asked whether I was sure I'd told no one. No one, I lied again. Not even your parents? the voice insisted. My parents are dead, I said. The voice went still again, then apologized in case he had upset me, adding that then I indeed did know how the cosmos dies. But now the moment has come for it to be reborn, I said, hasn't it? The voice asked how I would do that. I'd be gentle, I said, and I would never raise my voice. Good, said the voice. For a moment I thought he would not speak again. Might you, the voice inquired, go to the same place this evening? Sure, I said. At eight, said the voice, and hung up. I held the receiver to my ear a little longer, as if the pulsing of the telephone signal could explain something. Beyond the signal, somewhere very far away, I could hear inarticulate fragments of a conversation, and then they too faded. I put down the receiver and looked at the clock. I had more than two hours until the meeting, if we were thinking of the same place, that is: the quay next to the playground. I didn't want to believe that this might be a mis-understanding, a different slap altogether and a second, or a third, cosmos, so when the time came to leave, I grabbed my jacket and headed for the quay. The promenade at that time of day was full of people, despite the black clouds careening through the dark sky, which made it all the more difficult for me to keep an eye out for the person I was supposed to be meeting. The man I had spoken to on the phone sounded like someone who was getting on in years, though that impression might have been wrong, he could have been a young man with his voice altered by an old or damaged phone. Of course I might sound, and probably did sound, entirely different over the phone, and so the feeling of mutual betrayal was only to be expected. For that reason, and perhaps out of insecurity, I decided to go around the high-rise and approach on a trans-versal the shabby merry-go-round, from which came the sound of children shrieking, through a dark parking lot and between rows of cars. Along the bank, among the trees, as well as near the apartment buildings, especially by the high-rises, there were oases of dark shadows in which it would be possible to hide, though I could not imagine why someone who wanted to meet me would want to hide. I got closer to the playground, stepped onto the path, and turned right, toward the bench on which I'd sat then, and the bench, like all the rest, was taken, so I decided to stand right there, staring at the river and the glow of Belgrade, and wait. Fifteen minutes later I told myself I was crazy, and still I didn't budge. Meanwhile a group of teenagers got up from one of the benches, shouting and swearing, leaving a semicircle of spit on the pavement. I waited for them to move off, then walked over, wiped the bench with a tissue, and sat down heavily, as if I had been walking for days. I threw back my head and looked up at the sky. Straight above, between the clouds, I saw two stars. A moment later, a cloud moved and I saw a third star, and then, right behind my head, I heard a voice asking if the seat next to me was free. When I looked to the side, I saw an old gray-haired man, slightly stooped. He was holding a large envelope. He looked at me, cleared his throat, put the envelope down on the very edge of the bench, rested his head on his hand, and fell asleep. Marko didn't believe me, I saw it in the way he shook his head. I didn't dare move, I said, and I wasn't even breathing, just as I probably hadn't blinked, convinced that even the softest sound or the least jostle would wake him, which I sensed would have had catastrophic consequences, like the beginning of a new ice age or the ripping of the universe like a tattered handkerchief. Then I heard a voice by my left ear instructing me, gently, ever so gently, to take the envelope because it was time for me to go. I turned: no one was there. The voice went on whispering in my ear, though I could no longer distinguish the words. My head drooped, my eyelids shut, and when I opened them again, I was amid the stalls at the marketplace, in the darkest night. I was holding the envelope, which contained pages of a manuscript. When I tell Marko about all this, I thought, he will demolish me. And indeed, when I'd finished the story, Marko nearly fell off his chair. All that masquerade, he laughed, just to hand you a manuscript, hey, they could have delivered it to you at home, man, why waste your time on the quay, do these people know what century they live in? I'd wondered that myself, but I didn't say anything. I waited for Marko to leave. There was a limit to how much I could take of his commentary, and I was not prepared to push the limit that evening. For the same reason I neglected to tell him that as I placed the manuscript on the table when I first got home, I saw on the envelope the faint impression of that same geometric figure, but later it was gone. For me this might have been magic; for him it would have been one more chance to ridicule such thinking and to talk about the chemical reactions that could make a text visible or invisible, on request. I could not allow him to get to me. I had had disappointment enough when I had arrived home, cautiously opened the envelope, and pulled out the thick bundle of pages printed on someone's laser printer. I don't know what I'd been expecting, exactly, perhaps a mysterious inscription or a copy of a precious document, but I certainly had not imagined a computer printout. I leafed through it quickly, then slid it back into the envelope and dropped it into a drawer in my desk, where it stayed until Marko came over to hear what had happened to me. It was not until after he had left that I could finally give the manuscript my undivided attention; it looked different to me, it even felt heavier. On the first page there were only two words, *The Well,* while on the next page was written, A dream uninterpreted is like a letter unread. I didn't know whether the whole manuscript was an account of a dream—the writer's or, perhaps, why not, mine—but I did discover when I examined it more closely that dreams were central to it. If someone were to ask me to describe the manuscript, I am not sure I could. It started off as an historical narrative, then turned into a history of dreams, followed by a collection of Kabbalistic exercises, furnished with an assortment of lists of people and events and material expenditures, books and artwork and porcelain bowls, and the lists were followed by verses, anecdotes, and dramatic dialogues, supplemented by a brief epilogue and, at the end, a detailed index, which, I later established, had little to do with the manuscript itself. This suggested that there might be other parts to the manuscript or that it referred to parts, as Marko said, that had not yet been written. Maybe this is how all books should be written, Marko went on, because the index is their essence, and if one knows the essence of what one wants to write, it is easy to fill in the spaces between the entries and establish the connections. The manuscript reminded me of the infinite book of sand that Borges had so desired: each time I opened it, the manuscript changed, with a new beginning or a new end, and none of these beginnings or ends broke the continuity, rather, they became part of a whole. This is it, I remember saying to Marko as we leafed through the manuscript together, this is what I've always wanted: a text to which I can dedicate my life. Everything changed then, and if this were a book, only now would it begin to engage the reader, but this is not a book, it is a confession, which I am speaking into the wind at the edge of a forest, so that the words, threadbare as always, are vanishing, mingling with the nitrogen and oxygen and who knows what else, and even I, as I'm speaking, can't hear them. I should mention, however, that despite formal differences between some portions of the manuscript, two subjects dominated throughout: one was the history of the Zemun Jewish community, which originated in the first half of the eighteenth century when, after Belgrade again fell into Ottoman hands in 1739, Jews stayed on in Zemun in slightly larger numbers, while the other was a collection of several Kabbalistic threads that kept tangling and untangling, though for me, quite frankly, they always represented a perfect knot. There were other themes in one or, at the most, two of the chapters, though it may also be that I hadn't recognized them elsewhere in the manuscript or that I had simply not been able to grasp them. This didn't bother me, because those other themes played no role in the change that I mentioned, which could clearly be tied to the central themes of the manuscript. When I realized I would need to learn more about the Jewish community, I turned to the Jews I knew, the writer Isak Levi and the historian Jakov Švarc, who to begin with took me to the Jewish Historical Museum in Belgrade, where I was given copies of various writings about the Zemun

Jews. While we drank coffee and nibbled matzos, Isak Levi went next door to take a call. When he came back he told me the call was from Jaša Alkalaj, a painter who dabbled in the Kabbalah, who, when he heard of me, had suggested that Levi bring me to his studio. At the time I assumed the invitation was impromptu; now I am convinced it was not: Jaša knew I was at the museum, and I tumbled easily into the trap. We spent that entire night at his studio, cluttered with paintings, candlesticks, and colorful things he'd picked up on the streets. Isak Levi was the writer, but Jaša Alkalaj could tell a story, and once he'd started, he showed no inclination to stop. His answer to my first question, which had to do with the presence of Kabbalists in Belgrade, took nearly two hours. Then he went looking for another bottle of brandy and brought out a plate of cheese and olives, but he never stopped talking, though it sounded more like mumbling, like a person talking to himself. Just don't ask him about the Hasidim, Isak Levi and Jakov Švarc warned me, because then he won't stop talking till dawn, but by accident, if anything ever happens by accident, I brought up Martin Buber, and that's how we ended up staying at the studio till dawn. Isak Levi was snoring on a low sofa, Jakov Švarc was barely able to keep his bloodshot eyes open, and my head was about to burst when Jaša Alkalaj apologized; he could no longer talk with us, he had to run to the Art Academy where his students were waiting for him, but whenever I wanted to, he said, I could get in touch or, better still, drop by the studio, no need to call ahead, a key was under the mat, just lift the right or left lower corner, though sometimes it slid over to the side, but not often, he said, and I could unlock the door, go in, and wait. The only thing I mustn't do while I was waiting was paint. At that point we were standing by the door to the studio, Jaša Alkalaj lifted the corner of the doormat, we leaned over to see the key. Isak Levi started snoring again, leaning against the door frame, Jaša Alkalaj dropped the doormat and a little puff of dust rose, and we all hurried into the elevator, as if we were fleeing a sandstorm. Two days later, once I'd completed my piece for *Minut,* I went back to the studio, this time resolved to put several clearly formulated questions to Jaša Alkalaj, about the people and events mentioned in the manuscript, to prevent him from straying into his meandering associations. I rang the doorbell, but there was no response. I decided Jaša wasn't there and, following his instructions, I looked for the key under the mat. Then I changed my mind, pulled my hand back, and set the mat down. I couldn't go in, I told Marko later, because I am incapable of entering anyone's apartment in the owner's absence, so I walked to the elevator at the other end of the corridor. While the elevator was on its way down, it occurred to me that I should have left a note, but by then it was too late; and besides, it is better, in terms of fending off bad luck, not to retrace one's steps, or, in this case, to use the same elevator, and I was not about to walk up to the fourteenth floor. I thought about waiting for a bit at the entrance to the building, because who knows, I said to Marko, maybe he'd just stepped out to the supermarket or a liquor store, or to the corner kiosk, and would be back in no time. A boy in a leather jacket was perched on the entrance steps; he was staring, head bent, at a magazine spread open on his knees. I probably wouldn't have noticed him, or maybe I would have just glanced at him while pacing back and forth in front of the building, but he looked up, and his eyes opened wide in an expression of disbelief. I took a few more steps, and only then did I stop and turn. The boy, his back to me, was punching numbers into his cell phone. When he put the phone to his ear, he turned around. We looked at each other, and though I don't know why, as I told Marko, I started for home right away. I didn't look back, I didn't want to find out whether the boy was following me or still standing at the entrance, listening to what they were telling him to do, so I lowered my head, hunched my shoulders, and walked faster, and the only thing I could think about was that I couldn't think. My head was a vast, deep void in which the blood throbbed painfully, and where, despite the void, there was no room for thought. It was only after I'd crossed several streets that I had a clear thought: I'd escaped. Then I turned, looked to the left, looked to the right, and decided that no one was following me. No one is following me, I thought, but I wasn't sure. I'm not sure, I thought. I entered a shop and stood by the display window. Several people walked past in the street, but none looked like the boy. I ought to give Jaša a call, I thought, and then I remembered he wasn't home. He is not home, I thought, which was irrelevant since I didn't have his phone number. I went back into the street. The boy was not after me, I could breathe a sigh of relief. That is when I noticed, as I told Marko, that I was no longer thinking in sentences, single words were all that was going through my head: *house,* for instance; I thought "house," and not, as you might expect, "I am going home," then I thought "joint," though I wanted to think "I could use a joint right now," then I thought "solitude" and then I knew that what I'd really been thinking was "one of these days my solitude is going to cost me my mind." And how long, Marko asked, did that go on? When I got home, I said, I thought "water," though I wanted to think "I'm really thirsty," and after I'd gulped down a glass of water, everything reverted to normal. In the bathroom, looking into the mirror, I even smiled at my fears, but my hands, no point in hiding it, were shaking. If you had told this to anyone else, Marko said, they'd think you'd gone off the deep end or that you suffer from paranoid delusions; first the man in the black trench coat, then the mysterious ad, then some crackpot manuscript, and now this boy getting instructions on his cell phone. And you, I asked, what do you think? I'm your friend, said Marko, and handed me a new joint, and friends don't ask, they know. The next day, however, he shook his head, he didn't know how something like this could ever happen, he said. Scrawled on the front door to my apartment in heavy black marker, in letters of all different sizes, were the words THOSE WHO KEEP COMPANY WITH JEWS WILL BE SWALLOWED BY THE NIGHT. The message started in the upper-left-hand corner, the first three words were in the top row: the word WITH, written smaller than the previous words, was in the second row, alone, probably because of the desire to make sure that JEWS was prominent and suitably visible; that word took up the third line, but for some reason it was on a slant, as if aiming for my doormat; it was followed by the first part of the warning, written in what were surprisingly regular and even letters, almost pleasing to the eye; and then everything dispersed with the word NIGHT written in erratic letters, probably to convey the horror of the night. Around this word, like little celestial bodies, floated swastikas (three), stylized skulls (two), penises (two), various symbols I was unfamiliar with (four), and one eye, which Marko claimed was a drawing of a vagina. I didn't wish to discuss this any further, since we were soon joined by neighbors, and each had a suggestion for what I ought to do. The neighbor from the apartment across the way started rubbing at one of the letters with the tip of his forefinger. If it smudges, he said, no problem, it will wash right off, if it doesn't smudge, that means they used permanent ink, and you'll have no choice but to paint the whole door. The letter he was rubbing was the initial J in JEWS. It smudged and we all breathed a sigh of relief. That filth should be washed off right away, said my ground-floor neighbor, and that very instant I was about to go and get water, detergent, and a rag. I was stopped by my upstairs neighbor, who insisted that the police should be called first, or at least a picture taken of the door, otherwise, he said, we would be considered co-perpetrators with these evildoers, giving them the go-ahead to commit more reprehensible acts. Fine, I said. I brought out my camera, clicked twice, it didn't work the first time, then went to get my washing paraphernalia. While I was dragging the rag across the door in broad sweeping motions, I listened to my neighbors and Marko berating and cursing the government, and then someone spotted a rat in the stairwell and the conversation took off in a new direction, following the trail of filthy, overflowing garbage bins, neglected parks, unswept streets, and the general sense of things falling apart. Meanwhile I finished wiping the door. The letters were no longer visible, but the door was a shade darker, like a patchily erased blackboard on which the curving path of the sponge and layers of chalk are still visible, despite the class monitor's best efforts. Now that's better, said Marko. Go ahead and call the police, said the upstairs neighbor. Next time use more detergent, said the ground-floor neighbor. Those idiots should be put to death, said a neighbor I'd never met. Vim works wonders, said the ground-floor neighbor. It is astonishing that I didn't hear a thing, said the neighbor from across the hall. Scum of the earth, said the neighbor I'd never met. I would send them all straight to the quarry, and then you tell me if they'd ever do something like this again, said the neighbor who lived in the converted laundry room. Only a maniac would do something like that, said the neighbor I'd never met. Worse than maniacs, said Marko. Damn right, said the ground-floor neighbor. I took the rag out of the bucket, wrung it, and wiped the door once more. The stain turned a little lighter. The neighbors began to disperse. If you need anything, said the neighbor I'd never met, you know where to find me. I didn't, but I was reluctant to say so. Marko also had to leave; he had a date with a dealer near Hotel Slavija, and he was running late. In no time I stood alone in front of my messy door. I picked up the bucket, walked into my front hall, shut the door behind me, locked both locks, hooked the chain. I poured the dirty water into the toilet bowl. I went into the bathroom and washed my hands. Then I returned to the front hall, undid the chain, unlocked the locks, and opened the door. The stain looked darker, but otherwise nothing. I closed the door, locked the locks, and hooked the chain. I looked through the spy hole: the hallway was empty. The phone rang. It was Jaša. He wanted to know when we would be getting together again. I told him what had happened, and after a brief silence, he said that, sooner or later, everybody shows their true face. What mattered the most for me, however, he went on, was that I should pay no attention to that silliness, but stay on track. So which track is mine? I asked. In the Talmud it says that if you don't know where you are going, he said, any path will take you there. But what happens, I asked, if you know where you are going? Then the path doesn't matter, said Jaša, and hung up. Something stinks here, mumbled Marko. We were sitting in a pastry shop on Makedonska Street, across from the Youth Center, eating cream puffs and drinking *boza*. A woman sitting at the neighboring table gingerly raised a cream puff to her nose and sniffed it. An equation with too many unknowns, I said, is no longer an equation, but chaos. That's something for your friend the mathematician, said Marko, and ordered another glass of *boza*. Why not? I thought, though not just then but several days later, when I found a slip of paper in my mailbox with a yellow star and superimposed on the star, a fat black swastika. That morning in *Minut* a piece of mine had appeared about the necessity of tolerance if a civil society is to succeed, and I was sure that the clumsy drawing was in response to my suggestion that we should not suspect someone simply because he or she is Chinese, gay, Jewish, or a social outcast, for to doubt them means to have no faith in ourselves, it means having nothing. The mathematician, my former schoolmate, had nothing to do with this, but I hoped he could guide me. We learn sometimes from those we least expect to learn from, or from whom we expect something entirely different. However I didn't feel like chasing him around his high-rise, so I called the woman who had run into him from time to time before she moved to Banovo Brdo, and asked if she could somehow find Dragan Mišović's phone number for me. We all have phones nowadays, I said, he cannot possibly live without one. If he can wear a winter coat in midsummer, she said, he can live without a phone. She promised to call people who went to school with us, and whom she had seen more often before she had moved. She mentioned several names, but none of them rang a bell. Maybe you weren't in the same class, said Marko when I told him about it. He, said Marko, knew the first and last name of every single classmate of his, even the desk and row each of them sat in. I can draw you the layout of my entire classroom, he added, and if he had had a piece of paper and a pencil with him at the time, no doubt he would have done just that. The woman who used to run into Dragan Mišović got in touch with me the next day. She had managed, she boasted, to get his phone number from the first person she'd called, because she, meaning the other person, had organized our most recent class reunion and had everybody's phone numbers. She dictated the number to me, cautioning that Dragan Mišović seldom answered his phone and that I would have to be persistent and call repeatedly until he finally picked up. I called him immediately. My name meant nothing to him, and only when I reminded him of the interpretation of the circle and triangles did he remember who I was. That's not why I am calling, I said. So, said Dragan Mišović, everything's clear? I said nothing. I understand, said Dragan Mišović, sometimes mathematicians get a little carried away, like most professionals, though I should tell you, he said, that I later thought I might write you an addendum, because the next day, that diagram reminded me of the initial step in the iterative process of construction of one of the first known fractals, called the Sierpiński Triangle. Sure, I said. What else could I say? I won't get into the whole story, said Dragan Mišović, but that fractal grew from a random toss of a die, and many theorists of dynamical systems were entranced by it, believing that this procedure demonstrated how order comes from chaos, which served the members of the Brussels School of Ilya Prigogine as proof that the universe didn't have to obey the Second Law of Thermodynamics, or that the system need not ultimately end in chaos and collapse, but instead at a certain moment it would begin to organize itself into another form. Sure, I said again. Of course, Dragan Mišović said, I don't believe that at all, for the simple reason that it's extremely naive, even when expressed in this reduced form. He stopped talking, and for a while we were both silent. I could hear him breathe, just as he could probably hear me breathe, though I tried tucking the receiver under my chin, away from my mouth. Then Dragan Mišović coughed, and said, If that wasn't it, what did you want to ask me? I coughed too and asked, Is the number of unknowns in an equation limited, I mean, what happens with an equation in which there are too many unknowns? Those are two separate questions, said Dragan Mišović. The answer to the first question is simple: no. What about the other question, I asked, the same answer? Depends, said Dragan Mišović, on how you define "too many unknowns." I don't define them at all, I said, that's why I called you. Take, he went on, equations with two unknowns, you probably remember those, they describe many curves in the plane, so the set of pairs (x,y) that satisfies the equation $f(x,y) = 0$ makes a curve. For example, $x^2 + y^2 = 1$ is an equation for a circle with a diameter of 1 and its center at origin. In other words, said Dragan Mišović, that phrase of ours, "too many unknowns," represents a key idea of both Descartes and Fermat, which ties algebra to geometry or the equation to the curve. Your question, he said, contains analytical geometry in all its dimensions, and I would need several hours just to get started. Oh, I said. That's the reason, Dragan Mišović continued, it would be useful to know why you're asking me, because then I could be more precise. Let me put it this way, I said, over the past few days I have come up against a multitude of unknowns, and I am eager to understand just one, because if the unknowns keep multiplying, I said, soon it will no longer be an equation but sheer chaos. Sometimes chaos can be an equation, said Dragan Mišović, but we're better off not going there, let's try to look at it in a different way, or else, he said, let's assume that among those unknowns only one is a genuine unknown, the rest are its parameters. If we do that, he continued, it gets easier. I didn't know why it would get easier, but tacitly I agreed. Of course, that is possible only under certain technical conditions, said Dragan Mišović, which are given by the Implicit Function Theorem. Maybe, I mused, maybe I should never have called him. Don't worry, he said, as if reading my thoughts, I won't trouble you with all the particulars, and besides, I remember how much you loathed math in gymnasium. That's not true, I protested, it's not that I loathed it, it's that I wanted nothing to do with it. You can put it that way if you like, said Dragan Mišović, but memories are a lot like chaos, so it's better for us to leave them be. In this case, he continued, I will only say that this theory tells us that in the corresponding set of equations some of the variables are defined as functions of other variables, on condition, of course, that the Jacobian is nonzero. Sure, I said. So, said Dragan Mišović, if all those conditions are met and we isolate a single unknown in your equation, which we will call the privileged unknown, and we proclaim all others to be its parameters, then we arrive at a new function, we will call it function G, which satisfies the initial equation, even though, and this is the niftiest part of this whole business, we have no idea what that function is or what it looks like. In other words, and I'll conclude with this, said Dragan Mišović, there is a solution that can be expressed as a function, but nothing that tells us how to formulate it more closely. So you know, I said, yet you don't know. No, said Dragan Mišović, you don't know, yet you know. I don't understand a word of this, I confessed. It is pretty simple, he continued patiently, choose one among all the unknowns, and when you solve that one, the others will open. You mean to say, I asked, that they are interconnected after all? It is late for a conversation about paranoia, answered Dragan Mišović, then cleared his throat and hung up. I listened for a while to the white noise coming from the phone cables, then hung up. Did you really expect, Marko asked when we took a stroll the next evening, that he would give you a straight answer? No, I said. The promenade was packed with people, children were shrieking, girls zipped by on roller skates, boys whistled and shouted. Restaurant barges rocked on the water and blasted loud music, from turbo folk to reggae. The days were getting longer, and the sun hung motionless on the western rim of the horizon. I suggested to Marko that we buy ice cream on a stick, but he said he'd rather not, confessing to his fear of getting a splinter in his tongue. That can't happen, I said, but I got us ice cream cones. We perched on the steps going down to the Danube and licked our ice cream in silence. The steps continued into the water, as if descending into Atlantis. The river surface was covered in ripples, and small waves splashed soundlessly against the concrete. Someone at the top of the stairs called out, Look at the sky, it'll rain tomorrow! Everyone is a weatherman these days, Marko said. Two boats passed by slowly, on their way to the marina by the high-rise, and water splashed noisily in the corners of the steps. I think I knew what he wanted to say to me, I said. Marko raised his eyebrows quizzically. First of all, I said, my heart pounding, I must accept the possibility that everything is interconnected, that nothing exists in isolation, that everything is part of a whole, which means that what I don't know and don't understand, the questions and dilemmas I am up against, are also interconnected. Marko persisted in his silence, sticking his tongue as far into his cone as it would go. A white mustache took shape on his upper lip. Another boat passed by, moving along the river toward the high-rise, and again the wavelets gurgled in the corners of the steps. Just tell me, said Marko, how you'll decide what tie there is between the slap on the quay, the sign on the sidewalk, the manuscript on the Kabbalah and history, the anti-Semitic threats, this place that behaves as if it is a hole outside of time, and whatever else, I mean, how will you establish from which of these the others originate, or into which they flow, which is more or less the same thing? I said nothing; I didn't know. Even today I don't know. Jaša Alkalaj, however, didn't hesitate for a second when I asked the same question several days later at his studio. The Kabbalah, he said. Isak Levi sighed, and Jakov Švarc dismissed this comment with a wave of the hand. Ignore them, said Jaša Alkalaj, they are slaves of linear logic, for them it can only be one thing or another, they can never embrace the notion that something may be both one thing and another, at one and the same time. For them the glass is either full or empty, he said, and they don't understand that an empty glass is also full, just as a full glass is also empty. Nonsense, countered Isak Levi, if that were the case, you would be able to answer the question of what happens when I drink half the liquid from a full glass: is the glass then half empty or half full? Both, said Jaša Alkalaj, how many times do I have to tell you? He turned to me: This is how they torment me, he said, like true unbelievers. Who? chimed in Jakov Švarc, us—the unbelievers? You are the only one of us who never goes to temple. My body is my temple, said Jaša Alkalaj, what do I need a synagogue for? That's why the Jews are in trouble, said Jakov Švarc, instead of coming to God, they expect God to come to them. Isak Levi pounded the table, Are we going to argue, which we can always do, or are we going to listen to this man who in coming here is risking his life? If nothing else, he said, we ought to respect that. Sure, sure, said Jaša Alkalaj and Isak Levi, then both looked at me, probably expecting me to say something. Nothing came to mind. I thought it might be good to go out on the balcony and see if anyone shifty was hanging around the building entrance, but I didn't want to un-settle them. They were already worried by the anti-Jewish mes-sages scrawled on my front door; they wanted, like that neigh-bor of mine, to go straight to the police, and I barely managed to convince them that this was not called for, but I had to promise I'd write about that subject in my column in *Minut*.

So, said Jakov Švarc, what's going on? I licked my lips, sipped a little of Jaša's brandy, rubbed the tip of my nose. If the essence of everything is contained in some aspect of the Kabbalah, I said, how do I get to it? And how, I added, can I be sure that this is the right way, since if I don't know what it is I am looking for, how will I know I've found it? It is not easy, answered Jaša Alkalaj, but it's possible. He smiled as he said this, which stirred doubts in me, and Isak Levi noticed my distrustful look. Trust him, Isak Levi said, even though he may not strike you as the kind of person who merits your trust. Sometimes such people are more trustworthy than those who look trustworthy, Jakov Švarc backed him up. Fine, I said unconvincingly, then I will . . . If you have doubts, Jaša Alkalaj interrupted, then don't bother to begin. Doubt at the outset, said Isak Levi, is the same as defeat at the end. He who doubts early, chimed in Jakov Švarc, sheds his doubt late. If we spent the entire evening talking in this rhythmic pattern, each sentence of mine followed by their tripartite commentary, would I burst out laughing? Perhaps we sound silly, said Jaša Alkalaj, and winked, but that's because we have been together for so long, and we know exactly what each of us is thinking. How long? I asked. They looked at one another. Five hundred years, said Jaša Alkalaj, if not longer. I lifted my shot glass and sniffed it. Who knows, I thought, what they're drinking. Of course, Jaša Alkalaj continued, we can't remember everything, so our earliest common memory is our years in a prewar Belgrade gymnasium. Having said that, said Jakov Švarc, some graduated and some didn't. The man is interested in the Kabbalah, protested Jaša Alkalaj, not in our little differences. At any rate, he added, the only purpose school serves is to distance children and young people for a few years from their anxious parents who are running themselves into the ground to make ends meet. Let's leave school and the education system out of this, I said, let's talk about the Kabbalah. First of all, Isak Levi spoke up as he took hold of the brandy bottle, no point in being impatient. Let's start here, said Jaša Alkalaj, as he walked over to a stack of paintings in the corner, then came back with one. It is called *The Cloak of the Soul,* he said. The painting portrayed a genderless human, barefoot in a grassy clearing, a generous variety of symbols hovering around it. The symbols were probably all Jewish, I recognized a six-pointed star of David, a menorah, the aleph, and other Hebrew letters. Some parts of the body were exposed, as if in an anatomical atlas, so that the body's cavities were clearly visible, though they contained no organs, or else the organs were not depicted, instead the entire insides were lit with a radiance that came from within, from a central point located in the general vicinity of the bellybutton. A transparent glow permeated the interior and was visible at some of the orifices, but it didn't extend beyond the body layer, meaning the skin, and that space, the buffer zone between the body and the radiance, was filled with a second body, if the word *body* applies here, that was transparent, and identical in all but its transparency to the body above it. In short, this genderless body seemed to include three bodies, each tucked into the next, like Russian dolls, except that Russian dolls are all made of the same material, and the three bodies were not. I painted this, Jaša Alkalaj continued, after I had read the interpretation of Chaim Vital, a sixteenth-century Kabbalist and student of the celebrated Yitzhak Luria, that God, when he places a soul in a human body, has to insert an intermediary between them, an astral body of sorts, because if there is no shield, the radiance of the soul will scorch everything. Therefore, when a person wishes to speak with his soul, he said, he doesn't invoke the soul, for it would scorch him; rather he communicates with his astral body, which joins the reflection of his soul and the reflection of his body. But to see the astral body, and even more so to communicate with it, Jaša Alkalaj said, one must reach the highest level of purity. Then his eyes open to the beauty of God's nature, and he sees, he said, how beautiful he too is in his purity. So, now two things matter: first that one be cautious when invoking the astral body, for many cases have been recorded of invocations that took people to the side on the left, as it says in the Kabbalah, meaning the side of evil, while the other thing to keep in mind, he said, is that one's shadow is actually a projection of his astral body, which is why the Bible says our days upon the earth are as a shadow, which means, he said, that they are brief because every shadow lasts only a short while, but they are also a reflection of our astral body, in which are recorded all of our days, and everything that has been, and, most important right now, everything that will be. The prophets were people, he said, who could invoke their shadow, or, more precisely, their astral body, whenever they wished to, and it would tell them what was to come. But how does the astral body, I asked, know all that? By descending at the moment of conception with the soul, said Jaša Alkalaj, as its cloak, and in it, in the astral body, is registered the figure of the new being and everything that the life of that being will be in the days and years to come. In other words, chimed in Isak Levi, he who sees his shadow will see the course of his life. And he who learns to converse with it, added Jakov Švarc, will learn all he wants to know. It all sounded rehearsed, and for a moment I thought it would be best for me to leave, but then Jaša Alkalaj, turning away from me, said, One needs to doubt, but one needn't believe in doubt. I swallowed and sniffled. Is there any more brandy? I asked. When all the shot glasses were topped off, Isak Levi raised his and invited us to drink to the shadows. I waited until the bite subsided on my tongue, then asked, How long does it take to learn how to invoke one's shadow? I watched the three of them exchange glances and shrug. Twelve years, said Jaša Alkalaj finally, sometimes longer. To this day I don't believe that to be a true figure, and at the time I felt my mouth drop open in astonishment. I looked from one to the other and tried to decipher whether they were joking. There are those, said Jaša Alkalaj, who manage it in six years, but they are the gifted followers who have already succeeded in ascending the stages of the Kabbalistic Sephirot. If they need so much time to see the shadow, I said, how much time do they need to see the body that casts that shadow? The body is always visible, answered Jaša Alkalaj, as is the shadow, but they are looking with the wrong eye. Only when one learns to see, he went on, only when the eye is pure, can the body be seen as it truly is, but the shadow is no longer a shadow then but a cloak for the soul, a cloak that is acquired during conception and added to by the weaving of the days and the good deeds one performs in a lifetime. Isak Levi poured the rest of the brandy into our shot glasses. Things cannot be hurried, he said, and what needs to happen, no matter what it is, will happen when the time is right. For instance, he added, in this glass I am holding soon there will be no brandy. He raised the glass to his lips, downed it in a gulp, turned it over, and not a drop dribbled out. Jaša Alkalaj offered to open another bottle. Jakov Švarc was nodding in approval, so I quickly announced my departure. The brandy I had drunk, and I had had more than usual, had softened my knees and dulled my eyes, and I didn't want to test the reactions of my body to even more alcohol. I deflected their efforts to persuade me to stay and soon found myself in a taxi, which drove through the poorly lit streets to Zemun. There was no one at the front door of Jaša Alkalaj's building; no car followed us; no one was standing in front of my building; the stairs were deserted, the door to my apartment was locked as it should be, the doormat had not been touched. By then I was barely able to move, and all I wanted was to drop into bed and sleep, which I promptly did. When I opened my eyes again the clock next to my bed showed exactly three o'clock in the morning. What had woken me? Was it someone snooping around my door? I got up and padded out to the front hall, I leaned my ear to the door, held my breath: not a sound. I unlocked the door, opened it a crack without undoing the chain, and peered out into the corridor.

There was no one crouching on the doormat, no one's eyes gleamed in the dark. I locked the door and went back to my bedroom. I went over to the window, checked out the street and the buildings across the way: the street was deserted, all the windows were dark, only the yellow of the traffic lights blinked patiently. My mouth was bitter and dry, which I had not expected from the brandy, I admit. I ate a piece of Turkish delight in the kitchen and drank a glass of water. The clock showed that seventeen minutes had passed since I got up. I watched the clock face until the big hand shivered and moved a notch, then I remembered what had woken me: I'd been dreaming that I was standing on the bank of a rapid mountain stream, so different from the slow Danube of the plains, and that a voice was announcing numbers: seventeen, thirty-five, forty-three, ninety-eight. At the final number, on the river a woven basket swept by, in which sat, instead of an abandoned baby, the manuscript given to me by the mysterious old man. I reached for the basket, my foot slipped on the damp grass, I flew face forward toward the river, and as the water splashed my face I woke. Now it was nearly three-thirty. I went to my study to get the manuscript, repeating the numbers I'd heard in my dream. On page 17 I read that a young but wise man named Eleazar, a "mystic and a teacher," was part of a group of some twenty Jewish, mostly Ashkenazi, families who arrived in Zemun in 1739. Little was known of him, though he was probably the first, even before the arrival of Rabbi Jehuda Jeruham, to perform religious rites. Until that time, it said in the manuscript, there had been no Jews living in Zemun, or at least not in any significant numbers. In 1717, when the Austrians routed the Ottomans and captured Belgrade, several Jewish merchants settled there, along with a larger group of Austrian merchants and craftsmen. When the Ottomans recaptured Belgrade some twenty years later, however, these Jews withdrew from Belgrade and chose to make their home in Zemun. Eleazar's trace can be found there today, it said, but hardly anyone knows this, or even wishes to learn about it. The next passage dealt with the way the Austrian authorities treated the Jewish residents of Zemun, but there was no further mention of Eleazar. On page 35 of the manuscript, however, after a passage listing the rabbis who had served in the Zemun synagogues following Jehuda Jeruham—Israel Aleksandar, Joze Fridensberger, Šlomo Hirš, Jehuda ben Šlomo Haj Alkalaj, S. D. Tauber, Hinko Urbah, and Kantor Geršon Kačka at the Ashkenazi synagogue, and M. B. Aharon, Šabtaj, Moše Bahar, and Hakham Jichak Musafija at the Sephardic synagogue—there was an unrelated passage: here one must also remember that Eleazar still had Hermes' words in mind about how he, Hermes, was searching for the secrets of Genesis, and how he had gone into a cave deep beneath the surface of the earth, through which powerful winds blew, and there before him appeared an image of incredible beauty, an image of which it is written in the Torah that God made man in his own image, and this image, which represented his perfect nature, instructed Hermes in what he should do to obtain knowledge about the most exalted matters. Further, it was written, this is why Eleazar occasionally separated his self from himself, that is, freed himself from his body, until he could see himself, slender and transparent, illuminated by a wondrous inner light that came from the divine spirit. But what Eleazar was able to do, and with such remarkable ease, did not work for anyone else, so perhaps there is no point in speaking of it further. And truly, the next few pages contained no mention of him, until page 43, where the part about Eleazar began with the words "In the meanwhile," as if it were taken from some larger whole in which his life was laid out in chronological order, in much greater detail. And so in the meanwhile, it was written at the bottom of the page, Eleazar wondered more and more often why God, who was perfect, had not created a perfect world, but instead had made a world in which there was a place and a role for evil. Eleazar understood, it said, the Kabbalistic explanation that it had not been possible to create a perfect world because that would have meant that God, who is perfection, was duplicating himself, making a copy of himself, and God, in the nature of things, cannot be duplicated, cannot copy himself, he can only limit himself. Hence, it said, there is evil in this world, though not as a separate force, as pure evil, but always and only as part of all that is, therefore in man's soul, from its very inception, there are germs of both good and evil. God is none the weaker for it, the manuscript reads, but instead more generous; this didn't satisfy Eleazar, and after long periods of musing and going through all the possibilities, he decided to approach the left side, the side of evil. With this in mind, it said, Eleazar stood in the circle of light from a special source, but in such a way that he could see both his shadows, the one that was his astral body, and the one that held the living spark of the astral body and seldom shows itself, and for that he needed to say certain prescribed words, and that was when impure forces appeared, which took over Eleazar's shadows, and, with the shadows, Eleazar, and after that no one ever saw him. His name was not mentioned again until fifty pages later. Before that final mention, the manuscript dealt with the Zemun Jewish cemetery; then a brief history was given of the Zemun synagogue, so it's unclear why the piece about Eleazar's destiny is treated here. Today, it says in that chapter, somewhere in Zemun is a place where the forces of good and evil intersect, and where it is possible, if a person knows the right words, to pass from one world into the other, and even to move into the realm of endless possibilities, or into the realm of endless worlds that emanate from the ten divine Sephirot, endlessly multiplying and forging anew the reality we dwell in. Outside a new day had long since dawned. The clock showed seven-thirty A.M., which meant that I had spent four hours leafing through the manuscript I still had no clear sense of. If this is one of the books of sand, I told Marko, I should be finding grains of sand on my hands after reading it.

There was no sand on my hands, but plenty of dust and paper shreds. After I read that Eleazar's passageway to the other world still existed in Zemun, my first thought was of the corner in the courtyard on Zmaj Jovina Street. I hadn't gone there for several days, just as I hadn't thought about the woman from the quay, because the circumstances, the events connected to the warnings scrawled on my door, had pulled me in another direction, which might have been the cause of the nagging sense of impaired equilibrium that had been dogging me for weeks. I splashed my face with water, ate a piece of bread spread with honey while I waited for the weather report on the morning radio program (clouds, wind, with a chance of rain in the afternoon), I got dressed, put a piece of gum in my mouth, and left the apartment. I decided to walk to Zmaj Jovina Street, taking the shortest cut through the center of town. This exposed me to exhaust fumes, but I was too groggy and tired, after my nocturnal reading, to take the less direct route by the quay. On my way back, I thought, I might take that route, but first I should walk through the market and pick up some fuse cartridges and a new phone jack at the stall of the man who resells spare parts, and then, walking along the Danube, I could inhale and exhale the air as deeply as possible, swinging my arms vigorously to accelerate circulation, coordinate my equilibrium and speed the rhythm of my steps. Glavna Street was packed with people and cars, bluish clouds of fumes, and bustle, and the street vendors had opened their makeshift stalls out in front of the department store. The clouds the radio announcer so generously promised had not yet appeared, unless they were at the horizon, hidden from view by the rows of buildings, so that the sun, though still a spring sun, radiated a heat hard to bear, swallowing shadows like a Kabbalist. If somebody, I thought, had told me a few weeks before that I would be caught up in mystical teachings about good and evil, I would have thought that somebody mad. And now that same somebody could tell me I am mad and grasping at straws. It's only right, I decided, that I am thinking about this as I walk by Dubrovačka Street, which used to be the heart of the Jewish quarter of Zemun and where the young and old trees continued to cast shadows full of foreboding and promise. Once I am on the street, I thought, I should go to the synagogue, though they knew nothing of Eleazar when the temple was built, because it is always possible, and sometimes inevitable, that what is anticipated turns up where one least expects it, be it exalted celestial light or shards of the pottery in which earthly darkness was once preserved. I passed by the cinema and the hotel, and at the corner, by the shoe store, I crossed into Zmaj Jovina Street. The tai chi poster hung in the same place by the large wooden gate, but with a different starting date for the beginner's course and with no circle and triangle. The yin and yang were real, as I established when I tried to scratch them. The gate was ajar, the passageway leading to the courtyard radiated a pleasant freshness, the bench and barberry bushes had not changed, and water was dripping from the pump, as if just before I got there someone had been filling a bucket or, perhaps, a washbasin, and had slipped away upon hearing my footsteps. I went over to the bench and sat down, but the muted murmur from the street and market did not stop, nor did the music start to play. I looked up and saw a patch of blue sky. The sky is the same, I thought, even if everything else has changed. I closed my eyes, perked my ears like a rabbit, stopped breathing. Nothing helped. I squeezed my eyes shut even more tightly, breathed the air in deeply, slowly released the breath, then breathed in again. I must have fallen asleep, because when I opened my eyes a broom was in my face. The broom was held by a small, scrawny woman, wizened face, no teeth. Get going, you bum, she said, scram. What did you think? she shrieked, and brandished the broom, that this is a city park and any old bum can sleep here? I shoved the broom out of my face, but that further infuriated her, so she kicked me. I got up and turned to go down the passageway and she swung the broom and smacked me on the behind. In a story by Kharms, I thought, she would have flown out a window, but I wasn't in a Kharms story, I was in Zemun, and as her voice rang after me down the cool passageway, I tried to understand what had happened. I didn't ask myself why the old woman with the broom was there, but why the place no longer radiated its magic. What had changed, the place or me? Maybe nothing, said Marko, maybe it just wasn't a good day for the harmony of the spheres. But that old woman, I asked, what are we to do with her, especially if she appeared from the left side? Do you actually believe, grinned Marko, that the old woman is a witch? She had a broom, I said. The broom means nothing, countered Marko, and besides, why would only old women be witches, don't you think that's prejudice? I said nothing. Why an old woman? Marko went on. Why not the young woman who was slapped? I'd much rather deal with a young witch than with some old hag. We hadn't been spending much time together of late, at least not the way we used to, and that came across in Marko's edginess, in his readiness to lock horns with me, to keep a certain distance. I didn't know what to do about it. I was spending more time with Jaša Alkalaj; I was staying up late, reading an assortment of Kabbalistic books from his library; I was able to think of little else. Worst of all, I told Marko, nothing had proved to me that I was on the right path or that I was on any path at all. Maybe, I said, I am just kicking around in the dust. When I repeated this to Jaša Alkalaj, he raised his index finger and said, If there is a signpost to be found, it is not along a path, but in the heart. Remember that, he added, and for the next few days I kept saying "A signpost in the heart" as a sort of mantra. Nothing happened. I still didn't know whether I was on the right path or not; I still couldn't explain why nothing had happened when I last sat on the bench in the courtyard at Zmaj Jovina Street; and I was still groping in the dark. After my retreat from the old woman I again walked the streets that led from the quay to the Harbormaster's, carefully inspecting the entranceways to the buildings and looking under each piece of litter I came across, but nowhere did I find any trace of the geometric symbol, nowhere was there a hint that would lead me to the woman who'd been slapped. I was running late again with my piece for *Minut,* except that the editor wasn't his usual sympathetic self; he lectured me on the obligation of columnists to respect the rules, adding that if this were to happen again, he'd have no choice. Though I would have much preferred to go back to my pursuit of the sign and the woman, I wrote a piece on the upsurge of anti-Semitism in Serbia. Hatred of other ethnic groups is in effect hatred of oneself, was how I started. It is not the other we fear, we fear ourselves, we fear the changes the presence of others may impose. When I say that I dislike Jews, or Roma, or Croats — the list is endless — I am expressing the fear that under their influence, or under the influence of what they genuinely or symbolically represent, I will be forced to give up some of the convictions that matter to me. Their uprooting of my convictions, no matter how irrational, represents uprooting of my personality. And so, I went on, if I am not to change, they must be branded, isolated, expelled, and, if necessary, utterly destroyed. But a person who dislikes members of other ethnic groups, dislikes, I declared, his or her own people, hence, if I announce that I dislike foreigners, I am admitting that I live in a void, stripped of anyone's love. And a person who has no love, given or offered, is no longer human, for love is what defines us in the system of nature we inhabit. The rising number of anti-Semitic incidents, I continued, is still small in comparison to the number of such incidents in the so-called democratic countries, but these statistics, no matter how attractive and dear to the state and politicians, are no comfort whatever to the victims of anti-Semitism. It is high time, I concluded, for the authorities to realize that this is a fire which, if not extinguished in time, may easily become a blazing conflagration that will no longer be possible to put out. Then, of course, I wrote, it will be too late, so speed is of the essence, and while there is time, we must stomp on the viper. Not just the viper of anti-Semitism, but the viper of every form of hatred, whether rooted in ethnic, sexual, or ideological differences. I titled the piece "In the Snake's Nest." The editor read the text twice before he looked at me. Many people will not like this, he said. It is mine to write, I said, and the rest is up to them. Yes, said the editor, but who are they? We shall see, I answered, not knowing that I would not have long to wait. He published the piece several days later, and on that day, or more precisely, that evening, I went to the theater. I don't remember the title of the play, I think it was an adaptation of a novel by one of our young writers, something about voluntary exile and escaping war, but I know that it was performed at the National Theater to a half-empty house. Three or four seats to my right an elderly man smacked his lips in his sleep; in the row in front a young man with a crewcut and a red-haired young woman never stopped kissing; to my left, in the first seat in the row, sat a middle-aged woman: whenever I looked over, she was looking at me. Once she smiled, brushed a lock of hair from her cheek, pursed her lips, and blew me a kiss. As hard as I tried to focus on the chaotic scene changes and the constant dips into the past, in the end it was a mystery to me why the mother was dying and the protagonist, apparently her son, took his clothes off and ran naked around the stage. When the son finally stood still and his penis stopped swinging, the curtain dropped. There was a scattering of reluctant applause as the mother and son appeared in front of the curtain. The son was no longer naked; a colorful patch of cloth covered his loins. The applause died down, they bowed, then retreated behind the curtain. The elderly man to my right was still asleep; the woman to my left had departed before the applause; the young man and woman stood up and stretched; my foot had fallen asleep, so I moved slowly toward the exit, waddling like a duck. Outside it was drizzling, yet the square in front of the theater was thronged with people. I looked to the left and to the right but saw no one familiar. Many years ago, you could find people selling hash on this square, but now, even if they were there, I couldn't spot them. I found a table in one of the nearby cafés, and to blaring music, mostly classic rock, I had a cappuccino. That's thunder, said the man at the counter in the break between two songs by Cream. I couldn't imagine how he could have heard it, but I took this as a sign that it was time for me to head home. And sure enough, as I was walking downhill to the Zeleni Venac bus stop, there was another rumble of thunder, then it started to rain, and while I was on the bus to Zemun, the rain turned into a real downpour. When I got off the bus at my stop, I ducked and dashed to my building, and there, after I had hopped over the last puddle, I bumped into a man at the entranceway. In fact I spotted him at the last moment, which allowed me to slow down a little and diminish the impact of the collision, and he seemed to have seen me, because he greeted me with arms wide open. My face ended up on his chest for an instant, while my arms encircled his back, and anyone seeing us would have thought we were embracing after a long separation. I pulled myself up, ready to apologize, but the person gripped my arm tightly and, through clenched teeth, ordered me to keep quiet. Then over my shoulder, as if speaking into a void, he said everything was fine. I turned and saw three other young men. In the wan light of the street lamp, weakened by the gloom of the storm, they looked a lot like the man standing before me, gripping my arm ever more tightly. Let's go, he said, and shoved me toward them. I thought I would fall, but the men grabbed me with a practiced ease: the one in the middle went for my neck, while the other two each reached for an arm. I should, of course, have guessed what was coming, but the only thing I could think of was that I would burst out laughing if they took me to a car and tied a blindfold over my eyes. We turned into Teslina Street, where it was darker still because of the trees full of spring leaves. I tried to say something two or three times, but each time I was silenced by a squeeze to the neck or a jab in the side. At the end of the street, where a long time ago the railway tracks used to cross, we clambered through a twisted metal fence into a nursery school yard and through the bushes and came round to the back of the building, where it was pitch-dark. The men holding me stood so close I could hear them breathing. If I had leaned over an inch I would have been leaning against one of them; had I straightened my fingers I would have touched their faces. I didn't lean over, I didn't move a finger: I listened to the rain fall and pretended this was happening to someone else. Tell me one thing, said the fellow who had been standing by the door to my building, how can you bear to fraternize with those slimy creatures who obsess about one thing and one thing only? I wasn't certain whom he had in mind though I had an idea, but for the life of me I couldn't guess what it was these people were obsessed with. What thing? I asked. So we're playing a game, said the man, are we? Before I had the chance to say another word, his fist shot into my gut. I gasped for air, my mouth yawning, then my knees buckled and I dropped to the ground. The men behind me lifted me right up. Now you know what I am talking about, don't you? said the man. Sure, I said, though I had no clue. A rat is a rat is a rat, he said, and they go on living in the dark, all in the hope that one day they will rule the world. Sure, I said, just in case. However, said the man, there's one thing I will never understand: how an honest, true Serb can choose to side with them and then get on the case of other Serbs who criticize them and expose them for who they really are. When I had finally regained my breath, I understood whom he had in mind, but I said nothing, fearful I might be punched in the gut again. Say something, said the man, don't make me wait. I was silent. This time the blow came from behind, in the area of my kidneys. Did you hear the man's question? said a voice, or should we give those ears a twist? Instead of unmasking them, said the man, you defend them; instead of publishing the truth, you obscure it; instead of being true to who you are, you are being something else. Tell me, he went on, is this normal? I didn't have much choice: No, I said. So why do you call Serbia a snake's nest, said the man, and Serbs vipers to be stomped on? He didn't wait for my answer but slammed his fist into my belly. My knees betrayed me again. If it hadn't been for the men who were at the ready, and I must admit, practiced at putting me back on my feet, I would have lain there on the ground, gasping like a beached fish. If you've got to write, he said, at least write the truth; there have been enough lies. He dipped his hand into his pocket and for a moment I thought he was pulling a knife, but instead he produced several folded sheets of papers and pressed them into my hand. We're out of here, he said. The other men released me and followed him. I watched them walk away. My knees were knocking, pain was rising in my gut, my eyes were tearing. I tried to take a step, but every step ached. I had to stop by a plastic penguin with a spring for feet and a seat fastened to its head. I sat down and the penguin bounced. It was still raining. I finally made it home, stripped off my wet clothes, filled a hot-water bottle, got into bed, and spread the sheets of paper I had been given before me. I didn't have to read every word because after the first few lines I got the gist. The opening page dealt with the Aryan origins of the Serbian people and the need to preserve their racial purity, all those of mixed heritage, as well as members of the tainted peoples who lived in Serbia, and they included Jews, Gypsies, Muslims, and Albanians, would be sent back to their homelands, or else be relocated to special fenced-in areas. On the following pages, however, the Jews were the only group to receive attention. Here and there overt mention was made of the need for the world to rid itself of the Jews, who always found ways to control the governments of major countries, the flow of capital, and the mass media. We are living, it went on to say, in the claws of an international Zionist conspiracy, a conspiracy Hitler unmasked and brought to the verge of collapse. He did not succeed, it said near the end, in finishing the job, but he did show the direction all true Aryans must follow. Then a sketch of a skull encircled by a slogan: "Death to Zionism, freedom to the people." There are moments in life when one doesn't know whether to cry or laugh, I told Marko later, and that was one such moment. I clutched the hot-water bottle as if it were a life belt. What I had read could easily have been dismissed as the voice of a crackpot, but it was not a lone voice, it was one voice from a large chorus in which many, like the three who had looked after me in the nursery school yard, had no vocal talent and made up for their lack with skills of a different kind. I tried to summon their faces, which in the feeble light by the entrance to my building had seemed alike; their identical closely cropped haircuts, like those of soldiers, no doubt helped. The fellow who had addressed me, and who punched me in the gut several times, had a slanted scar on his forehead, that was all I remembered. The rain, the trees on Teslina Street, the smashed street lamps, made me remember what I had felt rather than seen. And I felt, as I told Marko later, something like grief, an emptiness that left me as limp as a straw doll. Did it ever occur to you, asked Marko, that they could have killed you? It did, I said, especially when they took me into the bushes behind the nursery school, I really was dead for a few minutes. So how is it, chuckled Marko, on the other side? I chuckled too, but Isak Levi and Jakov Švarc didn't. They read every line carefully, studied the sheets of paper on both sides, lifted the paper to the light, compared certain sections with other texts cut out of newspapers or photocopied from books. We sat around the kitchen table in Jaša Alkalaj's studio; Jaša wasn't in Belgrade then. The table was sprayed with an array of colors, mostly blue, though that color was rarely seen in his paintings, at least in the ones that hung on the walls. I don't like this, Jakov Švarc said, finally, it does not bode well. This is one big pile of nonsense, I said, and there is no point in paying attention to it. We paid no attention to another pile of nonsense, said Jakov Švarc, and look where it got us. The same thing would have happened, Isak Levi spoke up, even if we had paid all the attention in the world, and it is pointless to dupe ourselves with conditional sentences. Spare me the linguistic analyses, Jakov Švarc snapped back, the only thing a person can get from them is heartburn. History is not a novel that unfolds according to established rules. But it is also not a book, rejoined Isak Levi, that can be leafed through now from the beginning, then from the end. Experience tells us, continued Jakov Švarc as he waved the sheets of paper, that something like this always starts innocently and ends up in the most tragic way imaginable. So what now? asked Isak Levi, should we kill ourselves? No, said Jakov Švarc, we should keep ourselves alive. There was silence in the studio. Low tapping sounds could be heard, as if an alarm clock shut in a sock drawer was ringing, but when I went into the bathroom, I realized it was the sound of water dripping from the bathtub faucet. I tried to tighten it; I didn't succeed, it continued dripping onto the yellowed enamel. The rubber washer needs changing, said Isak Levi behind me, but Jaša doesn't see to things like that. He stood at the door, his hands crossed on his chest. You have to understand Jakov, he said, his experience in the last war was particularly painful. Which war are you referring to, I asked, when you say the "last"? I meant the big one, the world war, he answered, because little ones, like ours, don't count as real wars. For those who are no longer alive, I said, every war is real. That is correct, agreed Isak Levi, but a local war is actually abuse of the noun *war,* since it is most often an armed conflict of limited intensity being waged on limited territory. Of course, he said, most of the conflicts registered in history belong to that category, I admit, and there are few wars that were truly grandiose. You speak of wars, I said, at least of the big ones, as though you admire them, and I see no justification for that. He saw no reason to admire them either, Isak Levi replied, but if they did exist, there was no point in closing one's eyes to the fact. Did I think, he asked, that war, any war, great or small, would disappear if I were to shut my eyes tight? That depends, I said, willpower sometimes accomplishes fantastic things. I don't know about willpower, answered Isak Levi, but I do see that Jaša Alkalaj's influence has had its effect. I tried to protest, claiming he was wrong, that I knew nothing about the Kabbalah, or I should say that I didn't know the Kabbalah well. Jaša was a good teacher, said Isak Levi, and I had no cause to worry. I said I wasn't worried and that I would ask Jaša to confirm that my knowledge of Kabbalistic teaching was minimal. Forget it, said Isak Levi dismissively. There was something else, he added, that had just occurred to him: the possibility that Jaša had invoked the dark forces against the thugs who had beaten me up. He would surely, he laughed, be able to summon an entire army of golems and other monsters to steal the thunder from the racists and Nazis and send them scampering as fast as their feet could carry them. Meanwhile, he said, we must fight without their help, because every single wasted moment makes us weaker. I wasn't sure whom he meant: the two of us in the bathroom, the three of us in Jaša's studio, the two of them and Jaša Alkalaj, or all the Jews of Belgrade. So, I said, I should write about what has been happening to me? Isak Levi nodded. As soon as possible, he said, as soon as possible. I, however, was not convinced that this was the best solution, and when the deadline came up, I wrote a lame, halfhearted piece about the absence of musical taste in the most widely watched television programs. For some mysterious reason the editor was pleased, he beamed as he read the text and even stood up and thumped me on the shoulder. Utterly perplexed, I left the building and for a while stood indecisively on the steps. Then I decided to forget about it, as I already had to struggle with plenty of secrets, and editors are unpredictable creatures. I went home, stepped onto the balcony overlooking the yard, shooed away two white pigeons, sat on the deck chair, and tried to make some sense of what had happened to me over the past few weeks. This was not my first try, just as I felt it would not be my last. Jaša Alkalaj's advice to seek in the Kabbalah, or rather, to find in the Kabbalah the key to these events, advice I genuinely believed in, proved of no help. I knew slightly more than I had known about the Kabbalah, though what I knew was a crumb in comparison to its entire treasure. I understood the meaning of the Sephirot, the divine emanations; I had moved toward an understanding of the Infinite, or Ein Sof, which was how the Kabbalists referred to divine substance; I had carefully studied the interpretation of Adam's fall; I had got to know the principles of Gematria; but these pathways led me nowhere, and sooner or later I came back to the beginning, to the Danube riverbank and the slap that, though I hadn't been able to hear it, had deafened me. That slap led to the next, to the event I was fully prepared to accept as a misunderstanding, a comic misunderstanding, but it brought the manuscript into my life, which, I had to admit reluctantly, was related to a variety of things, as if it were constantly being added to and renewed. Then I realized, as I sat in the deck chair and propped my feet on the balcony railing, that I had never mentioned the manuscript to Jaša Alkalaj, though he would certainly be interested in the Kabbalistic parts of the text. I couldn't explain this to myself; the only interpretation I thought of was that, jealous of his apparently limitless familiarity with the Kabbalah and mysticism, I wanted to withhold the information about the manuscript until I could plunk it onto the table in front of Jaša with unconcealed glee. I pictured him leaping from his chair, grabbing the pages of the manuscript, and trembling with excitement. I laughed out loud and decided to tell him about it. I shifted in the deck chair and looked to the right, toward a neighboring yard, and noticed in the crown of a poplar a man wearing black pants and a white shirt. The branches and leaves partially concealed him, but if he thought no one could see him, he was wrong. His hands were in front of his face, and it took me a moment to figure out that he was holding binoculars, trained on me. I looked to the left, I looked to the right, I leaned over the railing, but there was no one but me on any of the balconies. There was the possibility, of course, that he was a jealous husband, trying to locate the window behind which his wife was languishing in the arms of a lover, though that was difficult to believe. I remembered I had my father's old binoculars somewhere, and dragging myself out of the deck chair, I went to look for them. I rummaged in the cupboard, checked some boxes in the pantry, poked around in the drawers of my desk, and, not having come up with the binoculars, I returned to the balcony, but the man was no longer in the poplar. I studied the other treetops, surveyed the roofs of the buildings, lowered my gaze to the yards overgrown in weeds, the man was gone. Maybe he was never there, said Marko when I told him, so I decided to say no more. Of course, I knew that people are sometimes victims of their own guesswork and prejudice, and that there are times when they think they see what they would like to see, and the man with the binoculars, so clumsily hidden in the crown of the poplar tree, might be nothing more than a projection of mine, a reflection of my hidden hope that I was part of a vast plot or scheme in which a large portion of the world was embroiled. I knew what Marko would say to that: he would laugh and say I had been watching too many American movies. He had said something along those lines a few days before when I had set out a theory about a different, though similar, version of a conspiracy. We've all seen too many American movies, I had told him then, which was true. This was not merely a worn phrase that Europeans use when, on their first visit to America, they feel they are in a movie, but even we in Europe compare our reality more and more often to the cinematic reality of American films. Who in Europe thinks about conspiracies, I asked Marko, in which ordinary citizens become the greatest obstacle to the monstrous plans of insatiable politicians? It's all small in Europe, said Marko, even conspiracies. I can't tell whether he meant that as consolation to me, but when I saw the man in that poplar tree, it was no consolation. Whether large or small, a conspiracy is a conspiracy, and if someone is caught up in it, the consequences may be dangerous. Fine, said Marko, when I'd made that argument to him, the consequences may indeed be dangerous, but we should be realistic and accept where we live. Conspiracy in Serbia, he said, is that even possible? Why should Serbia, I spoke in my defense, be any worse than any other country, why couldn't we have a nice, big conspiracy here? Serbia is already worse than many countries, said Marko, but I'd say you are missing something. Where have you been, he asked, these past ten years? On Mars? So, I continued, on the defensive, you have it all figured out, is that it? Nearly everything, said Marko, except a couple of murders among criminals turned patriots. And those, I said, aren't conspiracies? Just because I don't understand something, replied Marko, doesn't mean that some dark evil force is behind it, a mysterious organization in collusion with the government, army, police, or who knows what. Such things, he said, happen only in American movies, in which, by the way, the entire plot is reduced to the struggle of conspirators to strip free and honest American citizens of their right to information, to knowledge that supposedly belongs to them, if for no other reason than that they regularly pay their taxes, while in this country, he said, it is about silencing witnesses, and ordinary people like you and me are never in the picture. Besides, he added, in a country like ours, where everybody knows all there is to know about everybody else, conspiracies aren't workable, at least not conspiracies of the kind you've seen in the movies, because no one here can keep a secret. Someone, said Marko, don't ask me who, said that real history is what goes on between two people with no witnesses, but if that is true, then history here is what goes on inside a single person, who sits alone in a room and invents history. And if *that* is true, I said, then the single person's power is limitless. Sure it is, said Marko, and that's why our conspiracies aren't the same as the ones playing out in the world and in Hollywood studios. They're like a puppet theater with only one actor, well concealed behind the set, playing all the puppets and pulling all the strings. Marko was right, I had to give him credit, though I was still eager to understand who was pulling the strings of the people caught up in what was happening to me, including mine, and if they all had their little strings, as Marko put it, then I had strings too. And you too, I told him. In Serbia we are all dangling by a thread, said Marko, no one is spared. Don't tell me, I protested, that all the strings are held by one man. Of course not, countered Marko, he is at the peak of a pyramid composed of his mini clones, just the way every successful dictatorship has always functioned, take Stalin's in the Soviet Union, for instance, if it was to function successfully, there had to be, aside from Stalin himself, hundreds, thousands of mini Stalins, his copies or clones, each one controlling a handful of strings, while their strings, he said, were in the hands of someone else who was above them on the hierarchical party ladder, and their strings were in the hands of someone above them, and there were always fewer of those above than those below, and so it went, he said, all the way up to Stalin, who held only two or three of the main strings, but he could give one of them a tweak and all of the Soviet Union would rock as if it had been hit by a major earthquake. I tried to imagine this pyramid and all the strings, but they kept getting knotted up in my mind's eye, tangling hopelessly. Only Stalin was unscathed at the very top, grinning under that bushy mustache. Always the same story, said Marko, in the end, there are no big differences among the dictatorial pyramids and the networks of strings that make them. The only difference he could think of, he said, was that our dictators didn't sport mustaches. This thought moved him to air a theory about how most dictators had a mustache because the mustache was a symbol of masculinity. Dictators, generally spineless types, grow a mustache to enhance their masculine powers and justify their authority, he remarked, which raises the engaging question of the absence of mustaches on the faces of our dictators. He looked at me but I shrugged. Maybe they proved their masculinity some other way, said Marko, or felt no one was questioning them, there is no other explanation. He spoke a bit longer about the difference in significance between Hitler's little brush of a mustache and the bushy mustache on Stalin's face, but I was no longer listening. The next day, however, while I was on a city bus crossing the Sava, I thought back to the conversation and chuckled to myself. The man standing next to me scowled, then quickly touched his cheeks, nose, and lips, and when he found nothing on them to have made me laugh, he snapped, What's got into you? I turned serious, but a moment later my lips stretched again into a grin. You know what, said the man, I'll hit you so hard you won't get up again. Even though he said this in a voice that shook with rage, his eyes flashing, brandishing his fist, for some reason it struck me as so hilarious that, clenching my teeth to choke back the spurts of laughter, I dashed off the bus at the next stop. Instead of at Zeleni Venac, where I was headed, I found myself at the end of the bridge over the Sava, at the beginning of Brankova Street, and so I had to walk farther than I had planned. It was Friday and I was supposed to meet Jaša Alkalaj at six that afternoon in the courtyard of the synagogue on Maršal Birjuzova. That was the time, he told me, Shabbat began, and there was no more peaceful moment than when, like a bride, Saturday steps into the temple. I don't know what it was like inside the temple, but when I arrived at the synagogue courtyard, short of breath from my brisk walk, no one was there, only a hat on a bench beneath a spreading tree. I approached it gingerly, as if something might leap out from under it. The hat didn't move, or resist when I picked it up and set it on my head. It was too large and slid down over my brow, covering my eyes and resting on my ears. What do you know, I heard Jaša Alkalaj's voice, such a refined fellow, so well-mannered, yet stealing hats. I tore the hat off my head and turned: Jaša Alkalaj, grinning, stood by a graying older man. The hat belongs to me, said the man, extending his hand. I gave him the hat. If his hair had been completely gray, I would have thought this was the man who had handed me the envelope with the manuscript. I asked him if he had a brother living in Zemun. No, said Jaša, our Dača has no one, certainly not in Zemun. Though he had no relatives there, Dača was well versed in the history of the Zemun Jews, and he drew my attention to the fact that their fate for many years had been determined by the fact that Zemun lay on the Military Frontier, where they were not, otherwise, permitted to settle. For some reason, Dača said, putting on his hat, Empress Maria Theresa gave her permission for the first Jewish families who moved here, roughly a dozen, to stay on in Zemun, and this edict determined the life of the Zemun Jewish community for the next hundred years or so. As with so many imperial privileges, Dača said, taking off his hat, this one was based on defining the ban and on insisting that it be obeyed, so the whole century passed in attempts by the Zemun Jews to sidestep regulations and find a way to stay in Zemun, which was rich in opportunities for trade and other activities because of its border location. You see, said Dača, putting the hat on again, the privilege of staying here applied only to a small number of families, and though that number increased gradually through the decades, there were threats, even moves by the authorities to bring the number down to the few that had originally been permitted to stay. One way, Dača said, once more taking off his hat, was to switch names, in hopes of burying their traces in lists and documents, which infuriated the authorities of the time and historians today, who need to determine whether, for instance, Rafael Salomon and Salomon Rafael are one and the same person whose first name becomes his last name for a time, and his last name becomes his first, or whether the two are unrelated. The names on one list, said Dača, holding his hat in his lap, do not appear on another drawn up several years later, and several years on they crop up again on some new list. He stared at his hat, lifted it, then dropped it back in his lap. Tell me, he said to Jaša Alkalaj, why am I telling you all of this? Because of Eleazar, said Jaša. Ah, that's right, said Dača, and patted the hat, because of Eleazar. He turned to Jaša again and asked him if I knew who Eleazar was. Naturally, said Jaša, he came asking about Eleazar and found him. And lost him, I said. Dača looked at me sternly, as if startled that I knew how to speak, and I felt my cheeks blushing red. It's not that you lost him, he said, putting on his hat, but that he himself found ways of getting lost. I breathed a sigh of relief, the weight of guilt lifted off my shoulders. Yes, said Dača, he disappeared of his own volition, that was the best way he had of finding himself again. He took his hat off, scrutinized it on all sides, sniffed it. Hey, he looked over at Jaša Alkalaj, where did I get this hat? I was wondering that myself, Jaša replied. This is a pot, said Dača, not a hat. I laughed, but turned serious when my eyes met Dača's. Eleazar, he said, if that was indeed his name, unlike most of the other Jewish families in Zemun was one of the "Turkish" Jews, meaning a Sephardic Jew who had been an Ottoman subject. And as such, and especially because of the niggling that went on between the Ottomans and the Habsburgs, he was, at the very least, suspicious, so that is probably why when he was registering with the authorities, he came up with another name or, using Gematria, chose a name that had the same numerical value, so that he was Eleazar yet he was not Eleazar, and it is easy to assume that when a census was held fifteen years later of the Jewish inhabitants of Zemun, he was the very man registered as Volf, a water carrier, which was confirmed in a more detailed list drawn up a year later, in 1756, in which he was listed as Volf Enoch, only to disappear altogether or show up on a list in 1815, no longer as Volf, but as Nahmi the water carrier, who had apparently been living in Zemun for thirty years, with a family of four, which is, of course, rubbish, because where there is water, there is Eleazar, who slaked people's thirst, their thirst for water and their thirst for Zion, the thirst of the body and the thirst of the soul, because only in harmony between soul and body do the soul and body survive. He paused. I suddenly noticed that during that long sentence he had stopped touching the hat. He brought water to the Hertzls, said Jaša. And to Rabbi Alkalaj, said Dača. He got up, put on the hat, and licked his lips. After all this talk of water, he said, a person works up a thirst, but there are no water carriers any longer, though I wouldn't mind a lemonade at Murat's, if one of you two is willing to pay. I'd pay, said Jaša, but just as there are no more water carriers, so there is no more Murat. Really? said Dača, surprised, and took off his hat. When did he die? He didn't die, answered Jaša, he went back to Priština. Really? said Dača again, but why? Even you, as a Kabbalist, can't answer that question, laughed Jaša. Dača stared at the hat as if he no longer knew what to do with it. What about the pastry shop, he asked, finally, is it still there? It stands there, said Jaša, empty. I'd gladly give this hat, said Dača, and looked at us, for a couple of his baklavas. I preferred the *tulumba* myself, said Jaša. And then, I said the next day to Marko, what came next was the two of them going on about all the other delicacies, the cream pastries like *krempita* and *šampita,* the *sudžuk* and chocolate roll, the halva and chestnut purée, ice cream and *lenja pita.* Murat must have made all the pastries under the sun, I said. Marko shook his head. Let me get this straight, he said, on Friday evening, just as the holy day is beginning for Jews, you are standing in the synagogue courtyard quibbling about pastry? After all that, he asked, did you buy the man a lemonade? Yes, I said, but because Murat had shut down his shop, we went to the Majestic, where, as soon as we walked in, a friend of theirs showed up, an old actor, who sat at our table and regaled us with stories of what happens to actors when they tour the provinces. And then I felt certain again that I had seen the woman from the quay entering a gallery across the street. I said that a meeting had slipped my mind and that I would have to leave at once. By the time we'd said our goodbyes, and Dača had showed me the Parisian label in his hat, and the actor had launched into a story of what happened to them on a visit to Leskovac, there was no one left over at the gallery. It was dark upstairs and down. So it goes every single time, I had thought, though I didn't tell Marko this, either I get there too late, like this time, or too early, like the day when I went into the courtyard on Zmaj Jovina Street and sat down on the bench in the corner, thereby missing the opportunity of running into her when she came out of the building. I don't know why I decided not to mention any of this to Marko. We were sitting in his kitchen, drinking coffee and smoking hashish that someone he knew had brought him from Amsterdam, and just as I was retelling the actor's last anecdote, I felt myself sinking. It was not, in fact, a real slump, but a sensation of unexpected shrinking, as if the hashish had set something off in me, a little switch that had totally changed my perspective, making me see everything from a low, bottom-up angle, as if the people and things surrounding me, and even whole realms, loomed suddenly large or, at least, unpleasantly elongated. Marko knew about this, moreover, he had had similar experiences several times, though in his case, or as he told it to me, more often he seemed to be growing, while everything else shrank. We never sorted out whether in both our cases this was a question of original experience, or if one of the two of us had gone through it and then told the other what had happened, and the other then had had the impression that he had experienced the same thing, because neither of us could remember who had first had the experience we called "the Alice," after the episode in the cartoon of *Alice in Wonderland* in which she nibbles the mushroom, or was it cake, and alternately grows bigger and smaller. I've got the Alice, I would say, which came in handy, particularly when we were in company or in a public place, because the Alice could, at times, be headstrong and rocky. That day, at the exact moment I was describing what had happened the night I left the Majestic and crossed the street, I was hit by a wave of the Alice, and though in my story I stayed at pavement level, I began to sink, and when in the story I looked at the upper level, where it was also dark, in the Alice I also looked up and saw Marko's face towering over me, in a space neither light nor dark. I don't know if I am making myself clear enough. In any case, it would not be good for someone to think, when I describe the experience called the Alice, that I am trying to attribute to it a mystical property or profound significance. It was a minor, silly optical illusion caused by the action of some of the ingredients of the cannabis on who knows which brain cells, and like many similar insights caused by intoxicating substances, it readily lent itself to the most varied interpretations. This is our remarkable ability as humans to attribute a meaning to everything, as if nothing happens just because it happens, as if everything is a basis or a mirror of a secret, if not the secret itself, whatever that secret might be. The greatest secret, Marko once said, is that there are no secrets. Very few people, however, are willing to accept this premise, though I doubt many readers will have made it this far. Sometimes I'm not even sure I am writing this; perhaps I am only saying it; perhaps I am thinking that I am saying that I am writing; maybe not even that, but something altogether different, an interplay of images and sounds, a language that is no one's, least of all mine. Slowly, slowly, I have veered off course, soon it will turn out that I am talking to myself, like some drooling old man in the corner of a room, dirty and unshaven, in unbuttoned pants, no underwear, so that everyone can see his wrinkled penis and sagging balls. There, as soon as I mentioned Alice, that curious predecessor to Lolita, I knew we'd end up in someone's fly, searching for the mystical meaning of her name, a fall through a hole, a disappearing cat, and hysterical tea drinking. No, our Alice was an altogether minor, paltry experience under the influence of hashish, an illusion we knew to be an illusion, which does nothing to interfere with the real state of affairs, but runs parallel with it. So I looked at Marko from below, and I looked at him normally, with eyes that were level with his face, as always happens in the Alice, an experience that, now I see, we might think of calling something else. What frightened me this time, however, was the fact, the fact not the supposition, that on Marko's face hovered something so horrendous, an expression so rife with malice, that I felt my heart clench. It reminded me of the masks of New Guinea cannibals that hung above the bed of a girl I'd briefly gone out with some ten years before. When I first saw them, the blood froze in my veins. Later I got used to them, but when we made love I didn't dare look at the masks, I would close my eyes or twist my neck, terrified by the thought that one might come loose and crush me. Suddenly I no longer felt like talking, though Marko was pestering me with questions, and even when the Alice was over and all the perspectives leveled off, when I could see perfectly well how the gentle features of his face had, under the influence of the cannabis, taken on a grimace of horror, not even then could I force myself to keep going. I told Marko I was tired, that I was behind again with my piece for *Minut,* and though he tried to entice me to stay by rolling a new joint, I headed home. The night before, when I had gone to the gallery and found it dark inside, I had noticed the open door to the neighboring café, and there, at the bottom of the glass door, that same symbol I had found near the Zemun open market. It's hard to believe that I even spotted it in the half-darkness, as if I had developed special receptors in my brain that had only one task: spot the circle and triangles. How much time had elapsed since I'd first seen them? Sometimes it felt as if March 8 was only yesterday, at other times I thought that it had all happened years before; once though, when I'd dozed off, I believed that it was only about to start, while another time, just after I'd woken up, it was clear it would never stop, though the truth, as often happens, was simpler: it was still April, an Eliot-like April, the cruelest month, which meant that slightly more than a month had passed, five weeks, maybe six, from the moment I'd witnessed the unpleasant, and I must quickly add, unconvincing slap on the Danube riverbank. Everything that had happened, and that I had learned, still meant nothing to me, but I also knew, or, to be more precise, sensed that behind it all, there was something that would open at some moment, at a time extremely difficult to predict, just then, entirely certain in its uncertainty, no matter how absurd that might sound. But the absurd had become ordinary, commonplace, something we'd become used to these past ten years in a country that was not a proper country participating in a war that was not a real war, subjecting ourselves to a government that had anointed itself the government, becoming an island that was floating, set apart from the world like a leprosy colony that no one wanted to touch. There is your explanation, as Marko would say, the reason you are investing so much hope and expectation in that symbol, a mere geometric construct, which may conceal nothing in particular, but for that reason is powerful enough to draw your thoughts away from the chaos and commotion surrounding you. That may well be so, Marko is often right, indeed uncomfortably right, all the more reason for me not to tell him everything that had happened the night before. When I had caught sight of the symbol on the door of the café, I wasn't prepared at first to believe that it was the same geometric figure, the one that Dragan Mišović had explained, or at least tried to explain, to me. A startling likeness, I thought as I came closer to the café door and bent over to check. It even occurred to me that I should call him and ask how to explain the resemblance, and whether in mathematical terms there were, as one might say for people, kindred spirits. So, was there a spirit in mathematics? Were numbers conscious? I was thinking about this and similar nonsense as I bent down in front of the open door of the café and, kneeling, nearly touched the glass with my nose. There could be no doubt: it was the same symbol, drawn to the same proportions, even if some of the lines were a shade thicker. Once I was finally convinced, I ventured into the café, lifting each foot high as if afraid that I might trip over an invisible thread connecting the symbol to whatever and hoping at the same time for an explanation as to what it was doing here in the middle of Belgrade after the many sightings in Zemun. To my disappointment the café was empty. The only person there was a young man behind the counter, his head shaved smooth, dressed all in black, a small gold earring in his right ear. As I entered he was inserting a silver disc into the sound system, with his back to me. Everything gleamed in the gray semidarkness, the disc, the earring, and the back of his head, especially the back of his head, down which the rays of light slid as if alive. He caught sight of me in the mirror but turned around only after the disc had slid into the system, and then only to say, She's up there, and he gestured at the ceiling with his thumb. After that we were plashed by a wave of music from the band Morphine, a pounding bass and the moan of a saxophone. I stared at him. His lips moved again: I couldn't hear anything though I decided he wasn't addressing me, but mouthing the words of the song thundering in the café. Nonetheless I tried and I shouted as loudly as I could, Who is up there? The young man looked at me, scowled, then came close, nearly resting his lips against my ear. I can't hear you, he said. His breath tickled my ear and made me laugh. He moved his head and placed his ear in front of my lips. I smelled the sweet fragrance of lotion and saw the little hairs that had started traitorously growing. I was asking, I said, who is up there and why you told me. I tried carefully not to touch him but failed; my lips did touch the whorls of his ear several times. Again we changed positions, and his breath filled my ear. I don't know anything, he shouted, except she said I should send up the one who came in after her, dressed like you are dressed. He stepped away and gestured behind me, and only then did I see the beginning of a staircase leading to an upper level. I went over to the stairs, leaned on the banister, and looked up. There, I thought, reigned real darkness, but once I had climbed up I saw I'd been wrong. On each table was a lamp, so the room was filled with little oases of light, between which the dark was denser, but only for one or at most one and a half steps, which was all it took to move from table to table. Then I saw her hand. The lamps on the tables had low shades, so the heads and upper parts of the bodies of the guests were framed in a pale twilight, while the hands and lower arms shone with outlandish brightness, which is why I first saw her hands, almost unreal in their whiteness, and only then, above the edge of the light, her face, stippled with dark. I cannot recall how many tables were taken, perhaps there was no one else on the upper level, but I seem to recall a fragment of conversation, muffled laughter, which reached us when we fell silent and which persuaded me that someone was laughing at me. Each time I'd smooth my hair, feel my face with my fingertips, brush the corners of my mouth, press the tip of my nose. I think she never took her eyes off me. So all the while I was wondering, and here, that's the reason I was not prepared to tell Marko about it—sensing that, guided by male logic, he would have no understanding for such a subtle point—all the while I was wondering whether she could feel it in her fingertips, which rested on the table, how my heart was pounding, since I was seated at an angle and the left side of my chest rested against the table's edge. What did we talk about, or did we talk at all, or else did we take turns blurting out disconnected sentences? Everything was chopped, distinct, as if, while sitting at the same table, we were in different time zones and speaking to ourselves. I managed once or twice to bring up the Danube, but I didn't make it to the scene by the riverbank because she stopped me, lifting her hand or arching an eyebrow. May I at least know, I asked, your name? Of course, she said. I waited. Margareta, she said. She had two birthmarks on her left temple, freckles on her cheekbones, silken hairs above the corners of her lips, a small scar on the tip of her chin. I fell from a bicycle when I was small, she said, and touched the scar with the tip of her index finger. A scrap of someone's laughter floated over to us, and I quickly touched my cheeks and nose. The music in the lower part of the café swelled, the noise mounted the stairs, the drum and bass repeated the same monotonous, hypnotic beat, and I could feel the floor vibrate. I felt something else: nausea at the dense cigarette smoke, and I knew that I would wake up the next morning with a horrific headache. I wiped my forehead. I noticed worry flash through her eyes; I could see nothing when I took a closer look. I asked her if she would like to take a walk. A little fresh air, I said, would be nice. She nodded silently. But first I need to go and splash my face, I added, if she didn't mind waiting. She shook her head. I got up and went quickly down the stairs. In the mirror of the men's room I saw I was pale. I splashed my face and rubbed it with a paper towel. The paper was thin and tore, stuck to my fingers. How long did I stay there? Five minutes, ten, certainly no longer, not even that, but when I went back up she wasn't there. At first I assumed that she too had gone to the toilet, so I sat there calmly, legs crossed, sipping cold coffee. I stared at the table, Margareta didn't come back, the music got louder, and someone at a neighboring table swore ardently, someone else laughed, and finally I realized she was gone. I stood up abruptly, prepared to run, though I could barely walk for the misery of it, then, pressing against the table with the palms of my hands, I noticed a slip of paper protruding from under her saucer. I sat again. The paper, torn from a small pad, was folded twice, and it smelled just a little, when I sniffed it, of some long since forgotten perfume, something like patchouli or vanilla, no longer in fashion. I unfolded the paper and then quickly folded it again and turned to look around, and only then did I smooth out the scrap of paper and read what was written on it: A dream uninterpreted is like a letter unread. I knew the sentence, it had been on the back of the manuscript that the gray-haired man had given me. I turned over the scrap of paper and looked at the other side: nothing was written there, nothing sketched, despite my hopes to the contrary. I got up, picked up the check, and as I was making my way to the stairs I noticed a crumpled ball of paper under the table. A terrible silence suddenly reigned and all eyes were on me. In fact, no one was looking my way, the din had grown even more raucous, new guests were mounting the stairs, the waiter was carrying a tray with cups of cappuccino and little bottles of Coca-Cola, so I could bend down calmly and pick up the uneven paper ball. Just in case, however, I didn't smooth it out in the café. I shoved it into my jeans pocket, and there it remained until I got home. Even then I didn't smooth it out right away, but placed it on the table in the living room, sat in the armchair, and stared at it. For some reason I was sure that the crumpled paper held the real message and that the message left under the saucer had merely been a decoy, an illusion of a message, a distraction for someone who was not meant to learn anything. I tried to remember the appearance of the people sitting at the other tables, but they mingled, pale and paltry, always outshone by Margareta's face, and only one face came back to me in its entirety, the face of the young man at the bar, glowing with a light that, halo-like, reflected from his shaven head. I even recalled the earring in his right ear, slightly drooping, though nicely shaped. Perhaps Margareta's acts of caution were a routine she held to in every situation, regardless of whether there was real danger or not? I reached out to the paper ball, touched it with the tip of my index finger. Measures of caution, peril, a mask, and a distraction? What was I thinking? I looked at the finger with which I had touched the edge of the paper as if I expected to see a drop of blood on it. Then I licked it and raised it to the air, as I used to do when I was a boy, to determine which way the wind was blowing; where the saliva on the finger felt cooler, that was where the wind was blowing from. Nothing was moving in the room, of course, and the finger remained equally moist on all sides. I took a handkerchief out of my pocket, wiped my finger, then went to the window. I looked to the left, looked to the right, surveyed the street lit by the flickering light of the street lamps, and in the fragmented reflections in the windowpane I sought the reflection of the paper ball behind my back. Down there on the street, two pedestrians were moving from opposite sidewalks to cross the street at the same time, as if in a math problem, and I assumed that someone somewhere was calculating where they would meet. One of the pedestrians was much taller, which probably meant that his stride would be longer, but if he was melancholic by nature, then he would walk more slowly, which would give the second pedestrian, shorter and broader and irrepressibly optimistic, the advantage, despite the fact that his stride was shorter. Paying no attention to the demands of this challenging task, the pedestrians met precisely at the yellow line, which divided the street into two equal parts, and it even seemed to me that they nodded in greeting. I waited for each to cross over to the opposite sidewalk and walk on, then all there was to watch was the traffic light, but the pattern of its changes quickly became too predictable. There was no putting it off, I said to myself, but I waited for all three colors to follow one after the other once more. I went over to the table, uncrumpled the ball, and smoothed out the paper. I saw the familiar geometric figure, and below it, a six-digit number, which, there could be no doubt, was a phone number. I don't know what I was expecting: perhaps a few sentences, something more complex; this seemed simple, too simple for a story about the Kabbalah and cryptic occurrences. I took the paper, brought it to my nose, and sniffed. It had no smell. I checked the other side; it was empty, as had been the reverse side of the other scrap of paper. Now, easy, I said to myself, easy. Maybe there was something that should be done with that number, a mathematical operation, finding the right path, which would lead to the true meaning. A moment later I wondered what I was doing here: the country was in a state of collapse, threats of bombardment hung in the air like overripe fruit, people were snapping apart as if they had been made of Lego blocks, lunacy had nearly been declared the norm, and here I was tinkering with Kabbalistic mysteries and anti-Jewish conspiracies, and wasting hours and days to discover who had left tracks in river mud that had long since been washed away. I should have turned around there and then, shrugged it all off, headed in the opposite direction, forgotten Eleazar and his passage to the other world, returned to my messy, everyday life, to stories of politics and shifts in government, to exercises in the skill of survival, but just as I hadn't done that to begin with, so I didn't listen to myself now, and when I lifted the receiver my hand was shaking. The phone rang after only a few seconds, the first time with interference, then more clearly and loudly, until after the fifth or sixth ring it went quiet. Hello, I said, and my voice dropped like a stone into a void. I pressed the receiver against my ear: no more crackling, but now I was convinced that someone was saying something in a whisper or, perhaps, shouting from a great distance. Hello, I said again, feeling like a person who, leaning over the stone rim, speaks into the depths of a well. I waited a moment longer, then hung up. Where had I gone wrong? Again I remembered Dragan Mišović: perhaps more refined mathematical calculations were called for, more complex operations, a more sophisticated knowledge of algebra or whatever, something there was no way I could see when I looked at the numbers written on the crumpled scrap of paper. Then I picked up the phone again and dialed the same number, remembering the advice of the secretary at *Minut* when I complained that I had not been able to get through to them for hours. Never trust our phones, she said then, not when someone's talking, or even saying nothing, and less still when you get a busy signal. This time the phone rang straight away. It rang loud and clear, so loud, in fact, that I had to move the receiver away from my ear. And her voice, when she came on, was the same. Thank you, she said. I never knew what that meant, what she was thanking me for, so I said nothing. I remembered how her hands gleamed in the café, and I wondered what the light was like where she was sitting now. I imagined a great old-fashioned chandelier, full of crystal balls and tinkling decorations, through which the light was refracted, making fragile, little rainbows. It is dark, she said, it's dark in my room. My hands no longer shook; now my palms were sweating. So that's why I didn't tell Marko everything, it was because of Margareta's ability, I don't know what else to call it, to read my thoughts. At the time I thought of this as an ability; now, despite everything, I believe it was a skill, difficult but possible to master, yet as far as Marko went, nothing would have changed had I known that then. Ability or skill, none of this would have meant a thing to him, regardless of distinctions, because he would not have accepted it, and he would have produced a scornful smile, maybe even a loud laugh. Yoda from *Star Wars* reads minds, he'd say, that doesn't happen in everyday, normal life. High time, he'd add, for me to stop living in the world of sci-fi and come back to this planet, no matter how chaotic it might be. I would have told him then that he didn't know what he was saying, that I am not afraid of chaos, and word by word we would have sunk into the lull of hashish, until we fell silent, drained, or we pounced on a box of wafer cookies. Marko had once calculated that in the course of our many years of getting high we had eaten nearly a freight car worth of wafer cookies, though I never corroborated his figures. And it wasn't just wafer cookies we ate, often we had Turkish delight, tea crescents, and chocolate-covered raisins. These are from Freight Car Number 2, Marko would say, and as far as he was concerned the discussion would be over. Pressing the phone to my ear, I looked around as if I were in my apartment for the first time, and said that my room too was dark. In fact only one lamp was on, and its wan light could have passed for a thin dusk, the first stage of proper darkness. I may not have said that, or at least not in so many words, I no longer remember, though it was not so very long ago that this happened, but I, like most people, remember pointless details better, the circumstances leading to a goal, while the goal itself, even when I reach it, tends to elude memory, as if in a dream in which, no matter how far we walk, or run, or ride a white stallion, we cannot get close to the outline of walls on the horizon or the shore of the emerald river. Of course I should have jotted everything down and not allowed the writing, as is happening now, to turn into an archeological excavation. Words are the goods that rot the fastest, as the editor at *Minut* once said, and I stared, astonished, at him, not because he rarely declared such sentiments, but because those words suddenly illuminated a multitude of things to me and made me think about language as a cluster of bananas. Nothing, indeed, rots as quickly as language, though bananas that have gone soft do have their charm. I don't believe I brought up bananas in my conversation with Margareta that evening. In some sense we picked up where the conversation in the café left off, though she didn't explain why she had had to leave so abruptly, and just as I had felt at the café that we were not actually having a conversation, so this exchange too turned into a sequence of choppy fragments on the way to silence. Then we stopped talking, and a moment later, without saying goodbye, she hung up. In the rustling void that followed, again I thought I could hear someone whispering from an unreachable distance, and I kept the phone to my ear for a long time, so that my ear, as I could see in the mirror as I got ready for bed, turned red like a poppy and hurt at the slightest touch. The next day I told Marko other things, and in the end he advised me to stay away from it all, because pretty soon, he said, I'd be wanting to become a Jew, and then, he pointed out, I would have to be circumcised. He winked and laughed. Enough of this. I must go back to a few other things that happened, because if I don't do it now I'll never catch up. This story has too many threads as it is, and it probably will never become a proper story. Stories are orderly, the threads in stories are harmoniously arranged, what I am doing here is more a reflection of life, which is chaotic, with too much going on at once. Life, I heard someone say, is like a puppet theater in which many of the strings have snapped, so each of us is an unhappy puppeteer trying to pull together and reconnect the strings into a workable whole, but keeps making mistakes. Life comes down to untangling knots, and even more to tying them again, but that simple act grows more complicated as the years pass, the fingers thicken or get stiff, the sight grows feeble, the teeth drop out. The puppets stagger around on the stage, they raise arms instead of legs, they swivel their heads when they should be looking straight, in the summer they seek shade and in the winter they ask for gloves and scarves, they complain of gas pains, they wear two different pairs of glasses to read letters, and when that is not enough, they read only the headlines in the newspaper and then guess about the articles, and this makes their world more and more the product of their fancy, as perhaps it should be, because after that comes the moment when nothing matters, and the only thing left for the puppeteer to do is release the string that holds the funeral plaque and watch the little puff of dust rise above the empty stage. The performance is over. The end. That is not what I meant to talk about, but rather about something still far from over. The walls of the stairwell in the building where I lived were covered in splotches of different colors, irregular shapes, which my neighbors were using to try and cover the large and small swastikas, the six-pointed stars that dripped with gore, and the brief anti-Semitic slogan, if anti-Semitic best describes it: BOO TO THE JEWS. The messages in my mailbox had become so frequent and monotonous that I stopped saving them. One night, I found a little mound of excrement on the doormat. I bent over, then knelt down to examine it more closely. It was firm, compact, and I could just picture the effort with which the person had squeezed it out. Perhaps the squeezing was even accompanied by pain, the rupturing of a blood vessel along the rim of the anus, but the light in the stairwell was too weak for me to spot any traces of coagulated blood. Judging by the position of the stool, tidily coiled, the person had produced it while crouching over the doormat, and someone else, I assume, was keeping watch at the door to the building. If they had brought it there from somewhere else, surely the natural snakelike appearance would have been spoiled, at least smeared. I was not eager to carry it, so I picked up the doormat along with it and tossed them both into a large plastic shopping bag with the name of a fashion shop written across it. I bought a new doormat with the word WELCOME on it, but when I found it a few days later soaked in urine I gave up on any further purchases. So, maybe this was a victory for the monster, as Marko put it, and I believe that they experienced it as such; however, I would do better, I answered, spending my money on more useful things. I can always wipe my shoes, I added, on my neighbor's mat, nothing wrong with that. If I was being exposed to such things, then, I reasoned, the real Jews surely must have been suffering far greater abuse. Strangely, Jaša Alkalaj and Isak Levi had not known of any such incidents, or maybe, as Marko claimed, they preferred not to talk about them. Fear is the greatest censor, said Marko. I hadn't seen Jakov Švarc much at that point, but when I ran into him by chance on Knez Mihailova Street I brought the matter up. As I leaned toward him to hear better in the clamor and bustle of the street, I spotted two familiar figures by the entrance to a passageway that led through to Čika Ljubina Street. I could not recall at first where I knew their faces from, but then, as strains of an accordion wafted from somewhere, I recalled the rainy night when they accosted me at the doorway to my building. One of them, in the nursery school bushes, had punched me in the small of my back, right in the kidneys. The other had changed some, his hair had grown out or he had grown a mustache, but there was no doubt that he too had been breathing down my neck. Do you now understand, asked Jakov Švarc, why this is as it is? I looked at his lips, as if there were words on them that I had not yet heard. I noticed only a crumb of bread. It might get better someday, he went on, meanwhile, it is what it is. He had, he said, an appointment with a cardiologist, at his age, he said, every twitch was interpreted as announcing the ultimate absence of all pain. He patted himself on the chest, in the area of the heart, and left, and I looked again at the entrance to the passageway. There was no one there. I looked to the left, I looked to the right, I turned and kept walking toward Kalemegdan, spinning like a mindless weathervane. I had similar experiences over the next few days, not every day, of course, though often enough to make me anxious about going out into the street. The sequence of events was nearly always the same: here and there, alone or in company, I would spot the familiar faces, unobtrusive yet present, and the moment I was distracted they would slip away. Ignore them, Jaša Alkalaj said when I complained, they are spoiled rotten and have seen too many bad movies. I didn't believe him, sensing that he didn't believe himself. When I asked what was really going on in the Jewish community, he avoided answering, and when I said rumors were circulating around town that the Jewish cemetery had been vandalized, he said that I shouldn't believe everything I heard, but if I was so curious I could go to the cemetery and see for myself. The dead don't lie, you know, he said. So off I went to the cemetery. The metal gateway was freshly painted. I opened it with effort, stepped into the cemetery, and let it shut with a bang behind me. After all the noise and commotion of the traffic, the serenity of the cemetery was almost painful. The broad avenue, lined with evergreens, led to a large monument resembling the wings of a butterfly, or, more precisely, a gateway to heaven, a gate to the other world. The day was bright and warm, the path crisscrossed with shadows. I walked slowly, pausing, studying tombstones, but I couldn't shake off the sense that someone was watching me. Maybe that's how it is at every cemetery, what with the presence of all the dead and the feel of silence, but, just in case, I turned around abruptly several times, once I even crouched, determined to wait for the person to appear. No one appeared. I crouched until my calves and thighs ached, and then I straightened up with great effort and sat on the nearest bench. Though the avenue was not long, the winged monument looked as if it were far off on the horizon, as if I would never reach it. Then, suddenly, the branches of a pine tree above me began swaying, though I felt not a breath of wind. Two or three pine needles floated past me, and one, like an arrow, pierced the sleeve of my jacket, shivered, then tipped over. I looked up. There was still rustling, but now it came from the very top of the tree. That must be how the dead make themselves known, I thought. I no longer looked back. I lowered my head and hurried toward the monument. I wanted to get out of that tunnel of evergreens as fast as possible, to get to a place where no one was saying anything to me. I came out of the shadows and thought I saw someone pass behind the monument wings: he stepped from behind the right-hand wing and slipped behind the one on the left. I froze. I stood on the concrete path at the approach to the monument, staring at the empty space between the wings. Maybe those are the wings of an angel, I thought, but this did nothing to ease my terror. Only one possibility was left, and slowly, step by step, I walked along the path that led through the monument. I held my breath and listened. The only sound I could hear was the pounding of blood in my ears. Then I squinted and nearly galloped across the empty space on the path, shielding my head with my arms and kicking my feet up high. When I opened my eyes I was face to face with the cemetery wall. I turned around. Between the wings of the monument I could see the iron gate at the opposite end of the path. The pounding in my ears subsided, but my heart was beating furiously. There was nothing more stupid I could have done, I thought, than come to the cemetery and display my helplessness. I moved slowly among the tombstones. Some were standing at a slant, some eroded with age, but nowhere did I see any smashed stones or scribbled graffiti. In one corner I did see discarded hypodermic needles and wrinkled condoms, the sort of thing that can be found at any cemetery, and they did not seem to have any particularly anti-Semitic message to convey. I walked through another section and then came back to the shady avenue. There, by a modest fountain from which water was dripping, my attention was drawn to a monument in the shape of a pile of books. I leaned over to take a closer look and noticed that one part of the gravestone was lighter, as if it had recently been washed or scrubbed with a powerful cleanser. I crouched down and despite the best efforts of the person who had tried to scrub away the unwanted message, I was able to decipher the words DEATH TO THE JEWS. Instead of an exclamation point following the words there was an odd mark, probably someone's unsuccessful attempt at signing the message. I straightened up and wiped the sweat off my forehead. Why hadn't Jaša Alkalaj simply confirmed the story about the vandalizing of the cemetery, but instead sent me to see for myself? The dead do not lie, he'd said, and indeed, the dead did not lie. They also told the truth in the section of the cemetery near the entrance gate. Three tombstones were lying on the ground, all three smashed to pieces, and it was clear, though the pieces were laid out on boards as if awaiting repair, that an unnatural force had caused them to fall and break. Three tombstones do not topple on their own. I rinsed my hands at the fountain, shook them dry, and wiped them with a handkerchief. It took even more effort to open the gate from the inside, and as I pulled at the large iron handle, I was wondering whether someone might have locked it to shut me inside the cemetery, alone. Then the door creaked, budged, and when I pulled it to and stepped out into the street, a tram rumbled by. I looked to the left, I looked to the right, I looked every which way. In the days to come, as I said before, these motions preceded everything I did, and sometimes even today I look in every direction when I open the front door, though I am in a different city and no one is expecting me. Six years ago every gesture, every time someone broke suddenly into a dash, every word spoken loudly, to say nothing of whistles, all of it signified something entirely different from what that gesture, dash, or word seemed to mean on the surface. Never was reality farther from reality in Belgrade than during those years, and never was there greater insistence on the fact that this reality was the only true reality. And so I stood on the sidewalk, watched the tram trundling off into the distance, and strained to hear the murmur of the dead behind my back, and wondered how to fend off the aggressive flower hawkers who were striding my way. I never handled myself well in such situations, and usually I ended up buying everything they foisted on me. The only way to defend myself was to get away, so I turned in the opposite direction and moved quickly along the cemetery fence, but the hawkers also sped up, and their shouts reverberated in my ears, brief cries offering all kinds of flowers. Keep walking, a man said to me suddenly, as a woman shoved bouquets under my nose. When we come to the corner, continued the man, stop. I did. I stopped and said, What now? Now you buy the flowers, said the man. What you're looking for, said the woman, is in the bouquet. She lifted up the bouquet: carnations wrapped in damp paper. I asked, How much do they cost? The woman and the man looked at each other. Give what you want, the woman said finally. You wouldn't actually take his money, would you? asked the man. In case someone is watching, I interrupted, it must all look authentic. Fine, said the woman, then give me a piece of paper, give me anything. I dipped my hand into my pocket and pulled up a crumpled receipt for a registered mail package. The woman took it with the tips of her fingers, as if the paper were burning hot, dropped it into her pocket, and pushed the bouquet of flowers into my arms. They turned and walked to the cemetery gate, where other sellers were bustling with flowers and candles, and I stayed at the corner with the bouquet resting on my chest. And what, I later said to Marko, should I have done: gone back into the cemetery or kept walking, as if I had just decided this bouquet was for the living, not for the dead? Marko said he would have gone back, and he would not have neglected to see what was in the bouquet. A key, I answered, or actually, I added, a small plastic bag with a key in it. Good, said Marko, but for what? I'd like to know that too, I said. I showed him the key: an ordinary, smallish key of the kind used for a mailbox or a cupboard door. Marko was disappointed. He had been expecting a key to a safe, a key with an unusual mark on it, something to signal the complexity of any attempt at opening. If that's what the key looks like, he said, there is nothing of value hidden there. Shouldn't we first figure out what this key opens, I said, and then talk about what's there? You're right, said Marko, and suggested we smoke a joint of local grass. The grass, he claimed, was from Montenegro, and it had a nasty aftertaste and caused coughing, and that was the way it hit too: a sideswipe, slow, bitter. After some time, mostly spent staring at the ceiling, I wondered out loud how I would find the lock for the little key from the bouquet. Where do I start, I said, where should I look? Maybe there's something written on the little bag it was in, said Marko. It's a clear plastic bag, I said, there is nothing on it. Are you sure? asked Marko, sometimes it is hardest to see stuff that's in plain sight. I sighed, rose with effort, and weaving gently, went over to the wastepaper basket by my desk. When I knelt down, the entire room knelt with me, and when I bent my head to peer into the basket, I felt my brain touch my forehead on the inside. The basket was full of crumpled sheets of paper; the plastic bag was lying on top. I picked it up between my thumb and forefinger, and waved it triumphantly at Marko, and in that gesture toward Marko the bag was lit by a ray of light from the lamp by the sofa, and the letters KRSQ and the number 13 were clearly visible. I hadn't noticed them before because they weren't written with a ballpoint or a marker, but rather scratched on the inside surface of the bag with something sharp, perhaps the tip of a scalpel. Karađorđe Square, number 13, shouted Marko when I showed it to him. He suggested we go there immediately. He was shivering with excitement and some of the shivering affected me. I was barely able to tie my shoelaces, and my expression in the mirror wavered, as if I were shaking all over. Not bad, this Montenegrin stuff, said Marko as we stepped out into the street. He felt, he said, that he was trudging through layers of wool, that the soles of his feet never rested on solid ground. Maybe that is why it took us so long to walk to the high-rise. The entrance was dirty, buried in torn newspapers, plastic bags, and wrappers from wafer cookies and chocolate bars. The walls were scrawled with messages and scribbles. The mailboxes were on the right-hand side, many were broken open, some scorched with fire, some painted in different colors. Marko looked for box 13, but it was wide open and the door was dangling on a half-broken hinge. Someone beat us to it, said Marko, and I could do nothing but agree. Who knows how long we'd have stood there, alert to the despair we were feeling, had I not raised my eyes again to the mailboxes and studied them carefully until we found the one that had the right kind of lock. It was number 22, and the little key slid in smoothly, with no resistance. In the back of the opened box lay another key. This time there could be no doubt: unlike the first, the second key was clearly for unlocking and locking the door to an apartment. I looked at Marko and he nodded. Just in case, we went back to the front door and surveyed the area. We decided the apartment was on the fourth or fifth floor and Marko suggested we take the elevator, but I insisted we walk up, claiming that additional caution was not a bad idea and that the elevator might be more dangerous. Marko relented, though he did it because of a woman who had just entered the building, not because of me. We climbed quickly, skipping two or three steps at a time, and when we stopped on the fourth floor, we were both out of breath. Leaning against the banister, we waited to catch our breath and then went to the door with the number 22 on it. I looked at Marko; he nodded again. I put the key in the lock, turned it once, once more, and turned the knob gingerly. The door swung open to a dark front hall. Marko went in first, I followed. I closed the door, leaned on it, and wiped the sweat from my forehead. You entered an apartment when the owner wasn't home after all, said Marko, not hiding his sarcasm, as he felt the wall by the door in search of the light switch. He flicked it, and, with a crack that echoed like the sound of a rifle shot, light poured into the front hall. Our faces were reflected in an oval mirror. The two doors that led farther into the apartment were shut. One of them, the first one we opened, was the door to the kitchen, spotlessly clean and tidy, as if no one ever used it. Marko went over to the refrigerator and pulled open the door: empty. We stood a little longer before the open fridge and stared into its interior as if it held the answer to all our questions. Marko shut the refrigerator, we returned to the front hall and opened the other door. That led into the dining room, which gave access to two other rooms. However, at the doorway to the dining room we were startled by what we saw: all the walls, from floor to ceiling, were covered with shelves crammed with books. There were books on the floor, stacked in uncertain, wobbly piles. The same was true in the other rooms: shelves with books, nothing else. In the larger room were a small desk and an office chair with a seat that swiveled, that was all. Incredible, said Marko, just like that novel about the man who lived in an apartment full of books. He couldn't remember what novel, nor could he recall the writer's name, but he knew that it all ended in a big blaze, a fire that mercilessly devoured the books. I also didn't know which novel he had in mind, though for me, I said, the scene in the apartment evoked descriptions of the apartment where Salinger's heroes lived, the Glass family, or whatever their name was, they also had books lying all over the place, on the shelves, on chairs, the floor, even in the bathtub. It is always like that, said Marko, you put one book down somewhere, and two or three days later it's a pile, as if books get there by themselves. That had happened to him so many times, he said, that he decided to keep books in his apartment in only one place, otherwise, he said, they spread like mold, nothing can hold them back. You shouldn't compare books and mold, I said, but Marko rebelled, asserting that there are good molds and that everything that gets moldy needn't be thrown away. We were standing in the dining room again, not knowing what to do next. I didn't want to talk anymore about molds. Marko went over to the desk and looked into a side compartment, then he slid open one of the two drawers. There is nothing here, he said almost gruffly, then pulled open the second drawer and found an envelope with my name on it. I took the envelope and sniffed. I don't know what I was expecting, but it didn't smell like anything in particular, though I was convinced that my name had been written by Margareta, whose fragrance I would have recognized. Marko insisted that I open it immediately. I refused. He was startled, he pressed his lips together, said nothing. My refusal surprised me too, though I could have anticipated it after my decision not to tell him about the encounter with Margareta. Just as books attract other books, so confidences not shared attract other confidences not shared, and after the initial silence, others follow ever faster. Marko was, most certainly, my closest friend, someone whom I had known my entire life, but sometimes one should be cautious even with such friendships. In other words, there are moments when it is better to be alone, and I wanted such a moment for reading the letter from the desk. Marko made a last stab at changing my mind and offered me a joint, which he pulled out of his shirt pocket. A little more of the Montenegrin stuff, he said, and everything will be different. No, I said, and added that he should not be smoking grass in a strange apartment in which there were no ashtrays and someone might show up at any moment. Marko lit the joint anyway, and I went to the kitchen and opened a window. The kitchen looked out on the Danube and the path that stretched to Hotel Yugoslavia, and which, probably because of the clouds that had gathered over Belgrade, was almost deserted. Not far from the high-rise several boys were playing soccer. I heard Marko whistling behind my back, then a chair creaked and he coughed. Then I noticed that on a grassy slope by the hotel, where pillars were left standing from the old Zemun railway station, a group of people had gathered in an uneven, jagged circle, or so it looked from where I stood, and they were listening to a person who stood in the middle of the circle. Something is going on, I said, and called Marko over. Marko looked out at the scene on the slope, stubbed out the joint on the metal frame of the venetian blinds, and said that to him it looked like the meeting of some ecological party. No point, he said, in wasting our time. Besides, he went on, there's nothing for us to do here. At least for some of us, he added, and later, after we had left the high-rise, he said he had to run, said goodbye, and took off toward the center of Zemun at a fast clip. I watched him walk away and suddenly found myself thinking he was leaving forever. The thought was so awful that I nearly ran after him. Instead I called out his name. He didn't hear me, or pretended not to, and continued walking, zigging and zagging among the pedestrians and parked cars until I lost sight of him. I touched the pocket where the folded letter was. The paper rustled soothingly. I thought I ought to read it, I even started reaching into the pocket, but then I turned and headed toward the hill by the hotel. I walked past the boys playing soccer and cursing. A little dog was tied to a lamppost serving as the goalpost, and the dog whined and wagged its tail each time the ball flew by. I came out on the path and walked by a kiosk selling food and juices. The fragrance of frying fish wafted my way. Two pregnant women walked slowly by, holding hands. One mentioned the *košava* wind, though the day wasn't windy, and the other automatically lifted her hand to smooth her hair. A young girl on a bike rang her bell, then asked us to let her pass. High above, an airplane moved across the sky, leaving a shaggy trail, while along the river a boat slid by, reflected in the surface, so at one moment I thought that the boat underneath, not the real one, was carrying the one above. I wondered where Marko was, whether he had already reached home and whether he would be angry the next day when I went looking for him. Why the next day, I said out loud, I could see him tonight. An old woman sitting on a bench gave me a sharp look, then shook her head. She was knitting. The woman sitting next to her was crocheting. Of the dozen electric cars, only one was being used by two little girls waiting for the ride to begin. On the path someone had written WHOEVER LOVES VESNA MUST BE CRAZY in chalk. I passed by an inflated slide in the shape of a four-sided giraffe, near which a foul-smelling compressor was rumbling, and then the entire hillside stretched out in front of me. The people I'd seen from the window of the high-rise were still on the slope, perhaps more closely packed than before and still forming an irregular circle. The only difference, I thought as I walked toward them across the grass, was that no one was standing inside the circle. In fact, *circle* is not the right word, I saw as I got closer, and what had seemed from afar, from the window of the high-rise, to be an irregular circle was actually a complicated arrangement of men and women, a human stripe circling the entire small hill and slowly dispersing. The people from the group were gradually, unhurriedly, leaving their places, but efficiently enough that by the time I'd climbed to the top of the hill, there was no one left. The last couple, a graying man and a young woman who resembled him, passed me on my way up the slope. I stood by the old metal pillars alone, my ears humming as if I were standing at the foot of a church tower. For several minutes more I could follow the people as they moved away from the hill; soon enough, however, they began to mingle with those out walking, and when I looked back, the grassy surfaces were empty. I touched my pocket again. Go home, I said to myself softly, through my teeth, go home. I turned, walked down the hill, and headed toward the Danube riverbank. As I was crossing the path, I nearly bumped into a little girl on a bike, perhaps the same girl on her way back to the high-rises. I reached the steps, sat on the lowest one, so that my feet were nearly in the water, pulled the letter from my pocket, and tore open the envelope. The letter was short, disappointingly short, it contained three sentences. The first I knew well. A dream uninterpreted, was written in large, even letters, is like a letter unread. A letter when read, the second sentence began, opens the way to dreams. If dreams are not dreams, read the third sentence, what are they? Such expectation, I thought, only to find myself faced with yet another question. Maybe I should crumple up the letter, I thought, and toss it into the water? I was angry, really angry, which, hand on heart, was funny, because a person who receives a letter never determines what's in the letter, but once he opens it, there is no going back, because regardless of how hard he tries to stuff that letter back into the envelope, it can never be as it was, even if he reseals the envelope so expertly that it fools the naked eye. I didn't crumple it up, though for a while longer I toyed with the idea of folding it into a paper boat. A letter from an unknown sender headed in an unknown direction, and the twofold indeterminacy suddenly became a source of comfort to me. I folded it carefully, slid it back into the envelope, stood up, and tucked it into my pocket. A wave that splashed against the steps splashed my sneakers. When I climbed to the top of the steps and looked back, I saw wet footprints leading straight to my feet. Someone's following me, I thought, and then burst out laughing. I laughed again every time I recalled the thought, especially as I was walking by the old woman knitting. Hearing my chuckles, she looked up and shook her head. The woman who was crocheting didn't move. She's deaf, I thought, but then, as I reached the high-rise, I realized that someone was, indeed, following me. Suddenly I was sure that someone behind me was making an effort to keep me in sight. I was next to the first of the high-rises, not far from the spot where it all began, and I could see the playground and the parents shouting greetings and encouragement to the children in the caterpillar train. There was a man somewhere here, I thought, in a black trench coat, standing by the seesaw or the wooden horse with the broken ear, watching a woman who has just stepped into the water. I spun around, my hands raised high as if ready to strike a karate blow, and one of the people out for a walk said quite audibly, He is crazy. I'm not crazy, I said, though I was hardly convincing. The little train had meanwhile come to a stop and the children were getting off, shrieking, jostling with the children who were getting on for the next ride. Go home, I whispered again to myself, go home, and I headed home, though I sensed that someone, keeping a careful distance, was eyeing the back of my head. There are things one should ignore, I said to Jaša Alkalaj the next day, and that is the best way that they, at least for a moment, cease to exist. I suppose, said Jaša, without conviction. He got up and went to the window and looked out. We were sitting in his studio waiting for Dača, placing bets on whether he would come wearing a hat. I had not seen old Dača since the encounter in the yard of the Belgrade synagogue, and this time, at least so Jaša Alkalaj said, Dača had asked to see me, though Jaša didn't know why. I told him I had been to the Jewish cemetery, that I had seen the traces of vandalism, and that I didn't understand why he had been ambivalent about my going. It would be better, he said, for us to have some brandy, and went over to the shelf with bottles. He had told me, I reminded him, that the dead don't lie, and that their truth must be honored. But, said Jaša, to honor the truth there have to be people who wish to honor it. At the end of July last year several tombstones were knocked over at the Zemun Jewish cemetery, others were defaced, some soiled, and ever since, he said, there has been no end to it. I can speak anywhere I please, he said, and be listened to with the greatest commiseration, but short of head shaking and maybe even some clucking, nothing happens, despite their promises, he said, despite the promises they offer, not one of them will lift a finger. These are times, he added, when there is a lot of talk, and when there is a lot of talk, little gets done. He put three glasses on the table and began to pour the brandy, but his hand shook so hard he had to stop. I took the bottle and filled the shot glasses nearly to the brim. For every thing, Jaša Alkalaj said, there is a season, and life is, in essence, the skill of matching the season to the thing. Now is not the season for cemeteries, he added, let's hope the dead won't hold it against us. Then suddenly, in a bright voice, he announced Dača's arrival and in a gulp he downed the brandy. Dača was wearing his hat, though we couldn't remember who had bet that he would, so even Dača's willingness to wait outside the door while we placed our bets again could not take us back to our earlier levity. The brandy, in its unpredictable way, closed off every path and thoroughfare to a brighter mood, and soon all three of us were darkly silent, clutching our shot glasses. Cemeteries are bottomless wells, said Jaša, and if you begin to talk about them, you have no choice but to go on falling. I perked up my ears when I heard the word *well*. Jaša mused on his vision of falling through a well, but in his vision, or was it some old dream, at the end of the well he arrived in a new, shiny, and perfect world, which was the product of all Kabbalist Sephirot, in which an unerring wisdom reigned. The wisdom may be unerring, I said, but if the well is endless, the man's fall will never reach that end. Jaša countered that I was taking the words too literally, or that I understood the word *endless* to mean something that had no end, but that every word has countless meanings, so at different levels, in different worlds, *endless* could mean many things. No word, he said, is ever plumbed, it always contains within it all other words, and speaking of language, he said, I see it as a series of bowls stacked one inside the next. I didn't think of language as stacked bowls, but that's not the point. For me language is alive, so it doesn't stack in larger or smaller packages, since nothing alive tolerates restraint, and if something defines language, it is the freedom of the movement of words, a subject for another time and another place. Meanwhile Dača began to sweat from under his hat, and it was time to let him speak, because if we hadn't, he would have melted away, leaving only his hat and his shoes. This is how things stand, said Dača. He put his shot glass down on the table and smacked his lips. On Shabbat when we met in the synagogue courtyard, he said, actually later that night, I dreamed of Eleazar. He was standing on a dusty path, wearing a shoulder yoke from which hung two buckets, brimming with water, he pointed at the horizon and said, Go to Sremski Karlovci. I asked him, What will I do in Sremski Karlovci, I am doing all right where I am now, but he kept repeating: Go to Sremski Karlovci, so in the end I had to agree to go, and he stopped talking, waved to me, and vanished. Then I woke up, said Dača. He took off his hat and wiped the sweat from his brow. He peered into it, then set it down on the floor by the chair. I lay awake, he continued, and tried to understand why Eleazar was sending me to Sremski

Karlovci. For wine? said Jaša Alkalaj. No, said Dača, for the archives. Jaša looked at me, I shrugged; the last time I'd visited Sremski Karlovci I was in the seventh or eighth grade of elementary school and interested in everything but what the teachers were trying to teach us. There are archival collections there, said Dača, and, back when things were better, I spent many a day in those rooms. Eleazar, Dača went on, apparently was aware of this, otherwise why, of all the places in the world, would he mention that particular place in Fruška Gora? But as he lay there awake, said Dača, he realized that Eleazar knew something else, something that had once escaped him, Dača, or at another time hadn't seemed to matter. He could no longer go back to sleep, and tossed and turned until the day dawned, and then, he said, he went to the train station and took a train to Sremski Karlovci. When he entered the archive, the first archivist he ran into crossed herself, he said, and exclaimed that he looked like a ghost. She asked, he said, whether anyone was giving him trouble, or, was it that he'd finally married? They all knew him there, said Dača, as a sworn bachelor, which he had been, no question, but why marriage would have turned him into a ghost, he couldn't fathom, and so, he said, he stood in front of her desk, unsure of whether to strike up a conversation about the ups and downs of married life, or to go in search of what had brought him there, and who knows how long he would have hung around spinning his hat, had the archivist not struck herself on the brow and pronounced it a miracle that he had turned up that morning, for had he come a day later, or even later that afternoon, he would not have found her in the office, and no one would ever have known, she said, that waiting for him in her desk was an envelope that had arrived from Zagreb, who knows by what route, stamped with the seal of the city archive, she had not sent it on to him because no one knew what had become of him, of Dača, he'd stopped coming to the reading room, not having left a forwarding address or phone number or the name of a person they could get in touch with, so the envelope had stayed with her, unopened, of course, she said, no one would ever have considered opening it, she added, even if they had learned that the very worst, heaven forbid, had happened to him, to which he, Dača, replied that there are worse things than dying, for instance, betrayal or deception, and then the archivist, who knows why, he said, blushed, quickly bent down, and pulled a small white envelope out of the lowest drawer. The size of the envelope disappointed him, Dača confessed, because he'd expected a larger and heftier missive, probably because of her lengthy introduction. He set his hat on her desk, he said, took the envelope, and sniffed it. The archivist shook her wrinkled index finger at him. Dača tore open the end of the envelope and inched out a folded sheet of business stationery. Dear Sir, it said at the top, I recently came across the enclosed printout and remembered that you were looking for this information a long time ago. I don't know whether you are still researching this topic, but I thought this might be of interest. There are other archives now active, it said in closing, but I hope the old ones will not be forgotten, or, worse yet, destroyed. Sounds nice, said Jaša, but I don't understand any of it. You've never understood anything, Dača said, glancing at me as if seeking support, though all I could do was raise my hands helplessly. Now you'll tell us, said Jaša, that this message came from an old flame of yours? Nonsense, said Dača, though not without a smile at the corners of his mouth, she is a good friend, that's all, a person I often saw when I was leafing through documents many years ago at the Croatian Archive in Zagreb, searching, among other things, and here he looked at me again, for information about Eleazar. But, he said, first I have to tell you something else. He closed his eyes, leaned over, and I thought he'd fallen asleep. I am not sleeping, said Dača, just wondering where my hat is. Under the chair, said Jaša, where else would it be? At the time, Dača continued, I was obsessed with leeches. He knew this might sound peculiar, he said, but leeches used to be a precious commodity. It is hard to believe, for instance, that in one year alone, he said, and the year was 1833, French doctors imported over forty million leeches, and if you take all the other countries into account, over one hundred million leeches changed hands that year. Leeches had become so popular by the nineteenth century in Europe, he said, that they became an endangered species and were on the brink of extinction. Someone, of course, he said, had to go out and gather all those leeches, and unlike many of the other jobs that were off-limits for Jews at the time, or restricted to an elite, no one was fighting over gathering leeches, so among the Jews, he said, there were quite a few leech gatherers, people who went out and collected them in swamps, but also those who organized their purchase and further resale. Despite the distasteful nature of the work, however, he said, there were others who, as was the case with most occupations, protested the issuing of permits to Jews for this kind of work, and some of the most vocal, he said, were Serbian and German merchants who viewed the Jews as unpleasant competition. Good Lord, interrupted Jaša Alkalaj, who could possibly mind them gathering leeches? Leeches, he shuddered, I am disgusted at the very thought. One more person, shouted Dača, and clapped his hands, one more person who doesn't know anything about leeches! All I care about is that they are disgusting, said Jaša, the rest doesn't matter. You should care, said Dača, but, as always, you prefer to scratch the surface, just like your paintings. If you don't shut up, said Jaša, you might end up without your hat. Dača scowled, bent over, and peered under his chair. When he straightened up, his face was red. You wouldn't dare, he asked Jaša, touch it, would you? Jaša said nothing. You know what the Talmud says, Dača continued, that he who takes another man's hat may lose his soul? Are you a leech gatherer or a sermonizer? answered Jaša. Or are you just a hatter? Listen to him, will you? said Dača, turning to me, and all because he has never overcome his childhood phobias, his fear of a leech latching on to him when he was splashing in the puddles, though—he couldn't have known that at the time—they do everything to keep their victims from feeling pain, so along with an anticoagulant, which makes possible the unobstructed flow of blood, they secrete an analgesic, which helps the victim, or patient, not to feel anything. I looked at Jaša, who was frowning, but I couldn't be sure whether the frown was a sign of genuine ire or just an act in a well-rehearsed performance. In a sense, I might well have been the one to be angry because Dača's claim about the painless leeches reminded me of the opening lines in Nabokov's book on Gogol, where Nabokov gives a convincing description of Gogol's agonies as doctors let his blood and leeches were dangling from his legendary nose. Every time I read those lines I felt revulsion at the thought of those powerful leeches, no different, to tell the truth, from Jaša's disgust of a moment before, and I had always thought how excruciating Gogol's pain must have been, how awful and miserable and humiliated he must have felt, and suddenly Dača destroyed the image for me with the analgesic, making me doubt Gogol, whose nose was all that was still real, and Nabokov, who, I thought, should have warned me somewhere of this absence of pain. To convince you that I am telling you the truth, piped up Dača, I should put a leech on each of your legs. You're mad, shouted Jaša Alkalaj, you really are mad! That sent Dača into fits of laughter, except that this time he didn't clap, he slapped his thighs. I reached out and touched his elbow. Why don't you tell us what was in the document, I said, because everybody has the right to be afraid of whatever he wants to be afraid of. I knew a woman who fainted whenever she saw a photograph of a spider, and even the sight of a drawing of a spider sparked an unbearable headache. So why shouldn't someone have the right to be disgusted by leeches? Fine, agreed Dača, but I would like him to see a leech, he said, on the operating table of Pirogov, the Russian surgeon, who would fix as many as two hundred leeches on a patient. The document, I asked, what did the document say? Dača repeated the story of his interest in the unusual jobs that Jews did in Zemun and Srem, making a point of how he would tell us the next time about rag collecting, once a very lucrative business because rags were the raw material for the production of paper. Leeches, however, were not as appealing for Serbian and German merchants, regardless of the huge demand and good earnings, and it was while he was at the Zagreb archive, Dača said, that he came upon many documents about the Jewish leech gatherers, about whom, as in the material on the other trades, there was an assortment of permits and bans, support and suspicion, an invoking of legal regulations and an evident sidestepping of these same regulations. Since Jews were not allowed to reside permanently on the Military Frontier, Dača explained, they used every opportunity, even the smallest, the size of a leech, for instance, to find a way to rest with at least one foot on solid ground. In the case of leeches, of course, it would be better to say mud rather than solid ground, but even mud, he remarked, could sometimes be reliable. There was something about mud in the Talmud, he said, but now he couldn't remember where. He stopped talking and began to nod. Jaša and I looked at each other. Don't you look at each other, said Dača, I'm not sleeping, I am just trying to remember the name of the leech gatherer in the Brod regiment. Then he straightened up, opened his eyes, and said that the buyer's name was Marko Felner and that for the right to be a buyer he paid more than a thousand forints annually, while he gave the gatherers ten krajcars in silver for a standardized measure, which came to about a cup and a little more. No one, Dača said, no one dared catch leeches without Felner's go-ahead, and his privilege was supported by the military command, which, of course, was a paradox, he added, because the army should have been doing the exact opposite, meaning that they should have been encouraging Jews to leave the Military Frontier region. Clearly everybody cared more about pocketing a little spare change, he said, even if it came from leeches, because the dilemma of the leech gatherers crops up often in the correspondence of the Slavonian general command, and for instance, he said, there is mention of a case of two Jews who hung around Slavonski Brod for more than a month in 1833 without authorization, which was absolutely unacceptable according to the regulations of the day, and they were allowed to be in Brod only on the days the ferry ran, and even then, said Dača, only for as long as absolutely necessary for them to receive the leeches delivered from Bosnia, and on condition that no smuggling was involved, in which case the authorities would have been merciless with them, the Jews, not the leeches, and expelled them from the Military Frontier at once. Now here is where the additional information that arrived from Zagreb comes in, an extract from a document that had eluded me or else had been located at a later date, in which the Slavonian general command informs the Zemun magistrate's office that a young Jewish man who had been smuggling leeches was arrested in the vicinity of Slavonski Brod, and when questioned as to what his name was and where he was from, he replied that his name was Volf Enoch and that he was a water carrier by trade from Zemun. The command didn't believe him and sought confirmation from the magistrate that in the registry of Zemun Jews such a person with such a name was listed, demanding at the same time of the magistrate that if the detainee's claims were shown to be accurate, why he had been able to leave his duties in Zemun and come as far as Slavonski Brod, especially since no leeches in any considerable quantity were found upon his person, but he did have in his sack many manuscripts and vials with an assortment of liquids and powders, which made everything more suspicious and merited confidentiality and caution. The response of the Zemun magistrate, Dača said, has not been preserved, but even so we can clearly see that this could not be the same Volf Enoch, because the document refers to a young man, whereas Volf Enoch, if he were one and the same person, would have been about eighty years old at the time, and no one could have described him as a young Jew, unless, said Dača, it was, in fact, our Volf, but altered or refreshed in some way despite his advanced age. You see, he said, and by this time he was gesticulating excitedly, the extract quotes a part of a letter from the command dated January 1834, which states that the Zemun magistrate's office should make an effort to provide additional information about this Volf Enoch, because he vanished from the cell where he'd been held, and when they say vanished, said Dača, they remark that he vanished in the literal sense of the word. In that cell, you see, there were other people, and when they woke up one morning, Volf was no longer among them. No one had heard or seen a thing, there were no traces of a tunnel dug or bars broken, and his sack was missing from the office where it had been set aside for safekeeping, though no one had been in the office that night, since the key was in the pocket of a prison clerk who had spent the entire night in his bed, as confirmed by his wife. This disappearance, the document explained in closing, casts an uncomplimentary light on the work of the police and the corresponding segment of the Slavonian general command, and required of them to make an effort as urgently as possible to address the case of the Jewish leech gatherer who could not have simply melted into thin air. Except, of course, said Dača, and winked at me, if he was our Eleazar, for whom, as a Kabbalist, to move to another place was no hardship at all, no matter how far away. He leaned over, picked up his hat, and set it on his head. It's time, he said, as the doorbell rang. Dača immediately took off his hat, I got up, Jaša said he wasn't expecting anyone, and when he opened the door, there was, indeed, no one there. Not only was there no one there, I told Marko when I visited him later, but it was dark in the stairwell, so Jaša, when he opened the door, took a quick step back, just as he would have, I said, had he seen an unusual person or an unexpected sight at the door, and Dača and I, convinced that this was why he had stepped back, ran to the door, and then we too stepped back, faced with darkness. We peered for a bit longer into the darkness, then Jaša shut the door and asked if we'd like a drink. Darkness, he added, brings on thirst. Marko nodded, though I could see he was not listening as carefully as he had on previous days. I told him about what had happened on the hill near Hotel Yugoslavia, and here he seemed more willing to listen, he even asked a few questions about how the people were dressed, whether anyone among them was barefoot, whether there were more fair-haired women than dark-haired, but I had no precise answers. I was so vague in fact that Marko finally asked if I had been on the hill at all. I didn't answer right away; I was tired, I wanted to lie down and get a good night's sleep, and I was upset with myself for being upset by Marko's reproach, it being every bit as justified, I have to admit, as my own behavior of the day before. Perhaps I had forgotten some things, I said, finally, however, I remembered that their movement, which seemed arbitrary at first, was coordinated, even when they began to disperse, so I decided there was a message hidden in the shapes, forms, geometric figures, call them what you will, and that the movement, this traversing of imagined pathways to and fro, in other words everything up to their departure, represented a language that was being communicated to someone who knew how to listen. To watch, said Marko, because if this was geometry, listening wouldn't be of much use. He rolled a hefty joint and offered it to me like a peace pipe. While we smoked, he talked about grand geometric endeavors, such as the vast earthen drawings in South America or the magnificent hills raised by the Indians of North America, and in both cases, he felt, one could speak of visual languages, just as the pyramids had been elements of such a language, he firmly believed in that, both those in Egypt and those the Incas built to reach the sun, and then he rolled yet another joint, so the visual languages acquired yet another dimension, just as we two did, and the conversation meandered more and more, traversing a winding forest path, and at one point I wanted us to reach a clearing somewhere, to sit and catch our breath. Instead, I said goodbye to Marko and left for home. In the hallway of his building, as I was going down the stairs, I had to clutch the banister because I was finding it difficult to gauge the height and depth of each step correctly, which made me stumble, and I was afraid I would fall. By the end I was gripping the banister with my right hand, while swinging with my left as if I were walking on a tightrope, high above a ravine. Out on the street I raised my right hand high in the air, and only then did I feel the ease of equilibrium. I could go, I thought, anywhere I like, and I set out for the city park, but when I reached the main path, the barking of a dog that came from its dark depths prompted me to take a different route, by the hospital, then down along Dubrovačka, until I reached the main street. I looked to the left, I looked to the right. The traffic lights were blinking, several people were waiting at a bus stop in front of the department store, the McDonald's was gleaming, taxi drivers were sitting on a bench smoking, drunken men were singing, a little later a woman's voice joined in, then a man spoke of stars, perhaps he even gave their names, and suddenly I knew where I was to go. I headed for Zmaj Jovina Street. I walked back by the taxi drivers, crossed to the other side of the street, looked at the window of a stationery store, and turned by the theater, which seemed neglected in the dark, perhaps even more so than in daytime. I walked cautiously, as if wading through shallow water, and when I saw that the big wooden gate was ajar, I thought it would be better to keep going until I got to the riverbank where all this had started and where the water, I thought, would be deeper. But I did pause. I couldn't see the poster for tai chi classes, though for a moment I thought I spotted a light patch where the poster used to be. I looked to the left, I looked to the right. There was no one. Slowly I slipped into the dark passageway, took two or three steps and stopped, staring at the pump, which glowed as if all the moonlight were pouring into it and it alone. Everything else was pitch-dark: the flowerpots with the barberries, the side-wall of the facing building, the stoop, and the front door. I couldn't even make out the bench, the darkness had probably engulfed it, as it had everything else. Then it occurred to me that someone was sitting there. I don't know where I got the idea, but once it had occurred to me, I couldn't shake it, and I took cautious steps toward the courtyard, slightly hunched, as if fearful of what I would see. Very slowly I approached the end of the passageway, leaned against the wall, and inhaled and exhaled deeply. Out of my eye, my left, I could still see the silvery pump, its long handle, the decorated basin into which the water flowed, the foundation with partially chipped paint. I took another deep breath, but I didn't release it, and instead stepped abruptly out of the passageway, eyes open wide, pre-pared to surprise the person sitting on the bench. The bench was empty. Something rustled in the dark behind the barber-ries, and when I spun around the pump was no longer aglow. The moonlight, if it was moonlight, had disappeared and all that was visible on the pump were patches of old paint and layers of rust. I went over to the bench, sat down, lay my hands on my thighs, and shut my eyes. Nothing happened, no silence settled on me, no music struck up, no one's voice could be heard. I opened my eyes and looked at the walls around me. Nothing had changed, as if reality this time had decided to stay the same. I stood up, then sat down again. I shut and opened my eyes several times, even squinted once through my lashes and tried to hold my breath as long as possible, but nothing helped. It occurred to me then that I'd always sat on the bench in daytime, and that things might be different at night, which was a comforting thought, though inadequate to bring back the fine mood I'd felt as I had turned into Zmaj Jo-vina Street. I stood up, ready to go, and that is when I heard the music. It sounded different from the ethereal music I'd heard earlier, and when I strained to hear better, I realized it was the echo of music from a café nearby, or perhaps from the barges along the river. There was no point, what with the pounding rhythm and the rumble of bass and drums, to staying in the courtyard. The bench was sinking into a darkness so dense that it was as if the darkness meant to hide the bench. Then that same darkness seemed to be taking the shape of a body, of someone's presence, but when I moved and shifted my angle, I realized this was just the interplay of thick and thin shadows. I went down the passageway, headed for the entrance, and paused: the gate was shut and there was not a trace of light from the street. I was certain I had not shut the gate when I came in. More precisely, I had not even touched it, doing my best to slip through unobtrusively. I was also certain that no one had come into the courtyard after me, because I would definitely have spotted that someone; neither the pump nor the bench so held my attention that I could have lost touch with what was going on around me. But then if no one came in, did someone go out? Maybe the person was waiting in the dark of the passageway, maybe he'd been standing behind the gate or was crouching in a corner, and when I got far enough, or when I went over to sit on the bench, he sneaked out, pulling the heavy gate shut behind him? I took hold of the big latch with one hand, and with the other I pushed the gate open and stepped into the street. I looked to the left, I looked to the right. There was no one. But I still felt, I said to Marko on the phone, that someone was watching. I expected his mocking commentary, but all that came across the telephone receiver was the sound of crunching. I had called him at about midnight and our conversation went on for nearly two hours, so that at one point, just as I was wrapping up the account of my most recent escapades, Marko said he had to eat an apple. I didn't see a soul, I repeated, but the feeling that someone was watching closely was so real. And offensive, I added. You too,

Marko announced, should eat more apples, and he went on to talk about the beneficial qualities of the apple, and then, without a pause, remarked that he was still thinking of a newspaper article he had read about a man who had killed himself, and for no reason, it said, in a car parked in front of a clinic, and it wasn't even his own car but a car borrowed from a friend, allegedly to cart his old television set to his mother-in-law's. It's not clear, said Marko, why he stopped in front of the clinic, which is not near his mother-in-law's apartment but in a whole different part of town, and besides, where did he get the gun, sometimes it seems easier to get ahold of a gun than of household appliances. But it's clear, Marko continued, the times we live in killed him, what else could have? By the way, he said, no one knew the man in the clinic, which didn't stop the employees from making all sorts of pronouncements, and the mother-in-law from stating that she would cherish that television set as a memento of her son-in-law, though she had to go to great lengths to wash all traces of the blood off the screen and the buttons. I was supposed to laugh at that point, but there was no time, because Marko kept talking about wiping off the blood and removing traces, and then from the story about the suicide and the mother-in-law moved on to advising on the direction the talks should be taking between the authorities in Belgrade and the Albanian leaders in Kosovo. The newspapers at that point were forever running reports on the efforts of the government to establish a dialogue with the Albanians, thereby painting a more favorable picture of themselves for world opinion, and if there was a subject about which I had absolutely no desire to talk, Marko had found it. Now I realize that I was actually evading talk of reality and that everything that happened to me during those spring months six years ago—plunging into the shadowy world of mystical phenomena—was a form of self-deception, a form of solace or, more precisely, escapism from our reality at the time. The encounters with the unbridled nationalists were so surreal that I didn't even feel them to be a part of that reality. I was wrong, of course, because they, the violent young men, were just as real as the blows they dealt me, and just as real today, perhaps not quite so numerous, but certainly louder and more bold. Furthermore they are still where they were then, in a place they feel to be theirs alone, while I am somewhere else, it doesn't matter where, and words are all I have left, and this attempt at fashioning from them something that will have at least a semblance of permanence. Eleazar, if he were here, might have cast off words, though I am not altogether sure of that because the Kabbalah, like the entire Jewish tradition, is based on words, and silence is a realm into which Kabbalists have not been eager to venture. But what do I really know about the Kabbalah? What I learned from Jaša Alkalaj and heard from Dača, when I managed to wrest myself free of the hypnotic movement of his hat, and which, in terms of real knowledge, was barely a drop in the sea. Sometimes one drop, Jaša would say, is greater than a whole sea, a grain of sand more impassable than a desert, a snowflake more threatening than an avalanche. At those words Dača would take off his hat and add that the ignorance of an ignoramus is greater than the knowledge of a connoisseur, and a connoisseur will never know as much as the ignoramus doesn't know. Then he would put on the hat, maybe even tilt it, you would barely see his eyes under the lowered brim. My eyes were also barely visible, but in my case the reason was exhaustion, as well as Marko's endless, monotonous, boring monologue. At first I attempted to get a word in edgewise, then I only voiced my assent or disagreement gutturally, and finally I fell silent altogether, and waited for it to end, doing what I could to fend off sleep. All in all, said Marko finally, only madmen can't see that the solution to the crisis lies in partitioning Kosovo. Sure, I said, easy to say that to me, but go and say it out loud on Terazije and they'll skin you alive. I looked at the clock, it was almost two, I nearly ended the conversation, which I didn't do, because I felt I ought to show Marko some sign of devotion so that I could repair what I had damaged with the unintended misunderstanding at the high-rise. I turned away from the clock and pressed the receiver more firmly to my ear. You think I won't? Marko went on, and not only on Terazije but anywhere else for that matter. All right, I said. My mouth was dry. You know how all this will end? he asked. No, I answered, I don't. Those idiots will bomb us, he said, and maybe none of us will survive. What idiots? I asked. The Europeans or the Americans? Both, answered Marko. I said nothing. He said nothing. I tried to think what bombing would be like, I managed to summon images from archival footage on the bombing of Belgrade in April 1941 — the wing of an airplane and bombs dropping like logs, then the pilot turning and grinning a big grin. He had nice teeth. I could hear Marko breathing, breathing deeply and evenly, as if he were sleeping. It's sad, he said suddenly, when nobody loves you. I didn't know what he was talking about, how love came into it after the bombs. We are now the bowels of the world, he said, and I fear we are going to stay that way for a long time. The image was challenging, though I didn't try to picture it. I had had enough, what with the stench of excrement and urine that I continued to find, at irregular intervals, before my apartment door. The bucket and broom were now permanently stationed in my front hall. I had rubber gloves and a pile of old newspapers, and still needed to buy disinfectant. Your future is assured, said Marko when he happened upon me once with all my cleaning supplies, you'll always be able to find work scrubbing toilets. I pressed the receiver against my ear again: there was no sound. Marko, I called, where are you? You know what, Marko finally said, I'd like to be in another galaxy, but fuck it, I live in Belgrade and there's nothing I can do about that. I didn't know what to say, whether to console or reassure him, so I breathed a sigh of relief when he wished me a good night and hung up. I hung up at my end, then as I turned I snagged with my elbow the address book and pad that stood by the phone. They dropped to the floor, and when I bent down to pick them up, I saw that the pad had opened to the page where I'd jotted down Dragan Mišović's phone number several weeks before. That meant I should call him, I had no doubt. Maybe I should write about this, I thought. My next piece for *Minut* was due any day, and considering the historical circumstances, especially the threats of bombing and the efforts of the authorities to portray the threats as an illegitimate attack on the internal affairs of the country, a text on destiny seemed appealing. But what could I write about: that what was said made no difference, because what was bound to happen had been determined long ago, that any action on our part now would be a waste of time? Which, of course, was the opposite of what the government was saying to the nation: that we the people, all of us, were deciding what would happen, and if we said no to anyone or anything, we became the tailors of our own destiny. In other words, if the tailor was shown not to be real, and real bombs were to start falling on us, we would simply say this is not true and pretend to be living in another reality, in which the world was created to our own specifications. I completely understood Marko's desire to go off to another galaxy, though I would have been happy with a parallel time, a reality in which events were playing out in a calmer way. I went to the window and looked out. Lights were on in several apartments of the facing buildings. There was no one on the street, though the turn signal was blinking on a car parked in front of the pharmacy display window. It was blinking on and off with a slow, halting rhythm, and before long I decided that it was sending me a message, a little like Morse code. I watched a while longer, trying to divine the rhythm of the repeats, to measure the time between blinks, but then I got tired of it all, my eyelids began to droop, and I went into the bathroom. When I came back, the turn signal was no longer blinking. I looked to the left, I looked to the right. The city slumbered, and suddenly I felt terribly tired. I sat down in the armchair. Whether because of the late hour or my exhaustion, I thought I should forget all this, or give up on it, because it had begun to look like the poorly linked parts of a farce, comic in its efforts to be taken seriously. Even the manuscript that I had acquired suddenly looked like a pompous mishmash, a patchwork quilt, a toy that played games with itself. True, I hadn't looked at it for days, and maybe it would not be a bad idea, I thought, to leaf through it in the mood I was in now. I settled into the armchair, clenched my buttocks and released them, and then shut my eyes, anticipating a yawn. I was awakened by the clamor of the street. I opened my eyelids and saw a cloudy morning. I straightened up, stretched, probed my teeth with my tongue. Then I covered my face with my hands. My mouth was dry: I could do with a glass of water. I got up and went to the window. A fine rain was drizzling. A woman was standing at the bus stop, protected by a red umbrella. The car was no longer parked in front of the pharmacy. I drew the curtain, stepped back, and opened the window. People were going from kiosk to kiosk, buying newspapers, carrying bread from the bakery, somebody whistled, the buses rumbled, a boy and a girl were kissing, sparrows landed on crumbs, and then I thought that nothing could replace the fine warp and woof of life, that no government or system could completely unravel this fabric; at worst, some of the thread would be wound up in an irregular ball, but new ones would keep sprouting, even if they were only threads one of the Fates was drawing off her spindle, sometimes that's sufficient, a thread of life stretched in a void. I thought at once of the other two Fates, the one who decides how long the thread will be, and the one who snips it. A person is tied to the spinner of fate his whole life, and wherever he moves he pulls that thread along with him, and when he finally shakes free of it, he marches to death, as if by dying he earns his right to freedom. I shuddered at the thought, swiftly shut the window, dashed into the bathroom to wash my face and shave, nothing refreshes a man like a shave, even washing your hair doesn't feel as good, at least not for me, so, once I had done it all, I felt like a new man. Then I called Dragan Mišović. This time there was no need to remind him who I was. He asked what had happened with the sign made of the circle and the triangles, and how I was getting on with solving the equation with too many unknowns. Nothing has changed, I said, the sign hasn't opened up and the unknowns have gone on multiplying. And now you have a new question, said Dragan Mišović, and you think it will help you understand the other two? Yes, I said. Don't you think, he went on, that the unanswered questions will become too large an obstacle, which will, in time, become insurmountable? I don't like being lectured to and had I not shaved, which had put me in a good mood, I would have hung up on him. Sure, I said. That's what I always say when I don't understand something or I disagree with something. Dragan Mišović said nothing. I could feel he felt my lack of sincerity, just as I could feel that he felt I was feeling it. Sorry, I said. Forget it, he said, we all have moments we wish we hadn't had, and then he asked for the real reason I had called, he couldn't imagine I had called to ask how he was, and even if I had, he never answered such questions. Fine, I said, and took a deep breath, I'm interested in whether geometry can take the place of language. Geometry is a language, said Dragan Mišović. I don't mean the language of signs, I said. Me neither, said Dragan Mišović. I read somewhere, I said, that the body finds its way through space, whether geometric or emotive, by constantly drawing mental maps, and in that way space and feeling communicate with the body. So, now, I said, if we take this map out of the body, so to speak, will it speak to others the way it speaks to us? Sometimes I wonder, said Dragan Mišović, how you come up with such questions. I would like to know that too, I answered. And besides, he said, I am not sure your question really belongs to the realm of mathematics, because these mental maps, even though they can be represented as geometric models, come about in a complex interaction of physical and mental factors. And one more thing, he added, geometry implies a certain universality, while mental maps are highly individual, as individual, he said, as each of us is different, and here, I am afraid, there is no language. Yet if we imagine a group of people, I continued stubbornly, who are making the shape of the same mental map with their bodies, say, a map of feelings of love or serenity, couldn't someone else, who sees that, develop those same feelings? Maybe, said Dragan Mišović, though I am not entirely sure what you are saying, and I am no expert at feelings. I'm not talking about feelings, I said, but about the transmission of information, a process that happens with every reading, say, when you read a description of a sad scene in some novel and you start to cry. I wouldn't know, he said, I don't read novels. His tone had suddenly changed, as if he were losing interest in the conversation, or, which only occurred to me much later, as if someone were standing next to him and listening in. I asked him to give it some thought anyway, and he, sounding vague and unconvincing, promised to get in touch if he thought of anything. He hung up before we'd even said goodbye. I stared for a while longer at the receiver, then placed it back in the cradle. Had the time come, I wondered, to admit that I was at a dead end, that somewhere I had taken a wrong turn and found myself on the wrong path, and the only way to change anything was to go back to square one? So, I took an apple, just as I had a month before, and walked down to the quay. It was not Sunday, and it was not yet two P.M., but the day was every bit as fickle: the clouds parted as I left the house, the sun gleamed through, but by the time I reached the promenade, it started to rain. I lowered my head, swallowed the last bite of apple, except the stem, which I continued to nibble on and suck until it finally came apart. The water level of the Danube was not as high as it had been a month before, so I could not be sure where the man and the woman had been standing, and I wasn't altogether certain which bench I had been sitting on. There were three, and first I thought it was the middle one, which seemed too easy and obvious a choice, so I settled on the third, the one that was the farthest from the shabby little playground. The playground was deserted: maybe it was too early for the mothers with small children, or maybe they had already been here and the rain had chased them away. I went over to the third bench and from there looked out at the Danube. Yes, that was the angle, that was exactly the spot where I had been sitting when the young man walked past, and it was from there that I had stepped forward, ready and eager to go down the slope toward the woman who had stood with one leg in the water, but then I had stopped when I caught sight of the man in the black trench coat. Why had I stopped? What led me to kneel and start tying and untying my shoelaces, allowing the man in the black trench coat to get away? I looked at the damp seesaw, the little cars and the train, and the only explanation I could arrive at was that the man who'd been standing by the seesaw was so at odds with those surroundings that he couldn't help but arouse my suspicions, my alarm, and, finally, lead me to abandon my Samaritan descent to the woman who had been slapped on the riverbank. Maybe I wasn't supposed to have followed the girl, I thought, except that my later discovery of the signs could be interpreted as an outcome of my having followed her, as something she guided me to. Probably I wasn't supposed to notice the man in black either. He wasn't there because of me, but because of the young man and woman. But what was the connection between the two, if any? And had everything that had happened to me since then happened only because someone saw me follow the woman? Perhaps here on the promenade there had not been just one man in a black trench coat, perhaps there had been two? And why not an entire battalion, Marko would have asked had I told him about it, why be modest? And he would have been right, I have to confess, regardless of the role that he played in it all.

From this distance I can see, clear as day, but it's too late now, I've said it before, to change anything, life is only a handful of memories, after all, nothing more. The rain kept pelting, sharp and persistent, as if it were autumn, not spring, and the raindrops slid off my hair and unerringly found the space between my neck and shirt collar. I went home, dried my hair with a towel, ate one more apple, translated some, wrote for a while, watched television, and finally tumbled into bed. Two days later, armed with a pad and several colored pencils, I made a detailed inspection of the streets around the Zemun open market. I wanted to find as many traces as I could, or signs, and make a list to see whether, taken in total, they offered additional insight. The day before I'd done something different: I went to the *Politika* newspaper archive and pulled out the issues between the eighth and fifteenth of March. I didn't know what I was looking for exactly, but I pored over the city chronicle, the classifieds, and the death notices. I came across a brief news item in the March 10 issue that the body of a young male was found in the reeds along the Danube shore on the Zemun side, but there was nothing to indicate foul play. There was no follow-up of the news item over the next days, nor did I find anything among the death notices that could be tied to the young man. Then, in the March 15 paper, along with a news item about a man who'd been killed the day before in Surčin, I came across a mention of an investigation showing that the young man whose corpse had been found near Hotel Yugoslavia had been killed by a blunt object. The identity of the victim was still unknown. I put the paper down and rubbed my face. My heart was pounding as if I had come to a sudden halt after a horrific run; I felt dizzy, nausea climbed up my esophagus. I don't know how I got out of the *Politika* building. All I know is that I caught sight of myself in the window of a glass-cutting shop. The wan, rumpled figure smiling anxiously at me must have been me, though there was no indication that I had recognized myself. I turned and kept walking down the street that, as it turned out, led to Zeleni Venac. I got on a bus to Zemun, and not until the crowds around me grew larger did I finally pull myself together. If the news in the paper had been accurate, and there was no reason to think it was not, and provided this had been the very same young man, then what had happened was much more than a game. For a moment I even thought that I was to blame for the young man's death, for had I gone after him instead of pointlessly following the woman, he might be alive today. On the other hand, something else could have happened: I could be dead today, because clearly, the people the young man had rubbed the wrong way would have been just as sensitive about witnesses. Therefore, I should be pleased that I had followed the woman; still, I couldn't rid myself of the bitter taste of complicity or betrayal. The bus crossed the Sava Bridge and turned toward Zemun. In the distance along the promenade cyclists and strollers could be seen. A little girl was holding a string tied to a kite flying high above her. Big and little dogs romped in the bright green grass. Two boys tossed a Frisbee back and forth, and it wobbled through the air as if exhausted. The bus passed Hotel Yugoslavia. There was nothing at the top of the artificial hill but the pillars of the old Zemun railroad station, protruding like the ruins of antiquity. I got off the bus at the square, went into a supermarket, and spent about fifteen minutes studying the ingredients on various canned and processed foods. Nothing calms me so profoundly as the partially intelligible lists that reduce food to an extremely unappealing form. A cookie, for instance, becomes flour, sugar, vegetable shortening, cocoa powder, powdered skim milk, ammonium bicarbonate, sodium bicarbonate, lecithin, kitchen salt, natural coloring, and natural aroma. I read this in several languages: Serbian, Albanian, Slovene, Croatian, Macedonian, English, Hungarian, and Romanian. Then I bought some bread and yogurt and went home. Over the past few days and weeks I had been unsure how to act in certain situations, but now I felt I'd lost ground altogether. It did occur to me, I must confess, that I should flee; inevitable thinking in such situations, but never for a moment did I consider this acceptable. Later I did run away, that's true, but the circumstances were entirely different and flight was a necessity rather than a choice. I'll get to that later, there's time. Flight, therefore, at that moment was out of the question, as was my next thought: that I should go to the police. I had no faith in the system, I didn't side with the regime in power, which meant that I had nothing to hope for from the police: they had quite a number of unsolved crimes on their hands, after all, one more would have meant nothing to them. Maybe I could write something for my column in *Minut*? I had to laugh: after holding forth for so long on how postmodernism had broken with a more traditional approach to language and form, here I was considering a text to be a reliable source of information, prepared to believe in words. Besides, what could I say in such a text when I knew nothing? I had seen someone who was, perhaps, now dead, and except for that unconfirmed death, I had no other information. That meant I had only one choice: no longer to wait for things to happen or not happen to me, but to make them happen. It was high time, I thought, for all the diverse streams to become a single course, for everything to become something, no matter how unconnected it appeared, or to finally dissolve into nothing, a marvelous solution that would offer complete freedom, and was, I had to say right off the bat, the least likely. And so the next day, armed with a pad and colored pencils, I set out for a detailed inspection of the Zemun market. It was a beautiful spring day, pleasantly warm, with clouds racing across the sky, and the market, when I arrived, swarming with people. I intended to cover as many streets as possible, looking carefully around, to record all the spots where I saw the sign made of the circle and triangles, as well as all the places where there were possible traces of the sign. I had to bear in mind the likelihood that most of the signs had not been drawn using permanent materials, so those drawn in chalk, or perhaps in crayon, were likely to have disintegrated. For instance, the signs I had seen earlier on Zmaj Jovina Street were no longer visible, which didn't mean that they played no role in the overall constellation of signs. Once I had completed the list, I intended to draw their locations on a map of Zemun and by so doing gain additional insight or a sort of key for my future moves. To be frank, I had no notion of any further moves, but I did have the hope that they would take form in and of themselves or that they would suggest themselves in a clear light the moment I made a map of the signs. I walked toward the market along Beogradska Street, where I found no traces of any kind. I turned into Mornarska, took two or three steps, spun around and went back. I obeyed a murky feeling, I said later to Marko, that I would find no signs there. So I went back to Beogradska Street and stepped into the bustle of the market. I passed by the stalls that offered the most varied merchandise, items of food, hygiene, electrical and plumbing equipment, men's and women's underwear, wooden spoons and three-legged wooden stools, coffee and detergents. Behind them were the vegetable stalls. I dove for a moment into the crowd, then came back to the first row of stalls, where I bought some chocolate. If there was a sign inscribed anywhere in that part of the marketplace, it was pointless to look for it, so when I arrived at the end of the first section of the market I turned off onto Gospodska Street and headed toward the quay. On the quay, across from the Venezia, I saw a few chalk drawings on the sidewalk, one resembled a spiral and the other a tangled ball, which had nothing to do with my signs. My signs? I am always amazed at the ease with which we adopt things, even when there is no question of ownership, because if there is something that was not mine, it was those signs, that much, at least, is clear. I looked to the left, I looked to the right, then turned left toward the corner of Zmaj Jovina Street. Here, a few weeks earlier, I had come across the first sign, hidden under a button. I stopped and entered that fact in the notebook. I wrote in black: the black was to mark the absence, or rather the absence of a presence; I planned red for entering newfound signs, blue for the possible vestiges of signs, while green was to serve for lingering vestiges that may not have been drawn as parts of signs. There was nothing at the spot where the black button had lain, just as there was nothing on the steps where I had seen the sign when I leaned over to pick up the woman's potato. Now too the street was littered, so I had to pause at every step, shove aside crumpled newspapers, pick through heaps of trash, lift plastic bags. At the corner of Gajeva, at the foot of a traffic sign, I came across an unfinished triangle, drawn in chalk, which might have been part of a smaller, inner triangle, inscribed in a larger triangle. I jotted this down in the notebook, in blue this time. Not far from the remnant of the triangle was an arrow pointing to the opposite side of the market, to Dositejeva and Karamatina streets. As children we used to leave signs for friends: by following the arrows they would find where we were waiting for them. I walked down Gajeva and soon came across a new arrow, pointing to the left, to Dositejeva Street. I saw yet another arrow, and then a boy who, a little farther along, was drawing a new arrow on the pavement. When he saw me, he ran off. He shouted something, without turning, then ducked into an entranceway. I didn't even try to follow him. I went back to Gajeva Street, and as I passed by the old foundry, I finally caught sight of the first real sign. After that it got easier. From Gajeva I went into Karamatina and walked down its one side to the quay, came back along the other side to Muhar, and then along Glavna Street to Zmaj Jovina. By then I had recorded six or seven signs and several possible traces, including one triangle with a dot in the middle, which, I suspected, represented something different, but it was easier for me to consider it a remnant of a sign to which someone, either by chance or on purpose, had added a dot. Then I walked along Zmaj Jovina Street. On the fence around the construction site behind the theater, in a sheltered spot, I noticed four signs, as if someone was practicing drawing them. At the large wooden gate, where there had been the poster advertising tai chi classes, a much larger poster was up, announcing a concert of folk music. I studied the poster carefully; I found nothing; a part that was smudged suggested a trace of lipstick, the imprint of a kiss someone had planted on the cheek of a performer. I peeked into the passageway that led to the inner courtyard, went over to the bench, checked the water pump and the barberry bushes. No traces there. Back I went into the street, passed down one side and then up the other, and ended at the quay. I found another seven or eight signs along Zmaj Jovina, as well as two traces, both by the first market stalls. Before I went into Gospodska Street I circled around the Harbormaster's. The gallery was closed, half dark, and when I pressed my nose against the glass door, on the facing wall, next to a photograph, I thought I could see the sign, but when I looked again a moment later, the wall was an unblemished white. I continued walking and recording with the different colored pencils, and when I got hungry, I went into a bakery and had some *burek*. The *burek* was greasy; I had to lick my fingers. I licked them one by one, ignoring the woman behind the counter. Then I bought a crescent roll with jam and asked for a glass of water. The water was lukewarm. I sipped at it and leafed through my notebook. I still had to go through Pobeda Square, and I mustn't forget Piljarska Street, the narrowest of the streets around the market but full of handy places to leave signs. This proved true: I found as many as six on Piljarska, drawn at precise seventy-centimeter intervals. By now it was late afternoon, fewer people at the market, time to head home. Clouds were gathering in the sky, rain was on the way. I stopped at the stationery store on Zmaj Jovina and asked for a map of Zemun. They had only a commercial map of the city, with the stores and businesses drawn in, but it was large and comprehensive, and I was happy with it, especially because in the upper-right-hand corner it had a magnified insert of the city center. My feet were stinging by the time I got home. I spread open the map on the kitchen table and began marking the places where I had seen the signs. The part around the market, I noticed, consisted of nine different-sized blocks, of which one, the one that came out to the quay, bordered by Zmaj Jovina and Karamatina, was in the shape of a triangle. The number nine may have had special significance, but I didn't dare call Dragan Mišović again. I could have asked Jaša Alkalaj, of course; after all, numbers are numbers, whether it is mathematics or the Kabbalah. I leafed through the notebook and marked the dots in different colors. Most were red, a few were blue, three or four green, and three were black. Once I had put in the last dot, I stepped back to see the map from a distance. I didn't know what I would see, I didn't know what I expected to see, I didn't actually see anything. The dots, dense in some spots and sparse in others, surrounded all nine blocks; only the middle, which was roughly at the place where Gospodska Street ran into Omladinski Square, was empty. I was disappointed, I admit. I had expected that this pattern would immediately suggest things to me I hadn't known, but it told me nothing, though perhaps it was speaking an unfamiliar language. Once more I checked everything carefully, and then I rolled a joint, lit it, and walked over to the window. I looked to the left, I looked to the right, then straight ahead. The window of the pharmacy was already lit; not a single car was parked in front of it; I could take a deep breath, inhale in peace. Slowly, deeply, I inhaled, watching night conquer the sky and felt the cannabis rise in my body: my knees softened, my stomach sagged, my heart beat faster, my eyelids drooped, and when I felt it behind my forehead, I went to lie down. That night I dreamed a strange dream. I regret not writing it down right away; with time it faded, and now, no matter how hard I try, I can summon only details and cannot, for the life of me, reconstruct the whole thing. Nothing particular happened in it, as far as I recall, and one could say I was dreaming emotions more than events. I remember, for instance, that I dreamed I was sleeping and that I was waking up but couldn't open my eyes. I wake up, in the dream, because someone is sitting by my bed, leaning over me, and staring at my closed eyes. Since I am dreaming that my eyelids are shut, everything I see in the dream is dark. I am awake in the dream but I don't dare open my eyes, I'm fearful of what I'll see, and I remember saying to myself in my dream, Maybe these are ordinary human eyes. Then a voice, right by my ear, says: There is no such thing as ordinary human eyes. And then: Each eye is a story unto itself. Then I was really awake, unsure of who had heard that voice or who was feeling fearful. I dreamed the same dream several times that night, and in the morning I could barely stand up. Go back to bed, I said to my reflection in the mirror. The reflection didn't answer, and even if it had, it wouldn't have helped, because that morning I had to edit the piece for my *Minut* column. Recently everybody had been talking about a referendum in which the people, the government claimed, would decide whether or not the involvement of foreign powers in resolving the Kosovo crisis was acceptable, and the editor, remarking that political subjects didn't seem to interest me much, said that he would still find it interesting to read what I had to say. I finally chose a different topic: the problems caused by the vast number of stray dogs, including quite a few purebreds whose owners, unable to cover the cost of food and care, had simply cast out into the street. Of course, I didn't feel that deciding the fate of Kosovo was any less important than abandoned dogs, but anyone could see that the way the referendum was being run was a farce and that there was no point in wasting words on it. The consequences would not be part of the farce, but someone else would write that story, not me. The stray dogs were left to me and the dilemmas they posed for us—the question of goodness and a test of loyalty. I wrote without passion, using clichéd phrasing and attacking the class of the newly rich for squandering their wealth on rare and expensive breeds of dogs, then shunting their problems off onto society. The simplest solution, I wrote, is to put the dogs down, but this does not go to the root of the problem, it deals only with the consequences. The real question is what to do with the people who abandon their dogs, and I was leaving it to the readers, I wrote, to come up with the most fitting punishment. Such a shame that it didn't occur to me at the time to encourage readers to send in their suggestions, because this might well have resulted in a little encyclopedia of both well-meaning and vengeful cruelties, intriguing proposals, though it may not be too late for this, if one bears in mind that, judging by the news that reaches me here, the problems with stray dogs in Serbia persist. There is no more *Minut,* of course, it went the way of so many other daily and weekly papers unable to secure a large enough readership, so I would have to write for a different publication, *Evropa* or *Vreme* or whatever the periodicals published there these days are called. I couldn't believe that the editor of *Minut* liked my piece, despite the fact that he was a cat lover, and besides his own, he fed three or four other cats in the yard of the building he lived in. Later it turned out they had to cut the piece down, that's why I was at the editorial office that morning with the editor in chief and the copyeditor. While we were waiting for the edited text to be entered into the computer, the editor in chief told me he had divorced his wife because she didn't like cats. She tried, he said, but couldn't. Whenever Feliks, the editor's old tom, jumped on the bed, she'd scream, he said, and she'd scream until Feliks left the room or until the editor carried him out. She put up with it for two years, which was, he said, admirable, then she gave him an ultimatum: it was Feliks or her, one of them would have to go. The editor thought about it, he said, for precisely three seconds, then got up, took down two suitcases, and began tossing her belongings into them. She sobbed, he packed, Feliks meowed, the phone rang, the TV news blasted, he had never in his life been in such a tangle of sounds, but once she left, everything was quiet and, I might not believe him, but Feliks hadn't meowed since. I didn't know what I'd done to deserve this confidence; our conversations had always been limited to work, to remarks about my columns and discussion of future pieces. Maybe, I told Marko when we ran into each other in front of the Youth Center, I should have reciprocated in kind and told him something from my own life? The man is lonely, that's all, said Marko, and besides, like anyone with a measure of power and control over others, he sometimes has the need to show himself in a benevolent, gentle, human guise. Refer to that same story tomorrow, Marko continued, and don't be surprised if he tells you to mind your own business. We waited for the light to change, crossed the street, and, on the other side of the square, headed for Knez Mihailova. I paused at the corner, looked to the left, looked to the right, then hurried after Marko. Good, I said when I caught up, they are not here. Who? asked Marko. Or do you think everybody knows? I reminded him of the men with the crewcuts. He dismissed this with a wave of the hand. They don't matter, he said, and within the year they'll be gone, trust me. I don't know where Marko is now, but I do know how wrong he was. The nationalists have not disappeared, nor are they insignificant; on the contrary, they are more present than ever, and their influence is again on the rise and shows no signs of waning. That is how things now stand, judging by the meager news reports and rare email messages that I trust because they come from reliable sources, while back then, in the constant, exhausting expectation of change, Marko's certainty was understandable and acceptable. Oh Lord, when I think of the waiting, of the energy invested in faith and hope, my stomach clenches. How slowly it was all built, with how much effort, and with what speed it was all dismantled, stopped, mired in swamp. There are some things one should not think about, or maybe one must never stop thinking about them, I still haven't decided which of the two to choose, but whichever I choose, nothing can be changed anymore, life is a line that moves forward only at one end, while the other stays in place, rooted, and no matter what we do, what we say, we can't get near it, just as I already said, I mean, wrote, even though that was not wrong, because I often first say sentences aloud, turn the words over on my tongue, listen to them bumping and bouncing back from the empty corners, but whatever the case, I am repeating myself, no doubt, which should not be seen as a bad thing, since all of life is segments repeated from other lives, with only the order of the segments new and singular, bringing an element of surprise to life, and *surprise* is just another word for *uniqueness,* since we invariably think that what is new to us, or what we don't recognize, is unique, though the truth may be quite different and what we think is unique may be only one of many iterations, which is what I meant to say when I started this sentence, but which broke off and went its own way, not waiting, as I had expected, perhaps incautiously, for Marko and me to continue our walk along Knez Mihailova, and instead, like a disobedient household pet that has been let out for the first time in ages, now scampered along, one minute in front of us, and the next, far behind, so we had to turn now and then to check whether it was still there and had not gone wandering off or over to someone's beckoning hand. Once when I turned to look back, I saw Margareta. I didn't recognize her at first: she'd changed her hairdo, she was wearing high heels, a light trench coat belted at the waist, a shawl carefully arranged over her shoulders. When I turned a second time I could no longer see her among the passersby. I looked a third time and saw her leaving a book or stationery store, pausing to drop a wrapped packet into her handbag, and turning to head in the opposite direction. I tugged at Marko's sleeve and said that I had forgotten to check on something at the bookstore. He should keep going, I told him, and I would catch up in a minute, if not before, then certainly by the entrance to Kalemegdan. He was not pleased, I could see, but on he went. I waited for him to disappear among the passersby, then went chasing after Margareta. I caught up with her by the bookstore at the other end of the street; she had stopped by the store window and was looking at the books on display. I didn't approach her but paused instead at a street vendor's counter and poked among the costume jewelry. Margareta didn't move. She stood by the window, staring in as if trying to read a closed book. Then a tall man with a mustache joined her by the window and also stared in. People passing by interfered with my view of Margareta and the man with the mustache, but I was almost certain I saw his lips moving. To be almost certain means to be uncertain, this I realize, but I can't be more precise. A moment later, I am almost sure of that as well, their hands touched briefly, the man's left and Margareta's right, and it is entirely possible that something changed hands. The street vendor asked impatiently whether I was going to buy anything or just wanted to poke around among his merchandise, so I had to put down the chains and charms I had been running through my fingers, and when I looked over at the bookstore window again I could see that the man was leaving in the direction I had just come from, toward the Academy and Kalemegdan. Margareta stood there for a few more minutes, then tossed back her hair, turned, and walked off the other way. I felt like howling, like invoking a band of angels, because again I had to choose between her and a man, but this time, cautioned by the earlier experience and against my better judgment, I went after the man with the mustache. Before I dove into the dense mass of pedestrians, I saw Margareta once more as she moved off toward Terazije, while the shawl over her shoulders swayed cheerfully as if in greeting. Following the man with the mustache was no joke. He moved swiftly, skillfully sidestepping passersby, which forced me several times to elbow my way through the crowd. I assumed that because he was tall he could see what was ahead and adjust his stride accordingly while I was scampering along, and since I could not see what was ahead, I kept bumping into people who were stopping and talking and walking in the opposite direction. When we got closer to the Academy, the man with the mustache suddenly turned to the right, toward the Faculty of Philosophy, which forced me to stop. If I turn and follow him, I said to myself, I will anger Marko, who must already be waiting for me in front of the Belgrade City Library, but if I don't follow him, I thought, then what? Who was that man anyway, and why was I following him? Maybe I really had seen too many thrillers, maybe I was a victim of my own mistaken convictions and delusions? How could I be sure that something had gone on between that man and Margareta, and why, suddenly, wherever I looked, did I see indications of secrecy, the language of signs, fugitives and pursuers, plotters and madmen? I looked back and, just as I'd thought I would, I saw the two men with the crewcuts in a lively conversation, jabbing each other and doubling over with laughter. I wouldn't have been surprised, I thought, if it turned out that the man with the mustache was also being followed, nor would it have surprised me if someone were following the men with the crewcuts, which thought made me give up on the tall man with the mustache, whom I could still see at the far end of the philosophy building, and hurry toward Kalemegdan, where I told Marko the whole story. I started talking while still a few steps away from him, but he cautioned me with a raised index finger. Then he whispered that I should take a look down the other side of the street, and there at the entrance to Kalemegdan I caught sight of a man in a black trench coat and dark glasses. I wasn't sure whether it was the same man I had seen on the quay in Zemun. It was a coincidence, I said, not everyone was being followed, and I told him about what had just happened, avoiding, of course, any mention of Margareta. At that moment, the man in the black trench coat and dark glasses turned and strolled slowly into Kalemegdan. What is this, I said, shouldn't he be behind us? He is luring us, answered Marko, and if we follow him, somehow he will disappear. And that is precisely what happened. Marko claimed that we had outsmarted him, though he couldn't say how, and that we had not lost sight of him, he had lost sight of us. And now, said Marko, who knows where he is off to, wandering around the fortress? Maybe he has gone into the dungeons, he mused, from which he will never emerge to the light of day or the dark of night. I wasn't so sure myself, though I stopped looking back. We came out on the terrace that offered a view of the Sava and the Danube, New Belgrade and Zemun on the facing riverbank. I thought of Feliks, my editor's tomcat, not meowing anymore after the editor's wife had left. Was Feliks quiet because he was happy or because he was unhappy? The editor seemed happy enough, but the cat might have felt differently. Perhaps, I thought, the editor should have gone off and left his wife with the cat, maybe they would have found a way to get along, and the fear and anxiety would have turned into respect and esteem? I glanced out of the corner of my eye at Marko. What was he thinking about? Certainly not the editor's tomcat, just as it would never have occurred to him that I was thinking about a hairy creature at a time when I should have been obsessed with thoughts of conspiracy. I was tired of everything else, of the stories that fed on themselves, that never moved forward, just as the colored point on a spiral always appears to stay in the same spot, though it is constantly spinning. Every time I thought I was getting close to something or somebody, I would discover that the distance between us hadn't changed a bit, and if it were to change, it would grow rather than shrink. This is too much, I thought, for someone who until recently was dreaming of being a writer, nothing more. I could hear Marko breathing deeply and regularly, as if he'd fallen asleep, though his eyes were open wide. The sky drew back over Zemun and New Belgrade like the curtain in a theater in which the two of us were the only audience, concerned that the night would descend before the last act and frightened by the possibility that this might be one of those plays in which the audience participates, reluctant actors whom fate had dealt the role of losers. The sun slid across the sky as if it were oiled, and it looked as if it might collide at any moment with the horizon, though the day was still young. The afternoon, I said, has hardly begun and it's already over. Marko turned slowly to face me. What was that? he asked. The first line of a new poem? I wrote a few poems several years ago, and Marko had never forgiven me. At the time he had a girlfriend who was a real poet and she published a collection of poems in the First Book edition of the Matica Srpska publishing house, and his intolerance for poetic voices and forms followed after a sudden and extremely unpleasant breakup, when she hit him on the head with a Benson English-Serbo-Croatian dictionary, until streams of blood were coursing down his forehead and neck. Worst of all, this happened during a performance of a play by Miroslav Mandić, so that at first no one found it disturbing, convinced it was part of the performance. Even Miroslav Mandić stood by, unsure of what to do. Not until the blood began dripping down Marko's head did he wrench the Benson dictionary from the hands of the enraged woman, yet she kept lunging at Marko. After that, no doubt, I too would have lost my taste for poetry, though I would never deny the power of the poet to express the essence of the world and our existence most succinctly. Right now I could use that kind of artist, a master at expressing essence, someone who, in one sentence or possibly two, could summarize what had happened to me over the last few weeks. Marko was staring at me, expecting an answer. No, I said in the end, this is not the first line of a poem, but a summation of my despair, time is passing, faster and faster, yet I can't seem to move an inch. Despair is not going to help you there, said Marko, especially if you bear in mind that no one has swindled, cheated, or mastered time. Some have too, I shot back, but when Marko looked at me inquiringly, I could think of no one. Perhaps those, Marko added, who made a pact with the devil, which as far as I know you would never do. Forget the devil, I said, these are far more serious matters. How can you say that the devil's not a serious matter? Marko shouted. Over his shoulder I saw an elderly woman who, at the mention of the devil, froze in her tracks and turned to stare at us. No need to shout, I said, we are attracting way too much attention as it is. The elderly woman took a step toward us, then crossed herself and went on her way. I will shout if I want to, said Marko more softly. He turned his back on me like a pouting child. I looked at my hands: my ten fingers probably would not suffice to number the calamities in my life, and now I had to include Marko's unreasonable behavior. Or was it my behavior, perhaps, that had become impossible to understand? Maybe I attribute to others what I should be ascribing to myself? How many unanswered questions can a person absorb and still not change? There must be an upper limit, and after that a collapse. I looked to the left, I looked to the right, I looked down, I looked up. I saw no answer. I assumed the same was true behind me. I checked, just in case, and sure enough. No trace of an answer, just as there was no trace of the man in the black trench coat. Marko's back was still turned, the sky was taking on a darker shade, the clouds were scudding away with no promises, and down below, on the Sava, two boats moved slowly under the bridge. I touched Marko's shoulder. He would stay a little longer, he said, and held out his hand. I couldn't remember when we had last shaken hands. I gave him mine and our hands joined, limply, only for a moment. Enough, however, for me to feel that his palm was stone cold, as if he had been holding ice. So now, how can I write the next sentence and not sound ridiculous to anyone, myself included? When I touched Marko's icy palm, what occurred to me was that he was so bitterly prepared to defend the devil because he,

Marko, was one of the devil's acolytes. As I walked away from him, I saw that phrase clear as day in the realm of my consciousness: it shone like a vast neon sign, in different colored letters, blinking on and off in slow rhythm. If the man in the black trench coat and dark glasses had appeared before me at that moment, I would have waved at him cheerfully; compared to the devil, he was nothing; he did not, however, appear, and I soon found myself on Knez Mihailova Street, which was even more crowded than when we started out. I thought it might be good to go to the synagogue courtyard, but I also thought I should shake off the thoughts of the devil, so I changed direction by the Academy of Science and Art and walked to the park at Topličin Venac. There is nothing so soothing as sitting on a park bench, surrounded by cooing pigeons on the lookout for bread crumbs. I would close my eyes here and try to calm my breathing, focusing on an emptiness that purifies. These were simple meditation exercises, but they always helped, so that within ten minutes I'd feel as if I had sloughed off the dingy skin of the polluted spirit and breathed a pure breath, first through one nostril, then through the other. By that time the pigeons had given up on me and were gravitating to an old woman seated on a nearby bench, tossing them seeds. She looked like the old woman who earlier on, in Kalemegdan, had turned when I invoked the devil, but all old women looked the same to me, whether it was a matter of the devil or a flock of hungry pigeons. Pigeons, pigeons, pigeons, I could think of nothing else, and so, with pigeons on the brain, I entered the courtyard of the synagogue. It may have been a Friday, or perhaps one of the Jewish holidays, I can no longer recall, but several men were seated at a table under a tree in leaf, among them Jaša Alkalaj, Isak Levi, and Dača. Jaša waved, and when I came over, he made room for me next to him on the bench. I had come at just the right moment, he said, because they were talking about how to protect the cemetery from incursions by the barbarians. Why barbarians?

asked a man who was sitting on Jaša's other side. They are just plain scum. Barbarians, scum, makes no difference, interrupted a man from across the table, doesn't matter who they are, but what we can do against them, and I'm afraid, he said, that we don't have much of a choice. In any case we can't scrawl graffiti on their gravestones, said the man next to Jaša, the police aren't interested in helping, and what options do we have left, nighttime guard duty? Not a bad idea, said a man wearing a yarmulke, fight poison with poison. Nonsense, said Dača, putting on his hat, then taking it off again, no point in biting off more than we can chew. And who, he said, would be doing the guard duty, us? And what would we do, he asked, take them on? Look at yourselves, for God's sake, he said, and tell me what you see? We all looked at ourselves and, as if by agreement, we all looked down at the tabletop. We are a handful of misery, said Dača, and anyone who can't understand that, or doesn't want to, will have to ask himself if he's in his right mind. Then he pointed at me. Only he, he said, can think differently, but that's something he'll have to decide for himself. I asked whether I should leave, perhaps it would be easier, I said, for them to talk about such delicate matters without the presence of outsiders. That doesn't apply, said Jaša Alkalaj, to the people sitting on my right side and on my left side, does it? Everyone clamored in confirmation, so Dača had to pound on the table to quiet them. We can hope to receive help from only one place, he said. He straightened his finger and pointed up. We all looked up, into the tree. Not there, shouted Dača, up there, above us! He stretched out his arm and we all stared at his trembling index finger. A tiny beam of light, barely visible, shot from the tip of his finger, passed through the spring leaves, and flashed to the sky. I blinked, the beam was gone. I looked around, but no one else seemed to have noticed a thing. What will the rabbi say, said the man wearing the yarmulke at last, when he hears of this? How will he hear, asked Dača, if we don't tell him? The rabbi is the least of our worries, said Jaša

Alkalaj, it's deciding what we should be doing. By then evening had nestled into the sky and was spreading, changing gradually into night. Dača launched into a story, sounding like a local town-hall bureaucrat in the office for community defense, describing in detail the advantages of guerrilla warfare and the importance of surprise, only to say in the end that we should forget all that and focus on living tradition. If for centuries the Kabbalists and mystics had managed to create beings of earthen dust and breathe life into them, he said, then there must be a way for us to fight against these hoodlums. Don't tell me, said Jaša Alkalaj, that you propose we make a golem? I'm not proposing anything, he answered, but if that is the only way, then why not? Again silence reigned at the table. The dark was descending on our faces, pressing down our eyelids, and for a moment I was afraid I might fall asleep, right there, in front of everybody, with my forehead on the table. Dača's voice reached me from a great distance, as if he were shouting from the deck of a ship sailing away. As I recall, he was talking about how in ancient Kabbalistic writings there were recipes, that is what he said: recipes, for different forms of resistance or concealment, or for simply outwitting the enemy, all we had to do was find what suited us, then adapt it to our times and technology, because it was important not to forget, he repeated in a soft voice, that these documents date from the Middle Ages, and some from even earlier, and that nothing can be simply grafted from one historical period to another, but that, he whispered, everything would be fine as long as we knew what we were doing. Do we know, said Jaša Alkalaj suddenly, aloud, straight into my ear, or do we think we know? I started. Even today I don't know what was happening: I'm certain I had not been asleep, yet at that moment there was no one at the table but the two of us. I looked to the left, I looked to the right. They are gone, said Jaša, no point in looking for them. And the golem, I asked, what happened to the golem? He's not here yet, laughed Jaša, and neither is Godot. Then he grew serious: You don't believe in what Dača was saying, do you? He seemed pretty convincing, I said, I have to admit. It's easy to be convincing, said Jaša, anyone can be convincing, especially someone as eloquent as Dača. The dark had grown so thick I could barely discern the features of Jaša's face. I don't believe he would lie, I said. Of course not, replied Jaša, no one is talking about lying, everything he said is the pure truth, from the first to the last letter. And those recipes, I asked, for the different weapons, do they exist? Let's say, said Jaša, that this is a kind of poetic license, but the fact is that there are very precise instructions for making a golem, and if an obedient golem were made, such a creature could easily throw the ranks of the enemy into a panic, and panic is the first stage of defeat. Generally, I said. Always, said Jaša. All that was left of his face was a pale egg-shaped stain, and I felt that I was conversing with a ghost on the verge of vanishing. The most interesting thing about the golem, said Jaša's mouth, is that despite his origins in language and the recitation of magic formulas, he cannot speak, which is patently absurd, because you'd expect language to first make language, with all else coming later; however, Jaša's mouth went on, if the golem were able to speak, then he'd be a perfect being, which would be a direct challenge to God, who alone can create perfect, complete beings. That's why, Jaša's voice came out of the darkness, the golem must be imperfect, and if he doesn't speak, then he doesn't have the most essential component of a real being, in other words, he cannot be a creator and create the world by uttering it, which is to say in the same way that the Lord created his world, our world, this world. I could no longer see him. I stretched out my hand but reached nothing. Then I heard the iron gate creaking, and slowly, stumbling, I moved toward the sound. Even today, six years later, I still don't understand what was happening in the courtyard of the Belgrade synagogue that evening; I only know that the dark thinned as I passed through the iron gate and stepped out into the street.

When I tried to go back into the synagogue courtyard, I couldn't open the gate. That gate is always getting jammed, said a man who was passing by, high time they fixed it. I was about to ask how I might get back inside, if he knew that the gate jammed then he might know how to unjam it, but he had already moved on down the sidewalk and I didn't try to catch up with him. I crossed over to the other side of the street and started up the steps that led to Obilićev Venac. It occurred to me that there must be some connection between the synagogue and the sign I had seen at the café by the Graphics Collective Gallery, in the same way that there was a link among the signs left around the Zemun marketplace. In other words, I was convinced that all I had to do was keep an eye out and I would discover an abundance of new signs, but I didn't have it in me to start yet another investigation. Perhaps *investigation* is not the best word, though at that moment I truly felt like a worn-out police inspector who, at the end of his boring career, finally comes across a spectacular case that radically changes his life, the only difference being that I had no desire at all to change my life. This is perhaps a strange thing to say for a person who lived in such a troubled, shattered country, in which very few managed to sustain even a shred of hope, but if I were to attempt an explanation, I would fail. There are some things one either knows or doesn't know, that's all. Ultimately my life did change, which I say with no regret, there is no point to regret, but I am giving it as a fact, especially because I feel that every fact is welcome in a story that has so few facts, at least in the form to which we are accustomed, and by saying that I mean those facts that free us from doubt, not facts that encourage us to doubt. In any case, a sentence in which the same word is repeated four times cannot be a good sentence and is a reliable reflection of the anxiety and powerlessness of the person who wrote it. I experienced that same powerlessness as I wrote the pieces for *Minut* those last weeks. When I refer to the last weeks, I am thinking of the weeks during which the events set in motion by the slap along the river-banks of the Danube were brought to a close. I recently got hold of a calendar for the year 1998, counted the days following the eighth of March, and established that it all took a little over nine weeks. What is nine weeks? Nothing. At the time, however, it seemed to be taking far longer, I even sometimes thought with despair that it would never end, that I would stay caught up in that merciless spiral for the rest of my life, which, tornadolike, sucked up everything in its path. In that chaos, which I am not doing a good enough job of conveying, I realize, the only constant was the pieces I was writing regularly and handing in every Wednesday by three P.M. at the latest. And of course, as time passed and I handed in each new piece later and later, they all screamed at me when I would come into the editorial office, text in hand. I mention this only because after the evening in the synagogue courtyard, as I climbed the stairs to Obilićev Venac and thought about the new cluster of signs, I remembered that when I had studied the map of Zemun, I had established that the neighborhood around the market, where I found a concentration of signs, consisted of nine city blocks. Why did that matter? Because nine men were seated around the wooden table in the courtyard of the synagogue; I was the tenth. At that point, of course, I didn't yet know that these events would last for nine weeks, but even so the coincidence was enough to prompt me to write about the role of numbers in our lives, which is what I told the editor in a phone conversation the next day. The editor was not thrilled, claiming that the subject matter was too obscure for your average reader, but I stood my ground, convinced that it was precisely the sort of subject that did engage readers, especially speculating about what might affect their lives. Other than Slobodan Milošević, of course, I added. The editor smiled, even so it took my asking about Feliks the cat and his meowing before he relented, with the caveat that he would publish no esoteric writing. We have more than enough of the esoteric in our day-to-day lives, he said at the end of the conversation. The first thing I thought of was Dragan Mišović, though after our last conversation, in which I didn't come off too well, I was not overly eager to talk to him. On the other hand, who else could tell me more about numbers? He was the only mathematician I knew; no one else cared about numbers, and as things stand in today's world, mathematics will become a secret language only for the initiated. In many countries, I recently read, children are no longer able to do calculations in their head, by heart, and the multiplication tables are no longer the foundation of knowledge the way they used to be, because everybody has, or can easily get ahold of, a calculator, and calculate all sorts of things while essentially having no understanding of what is involved. And while some say this is good, because knowledge need not be the exclusive property of the educated minority, I see this as the ascendancy of mediocrity. The mediocre rule the world, no doubt, and it is normal that they adapt the world to their needs and intellectual capacity. In a store, for instance, there are times when I can add up the prices of the groceries I am buying faster than the woman at the cash register can, which always wins me the admiration of the salespeople and other customers. I wouldn't be surprised if one day they all burst into applause. But I digress. It is always easier to make plans than to follow them up, and this was something that forever plagued me in my earlier life, the life I had to leave behind six years ago when I started this new one, which doesn't much resemble life. I was sometimes known to say that I dreamed of a life far away from historical divides and would be happiest to spend all my days reading and writing and listening to music, and now, when I am living far from history, when my time is all my own, I'm trying to reconstruct the events that led to it and am shamelessly saying, here and now, that I can imagine no other life, that I long for what I used to consider useless sludge. But back to the question of numbers, they are at least impartial, feelings mean nothing to them, one number is like any other, though, on the other hand, each is unique. It sounds as if I am talking about people, and that may have been my thinking when I proposed to the editor of *Minut* a piece about the role numbers play in our lives. It is amazing that something that doesn't exist in nature, in any form, plays such an important role in our conceptualization of the world. It would be more natural not to know numbers, which probably was the case long ago, because that brings us closer to the original construct of the universe, and this was recently confirmed. I read in *Politikin Zabavnik* that a tribe was discovered in the jungles of the Amazon who had no notion of numbers and could not count. If a member of the tribe caught two fish, a second one caught three, a third one caught five, they made no distinction. Fish are fish, and that was that. It is a long way from there to the numbers tattooed on people's skin in concentration camps, and I wanted to write the piece for my column in *Minut* about that journey, from a number that does not exist to the number that was the entrance ticket to the death chamber. When I did write the piece, it looked different, as so often happens when we write, and I focused mostly on numbers in the Jewish tradition and on the fact that many things in their religious practice are defined in numbers, such as, for instance, the Thirteen Divine Attributes, the Ten Commandments, the 613 commandments, or mitzvoth, the 231 permutations in the order of the alphabet through which the world is created, and here I also had to mention, which I now see as an exceptionally important detail, the ten Sephirot, or degrees, through which God is manifested in the world. The editor had worried needlessly; the piece did draw readers, and the same day it was published email began pouring in, followed with a lag of several days by real, old-fashioned letters, two or three postcards, and even a small package, which, for reasons of security, I never opened but tossed into the nearest trash basket on my way out of the editorial office. The messages were mostly voicing praise and respect for the Jewish tradition, though there were also unfavorable comments, even open attacks and accusations of excessive love for "Jewish scum." One letter looked like a ransom note from a crime novel, it was composed of letters, words, and parts of sentences cut from the daily and weekly press. It was long, and I felt a begrudging admiration for the person willing to spend so many hours with all that finicky cutting and pasting, probably while wearing plastic gloves to avoid leaving fingerprints on the scissors, glue tube, and newspapers. After finishing the job, when he had finally taken off the gloves, his skin must have been all puckered and wrinkled from sweat. Some of the phrases in the letter irresistibly reminded me of what I had heard in my encounter with the hard-core nationalists, and I had a feeling they would soon reemerge, which was promised, more or less, in the final sentence in the pasted letter. We will see who is right, the sentence said, composed of eight little slips of newspaper, among which I recognized two letters cut from *Politika* and one word cut out of *Danas*. A day or two after the piece was published, graffiti appeared on a building near the editorial office of *Minut,* which said, JEWS ARE NOTHING BUT NUMBERS, and under it the next night someone added, AUSCHWITZ COMMANDER, and out in front of my door I was greeted by foul-smelling excrement again, wrapped in a photograph of the Dead Sea, but, I confess, I didn't understand what that meant. I had never been good at interpreting symbols, and for the life of me I couldn't divine whether the excrement was an allusion to death, as suggested by the name of the sea, or to a surfeit of salt, a spooky atmosphere, a depression on the earth's surface, which could possibly be associated with hell, or whether the purveyor of the excrement, perhaps better the producer of the excrement, had no other picture of Israel handy, so the picture he did have, a somber view of the empire of salt, had to suffice for the wrapping. In any case, the shit lay over the photograph as if it were floating on the surface of the sea. The excrement, the writing, the irate messages warned me that there were worse things to come, and indeed, in the next few days I noticed those young men trailing me more often, and I tried to avoid coming home late at night or taking solitary walks along the river. At night I heard sounds in the hallway of my building, as well as in front of my door, which prompted me to position things useful for self-defense around the apartment: an umbrella, a board from the cellar, a hard plastic pipe, a hammer, and a wrench. And as I was placing them strategically, I had to laugh, because I knew I'd never use them, or if I were to use them, I'd be more likely to hurt myself. The hammer fell on my foot more than once. However, when the phone rang the next night, I grabbed the rolling pin from under the bed and started for the door. I stood there in the dark for a while, listening to the silence in the hallway, and only then did I recognize the sound of the phone ringing behind me. I walked over to the phone, rolling pin raised, as if, when I picked up the receiver, someone might leap out, but when I put the receiver to my ear, I heard Margareta's voice. Chagrined, I hid the rolling pin behind my back. She apologized for calling so late, especially if she'd woken me, she said, but she'd just read my piece in *Minut* and had to call me that instant. She enunciated words by separating them into syllables and spoke as if she were humming. That's all right, I said, wondering what to do about the rolling pin. Why did I own a rolling pin in the first place, a rolling pin that looked old and battered, though I never bake, and the making of pastry dough, which is what, as far as I know, the rolling pin is generally used for, I consider to be an undertaking more challenging than the efforts of an alchemist at making gold? Margareta, however, was interested in the Sephirot, as far as numbers were concerned, she said, she knew nothing, and even an ordinary visit to a market was torment because of the awkwardness she felt when the woman at the cash register handed her back the change. Some things, I thought, we will never know, and while Margareta was talking about her wanderings through the deserts and the primeval jungles of numbers, I was putting the rolling pin back under the bed. But, Margareta then said, back to the Sephirot. Did she think, I asked, that I should have said there were in fact eleven, and should I have mentioned the hidden one, Knowledge, situated between Wisdom and Understanding? Hey, said Margareta, about such topics we are better off talking without an intermediary. It so happened she was in the apartment in the high-rise by the Danube where Marko and I had found her message, and she would like us to go on talking about the Sephirot there if I didn't mind getting dressed, of course, and going out so late at night. How did she know, I asked, that I wasn't dressed? I know all sorts of things, said Margareta, but I don't let on. I said nothing. I wondered whether she knew about the brandishing of the rolling pin. I would not be surprised. Fine, I said, and started pulling clothes on even before I'd hung up. All the while, even once I'd gone out into the street, I could not get the rolling pin off my mind, though what worried me more was completely forgetting something. I've always been fascinated, I later said to Margareta, by the mechanism of forgetting, or rather the question of how to check whether something is forgotten or not, because if it has been forgotten, I said, it is no longer in question, which means, if it is still in question, then the oblivion is not complete. Just as it wasn't complete in the case of my rolling pin, I said, if, indeed, it was mine at all. Margareta laughed with a full-throated laugh that I didn't entirely appreciate at that time of night, maybe because her teeth flashed sharply in the gloom of the apartment in the high-rise. I didn't mention that when I entered the high-rise and found that the bulb in the stairwell was out, I regretted not bringing the rolling pin, especially when it seemed that someone was breathing in the dark not too far from me. I didn't dare use the stairs, I would have been quaking at every corner, so instead I called the elevator and took it to the fourth floor. Margareta opened the door before I had had the chance to ring the doorbell or use the key from the mailbox. She was barefoot, and, trying not to look at her feet or at my pale image in the oval mirror, I started talking about the rolling pin while we were still in the front hall. Numerous lamps were on, so that, dappled with shadows, the apartment seemed buried in books. More books on the floor than before: some piled high had toppled, so in places it was barely possible to wade through. A lamp was also burning on the small desk, casting light on a volume of an encyclopedia, next to which there were pages of writing. Margareta offered me tea, and when I accepted, she went into the kitchen to put on the kettle. I went to the window, looked to the left, looked to the right, night was everywhere. The lights of the capital city were squinting as if ready to go to bed. I turned when I heard clinking; Margareta set the tray on the floor, then sat beside it. Her skirt momentarily slid up her thigh, baring a dazzling whiteness, which forced me to look up and study the expanse of ceiling. Jasmine tea, said Margareta, and passed me a cup. She'd tried any number of teas, she said, but jasmine she liked best, and in any case, she added, there is nothing better for a conversation about good and evil. If she was thinking of my rolling pin, I said, that would be the embodiment of good, and it would only have something to do with evil if it were to land on a bad skull. There is nothing absolutely good or absolutely bad, answered Margareta, even in a rolling pin, though she believed, she added, that there were rolling pins that had pressed evil to the very edge of their cylindrical form. I laughed. I could not believe, I said, that she had got me up at three o'clock in the morning so we could talk about good and evil rolling pins. That is because, Margareta said, I thought I'd left my rolling pin at home, but I still had it with me. Many people, she felt, do not understand that things rule us only because we are careless with them. When you leave something, she said, then it must be left behind within the self and outside the self. She stretched out her hand, plucked a book from the nearest pile, lifted it, then set it on the floor. I am leaving it here, she said, but I am also leaving it in myself. She touched her stomach, as if she'd swallowed the book. If she were to walk away now, she said, and stood up abruptly, the book would remain, both outside and inside, and when she returned, she said, and sat back down, she would pick it up as if she'd never left it, in the room or in herself. As she was sitting, the whiteness of her thigh shone again. Margareta sipped her tea. Next time, I said, I will be more careful. No, said Margareta, it has nothing to do with being careful, and there may be no next time. She looked hard at me, and I had to make a major effort to sustain her gaze, not knowing what was expected of me. She had gray-blue eyes, more gray than blue, now that I think of it, though after all these years I'm not sure of that either. All right, she said, now listen. I'm guessing she talked for more than an hour; then she went off to brew fresh tea. What did she talk about? About the Kabbalah, the system of the Sephirot, the emanation of divine substance, about the system of everything in existence, the notion of good and evil, the migration of souls, the harmony of the spheres, the influence of the planets, prayer and silence. Some of the things were familiar, while others I was hearing for the first time. I got up, lifted my arms, stretched, then began pacing back and forth by the bookladen shelves. I passed by the desk, eyed the pages of writing, but didn't dare stop and study them more closely, though the sounds coming from the kitchen confirmed that Margareta was still busy preparing the tea. I did, however, recognize the open book; it was the volume of the *Jewish Encyclopedia* dedicated to entries starting with the letter *G,* as confirmed by the title of the entry "Gilgul," which I did manage to glimpse in passing. I paced a little longer, stared into the dark windowpanes, glanced at two or three books, leafed through Moshe Idel's study on the golem, and promised myself that I would definitely read it at some point. I notice that I am inventing reasons more and more often now to digress from the story, or slow it down, or even to avoid telling it at all, as if keeping a record can be called storytelling, and as if all this sounds like a story to anyone but me. After all, what is a story? A question to which, of course, I will not respond, because that answer too would only be yet another form of postponement, unlike the answer I got from Margareta when I asked her, pointing to the open volume of the encyclopedia, whether she was getting ready to travel. The question was meant to be witty, but Margareta answered in all seriousness that preparations mean nothing here because souls are traveling all the time, and it is certain that we do not make those decisions. The only decision we make, she said as she poured the tea, is what we'll be like in this life, because good souls seek out good people, just as evil souls search for the bad. That, she said, is one of the explanations as to why a good person becomes better sometimes, or why an evil person suddenly feels the evil urge. I sipped my tea. There are souls, Margareta continued, who circle the world for centuries doing whatever they can to contribute to the spread of good because that is the only way for evil to be gradually crowded off the face of the earth, to make the whole world a mirror for the good. She spoke with a fervor that in those years could only be heard, in an entirely different context, in the rabid tirades of political agitators on television news, and it was astonishing for me to find that such earnestness still existed in some other realm of the spirit. Margareta suddenly stopped talking, and tilting her head to one side, she looked at me intently. I hope, she said, that I'm not burdening you with things that don't interest you. There is nothing worse, she continued, than making people listen to something that means nothing to them, and it had seemed for a moment to her, she said, that she detected a shadow of boredom in my expression. I touched my face with the tips of my fingers, as if to check whether such a shadow was there, but the only thing I felt was the rough tips of my fingers on my chin and cheeks. If she had seen something, I told her, then it was fatigue, because if I'd been bored, I would have left long ago. In that case, Margareta told me, she would like to hear how I explained the presence of evil in the world. I shrugged. It is here, I said, like everything else, and if there is an explanation for other things, then the same holds true for evil. Margareta raised the cup to her lips, sipped a little tea, smiled. She had already taken note, she said, of my skill at speaking without saying anything, while leaving space in the process for further maneuvers, for affirming or denying or for totally withdrawing from further conversation. Now it was my turn to smile and raise my cup to my lips. I'd noticed, I said, that she never used more words than necessary, so that in some sense we complemented each other because I used the largest number of words, while she used the least possible number, which meant, statistically speaking, that on the average we used the same number of words. We'll never get anywhere if we fall back on language games, said Margareta. I agreed and took another sip of jasmine tea. The problem with evil, she said, is that its existence brings into question the assertion that God is good and omnipotent, because if he truly is, why did he need to create evil in any form? Maybe he didn't mean to, I replied, and instead, all on its own, evil transformed itself into a force opposing the one God had intended for the world and people? Margareta said that there were such interpretations in all religions, and that many rabbis, among them Kabbalists such as Moshe Chaim Luzzatto, felt that evil had been created so that the very act of overcoming it would bring people to understand the oneness of God. The Kabbalists determined the place within the system of the Sephirot where the source of evil lies, she said, and that is the Sephirot of Chesed and Gevurah, as shown by Rabbi Isaac the Blind. She spread her hands to remind me that these Sephirot assume the realms of the right and left hands on the human body, that the white and red colors belong to them, which she, for some reason, called angry colors, and silver and gold, or water and fire, all of them opposites, which, she added, through their friction probably encourage the emphasis on evil. All in all, she said, lowering her hands, whatever the sources of evil may be, no one can gainsay its existence, so there is no point in dwelling too long on the question of where it comes from, especially, she said, if the source is taken as Adam, or his tasting of the fruit from the tree of knowledge of good and evil in the Garden of Eden. Even if we wanted to, she said, we couldn't go back in time and stop him from separating the tree of life from the tree of the knowledge of good and evil by his action, so by picking the fruit he was sundering the thread that connected the fruit to the original source, which led to the creation, in his heart, according to the Kabbalists, of malicious intention. After that, she said, after taking apart what should have been joined, evil could have easily used the newly formed conduit to pour into the world, where it would then keep growing, establishing a counterbalance to good and offering itself, shamelessly, to the human race and its right to free choice. I'll never understand, I said, how someone, faced with a choice between good and evil, chooses evil. She couldn't understand either, Margareta replied, but the fact remained that human history is a series of disgraces springing from wrong choices. She sipped a little tea, wiped her mouth, and repeated that no matter how interesting the question of evil might be, what really interested all of us here was how to respond to it, how to stand up to it, and, finally, how to overcome it. I asked, staring at her feet, whom she had in mind when she referred to all of us here. Margareta fell silent for a moment, took another sip of tea, and said we would talk about that another time. Behind her head, through the window, I saw the sky begin to lighten. There are some, Margareta continued, who see no point in tangling with evil and feel that a focus on doing good deeds is all that is needed, leading to an increase in the quantity of goodness and a total liberation from evil, therefore, to an establishment of a world in which there will be nothing but goodness, not even free will, because there will no longer be a need for man to choose. There will be nothing to choose from, said Margareta, because everything a person does will be good, and each person will be good, and so will the whole world. Regrettably, she sighed, in the times we live in we don't have the luxury of waiting patiently for that day to come, because the lunacy of evil is growing, and there is nothing left for us but to take on the fight with evil, not just individually, each in our own heart, she said, but more broadly, just as the sons of light battle the sons of darkness. And what, I asked, does this have to do with me? Margareta hesitated for a moment, then shook her head as if she was persuading herself of something. This was still not the right time for an answer to that question, she said, but soon enough it would be, she couldn't say when, but she could promise that I wouldn't have long to wait. So does that mean, I persisted, that there's an explanation for everything that's been happening to me? There is always an explanation, Margareta replied, nothing happens outside the larger flow of all things. I know that, I said impatiently, but there are ways to channel that flow, to guide a person to a path that someone else has defined, and what interests me is which path that is. Margareta touched her finger to her pursed lips, then reached over and with the same finger touched my lips. There would be time for that, she said, first she had to wrap up the description of the fight between good and evil she'd begun, and she had to finish it before the day had fully dawned. We both looked out the window at the pale sky. Whatever the evil is, however it came to be, said Margareta, it is always growing, threatening to squeeze all the good out of the world. In the process, the evil is nourished, if one can put it that way, by the evil deeds people do, even by their impure thoughts, especially thoughts of committing sins, and as the evil gains in strength the bond is severed between the lowest of the Sephirot, called Malkhut, or Kingdom, and the other Sephirot, and this redirects the emanation of the divine to charging and boosting evil, while the feminine nature, designated as the Shekhinah, is threatened and forced into exile, and when it is exiled, we become one-sided, stripped of the balance of oppositions, and we become easy prey for surging evil. The entire system of Sephirot is threatened, said Margareta, from the Crown to the Foundation, in other words, from the top of the head to the genitals the world goes awry. And to keep that from happening, she added, the Shekhinah must become a part again of the system of divine meaning, so the feminine presence of reality has a role equal to the masculine presence. She turned and looked at the sky, now bright. Even to herself she was sounding like Scheherezade, she said, but her story had to end as morning came. If we were going to spend another night awake, I said as I stood up with effort, she might as well be Scheherezade, because I was not the kind likely to lop off heads, the kind that had to be distracted from the sword. Margareta didn't answer. Morning, apparently, contributed to her change: she was no longer talkative, the smile vanished, and as she hastily rinsed out the cups and spoons, it was as if her whole body went stiff, she became formal. A little later, as I kept talking, she put on white socks. When I saw that my attempts to keep our conversation going were floundering, I too fell silent, and the brief ride in the elevator was extremely awkward. There is nothing more unnatural than two people standing next to each other, nearly touching, saying nothing and looking for something to stare at. How many places to stare at could there be in a filthy, close, graffiti-covered elevator cabin? I could not understand Margareta's unexpected transformation, though I decided immediately, as both of us, were staring fixedly at the same upper corner of the elevator cabin, that I would pay it no mind. The fact of the matter is that the number of unknowns in my equation was no smaller than it had been, but that didn't mean that I should allow it to grow. So, showing nothing, I said goodbye to Margareta, though I couldn't resist turning to see the direction she took as she walked away from the quay. It occurred to me to follow her, it wouldn't have been difficult to do, and following her might have helped to resolve the dilemma that Margareta hadn't wished to speak of, meaning the question of what all these events had to do with me; but after she had opened up to me that night, it seemed dishonorable to follow her. If I had made it this far, I thought, I could last a little longer, so I went home. If I had known just how far off I was in my estimate of how long this would go on, I probably would have set off after her, regardless. Now, of course, it's too late, as I've said, or written, I'm not sure because several times I noticed I've been talking to myself, even as I sit at the table bent over the paper. Somewhere I read that this is called mixing the real and imaginary levels, and that movement between what is real and what is imaginary is most common in children, not counting mentally disturbed people. If that's true, I hope it's a child I'm becoming, and not a person with a dislocated consciousness, though it is the same either way, because no change can alter the past that preceded it. I used to think about that a great deal more, especially at a time when I dedicated myself to studying the Chinese Book of Changes, and I did what I could to find an arrangement of the hexagrams that would prepare me for the arrival of future changes, so that when they occurred I would not experience them as changes but as continuity. I do not remember whether I found the best arrangement of hexagrams; most probably not, because I never really understood the system of broken and unbroken lines, just as I do not now fully understand the system of the Sephirot. If the Chinese hexagrams represent a picture of the world, and if the Kabbalist Sephirot also represent the world, do the hexagrams and the Sephirot reflect the same world, or are these worlds so different that one could say with certainty that each of us has our own, unique world, which is not repeated anywhere? I know that in the end everything comes down to moral purity, and that between the Jewish tzadik and the Chinese superior man one could place an equal sign, but what about all of us who do not attain these pinnacles of virtue? I never had a chance to

discuss this with Margareta; when I went off to see Jaša Alkalaj with the same question, I learned he was preparing for an
art show. These were the paintings, he told me at his studio, he
had been working on for the past few months, and most of
them were dedicated, he remarked, to the theme of racial misunderstanding and prejudice. Until that moment I'd paid no
particular attention to his work, because what I'd seen earlier
had little appeal for me, and he was still convinced that, be-
longing as we did to different generations, guided by different
poetics, we had nothing to offer each other. He invariably dismissed postmodernism with a shrug, while I was prepared at
any moment to swear by that same postmodernism, and with
the same intolerance I heard his positions on the political and
social engagement of the artist. Our discussions, therefore,
about the Kabbalah and mysticism had not strayed into the
realms of art and politics. The art show was something very
different, just as the paintings he showed me were altogether
different from my simple-minded impressions and ill-con-
ceived notions. Unlike the earlier paintings, many of which
were abstract, not including the Kabbalistic canvases I had
seen on my first visit, the new pieces, which Jaša showed me
one by one, embraced the most varied influences and styles;
they included direct references to other works, ranging from
impressionism to pop art. Instead of a connection through sty-
listic expression, the paintings were linked by an openly political theme. Two or three paintings were references to famous
canvases by the painter Mića Popović, while Slobodan and
Mira Milošević appeared in a direct quote from Warhol's
works portraying Mao and Marilyn Monroe. The most interesting, at least for me, were paintings using hyperrealism tech-
niques, I wasn't sure of the source, to respond to the recent
upsurge in anti-Semitism. I assume these were based on photographs, though I'd never seen the original photos, except one.
A group of paramilitaries poses next to vandalized Jewish
tombstones, for instance, one of them holding a severed hu-

man head. The damaged tombstones, I sensed, were photographed at the Zemun Jewish cemetery; I don't know where the paramilitaries were from because they wore no insignia on their clothing or uniforms, but regardless of who they were in the original photograph, the accusation of racism and intolerance referred to the many irregular troops that had gone into the war from our regions. One of the other paintings depicted a fragment of a slogan scrawled across the wall of the Belgrade Jewish cemetery, and in front of it a group of young men with closely cropped hair; some were sneering with hatred, others had their hands raised in quasi-Nazi salutes, yet others brandished a banner, painted as a reverse pirate flag: a black skull and crossed thigh bones on a white ground. The photograph looked familiar: they were soccer club fans before a match in the cup finals or perhaps qualifying matches for the World Cup. In these paintings, as in the others, there were Kabbalistic symbols here and there, Hebrew letters, illuminations from ancient books, six-pointed stars, menorahs, and mezuzahs. Meanwhile, Jaša poured brandy into two glasses, we clinked our glasses, raising them to the paintings, which, as he said, through the art show were becoming a part of the world, we drank to the show, and to him, and, he added, with each of his paintings a piece of himself was subtracted and hence he was becoming an ever smaller part of the world. When he put together all he had done, he said, a few crumbs were all that was left of him, a handful of bits. They shouldn't even be calling him Jaša anymore, he said, but Little Jaša, there was so little of him left. I laughed, he was serious. What's going on, I asked, with the show coming up, shouldn't you be in high spirits? Jaša went over to the table, brushed the papers and newspapers aside, and handed me a folded envelope. Inside, on a sheet of red paper, in letters cut out of newsprint, was a brief message: You haven't got much longer, Judas!!! I noticed that each of the three exclamation points was different, the one in the middle was thicker and the one on the right-hand side was longer. It's no picnic finding the right-sized punctuation marks in newspapers, as anyone would agree, except in the gossip rags with those bombastic headlines, a gold mine of question marks and exclamation points. And besides, the size of the lettering in messages like that isn't coordinated anyway. I turned over the paper, there was nothing on the back, only several uneven blobs of glue. First I said, This is ridiculous; then I said, We should go to the police. Nonsense, said Jaša, what can they do? I said nothing. I could hardly praise a police force that was interested only in propping up the regime in power, motivated solely by their own survival, because if I did, I'd be flying in the face of my own actions. After all, I hadn't turned to the police when I was beaten up, nor did I call them to take a look at my shit-covered, pissed-on doormat, and I made a point of dissuading my well-intentioned neighbor from calling them for me. In return, sometimes I would wash the entire stairwell. Cleanliness is always calming. I asked Jaša whether any of his acquaintances had received similar threats, had Isak or Jakov, or maybe old Dača? But Jaša shook his head and said, If I was keeping silent about it, why would they say anything? And what happens next? I wanted to know. Jaša shrugged. One death threat, he said, is not the end of the world. The preparations for the art show are coming along, the catalog is at the printer's, the invitations too, life goes on and there is no point in paying this any mind, which has always been the case and always will be. Isak Levi wrote the text for the catalog, said Jaša, and the art show was planned for the following Tuesday at the Jewish Historical Museum. Perhaps that space, he said, wasn't the best possible, but I would surely agree that there was no more fitting place for such a show. I agreed, and then we washed that down with our topped-off glasses of brandy, drinking to the prosperity of the museum, the success of the show, and good reviews, for peace on earth and a speedy change of government in our country. For this last wish Jaša filled our glasses yet a third time, so from that moment on my recollections fade, and no matter what I do, I can't bring them back into focus. I remember, and only with great effort, the moment when I left his building to wait for a cab: I looked to the left, I looked to the right, and though I'd done this slowly, looking to the side made my head spin. I had to sit down, and I sat on the highest step. I kept thinking I was hearing leaves rustling, though when I looked at the treetops, they were still. Is that, I later asked the cab driver, the sound of alcohol in my bloodstream? The cab driver glanced at me sullenly in the rearview mirror. He was probably afraid I'd throw up on the seat next to me, which was not out of the question, so, just in case, I opened the window and took a deep breath. There is another bit that has since vanished from my memory, because all I remember is how I suddenly opened my eyes, how I stared at the cab driver's hand on my knee, shaking me, and how, little by little, his words reached me. I paid for the ride, tried to kiss his hand, which he had extended to take the money, got out of the cab, and then I emptied the contents of my stomach by a newspaper kiosk. As the last droplets were spewing from my mouth, I thought I should get my cleaning equipment and restore everything to order. I mustn't forget my plastic gloves, I kept repeating to myself. Of course, as soon as I stepped into the apartment, all such thoughts vanished. I flopped into the armchair, and I was still there when I opened my eyes the next morning, stiff, with a disgusting taste in my mouth, pain in my stomach, tacky fingers, and a headache that threatened to blast my skull to pieces. I'd been wakened by the reflection of the sun's rays, which had found their way to me from the windows of the facing buildings. I squinted at the sunshine, belched and groaned, hoping that by some miracle I might start to feel well again. I was hoping in vain. Some people don't even know what a hangover is, but I am of the kind for whom every hangover is a disease, and when I finally managed to get on my feet, I filled a hot-water bottle, got undressed, and crawled into bed.

The next day, Marko gave me a lecture, his favorite lecture on the theme of how impossible it is to reconcile cannabis and alcohol, and how my hangover and headache, which caused me to open the door to him with my eyes nearly shut, was one more proof that he was right. According to him, the earth was divided into regions of unequal size in which various means for altering consciousness dominated: the Near East, for instance, was a hashish region; the Far East an opium region; in South America it was coca; alcohol ruled in Europe; the native populations in North America had tobacco. However, he maintained, one's background does not necessarily oblige one to embrace the preference of a particular geographic region, rather, each of us was born with a predisposition, and if that predisposition were to connect one to, say, cannabis, then the other substances would hold no interest. In a search for the right substance, Marko explained, you try different mind-altering substances, and when you find the right one, all others become unappealing or damage you, as my poor reaction to Jaša's brandy demonstrated. He offered me his cure for a hangover, a plump joint of marijuana, but I waved him away: the very thought of smoke made my gorge rise, and I was in no mood to test what real smoke would do to me. The headache settled like a veil over my eyes, and I felt I was looking at Marko through my lashes, eyelids half closed, from a great distance. All right, said Marko, if you won't, I will. He lit the joint and for a moment his head disappeared in a cloud of smoke. I closed my eyes and pinched my nose, which was the only way I could shield my stomach from temptation. I even turned my head to the side and tried to point my mouth as far away from him as possible. In the end, fearing I might succumb, I went to the kitchen to make some mint tea, but once I'd made it, I stared into the cup, unable to bring myself to lift it to my lips. Meanwhile, Marko had smoked his joint and had joined me at the kitchen table. He had clearly read the papers that morning, he showered me with minute details on what was happening locally and in the world. The members of the Atlantic Pact had yet again threatened to bomb Serbia if there wasn't an acceptable resolution to the Kosovo crisis; the German mark was still worth six dinars, which was what a liter of gasoline cost; stray dogs were a growing problem; in an apartment frequented by the homeless, in the heart of Belgrade, the dead body of an unknown male was found; the preparations for the referendum were underway; the weather showed no sign of stabilizing; Chinese merchants were flocking to the Belgrade markets; the taxi drivers were calling for higher rates and were threatening a strike that would paralyze the city, as if the city, Marko said, was not already paralyzed. Depressing news sometimes has a bracing effect, if for no other reason than because you realize how paltry your troubles are compared with all those tragedies and cataclysms, so I perked up, sipped some tea, and finally was able to see Marko clearly. Marko, naturally, offered to roll another joint, but my insistence in turning him down surprised even me. All right, said Marko, he had come to show me something, or take me to where he'd show me something, something he felt I had to see, as it was directly related, or at least that was how he perceived it, to stuff that had been going on with me recently, and even if he'd read it wrong, which was not impossible, he said, anyone can make a mistake, I'd be interested in what he had to show me, and we should get going as soon as possible, so he was getting up, which was a good thing because tangled sentences like this were terribly draining for him. All right, I said, went into the bathroom, washed, confirmed that I looked haggard, brushed my teeth, splashed lotion on my cheeks, and came back to the kitchen. I'm ready, I said. Marko looked at me slowly, and suddenly, as I saw his bloodshot eyes, it crossed my mind that I shouldn't trust him. It's a horrible moment when you doubt a person you think of as your best friend, especially when it's not you doubting him over facts, but something inside you, some minuscule signal warning you, so at first you want to ignore it, persuade yourself that it is all a mistake, a short circuit, a disturbance sending you a false image as a foil. But had I not already decided not to tell Marko everything, especially when it came to Margareta? Now my intuition was merely confirming something my subconscious had known for a long time, as it knows everything else, both what has already happened and what is to happen. I am not talking about destiny here; I am not a believer in destiny, I have always favored the notion of free will and the freedom of choice. The blind given, a life spent in writing out an unchanging destiny, I never found such notions appealing—they reduced me to an automaton who goes through life simply to acknowledge that he's but a grain of sand swept along by events, stripped of any meaning. That biologist, I can't recall his name, hit the nail on the head when he said that destiny does exist but is not predetermined, we are the creators of our destiny, but what we choose to do, seen in retrospect, becomes an inevitability, not because of divine intervention but because the past can no longer be altered. Enough of that. Marko waited patiently for me to get ready, then got impatient. He kept hurrying me along, urging me to walk faster, he grew nervous and agitated as if he had snorted cocaine. He was taking me straight into the lion's den, I remember thinking at the time, though now I have to laugh, because there were no lions nor did the place we went to resemble a den. I was still hung-over, and I had the feeling that my stomach was an inflated balloon that I was carrying on a string, high above my head, and my head throbbed whenever we hit the bright sunlight. At the same time, I admit, I was figuring out how to run away at the slightest sign of danger, and I kept lagging a few steps behind Marko. Of course, this bothered him, so he'd grab me by the elbow and pull me along, cursing, though he never once explained why the rush. Even so, we made progress: we passed by the Faculty of Agriculture, entered the city park, then left the park near the hospital and turned onto a street that led to the synagogue. Once long ago, when a discotheque was located in that building, Marko and I went dancing there, as we used to say, to reel a girl in on our fishing line. The past few years there had been quite a public controversy over the synagogue, because the municipal authorities at the time were accused of having illegally taken over the building, but then it turned out there had been no violation of the law, though the story about the scandal resurfaced from time to time, always tinged with political overtones. As we approached the building, I wondered what Marko had in mind: a nostalgic return to the discotheque where Zoran Modli used to be the disc jockey, if I am not mistaken, or an attempt to draw me into some resurgent political dispute. It turned out to be something altogether different. We stepped into the courtyard. Though it was not an enclosed space, I felt a change from the street, as if the air was denser, no, as if something was in the air that could not be felt outside that space, a condensed sanctity, as Marko later said. He was surprised that I hadn't felt that change when I entered the courtyard of the Belgrade synagogue, though that didn't necessarily mean anything, since our reaction to the sanctity of a place, he said, need not always be the same. When he visited famous monasteries, he said, he seldom felt a thing, while, on the other hand, the pressure of sanctity would be nearly unbearable in a ramshackle little church in a village off the beaten track. Everything can be explained, he said, all you need is the will to do it. We were standing in the yard in the increasingly warm sunlight, looking at the synagogue as if expecting it to address us. I still felt a fast-paced throb in my head, but the pain had mostly subsided. I was even able to look at a window reflecting the rays of the sun, and the glare didn't make me nauseous. Marko called me over closer to the building and pointed to a rock with the number 1863 carved in it. He said he wasn't sure what that number meant, but that it probably was the year the synagogue was built. I knelt and touched the number, as if it could tell me something by touch. The number said nothing, instead it scratched the skin on my fingertips with its rough edges. Marko mentioned that the sum of the first two numbers was nine, as was the sum of the second two, and he was convinced that between those two sums there was a connection. I thought of Dragan Mišović. But why would every combination of numbers have an additional, hidden meaning? Couldn't a number be a number and nothing more? How could each number seem mystical, as if filled with secret missives, while words seem like a parody of reality, and the more words there are, the more ridiculous they are? Perhaps I should have wondered how Marko had discovered that number, what he had been looking for in the synagogue courtyard, or, who knows, in the building? I was passing by here the other day, said Marko, and suddenly it looked to me as if someone was waving to me from the corner of the building. And you wondered, I said, whether it was me? Exactly, answered Marko, how did you guess? Who else would have been waving to you, I said, from the synagogue courtyard? Whatever the case, he went into the courtyard and looked behind the corner of the building. No one was there. He had noticed the rock with the numbers, bent over to take a closer look, then heard a voice behind his back. He turned and saw an old woman in black: she even wore black lace gloves and a little hat with a short black veil. She raised her hand and pointed to the top of the synagogue. There, she said, by the chimney, you can see a light at night and those who know how to listen can hear a banging, rattling, and garbled words. Marko tried to ask for details, but she said the light was like no other light, it sometimes burned all night, and the sounds would become so loud that sleep was out of the question. Suddenly she fell silent, pointed up at the roof of the synagogue again, and with quick small steps, left. And you, I said, you came the next night to see what was going on, didn't you? Yes, said Marko, but I didn't see anything, I didn't hear anything, some commotion and the cooing of pigeons. And what did he expect from me now? I wanted to know. I have enough mysteries going at the moment, I said, that I don't know what to do with, I don't want to add one more to the burden. And besides, I continued, isn't there a bar here that stays open until late at night? All those sounds, the racket, the trembling light, doesn't that sound like a bar or club making noise and music? To a lady in black lace gloves, that might seem like the devil's work. Clearly I had not convinced him. He shook his head, blinked, wiped his nose. I suggested we find a café, and reluctantly he agreed. He stared up at the roof and stood on tiptoe, as if that would help him reach the attic. We set out along Dubrovačka Street, but at the first corner we bumped into a man, someone Marko knew, who apparently had something more attractive in mind for Marko than the planned cappuccino, because after conferring briefly they headed off in a different direction. I was left alone. I looked to the left, I looked to the right, then turned to look back at the synagogue. I thought of Dača's story about making a golem or finding some other Kabbalistic weapon; could there be a better place for work on that assignment than a synagogue? Then I remembered Volf Enoch, the water carrier, who passed through these same places more than two hundred years before, changing names the way someone else might change hats. Perhaps he was still walking around, under yet another name and with another occupation. What if, I said to myself, I am Volf Enoch, and that thought made me stop. I am Volf Enoch, I said aloud, and I didn't feel that I was not speaking the truth. But, I went on to say, how could I be Volf Enoch when I'm not a Jew? How do you know, I asked myself, that you're not a Jew? Just as I was about to voice my response, I noticed a little boy and girl staring at me, probably happy to see a crazy man talking to himself. I turned and started running. I don't know why I was running, but when I stopped, my head was clear, as if the increased amount of oxygen that had entered my lungs and blood as I ran absorbed every remaining trace of the discomfort from the hangover. And not just my head; my vision was sharper, more precise, so that I saw everything, as they say, as clearly as if it lay in the palm of my hand. My palm was sweaty, however, and so was my forehead, my lungs were still huffing with effort, my leg muscles quivered, my knees were buckling gently. I looked around: I didn't know where I was. I didn't know how I'd arrived there, obsessed with the thought that no matter how it had happened, I was in fact Volf Enoch. To the left of me was a toolshed, to the right a rickety fence, in front of me were tended garden beds. I was standing in the backyard of one of the old Zemun houses, that much was clear, all I had to figure out was how I'd got here, if I'd got here. I turned again and saw the house to which the backyard belonged. The door was closed, the curtains drawn, a broom and shovel lay next to a cracked set of stairs, a washbasin with a hole in it was on the roof of a vacant doghouse. I saw a pair of old slippers, though I couldn't tell whether they were a man's or a woman's. As I took note of all that, the door opened and an old man appeared, with a rag in his hand. The rag had probably served for dusting, because as the door creaked open, he thrust out his hand and shook it out. When he caught sight of me, he lifted his other hand and waved, as if strange people walked into his backyard every day and stomped around his garden. We exchanged glances until my breathing had slowed and he had shaken out the dust rag, and then I moved slowly toward him. The whole time, however, I couldn't shake off the feeling that I was sleeping and that none of this was happening, but when I got closer to the house, the old man, instead of vanishing as in a dream, came down the worn steps and held out his hand. I took it, expecting my fingers to find only air, but his hand was real and warm. He asked if I'd like to come in. I answered that I didn't know, because I genuinely didn't: I had not the slightest idea how I got there, so how could I know what I'd like to do now? The only thing I wanted was to ask where we were, but I couldn't bear to ask the question, because, as usual, I was embarrassed by my ignorance. So I stood in front of the old man, smiling, waiting for his next question. The old man asked if I'd like something to drink. This must be a dream, I thought, only in dreams do things like this happen, but if this is a dream, how could I have fallen asleep midstride, and if I really am asleep, then am I back there, still running? The old man was patient. Two or three times he rubbed his hands together, he coughed once, he scratched himself once, but he didn't rush me, just as he didn't prompt me to answer. Thank you, I said finally, a little water. The old man clapped his hands, and went back into the house. He closed the door and I heard him turn the key. A minute ago he was inviting me in, I thought, and now he is doing everything to make sure I don't follow him. So I stood there and waited for him and got more and more thirsty. The old man didn't reappear. I suddenly recalled the pump in the courtyard at Zmaj Jovina Street, and the thirst became unbearable. I went up the steps and knocked at the door. There was no sound, even when I leaned my ear against the peeling surface. I knocked again and pressed my ear even more closely to the door, and stayed there until my ear began to smart. I'll be going now, I said to the door, and stepped back. When I turned around, meaning to go down the stairs, I saw that I was in a city park. I sat down on a bench near a children's playground, a little dog sniffed the leg of my pants, two girls were making a sandcastle, a flock of pigeons waited at a safe distance, a woman on the next bench over was embroidering or crocheting, I was never sure which was which, and when I looked up, I saw blue sky and curly clouds. To this day I have not been able to figure out what really happened—had I run, or had I been sitting on that bench the whole time, and if so, how did I get there, and did it all happen because I, or at least something inside me, was truly Volf Enoch? But how could I have become Volf Enoch, and why me, of all people? Perhaps that was why I'd suddenly found myself caught up in these events, as Marko would say, though helpless to extricate myself from them. The universe is a weird place, said Marko, and there is so much stuff in it that makes no sense, which never bothers us except when the lack of sense comes crashing down on us. I had always felt this was empty talk fueled by cannabis smoke, but as it so happened I had personally experienced how emptiness can turn into fullness. I sat on the bench, wondering whether to approach the woman who was crocheting or embroidering and ask if she knew how I'd got there. Of course I didn't, but I could imagine how she'd have looked at me, and who knows, thinking I was attacking her, she might have brandished her crochet hook or embroidery needle, or whatever the device was that she was holding, as a weapon. So I sat there quietly, looking up from time to time at the clouds and waiting for my muscles to stop twitching. The little dog had by that time sniffed his fill of the fragrance in the cuffs of my pants and started sniffing other things in the vicinity. Volf Enoch, the water carrier, I repeated to myself, and tried to imagine what his work had been like back then. Did he have a barrel he filled with water, then lugged on his back from house to house? Where did he fill it? Did he receive a wage for his labors from the Zemun Jewish community, or did he charge by the water flask, bucket, or trough, depending on what he poured the water into? Later, of course, the leeches had their day, and when I remembered them I shivered. It was agonizing enough for me to be the person I was, and now I had to be a water carrier and a leech gatherer, too. That was not all, as it turned out. I stopped by the courtyard of the Belgrade synagogue on Saturday morning, hoping I would find Dača there and perhaps learn more about Volf Enoch. Dača was indeed there: he was sitting at the table, under the tree, wearing the hat. For two days now, he said, he'd been waiting for me to get in touch, and had I not turned up that morning, he would have gone out looking for me. Where would he have looked for me, I asked, since he didn't know where I lived? He would have looked for me where he'd find me, he said. He raised the hat, wiped his brow, then lowered the hat onto his head. I sat on the other bench, right across from him. Crumbs were visible on the table, left there after a meal. The crowning success in the first Serbian uprising, said Dača, was the taking of Belgrade, as any historian would agree, but history is always a mother to some and a stepmother to others, he said, and it was stepmother not only to the Ottomans, but also to the Jews, who were accused of having served the Ottomans, for which some were killed, others forcibly baptized, and some crossed over into Zemun. And now, said Dača, there are documents in which a certain Solomon Enoch is mentioned as the person who brought the ransom for the group, mostly women and children, though in the registers at the time of the Jewish families of Zemun there is no mention of a single Enoch. There is, however, a Jakob Volf, a widower and trader in used goods, but he surely could not have played that role because it is said of Solomon Enoch in one place that he was very young, while this trader must have been older if he had had the time to marry and, regrettably, bury his spouse, who died young. So who is Solomon? asked Dača, taking his hat off and looking at me as if I knew the answer. I don't know, I said. Of course you don't, replied Dača, but we can believe in the possibility that it might have been Volf Enoch, or, he added, putting his hat on again, whoever represented his essence. He saw my confused look. I am thinking of his soul, of course, he said, what were you thinking of? Nothing, I answered, I stopped thinking ages ago. Dača grinned. It won't help you, he said, especially when I tell you one more thing. He leaned toward me as if to impart a secret, so I leaned toward him, feeling conspiratorial. When, at the start of the uprising, said Dača, Father Matija Nenadović crossed secretly over into Zemun to ask Bishop Jovan Jovanović for a cannon, involved in all of this was a Jew, as Nenadović writes in a letter, a man named Enoch who was damned capable, though Nenadović doesn't specify capable of what. It appears, Dača continued, that he was involved in supplying a second cannon, a cannon that Father Luka Lazarević had helped bring to Serbia, which, he said, is strange, to say the least, because later the Belgrade Jews suffered at the hands of the Serbian rebels, but so it goes in history, at one moment you're up, up high, then you're down, very low. So it came about, he said, in Belgrade too, where, when Prince Miloš came into power, better times came for the Jews because the prince granted them full civil rights while they were in Zemun; in the other empire, they were still undesirables, which would last, he said, another thirty years or so. He took off his hat and wiped his forehead again, then he flipped the hat over and set it on the table, as if expecting a piece of fruit to tumble into it. I looked up into the crown of the tree. Dača was quiet, his eyes were closing, so I hurried to ask the question I'd come to ask. On the basis of what he'd told me, was I to conclude that Volf Enoch was not one man, but several, and if this was so, how many people were we talking about, no, that's not what I meant to ask, the number was moot the moment it went beyond one, but could he, I asked, explain how this had happened? Where had all these Volfs and Enochs in different places and times come from, and how did water carriers evolve into gun runners? Dača sat bolt upright when I said this and swiftly put on his hat. What runners, what guns? he asked, he had never said any such thing, and if Volk Enoch had ever run anything, it was leeches. Fine, I said, leeches and guns aren't so different after all, both subsist on bloodletting, but what I really want to ask, I added, is where Volf Enoch is now, today, at this moment? Dača stood up and spread his arms. If we knew everything God intended, he said, we'd have no need for him. He turned and walked toward the gateway, bent, tentative as he negotiated the uneven surface of the courtyard. At one moment he paused and called to me over his shoulder not to forget the opening of Jaša's art show on Tuesday. No need to worry, I called back, I am thinking of Jaša even when I am not thinking of him. I stayed a while longer in the shadow of the tree, then set off on my Saturday stroll. This was one of my little rituals, one of those intimate routines that help us, or at least helped me, preserve my sanity during the recent years in Belgrade, the lunacy years, as a friend of mine dubbed them. That friend managed to alert me but not himself, and at a moment of distress and confusion, in the middle of the day, he leaped from the terrace of a New Belgrade high-rise. The *košava* wind was blowing at the time, as it was blowing several days later when he was buried, and I remember the voice of a woman saying in muffled tones, If this curse doesn't end, I too will kill myself. It was around then that someone told me how important rituals were in sustaining a certain level of normalcy and keeping one from sinking into despondency and despair. I don't remember who said it, but I know we were talking about the ordinary activities, such as taking walks, visiting museums and galleries, reading classics, listening to music, or, and why not, the routine dusting of the apartment. That is when I began my ritual Saturday stroll, which, unlike my other walks, did not take me to the quay. Every other day belonged to the Danube; Saturdays I explored the less well-known parts of Zemun and Belgrade, sometimes walking quite far afield, nearly out to the edge of town. I walked like an old man, a pensioner, one foot in front of the other, hands crossed behind my back, and those walks had a remarkably calming effect, like, I'm guessing, the practiced moves of the Eastern martial arts. I don't believe my walks could be described as a part of the Samurai codex, but in the course of those walks my senses became purer, and at the end I felt as serene as Buddha. That particular Saturday I decided to walk along Kosančićev Venac and through the neighboring streets. Something about walking on cobblestones is different from walking on sidewalks; a person who walks on cobblestones is more mindful of his body, keeping it in balance and coordinating the movements of all his limbs. Many people slump as they walk on paved surfaces, their spine is curved, their legs unstable, so they easily fall, and sink into a bad mood. On cobblestones a person is always spry, poised to adjust his step, his spirit is alert and attentive, the eye sharp, the ear attuned, the nostrils flared. On cobblestones, I once said to Marko, I am a hunter, on the pavement I am merely the prey. Ah, how Marko laughed. We were younger then, of course, and the young find it easy to laugh; as the years pass, laughter often cloaks itself in sneers, disdain, caution, sarcasm, cynicism, and other garments. When you are young it is nicest to be naked; later taking your clothes off is agony because it's not easy to face the creature staring at you from the mirror. I don't know why I am thinking of this now. I have definitely never walked around naked on cobblestones: a swaying penis, no matter how large, will more likely provoke a snigger than an erotic response. So I walked down to Kosančićev Venac, walked to its far end, came back, having passed the Faculty of Theology twice, went down Zadarska Street, then down Srebrenička, and down the stairs to the bus stop at the foot of the bridge. I hated the jostling buses and the crowds, but I didn't have much choice, or actually it was money I didn't have, so taking a taxi was out of the question, as was walking all the way to Zemun. It was time, I thought, to write a new piece for *Minut*. I couldn't have known it would be my last. What I am writing now, of course, doesn't count because this is not a piece like other pieces, this is a whisper into the dark from my window, a dark so dense that no light can penetrate it. So I stand by an open window, I utter the words and watch them burrow their way molelike through the dark. I bit my tongue before I'd even finished that sentence, not because I dislike the notion that my words are blind, but because I remembered that years ago I helped a neighbor, who had a weekend house just outside of Belgrade, get rid of moles. He poured water into one end of their underground tunnel, and I waited at the other end, shovel in hand, and bashed each mole that emerged until it was a bloody rag. And we were laughing as we did this, we even took pictures of ourselves with all those mashed little bodies, first he took a picture of me, then I took a picture of him, and no doubt those photographs still exist somewhere. Someone is sure to hold on to what we'd most prefer not have saved. One day I'll open a newspaper and on the front page I'll see those photographs, I'll see my face triumphantly grinning above the mangled moles, and I will know that the entire world, along with me, will be horrified at my heartlessness, despite the fact that moles are the most ordinary of pests. Fine, I'll use a different comparison then, and say that my words were twisting their way through the dark like corkscrews through cork, though it sounds as if the words are tied by threads to whoever is saying them, as if that person can easily, whenever he'd like to, yank them out and return them to his embrace. Nothing is further from the truth, because words, once they venture into the dark, even when the light is the brightest possible, never return. I don't know precisely where they go. Maybe there is a cemetery for words somewhere, I wouldn't be surprised. I have no more time for surprise. I have no more time. Being alive is being constantly amazed at life itself, and once the amazement is gone, so is life. A text isn't life, is it? No point in cocking my ear to listen: no one here will tell me anything, and the dark never has any answers anyway. I can sit again at the table and hold on to a glass of water, as if it will keep me floating. That night, the night after the encounter with Dača and the stroll along Kosančićev Venac, I couldn't fall asleep. This had happened to me before, there was no cause for alarm, I could explain it by restlessness, insecurity, uncertainty, ignorance, and I could lie there hoping to fall asleep at some point. I lay on my back, my hands crossed behind my head, breathed deeply, and stared at the ceiling, barely visible in the dark. I did what I could yet again to pull myself together and find an answer to what had gone on in my life over the past few weeks, but I kept coming back to the questions. Had someone truly tried to make a golem in Belgrade, and was this intention somehow re-

lated to the group on the ridiculous artificial hill by Hotel Yugoslavia? And what sort of role was Volf Enoch playing in all
this, if indeed he was involved? The thought of Enoch un-
nerved me, as if someone were stretching inside me, straightening up to see who was summoning him. This time I reacted far
more calmly to the possibility that I might have become Volf
Enoch, my breathing may have quickened for a few minutes,
but that's all. Margareta I couldn't forget, never would. I
sensed the diagonal whiteness of her thigh, then her bare foot,
but had to make an effort to recall her face. Then again I saw
her thigh and felt my penis stiffening, until like a bar it reached
across my belly. I should have called her, I thought. I didn't
move. I trembled, stared into the darkness, and waited for the
blood to seep back out of the spongy tissue. That was the first
time I thought that Margareta might actually be the Shekhinah,
the female presence of the divine, tied to the tenth Sephirot,
Kingdom, situated on the map of the human body in the soles
of the feet. Wasn't Margareta barefoot during our conversation at the apartment in the Zemun high-rise? But even if she
was, does that really mean anything? People go barefoot, after
all, because they like to and not because they mean to carve
the shards of a secret message into someone's consciousness.
The times we were living in required a haven from reality,
which could be found only by living everyday life in a fantasy
or by reading meanings into reality. If I go on this way, I
thought, I will never fall asleep. My penis had wrinkled and
curled up by then like a pup weary of chasing cats. I touched
it with my fingertips; it raised its head sleepily, then flopped
right back onto my crossed hands. Good, I said, at least you're
asleep. My voice sounded hollow in the dark, like any voice
that knows it can expect no answer. My eyelids were starting
to droop, my head lolled on the pillow, my limbs grew heavier,
and I could tell myself that finally I was on the verge of sleep,
and, of course, the minute that thought occurred to me my
eyes snapped open, the ceiling stared me in the face, and I

knew beyond a doubt that I'd greet the morning. Now when I think about it, I am amazed that anyone slept at all in those days, or rather, those nights. Reality had reached a mind-boggling degree of ugliness: we were living under a dictatorship pretending to be a democracy, which was closing in ever more tightly around anyone who dared voice a divergent opinion. The divide between the cynical government, obsessed with material possessions, and the population pushed into gloom and poverty was deeper than the Grand Canyon, and the feeling of powerlessness to change anything ate at people like a stomach ulcer. You couldn't see all of it in Belgrade yet, but in the heartland of Serbia a true darkness reigned, both spiritual and otherwise. Such thoughts unsettled me all the more, so I got up and started pacing around the apartment. I didn't turn on the light; I shuffled around, though not barefoot like Margareta, but in soft slippers, until I got to the desk and the manuscript, which, it occurred to me, I hadn't looked at for a long time, so long, in fact, that I felt I'd never read it at all. I got back into bed, switched on the light, opened to page 1, and read yet again what was written on the facing page: A dream uninterpreted is like a letter unread. I resisted the temptation to look again at the pages I'd dreamed of, so I flipped ahead to page 223. Enough about the soul, it said at the top, though it should be noted that the soul of a deceased Jew will not stop migrating until it fulfills all commands and gains insight into the many secrets hidden in the Torah. Those who know, it said, know that there are 613 commandments in the Torah, of which 248 are positive and 365 are negative, which, as it was once believed, correspond to the number of 248 bones and 365 sinews in the human body, and they will therefore know that a human body that fulfills all the commandments is like the Torah itself, or that he who achieves spiritual perfection creates and repeats God's form within himself. In other words, he who accomplishes this, whose body blazes with heavenly light, allows the Shekhinah to dwell within him. There will be more on the subject of the Shekhinah, it said, because one might assume that the way to her is easy, bearing the water carrier in mind, but this is a task measured not by hardship or complexity but by the way it is performed; a person carrying water may do so with more dedication than a teacher who pursues his high-minded job in a laggardly manner. It should also be added here that Rabbi Chaim Vital instructed how one, or two, or three, or four souls may enter into a single body, but never more than four. Here I stopped. The next section, judging by the opening sentence, was about lighting the Saturday candles, and that was not a skill I needed. I reread the passage at the top of the page. The connection between the migration of souls and the fulfilling of the commandments in the Torah was easy enough to see, though I couldn't figure out why that section ended in Chaim Vital's words. Four souls in one body— that concept had never crossed my mind. As it was, I wasn't doing too well with one; what would I do with several? However, I was most confused by the sentence referring to a fuller description of the Shekhinah and the water carrier who could have been none other than Volf Enoch. Perhaps Vital's reference is to him? It is also stated that he, the water carrier, found it easy to reach the Shekhinah, whatever that means, as the reader is cautioned that the path is not easy. How, then, did the water carrier accomplish this? Toting a yoke with pails, maneuvering a wheelbarrow with a barrel, lugging pitchers and gourds brimming with water? I turned to the preceding page and, of course, as I might have guessed, on that page, though it was marked as page 222, there was nothing about the soul, the Shekhinah, or the water carrier; instead it was mostly about the building of the Sephardic synagogue in Zemun, the corner stone was laid in 1871 and built according to plans by a Josif Marks. The synagogue was damaged in the Allied bombing of 1944, it said in closing, and has not been restored; it was in fact razed to the ground, except for a few fragments near the Well, for those able to see them. I should put this manuscript aside, I thought, for if I come across one more ambiguous reference my difficulty sleeping will become chronic and I'll never shut my eyes again. Until that point I'd understood the title of the manuscript to be symbolic, the manuscript to be a well of sorts in which all of us dwell, the entire world, and now I had to forget that thought and accept that there really was a well somewhere from which that manuscript derived and to which it was heading. The pale morning light began slowly seeping through the window, as if to help me illuminate the words that were pulling me into the depths of the Well. Alas, there is light that obscures instead of illuminating. There was no longer any reason to stay in bed. I got up, made the bed, made coffee. I didn't feel like going down to get a paper because I knew what to expect: the regime newspaper would be trumpeting its referendum, the opposition newspaper would be mocking the referendum, which meant that, regardless of my political orientation, I would be reading the same story, only told from different angles. That is when I remembered that, more than thirty years ago, Filip David had published a collection of stories called *The Well in the Dark Forest*. His stories were full of Kabbalistic themes: perhaps he knew something about wells, I thought, could his well be the well I am after? Nonsense, I said aloud, I am beginning to behave like a paranoic obsessed with the idea of conspiracies. The words rang in the room, bounced off the walls and windows, dropped to the floor, as they do here when I stop writing and start talking to myself. Sometimes so many words are on the floor that I have to lift my feet high as I cross this sparsely furnished room from end to end. One of these days, it occurred to me, I might slip on a squashed word, fall, and lie there, buried under the detritus of language, and no one would find me until we started to decompose, the words and I, one corpse next to the others. I should have made stronger coffee, I said, my thoughts would be more upbeat, though words probably have nothing to do with it, nor does lack of sleep, it was simply Sunday, a day with no future, as Raša Livada wrote many years ago. Did he write a poem about the Zemun synagogue, or about Rabbi Yehuda Alkalai, the forefather of Zionism, or maybe about the destiny of the Zemun Jews, or something along those lines? Now, according to the logic of paranoia, I should find him and ask about the well, or, better still, about the sounds and lights that emanate from the attic of the synagogue, or about the water carrier. Nonsense, nonsense, nonsense, I repeated, then sipped a little coffee, closed my eyes, and leaned my head on my hand. The day of the week didn't matter, I had to admit, Sunday or Tuesday, Wednesday or Saturday, the calendar was of no help, I had reached a dead end. The world, or so it seemed at the time, had an end. It seemed so then, and it seems so now, nothing in that regard has changed. I am far away from it all, yet from time to time it feels as if I have never been closer. In short, I think more and more about my childhood, about little moments of happiness, such as when I ate rice pudding with raspberries at a restaurant called Zdravljak, or something similar, at the entrance to the Zemun marketplace, or when I had ćevapčići at the Central, while music that I can no longer recall, probably old standards, blared from a small stage. I read somewhere, who knows where, that childhood recollections multiply as life draws to a close, and the closer it draws, the more numerous the memories, as if we were trying to slow down the passage of time and keep ourselves on this shore a little longer. On the other shore, after all, we'll be spending, I almost said, our whole life, when it's our whole death we'll be spending there. I'm tired, who knows what I'm saying and writing, but I myself noted the absurdity of the rapid transition from raspberries to heavenly perfection. None of this contributed to my ruminations about the Well, here I was at a standstill, until Marko, in a phone conversation later that afternoon, said that I should think about the Well as if it were my own body. Your body is a well, said Marko, if you toss a coin in, after a long silence you'll hear it plunk on the surface of the water, with the same sound you'd hear if you dropped a coin into a real well. You might even make the same wish, he continued, which won't come true any more than the wish you'd say over a real well would. Yes, I should have thought of that, I said to myself in an almost chiding tone. Margareta said something similar to me, I believe, though she didn't compare my body to a well, but rather to a cosmic tree full of Sephirot. It comes down to the same thing, because if our body corresponds to the entire system of the cosmos, why wouldn't it correspond to a well? This offered no answer to the question of where the Well was located, or to the question of how one finds one's way in. A leap from a great height would not do, and as far as I recall, there was no mention of ladders in the manuscript. Ladders, Marko said, are a system of exercises to achieve a goal in a given religious or mystical system, and I almost hung up on him. Of course ladders represent an upward or downward system, he couldn't have been thinking that I would load an honest-to-goodness ladder onto my shoulder and, like a chimney sweep, clamber up to the roof. That reminds me, yesterday I saw a chimney sweep here: he looked the way chimney sweeps looked there, sooty, with a jaunty black cap, and his teeth, as he spoke to my landlady, gleamed like polished ivory. I quickly reached for a button, then realized that on the clothes I was wearing I didn't have a single button: a long-sleeved T-shirt and a blue sweatshirt both pulled on over the head, a zipper on the jeans, and shoelaces on shoes don't count anyway. So I stood there by the window, feverishly patting my body, wondering if I had the time to take the sweatshirt off and pull on a button-up shirt, but by then the chimney sweep's conversation with my landlady was over and he walked away with a jocular salute. A red ribbon dangled from the top rung of his ladder, probably a warning to passersby and vehicles, and as I watched it leaving, I said to myself that my happiness too was leaving, never to return. But back to the Well. It was one of those things where, the closer we get to them, the farther they are from us. Luckily this was not a real thirst, because I'd never get a drink of fresh water at that Well, I kept seeing it in the distance, in the morning or evening haze, and no matter how far I walked, I got no closer. The sun would cross the sky, followed by the moon, the haze would be a golden net at one moment and a silver spiderweb the next, and I would continue to be just as far off, like the people who stride along on the moving strip at the fitness club, while always staying in the same place, Sisyphuses unaware that they are Sisyphuses. This is, perhaps, fine for the heart and physical fitness, which would be useful if one were to dig a real well, but I was interested in the Well within me, which was at once a reflection of the one outside me, and I doubted that a fitness club would take me in the right direction. The day was passing, I needed to write the piece for *Minut,* and all I could think of was that I was sinking into a swamp and that the only way I could extricate myself was the way Baron Münchhausen had done when he was in a similar predicament: grab my pigtail and wrench myself free of trouble, however, my hair was so short at the back that I had nothing to grab hold of, let alone to tug at and yank myself up into the heights. I might as well, I thought, admit that I was lost; admission of defeat is sometimes the greatest victory and may offer possibilities earlier hidden or inaccessible. I didn't know where all this was headed, which was probably the most appropriate feeling for that aimless Sunday morning, or afternoon, keeping in mind how fast the time was passing, in fact by then it was nearly evening, with night in tow, just as a mother or father drags along a child reluctant to go shopping or to visit people with no children of their own, where the child is painfully bored despite being plied with cookies or ice cream. At the thought of ice cream I licked my lips and thought of how with the first nice days of spring they started selling a variety of ice cream treats out in front of my building. Unlike the dreary newspapers, the ice cream had magical power, and I soon found myself, still in my slippers, on the sidewalk. The ice cream vendor, however, was not where she was supposed to be. The refrigerator was locked, the sunshade down, the chairs chained to a nearby tree. I looked to the left, I looked to the right, and next to the newspaper kiosk I saw a man in dark glasses. Unlike the earlier figures lurking in dark glasses, this one was not wearing a trench coat, though he was in a black suit. No, I said to myself, you will not add him to your list of plotters; this is Sunday, the man may be going to a wedding and has stopped to buy mints or chewing gum. The man looked at me. Suddenly I felt awkward being on the street in my slippers like some old curmudgeon, and I turned to go back in. The man kept staring at me, no, the man was fixed on me, that is how I'd describe it, and suddenly I desperately wanted to go up to him and pluck those glasses off his face, and just then he lifted his hand, removed the glasses, and smiled. I turned to check whether there was someone behind me. There wasn't. I looked again at the man, who was now approaching, still smiling. I can always take off my slippers, I thought, and if need be, sprint barefoot. I have never cared for being barefoot, even as a child, but if that was the only way for me to flee, being barefoot wouldn't bother me. Margareta and her bare feet flitted through my mind, and I wondered what a barefoot flight would mean to a Shekhinah, or more precisely, would the Shekhinah aid or obstruct the flight, and then I had to stop moving and thinking, because the man was in front of me. He had sky-blue eyes. What, he said, you don't recognize me? No, I said, and I truly had no idea who he was, though his voice began to take shape in my consciousness, and the longer he spoke, the more the oblivion waned, and finally, when he mentioned Paramedium, our gymnasium biology teacher, the name and nickname hit me: Steva the Horse. There was nothing horsey about him, and while he chattered on about old friends, and about how happy he was to see us, and about how much it meant to him when he returned to Canada, my only thought was the delicate question of his name's origin. Would I hurt his feelings if I reminded him of this nickname? He'd eagerly carved it into old and new school desks, and even, in some instances, into the blackboard and the lectern. One of the things he'd started appreciating more since he'd moved away, he said, was the marvelous informality of the people here. To come down in slippers like that, he said, went beyond anything he'd seen in Edmonton. I don't know where Edmonton is, but if I were there, I said, I would not so easily abandon my comfortable slippers. Steva chuckled, and then I remembered how he'd acquired the nickname Horse: he didn't laugh, he neighed, though by now it sounded more like a frog's croak. In any case his laugh was awful, much worse than my slippers. All the while I was inching toward the door to my building, but he followed me, never letting the distance between us grow. I don't know why I wanted to put space between us, maybe because of those sky-blue eyes whose translucence had always stirred distrust in me. The lighter someone's eyes, the greater my suspicion. A prejudice, naturally, though harmless, if that's any consolation. I nudged open the door to the building with my back, preparing to slip in, but just at that moment Steva started listing everybody he'd seen, and after a few women's names, which I didn't recognize, he mentioned Dragan Mišović, with whom he had spent a marvelous evening, he said, only yesterday. I stopped pressing against the door. A marvelous evening with Dragan Mišović? I asked. Was he sure it hadn't been someone else? No, Steva replied, he was sure, Dragan the mathematician from whom we always cribbed solutions in math and mechanical drawing tests. He asked after you, said Steva, and said something about parallel worlds, repeating patterns, that sort of thing. The door suddenly felt so heavy, I thought it might snap my spine. Had I made the wrong choice, perhaps, when I recently decided not to call Dragan Mišović? I can't remember when that was, but I do recall the alacrity with which I had made that decision.

Now I dared admit that it was out of vanity, anger that he'd so casually blown me off two or three times, or sneered at me because I couldn't keep up with his mathematical reasoning. Are you sure? I asked Steva needlessly, that Dragan mentioned me? Actually I was trying to gain time, to figure out what to do, to evaluate everything from a new perspective. Steva didn't hesitate. Of course Dragan Mišović had told him all that, he even made a special point of saying, Steva added, that he was very pleased to be in touch with me again. He looked at me with those sky-blue eyes and blinked as if wind was blowing in his face. Was the blink a sign of insecurity, or was he not telling the truth? Who knows why Steva blinked? He realized, said Steva, that he'd run into me at an awkward moment, being in slippers on a Sunday was a sure sign of a wish for rest and relaxation, but would I be willing perhaps, he asked, to join a group of old school friends for dinner in a restaurant by the Danube? They had agreed to meet at the Harbormaster's at seven o'clock, then decide where to eat. And Dragan Mišović will be there too? I asked with a dose of incredulity, are you sure? He promised, answered Steva, and as far as he knew, and he was prepared to stand corrected, Dragan Mišović always kept his promises. I couldn't muster a single example, but all the same I nodded. So, said Steva, you'll join us? I consented, and he reached forward and patted me on the cheek. Leave those slippers at home, he said, and neighed again. Once a horse, I thought, always a horse. Little things are sometimes the most telling about the truth of people and the world, the tiny cracks signaling the advent of huge catastrophes. As I climbed the stairs to my apartment, questions were jostling in my mind about Dragan Mišović's unexpected willingness to appear in public, and to go, no less, to a restaurant. I remembered clearly how the person who had helped me find him several weeks before, and who had moved to Banovo Brdo, had cautioned me that he was odd and that he never, which I knew, attended group gatherings or alumni reunions. When I add to

that the fact that Mišović had asked after me, it was a miracle
that I had not instantly gone to the Harbormaster's. I managed
to hold off until six o'clock, and at six-thirty I was out there
in front of the gallery. My head swung left-right like a pendu-
lum, and even so I missed seeing Steva the Horse arrive with a
plump woman whose hair was tied in a bun. I could have
sworn I'd never seen her before, but she claimed we kissed on
New Year's Eve when we were fifteen. Steva neighed when she
tweaked my ear and said it was never too late to pick up where
we had left off. Pick what up, I asked, and Steva nearly fell on
the floor. The woman with her hair in a bun giggled, hands on
hips, her belly shoved in my direction. Who knows how long
this torment would have lasted if two other women hadn't arrived and I recognized them as Zlata and Dragana, best friends
and straight-A students. I had never kissed either of them, that
I knew, though I wouldn't mind, I thought, kissing them now.
There is nothing more beautiful than middle-aged women.
Sure, the body no longer has the firmness and flexibility it had
in youth, but there is that fullness instead, the stable hips, the
generous bottom, and the air of well-being. Zlata and Dragana
squealed when they saw us, and as we were hugging and kissing three times on the cheeks, Svetlana and Radomir arrived,
frowning as ever. Though we knew that the frown was a mask
of sorts, every time I saw them I thought that their identical
frowns must have brought them together. They had been, one
might say, the mascots of our class: they had started dating in
our first year, married a week after graduation, and had stayed
together ever since, judging by an email I received, don't ask
how, from Zlata and Dragana. Over the past few years Zlata
and Dragana have been tirelessly organizing annual reunions
of our class, and several weeks before the gathering they send
out bulletins with up-to-date information about the lives of
our former schoolmates. By my name it says "gone," which
means nothing, and suits my desire to lay low. "Gone" is certainly better than "deceased," which is what they wrote, re-

grettably, next to some of the names, including the name of the homeroom teacher, Milenko Stojević, whose heart, someone said at one of the earlier reunions, broke when the new war started in Yugoslavia. I don't know if that's true, though I believe that many hearts were broken when that happened, some forever, as was the case with Milo the Silo, as we called our homeroom teacher, some temporarily, though with a permanent scar, while some only pretended, feigning a despair that didn't leave a mark in their atria or ventricles. They said nothing about my heart, what matters is that it still beats evenly, and that, knock on wood, it shows no strain at maintaining a regular rhythm. To knock on wood I had to get up from the old armchair and go over to the windowsill, just as I rose at the restaurant back then, to go to the door, restless because Dragan Mišović was late. I looked to the left, I looked to the right, but there was no sign of him. I came back to the table, where the conversation was in full swing, and where the plump woman with her hair in a bun managed to maneuver Svetlana away and sit on the chair next to me. Until then I hadn't joined in the conversation, but when she began leaning her breasts against my left elbow, I completely shut off. No, it was not her breasts I was thinking of; what bothered me was that Dragan Mišović had changed his mind, assuming, of course, that what Steva had told me was true. He was sitting at the head of the table, ruddy with many glasses of red wine, and when he saw me looking at him, he winked. I don't need winks, I thought as the plump woman pressed against me, I already have more than enough of those, what I need is something clear, tangible, something authentic beyond any doubt. Was I prepared to interpret Dragan Mišović's arrival that way? I didn't know. The desperate, as the saying goes, grab at straws. The saying presumably refers to people who are drowning, but wouldn't anybody drowning be desperate, even somebody who had voluntarily gone into the deep water? Suicide may be a choice, but I'm convinced that no one walks calmly to death, there must be a moment at which the body sheds the raiment of consciousness and rebels against the inevitability of the end. Somebody might assume that I was suicidal because Dragan Mišović hadn't made an appearance, which, I assure you, never for a moment crossed my mind. Not then, and not now. Actually, during the years when I was growing up with the people who were now sitting around our table at the Sent Andreja restaurant, who were not heavy back then or balding, I chose as my mantra a line from Faulkner's *The Wild Palms*—given the choice between the experience of pain and nothing, the protagonist said he would choose pain, and I have stayed true to that mantra ever since. I would never lift a hand against myself, I thought, as the plump woman's bun tickled my nose, stirring in me a wish to flee as far away as possible. I probably would have done so too, had a hush not settled over the table. I turned and saw Dragan Mišović in an oversized greatcoat, buttoned to the chin, as if out there it was still winter. He was not wearing a cap, which surprised me, though I couldn't have said why, maybe because I had been convinced that he was never, even while sleeping, without a cap. Well, cap or no cap, the coat was so capacious that it looked as if it were walking on its own, as the person said, if I remember correctly, who had moved a while ago to Banovo Brdo, and who was the one to reunite me, if I can call it that, with Dragan Mišović. Judging by the silence around the table, he startled and confused everybody, not just me. Meanwhile, the waiter came over and helped him out of the coat. I knew he would be in a pristine, pressed shirt, but I didn't expect the tie, with an equally pristine knot. The tie was multicolored, with abstract designs, which, I was sure, he could express instantly in a cluster of equations or other mathematical concepts. Even more surprising was the fact that he grinned at all of us as he shrugged off his coat, joined us, greeted everybody, and finally sat down. After a few minutes of pained silence, the conversation picked up, coursing fast in many directions. I glanced at Steva, he winked back again, this time with a discreet nod to Dragan Mišović, who had taken the seat next to him, where Zlata had been sitting. Steva whispered something to her first, I saw it out of the corner of my eye, Zlata got up and asked the waiter to bring her another chair and placed it between the heavyset woman and me, despite the woman's half-joking protests. You've had your turn, said Zlata, now he is mine and only mine, and so a new pair of breasts now rested at my elbow. I suffered the rotund warmth patiently, or more precisely, the warmth of mashed flesh. Not that I fail to appreciate women's breasts, not at all, I could speak or write about them for hours on end, but there are moments when what we love the most bothers us the most, and if there was something far from my thoughts at that moment, then it was breasts, and their pressure on my arm turned into a sort of unpleasantness, a fire that failed to convince my penis to stir and offer to put out the fire, but threatened instead to leave burns all over me. I am exaggerating, of course, but some experiences can only be defined in hyperbolic terms—we speak of a mosquito that has been pestering us at night as if it were the size of an airplane or as big as an eagle, or we compare it to a rocket, because it's ridiculous that such a puny creature could torment you and not let you sleep for hours. Indeed fear has big eyes. My eyes too were big, or so they felt as I stared alternately at Dragan Mišović and at Steva the Horse. This was yet another unknown in an equation so vast it would not fit on the largest page, and the solution could evolve into a tapestry that, as in a certain novel, was an image of the world, or perhaps the world itself. Again, I am taking this too far. Doing something for the first time is always hardest, to tell a lie or go too far or exaggerate, then it gets easier. For instance, I take cold showers and I remember how I used to have to muster the courage to step under the icy jets, and now I do it without hesitation, I even let the water run for a while because that first burst of cold no longer satisfies me. Man is a strange beast, as Marko would say, and as I listened to Steva neighing, leaning his head on Dragan Mišović's shoulder, I thought how unfair I'd been to Marko, and that if I wasn't careful I might easily lose my only friend. I know that "only friend" sounds grim, but the truth is most people don't even have that one friend, while many declare mere acquaintances as friends, just as if I were to say now that Margareta is my friend, though I barely know anything about her life. I could describe her, I could say she's absorbed in some aspects of Jewish mysticism, I could talk about how I feel in her presence, but no one would be able to find her based on what I say. Even as I gave her description I would be stuttering, uncertain if she had pink cheeks, arched eyebrows, and fragile earlobes, or if all that was my imagination. It took no imagination, however, to conclude that between Steva the Horse and Dragan Mišović something was going on, and my only hope was that this new thread had nothing in common with all the other threads stretching my way. Zlata and Dragana called to each other across the table, Svetlana and Radomir frowned, Dragan Mišović explained something to the plump woman with the bun, Steva went to the men's room, and all I could do was gaze at the ceiling, that artificial sky that has given many unexpected inspiration. I hope, I thought, I don't feel the impulse to write a love song or an erotic poem, dedicated to the breasts that had so generously nuzzled up against me. I waited until my neck ached. Nothing happened, no line of verse sped through my mind, I could breathe a sigh of relief. I had long since given up writing poems; I didn't even attempt to write them anymore; short stories were good enough for me; novels, I felt, were beyond my ken. Here, at night, when total serenity reigns, I sometimes hear a voice from the silence that utters fragments that could only be parts of poems, but in the morning, as I splash my face, I try to rinse them off, especially "the leaden sky of hope" and "only the barest tender kiss for puckered lips," which stick to my wakefulness like burrs. Luckily, nothing like that engulfed me at the Sent Andreja restaurant, what I felt on my shoulder was the touch of Dragan Mišović's fingers. I hadn't noticed when he got up and came up behind me, and I nearly jumped at the sudden touch, but it all ended when I spun around and faced Dragan's smile. Everything's fine, he said, and patted me on the back, as if I were a baby whose sleep he didn't want to disturb. Then he bent down a little more and whispered that we had to talk. The triangles have started opening, added Dragan Mišović, then he squeezed my shoulder and went back to his seat just as Steva the Horse was coming back from the men's room. Was it my imagination, or did they exchange small gestures? Dragan touched the lobe of his left ear, Steva smoothed his right eyebrow with his index finger, they nodded to each other, sat down at the table, and almost simultaneously ordered another bottle of red wine. The waiter, of course, brought two, claiming that each had ordered one, and this quickly turned into one of those wearisome and unpleasant café tiffs that are remembered far longer than what led up to them, like the quarrel between Jack Nicholson and the waitress in *Five Easy Pieces,* which I remember, though I have forgotten what happens before or after. The waiter refused to take back the second bottle, Steva would not allow it to be put on the bill, and though we pretended not to notice, soon we were all taking part, and who knows how long it would have gone on, had Dragan Mišović not said that he would take the bottle, he had things to do, and the wine would come in handy. He looked at me as if I knew what he meant. I didn't. I was thinking feverishly about what the opening of the triangles might mean, but nothing came to mind. The one thing I could think of was that paper pinwheel attached to a stick that we toted around as children. They weren't triangles, of course, but when we ran, the pinwheel spun around, and, shrieking with joy, we imagined we were helicopters. This didn't include any opening, which, obviously, was the substance of Dragan's message, and judging by the look he sent my way as he raised the wine bottle victoriously in the air, I would learn the truth with wine, whether I wanted to or not. The quarrel with the waiter brought our party to a close; after all that had been said, there was no reason for us to stay there any longer. Steva tapped the rim of his glass with a knife, and once the conversation died down, he thanked us for easing, if only briefly, the pain of living abroad, and he hoped we'd get together again the next time he visited. He did live out in the middle of nowhere, behind God's back, but as long as God was there to be seen, things couldn't be so bad. Zlata started sniffling, real tears rolled from her eyes, her face contorted in an ugly grimace, and with a trembling voice she said to Steva that he shouldn't go back, that we needed him here, there were fewer and fewer of us with each passing day, and we were getting weaker. As she said this, choking back sobs, she kneaded my thigh with such ferocity that for days I had to nurse my bruises. There was no mark, however, on my lower arm from the three-hour nuzzle of the assorted breasts. Outside, in front of the restaurant, rain greeted us, so our goodbyes turned into a frantic exchange of hugs, kisses, handshakes, and waving. No one had an umbrella, so they all rushed to their cars, bus stops, houses, and apartments, including, to my great surprise, Dragan Mišović, who caught up with Steva the Horse at a gallop down Zmaj Jovina Street, the tails of his greatcoat flapping. I was left standing there alone. I hadn't expected this to happen and had no idea what to do with myself. I was convinced that Dragan Mišović would take me somewhere, maybe off to a sheltered bench on the quay or to another restaurant to explain the real meaning of the opening of the triangles, and when this did not happen, I almost felt paralyzed. It was raining harder and the drops pelted the pavement, turning into bubbles. I stuck my hands into my jacket pockets, and, in the left pocket, felt a slip of paper. I pulled it out and opened it. Judging by the initials at the bottom, it was a message from Dragan Mišović. He must have slipped it in when he whispered to me that the triangles were starting to open. The rain and gusting wind kept me from reading it, I folded it and put it back in the pocket. When I got home, soaked to the skin, I looked for it desperately—it must have dropped from my pocket as I hurried along the Danube, lashed by the rain and the wind. My thought was to go straight back to the quay, though it was highly unlikely, with the weather, that I would be able to retrieve the misplaced note, and even if I were to find it, snagged in a bush or under a bench, who knows whether the note would still be legible. I feared that now the writing was no more than a blot, but I was prepared to search for it nevertheless, because in the blot, as in a Rorschach test, there might be meaning, a message that could be a signpost for a traveler who had no idea where he was headed and why. Clearly, desperation had taken hold of me and threatened to turn into downright depression. Marko, if I had said that to him, would probably have just rolled his eyes. So what, he would have said, everybody is swallowing pills anyway, pills for sedation, pills for a better mood or against a bad mood, one more or less doesn't mean much, especially when the entire country is on one big psychiatrist's couch. And then he would pull out a joint, the cure for everything but fractures, as he often said, and he would offer to calm me down. I would have enjoyed the joint, no doubt, but first I had to face the elementary calamity, like a fireman in an American movie, and venture out to save the lost message, and then, as I put my jacket back on, I felt the paper under my fingertips. Dragan Mišović's message. Sometimes things know how to toy with us. I've no idea how the paper had vanished from my left pocket only to turn up there again; maybe I moved it unconsciously from pocket to pocket as I hurried along the quay, I'll never know. Secrets, after all, should remain secrets. I took off the jacket, hung it on the coat hook, went into the living room, sat down in the armchair, and started reading. Fifteen years ago, the message said, a Belgrade artist came up with a piece of conceptual art: he wrote the same sentence over and over again on adhesive stickers. The stickers too were identical, but the sentence on each sticker was written differently: in block letters, in cursive, typed, glued, colored, uneven lettering. The artist put the stickers up wherever he happened to be: in a bus, on the front door of a house he visited, on the sidewalk, on newspaper kiosks, shop windows, lampposts, park benches. The sentence, which he wrote out countless times, was WHERE IS ALL THIS TAKING US? It never occurred to the artist that this might be construed as political provocation. It had come to him when he was sitting in the kitchen, drinking coffee, watching treetops sway in gusts of wind, thinking about life. Where was all this taking us, humankind, the entire system, evolution, everything we know and don't know? Is there a goal, he wondered, and if there is, when will we reach it? He decided that there no goal, but then suddenly realized that everybody should be asked this question, so that once everybody was thinking about it, someone might come up with an answer. From there to the notion of stickers was a small step, and before long there was a trail behind him of stickers with this, as he saw it, pressing question on the essence of human existence and survival on earth. The only thing he did not anticipate was the possibility of a political reading and interpretation of his sentence, yet that is precisely what happened. The 1980s were on the way out and the foundations of the former country had already begun to wobble and crumble, the intelligence service soon developed an interest in this person who, in the opinion of those in the know, was cleverly stirring the population to doubt and unrest with the stickers, found in many places, including a public restroom at the bus station and a ticket counter at the train station. The artist was arrested, just as he was gluing stickers rendered in psychedelic colors to the glass wall of the swimming pool at the Sports Hall in Zemun during a Zagreb rock band concert. He didn't resist, he confessed to his activities, holding fast to his assertion that his intention was purely artistic. During the search of his apartment several more stickers turned up, as well as a large quantity of drawing supplies, a typewriter whose letters matched the letters on the posted stickers, and a map of Belgrade that included Zemun and New Belgrade indicating the locations on which the artist had left or planned to leave his mark. Of special interest, and we need to pay attention here, is that the artist's project, once finished, was meant to describe the shape of an equilateral triangle stretching from the old core of Zemun to Palilula and Košutnjak in Belgrade. The map was the main evidence of the artist's evil intentions, though no one could put a finger on what precisely these intentions were, but the district attorney understood that there was nothing behind it all, and the artist was quickly released from jail, packed up his belongings, and left for the Netherlands. However, the map, stickers, and drawing tools, including his portable typewriter, were never returned, and no one knows what happened to them. Before his departure the artist apparently said he found the inspiration for his work in a mysterious triangle with a point at its center that had appeared on the Belgrade streets and on public transportation in the late 1960s and early 1970s and about which to this day various theories and rumors were circulating. Here you should note, the letter said, switching to address me directly, in both cases these were triangles, which is key to understanding what came next. As most people do, you assume math to be a waste of time and you don't see the point of it, except in its more practical aspects, such as counting money or calculating interest rates, and I'd be glad to convince you otherwise, but this is not the moment. You have many other problems ahead of you, no point in my adding another. Back to the triangles. At the beginning of the last century, Helge von Koch, a mathematician, found a curve that was infinite in circumference, yet enclosed a finite area. This would mean, at least in theory, that you could pick it up and put it in your pocket, which would mean that the pocket would contain infinity. You could put it in an envelope and send it to someone who wanted infinity or who hadn't yet had a chance to see it. The Koch curve is made by dividing the given segment of line into three equal parts, and then replacing the middle part with the sides of a triangle in such a way that we get four segments, of which each one is equal to one third of the original segment. By repeating this procedure, one gets Koch's infinite curve, and if we start with an equilateral triangle and apply this procedure to all three sides, we will arrive at what is called the Koch snowflake, which some call the Koch star. What is of particular interest here is that the first shape formed in the opening of the triangle is a six-pointed star, and though the sides curl, if I can put it that way, they retain a recognizable six-pointed shape. At one moment it may assume the shape of a circle, which means that, in a reciprocal process, a circle can be turned into a six-pointed star. It is here somewhere that the explanation of the sign you showed me several weeks ago is hidden. So triangles can open, perhaps they have already started to do so, and the one thing that must not be forgotten is the point. I know there is no dot on the above-mentioned sign, but if you can't see it, it doesn't mean it isn't there. Apparently, with his curve Koch intended to demonstrate the limitations of classical mathematical analysis, which shows that sometimes a single snowflake can cause more trouble than an entire snowstorm, and that's the way to look for the apparently missing dot. In other words, the opening of the triangle leads to the rediscovery of a point that I would gladly call the Borges Aleph, but it is at the same time both more and less than that. So let's never forget that everything, even the infinity you have put in your pocket, must in the end come back to the point from which everything emerged. I put down the paper and took a deep breath. I'd never been good at math, I barely got by in secondary school, and now I had to recognize in a mathematical description a signpost for my destiny. I could feel a throbbing in my temples, after which,

I knew, a nasty headache would follow if I didn't immediately take something to kill the pain. I staggered off to the bathroom, took two painkillers, staggered back, glanced out the window, sat again in the armchair, got up again, went into the kitchen and ate a square of chocolate, went back to the window, looked at the facing building, then flicked on the TV. If I'm lucky, I thought, I'll find a porn movie, and sure enough, after two or three clicks on the remote I caught sight of interlaced limbs and heard a woman's voice modulating the sounds of *a, o,* and *u* with such skill that Yma Sumac might have envied her. I know what people think of pornography, but I am not at all interested in what goes on in the movie, not even if the plot gets intricate or ends in a mass orgy. At first I used to feel a certain measure of excitement that soon turned to boredom, what with the endless repetition of the same movements; the pornographic movie then lost all its erotic power and turned into a medley of attractive geometric patterns, which helped me think calmly about other things. About a pocket full of infinity, for instance. I turned the sound down, and while the unsheathed members of two detectives penetrated simultaneously the vagina and anus of the female protagonist, I reread Dragan Mišović's message. So the triangles are opening, fine, but where? And what does infinity have to do with it? Or maybe, I thought, as the heroine gnawed the corner of the pillow, everything should be understood as a sign of transformation, as an introduction to change. The six-pointed star, of course, has a clear meaning; something, however, was eluding me here; I knew that individuals from the Jewish community were involved, but clearly there was an aspect to their involvement I had paid no attention to, or else had not realized was there. Perhaps there was more than one aspect? My eyes began to shut, though on the screen the rhythm of ins and outs with every possible orifice was growing overzealous. The camera slid almost tenderly over the female protagonist's face, and her gaping mouth and darting tongue, probably meant to suggest passion at its peak, are the last images I remember. I know it is not healthy to sleep in an armchair in front of the television, not only because of the radiation emitted by the television, but also because of the consequences to the anatomy, the twisting of the spine and the harmful pressure on the joints, but this is a habit I cannot shake. So I fell asleep, and when I opened my eyes, electronic snow was streaming across the screen. I struggled up, my body cramped, my mouth dry, and went over to the window. Across the street, in front of the pharmacy not a single car was parked. I looked to the left, I looked to the right, then up at the sky. Gray, black in some places, it offered no hope of clearing, and I nearly retreated again to the armchair. I had to write that piece for *Minut*, which was threatening to turn into a nightmare: I hated writing in bad weather. It sounds childish, I know, but creativity is a game, and some games can't be played unless certain conditions are met. In my case, the game of writing was tied to weather. Some people require a particular kind of pencil, some absolute silence, others have to shut their eyes for a long time; I expect the sun's rays to fall on the paper and my hand, or on the keyboard and my fingers, and if the sun is not there, writing turns into torment, greater torment, because writing is a torment like no other in and of itself. I know what Marko would say: he would laugh and say with scorn that everybody wants to be a martyr: the writer, the baker, the postman, and the hatter. I'd like to know where Marko is now. The void I feel from his absence is as enormous as the mountain I stare at every day from my window. Absence is absence, he'd say, why measure it, and that, along with his lack of presence, is what disturbs my equilibrium. It was his commentaries, sometimes biting, sometimes searing, often on the mark, and seldom malicious, that held me back from plunging into all sorts of ventures, they forced me to question myself and tested my every flight of fancy. There are times when I think that if anyone were ever to come knocking at my door, this door here, it would be Marko. I am waiting in vain, of course, because if someone does knock, it will not be Marko, nor should I open the door but rather leave by the planned escape route. The details don't matter, let it suffice to say that it would begin with my pulling up the trapdoor in the kitchen floor. So I raged at the overcast sky, I raged at raging, I raged at admitting this and I raged because of something that was beyond my control, and who knows how much longer I would have gone on raging had the phone not rung. I didn't recognize the voice at first, but then caught on that it was Jaša Alkalaj. It would be good, he said, if you could come to the Jewish Historical Museum right away. He didn't say anything more. I scrambled to change my clothes, wash and shave, ate a piece of bread spread with margarine and honey, then hustled down the stairs and straight out into the street, where I flagged down a taxi. The taxi, a prehistoric Mercedes, was on the verge of falling apart, it looked as if only its own supernatural will was holding it together. The taxi driver, who tapped the ash off his cigarette into an ashtray above which there was a THANK YOU FOR NOT SMOKING sign, said not a word as we drove into Belgrade. He nodded when I opened the door; he nodded when I gave him the address; he nodded when we stopped at Kralja Petra Street; he nodded when I handed him the fare; he nodded when, saying goodbye, I left his vehicle. I thought that I ought to jot down his number; by my standards he was the perfect driver; however, as I patted my jacket pockets for a pen, the taxi dipped into the next street and the number soon evaporated from my memory. I nodded in parting and walked into the museum. At the entrance I was stopped by two young men. The museum is closed, they said, but when I gave Jaša Alkalaj's name, the shorter man of the two stepped into the glass booth and called someone. That's fine, he said, Jaša was expecting me, but up in the offices of the Jewish Community Center rather than in the museum. I called the elevator, one of those old-fashioned elevators in which the ride is always unpredictable, and slowly, as if I had several eternities before me, it took me to the third floor. The door opened, and I headed toward a room from which I could hear voices. I walked cautiously, as if afraid someone might jump on me through one of the many doors, until I made it to a large room where chaos beyond description reigned. No chaos lends itself to description, but how many instances of it had I witnessed in my life? Not counting the chaos in one's soul. No theories or mathematical explanations can describe that chaos, even if it can be simulated in a laboratory or in hospital and prison camp conditions. I stared in disbelief at this chaos, overturned tables and chairs, strewn papers, smashed glass, slashed paintings, and spilled paint. The words JEWS ARE VERMIN were scrawled on one of the walls, while on another wall was painted a yellow Star of David crossed with a black swastika. Not far from me, on the floor, I saw a painting by Jaša Alkalaj that had portrayed the figures of Slobodan and Mira Milošević; where the figures had been, there were yawning holes. Just beyond, on another painting full of Jewish symbolism was a yellow fluid, which, thanks to my experience with the doormats in front of my apartment, I recognized as urine. I saw Jaša Alkalaj and Isak Levi in the far corner with a group of people speaking in whispers, and I made my way toward them, carefully stepping over the rubble. Jaša saw me and came over. His face was part of the surrounding disarray: it looked as if it had come undone and then been slapped back together again. I extended my hand to convey my condolences, and he clutched it as though he was on the verge of an abyss. Meanwhile, the police arrived and generated even more chaos. In short, three or four days earlier, Jaša had brought the items to be exhibited to this room. The show, he said, was supposed to be set up on the floor below of course, in the museum, but since the space there was limited, it was agreed that over the First of May weekend they would leave everything in the room, and that on the Monday following, all the preparations for the opening would be made.

That night, some people climbed up the courtyard side, no way of knowing how many, said Jaša, smashed the windows, broke in, and did this. He gestured around, even stepped aside so I could get a better view. But why? I asked, needlessly. They didn't destroy everything, he said, maybe because they didn't have the time or because they weren't interested in certain paintings. We'll wait, he continued, for the police to finish their investigation, then we'll have a look at what can still be shown. Wouldn't it be better, I asked, to cancel the show? Jaša gave me an angry look. Why cancel? he asked. Everything is ready, the invitations have been sent out, the catalog printed, people are curious; giving up now would mean admitting that those who did this accomplished what they set out to do. I looked around, scratched my head. His eyes less angry, he asked whether I thought that giving up meant admitting defeat. Yes, I said. Jaša looked at me again, this time without a trace of anger, and urged me to go home. This would take time, he said, and at home, he added, I had work to do. What? I protested, I have nothing going on. The piece for *Minut,* said Jaša, and he spun around and left. I left too. I took the stairs, sidestepping people and the police. The elevator was stuck between the first and second floors: I assume that they'd had to pull someone out of the cabin. I thought I heard the meowing of a cat but couldn't place the sound. In front of the building several policemen were milling around; a police car was parked by the hotel across the street; passersby paused and looked up at the roof, as if expecting someone to jump. I hate Mondays, I thought, and walked to Student Square Park where I had once got so stoned that I had tumbled off a bench. The bench was still there, though perhaps not the same one; two girls were sitting on it and when I passed them both crossed their legs, as if on command. That reminded me of the dazzling flash of Margareta's thigh. The flash was so emblazoned in my memory that I had to close my eyes and pause. When I opened them, the girls were no longer there, but I had already grown used to the vanishing, nothing could surprise me. That was also how I began the piece for *Minut:* I recently thought, I wrote, that nothing more could surprise me. We live in a time in which the absurd and the irrational have been expanded to ridiculous proportions, and in which the imitation of reality has become more real than reality itself. Not to speak of life. It's not an imitation, or a simulation, or an improvisation, it's nothing. We live in a country that does not exist, composed of refracted reflections in a game of light and dark, and so we do not exist, or rather we exist only as shadows on a wall, with no substance or duration. And the wall is so slippery, the shadows cannot cling to it for long. They slide down before they've climbed up. Yes, some might say, life with no support is no life, and many will agree, but what about those who slide down the wall? Should they be denied even a moment of desperate clinging to the slippery surface, should they be denied the hope of an uneven patch that might delay the inevitability of their plunge? No need to couch this piece in such abstract terms. Things have names, and these names should be said clearly and precisely, especially today, in a country in which clarity has become a negative category. From one day to the next we are witnessing, at all levels of society, especially in the government and church, an indifference to the flood of ethnic intolerance. Usually those who are indifferent are drawn to the opposite course of action: obstructing any attempt at ending the intolerance. Hordes of young people with similar haircuts on square heads are attacking Gypsies and Jews, taking to task all those who think differently, especially if those who think differently are themselves Serbs, claiming all the while that they are doing this for the good of the government, invoking the support of the church. The church is silent, the government is silent, we all are silent. Isn't silence a sign of consent, or have I got something wrong? Does the silence of the church imply that they acknowledge in their ranks an inflexible anti-Semitic current, ready to assume complete control in the new ecclesiastical hierarchy? Does the silence of the government imply that the surge in anti-Semitism has come in handy, as they assign guilt to the "worldwide Jewish conspiracy" for all that happens in this country, as a way of shrugging off responsibility for the insane political decisions and provocation of the world powers? Last night a hard-core detachment of fellow thinkers tried to destroy the works of a painter whose only sin is being born a Jew. Tomorrow, I assume, they will be burning the books of Danilo Kiš, Isak Samokovlija, and Stanislav Vinaver. The day after someone announces that all Jews are parasites who suck the blood of the Serbian people. By the end of the week, who knows, there may be calls to bring out the yellow armbands, and lists will begin to appear, there will be attacks on apartments, property confiscated . . . Then, finally, a trembling voice will say that history is repeating itself and that we have reason to be concerned, but by then it will be too late, because history began repeating itself the moment none of us said a word. Here I stopped. It occurred to me that I ought to devote part of the article to the opening of the show. I submitted my pieces Wednesdays for the *Minut* column, which left me plenty of time. I already knew the end, all that was left was to write it. The last moment is near, would be the words at the start of the last paragraph, for us to understand that those who present themselves as the great caretakers of this country, invoking attacks based on ethnic minorities, have caused the greatest damage to the country. Regrettably the entire system of government has been corroded by moral and political corruption and no one feels called upon to comment or condemn the events of which I am writing. Perhaps, who knows, they are afraid to, because the connection between organized crime and the political hierarchies is an open secret. Everyone cares about his or her life, that much is clear, especially in a country where human life is cheap. If we all react, if the protest catches on, and hundreds of thousands of people join, there will be no more fear. And so on, in the same vein, with no shame. All that remained was for me to decide: should I name the names of the politicians, criminals, and waffling intellectuals? I wouldn't be saying anything new, but if the piece was not precise in attributing responsibility, then I ended up colluding with those against whom I inveighed. Vague allusions work in café arguments; in a text like this they are ballast that undermines every good intention. No surprise that I dreamed strange dreams that night, including an exhausting sexual adventure with a red-haired woman whose name was Hilda and a battle with a creature covered in leeches. I got up gingerly from bed, as if putting my feet into water teeming with the little bloodsuckers. The leeches, of course, put me in mind of Volf Enoch, and that instant something moved in me, came unstuck inside my skin, and I felt like one of those figures they carve in India, an identical smaller figure inside each successive figure, until the last one is so small that no one notices when it steps out into the world. I am making this up, of course, but had I not entertained myself this way, I would have stopped writing long ago. There is nothing more tiresome than a gloomy story that has nothing, aside from the story line, to steer us briefly in another direction, where it tricks us and shunts us onto a sidetrack, and then, just as we think we are forever lost, opens a door and leads us back to where we began. We may not have distanced ourselves from the gloom, but for a few moments at least we breathed fresh air. My day was not like that and it passed slowly. I had breakfast, bought the paper, and read it carefully—nothing on the Jewish Community Center burglary. Not a word. I didn't turn on the television; if the papers ignored it, the television stations would have nothing to say either, except for the rare independent programs that broadcast news outside the system, but I couldn't get them with my little indoor antenna. Marko had offered to set me up with an improvised antenna using a washbasin and an umbrella on the terrace, which, he maintained, would work perfectly. I stubbornly refused, and now I wonder why. Sometimes we reject the help of others because we think we are thereby protecting our integrity. I now know this is jealousy rather than a defense of integrity; jealousy because someone knows how to do something we don't and because no matter what we think of him or her, that person reflects us more than we do ourselves. It sounds complicated, but why should anything be simple? No one promised us when we came into this world that our lives would be simple, the world comprehensible, dreams clear, death merciful. We get the starting point, that's all, no signposts to the next, the one where the path ends. All in all, living is groping in the dark, blindness despite the seeing eye, a tightrope walk, a slide down a bumpy banister. In the end all that's left is pain, which corresponds to that sentence of Faulkner's, or to the choice I made in relation to that sentence. Pain is the antidote for the void, is what I meant to say. For lunch I prepared chicken soup from a packet. I used less water than the instructions called for, because I wanted it to be stronger. I also ate a slice of Gouda, the cheese I like best. After lunch, having placed the dishes in the dishwasher, I felt drowsy, but I boldly defied the weakness of my body and set about organizing the papers on my desk. The last few weeks, pulled in all directions by unpredictable events, I'd neglected my papers, files, and notebooks, and now I tried to file away copies of articles I'd snipped out of the newspaper, the letters and notes. The only thing I didn't touch was the manuscript of *The Well*. There wasn't a folder large enough for it, and I was afraid that if I tried to move it, it would turn to dust or sand, like a genuine book of sand. That made me think of that magic corner in the yard of the building at Zmaj Jovina Street. Had I already been thinking about it before that day as a passage to another world? I can't remember. In any case, I was thinking of it then: there must be a way to move from there to another reality, I just needed to find it, provided I didn't forget how to get back. I wouldn't want to stay where I didn't belong, though I could imagine several worlds from which I wouldn't want to return.

In one there would be a lot of scantily clad women, in another no one but me, and in the third only my spirit. I checked my watch. The afternoon was aging; soon I would have to leave for the opening of Jaša Alkalaj's show. I went into the bathroom, combed my hair, made sure I had no need to shave, slapped a little lotion on my cheeks, then washed my hands. I took my jacket down from the coat hook, locked the door, and walked to the bus stop. Two police cruisers were parked near the Jewish Community Center: one across the street, by the entrance to the hotel, the other a little farther along, partly up on the sidewalk in front of the grocery store. Police were also at the entrance and in the hallway that led to the courtyard building. Crowds of people were there, and after several steps I could no longer move. Pressed on all sides, all I could do was let the throng carry me, step by step, up the stairs. When I finally reached the museum, I was in a sweat. Inside, under the glare of the television spotlights, it was warmer still. I wouldn't have been surprised to see pools of sweat. Somehow I managed to maneuver myself to the back of the room, closer to where Jaša Alkalaj was standing. His face had undergone yet another transformation, and now looked more like the face I'd known. The man standing next to him had just finished a speech and the applause resounded through the room. He was followed by a critic: in a few sentences the man summarized Jaša Alkalaj's entire opus, gave his assessment of several new paintings, then lifted a piece of paper, for a moment I thought he was hanging out a white flag of surrender. This, said the critic, was the text he had prepared for the occasion, but the new circumstances left him no choice but to rip it up, which he did, tearing the page in half. I could see the shreds of paper floating through the air. When you take a look at the paintings hanging here, said the critic, you will notice that some have been vandalized, that the forces of darkness were trying to steal their light, believing it possible to crush creative spirit. In their shallowness, he continued, they believe fear to be the father of obedience, a misconception they would not be prone to if they knew anything about history. But this is no moment for lectures and sermons, said the critic, this is a moment when the paintings, both the untouched and the damaged, will speak for themselves. Conceived to demonstrate the power of defiance, he said, marked by this new assault, aimed at that spirit among us, they now send the same message, but louder and more assertively to all willing to listen. Often in history, said the critic, books have been burned and artwork destroyed, but each time art managed to rise from the flames, and so it would again. The opening of this exhibit, he said, will dilute the darkness that tried to engulf it, and along with it, all of us. There was more applause, and new beads of sweat erupted on my forehead. People began milling around, looking at the paintings, the cameramen besieged Jaša Alkalaj, a woman said she'd faint if she didn't get some air, the hubbub became louder, unfamiliar ruddy faces alternated with the ruddy faces of well-known public figures, actors and writers of Jewish background, politicians who had sniffed out an opportunity, bored newspapermen, then someone shouted that he had a number on his arm, a gaunt man who had rolled up his shirtsleeves, someone came over to him, gently tugged at his arm, and pulled down his sleeve, the man began sobbing, and as the visitors parted before him like a sea he staggered to the exit, his words breaking between sobs, until he fell silent, and that silence became loud. The television reporters also headed for the exit, the spotlights were turned off, space opened up, waiters appeared with trays, with glasses full of wine and apple juice, slender gusts of air coursed through, it was possible to move from painting to painting between the clusters of people fanning themselves with folded catalogs, the only crowd left was around Jaša Alkalaj, but I was patient, I could wait. That is when I saw Margareta. She was standing in front of a painting, craning her neck to examine a detail more closely, then stepped back and approached it from the other side. Access to

Jaša Alkalaj opened just then, and though I would have liked to go over to Margareta, I walked the other way. His face, closer up, looked like the cracked bed of a dried-up river, his eyes were bloodshot, his lips blue, his eyelids wrinkled. His hair was plastered with sweat, he was breathing with effort, raggedly, as if fighting for each breath. I tried to congratulate him on the show, but he dismissed this with a wave of the hand. A Pyrrhic victory, he said, nothing more, no point in wasting words. I asked whether the police had come up with anything. Did I really believe, Jaša asked, that they would? I said nothing. To some questions there is no other way to respond. Two older women approached Jaša, so he just said that I should come to his studio later to celebrate the opening. Fine, I said, and with the tips of my fingers brushed off the sweat that had pooled above my upper lip. Now that I was used to the vanishing, I didn't believe I'd catch sight of Margareta again, but there she was, standing in front of the same painting, sipping juice. I went over and stood by her. The painting she was looking at was nearly all black; in the upper-right-hand corner was a window from which light shone like a beam from a lighthouse; the light illuminated a cloud in the sky, and on that very spot, partially hidden by a curly wisp, was a triangle in the center of which was an eye; the eye was blazing, the fire had already caught the eyelid, and the flickers rose from the lashes as they rose from the candles in the menorah pictured in the pupil of the eye. If God's eye burns, Margareta spoke up as if she had been waiting for me, then it's all over, what use is a blind God? God didn't have to see, he saw without eyes, from within, with the heart, I said, or with who knows what. No one's perfect, said Margareta, not even God. Her sentence had a vaguely sacrilegious ring. I didn't know the Kabbalah well enough to be able to say that the Kabbalists doubted God, but didn't the Zen Buddhists say that Buddha had to be shit, just as he had to be all other things? In other words, he who desires to be perfect must also be imperfect; he who desires to be in everything must be in things he doesn't want to be a part of. God is either all or nothing, there is no third possibility. I stood next to Margareta and stared at the burning eye, and all I could think of was that the pain must be excruciating. I would like to know, Margareta said, what the painter really had in mind. We can ask him, I said. We'll ask him later, said Margareta, no rush. She finished her juice and looked at me: You see him now and then, don't you? Yes, I said. And you? She nodded. I didn't know you two knew each other, I said. You never asked, said Margareta. So, I asked, how long? hoping the tinge of jealousy in my voice would not be audible. Forever, said Margareta. Jaša's my father. There are situations in which we suddenly catch on to a word or concept, the real meaning of which has been eluding us for years. There, in the Jewish Historical Museum, standing in front of the painting Jaša Alkalaj had titled *Fire,* as listed in the catalog that I brought with me here, though there were many more important things that should have found a place in my modest luggage, I understood the meaning of the phrase "out of the blue." For a moment I could no longer feel the lower part of my legs, as if I was standing on my knees, my lips trembled, I shook all over, electricity raced through my body and instantly drained from me. I raised my eyes to Margareta, and in her face I saw the lines of Jaša's face. I couldn't believe I hadn't noticed it before, though I know that no matter how much we look, we don't see what is most obvious until someone literally points a finger at it. From the moment she told me that Jaša Alkalaj was her father, I saw nothing but a growing resemblance. I noticed the same mild twitch of the left corner of her lips when she talked and a tiny quickening tremor in her anticipation of an answer. Who knows what Margareta was seeing in my face. She said she knew it would surprise me, though she hadn't expected it would surprise me so *much.* She emphasized the word as if it were a legitimate measure for surprise, a unit for calculating the extent of incredulity. My lips were dry,

I thought of sandpaper. I asked Margareta to wait and went into a room where a woman wearing glasses with blue frames was pouring juice and sparkling water into glasses she had set out on a tray. I had some juice, then sparkling water, then rejoined Margareta, who was still there, confounding for a second time my expectation that she would not be. She suggested we leave, she wouldn't be able to breathe before long, she said, there was so little oxygen left that it wouldn't have surprised her if the fire on the eyelashes of her father's canvas went out. Her father's canvas: the words sounded strange to me, unreal, untrue. But they were true, I later ascertained with the help of people I knew, who checked in the records of births, never admitting to her that I held on to the suspicion for so long. Apparently I didn't even admit it to myself, nor do I understand why I resisted the simple fact that one person was another person's parent. One more question I can't answer. If everything comes down to questions, then is an answer a question? I am not thinking of the oft-repeated story of how Jews like to answer a question with a question; that doesn't mean that a second question is an answer to the first, though sometimes it may seem that way, and besides, I am not a Jew and cannot claim as my own something that is not mine. I can only assume that some people manage to tell their story in such a way that it is understood as an answer, or as an opening to an answer, while others, among whom I clearly belong, turn the story into a question, or as Marko said, into evading an answer, as if they want to say to the person listening to them, or reading them, that the question is here, but that all the rest is up to him. Or her, if the listener or reader is a woman, and more likely it will be a woman, judging by the latest statistical data, which unequivocally confirm that women dominate as readers and that the number of men who read is rapidly declining. Hence, say the experts, the growing number of books of family chronicles, culinary novels, full of recipes and stories about a search for existence based on diluted Eastern philosophies. Even if I wanted to introduce a recipe into this text I wouldn't be able to because I never learned how to cook, and I am in such awe of Eastern philosophical teachings, as of all others, that it would never occur to me to abuse them in a novel or a short story. I have long since acknowledged that it would be better for me to occupy myself with something other than writing. If your heart is not in what you do, give it up. I don't remember who said that, but there is truth in it. I know that it is now considered old-fashioned to talk of the human heart, as if modern man no longer needs the human heart for anything but heart attacks. Whenever I mention the heart, someone pushes under my nose a cross-section of the striated muscle and asks if I see anything other than ventricles, atria, veins, and arteries, and I tell them that this is precisely what I don't see, even if the image were so large that it covered the entire surface of the sky in the west. I also know that many feel the heart to be the concern of the cardiologists, not the writers, and there is some truth to that, so it would be wisest to say that both are concerned with the heart, each in their own way, because all of us must accept certain limitations in the job we do and take care not to step over into another's territory. This sounds as if I see myself as a writer, since I'm certainly no cardiologist, but I would never go that far. I don't know whether I'd be able to define what a true writer is. Wherever I start from, I get lost halfway. Yet again a moment when Marko's advice would have been useful, but Marko wasn't around. I called him repeatedly: no one picked up. I went to his apartment: no one came to the door. One morning it occurred to me he might have left the country, so many people were leaving, why wouldn't he, though it seemed incredible that he'd leave without saying goodbye after all the years we'd spent together. Who knows, maybe it's best to leave that way, without a word, without a farewell, at night, sneakily, like a criminal, even when there was nothing anyone could blame you for. That was the way Margareta and I left the exhibition,

I mean a departure without goodbyes. The police car was still in front of the hotel; the other that had been parked in front of the grocery store was gone. Several police officers, one of them a woman, talked and smoked in the hallway. There were two guns on a small table by the entranceway, gleaming in the feeble light of the stairwell. We went into the street and set out uphill toward Student Square. The air was not cleaner outside than it had been in the museum, but it was fresher, and an explanation from Margareta didn't seem nearly as urgent. I'd been struck by lightning, I could wait. We were among the first to arrive at Jaša's studio; we were also among the first to leave. There weren't as many people there as had been at the opening, but the crowd was too large for my taste. The commotion made any serious conversation impossible, and all talk was reduced to shouting single words in someone's ear. Isak Levi somehow managed to convey to me that the police had arrested the people who'd broken into the building of the Jewish Community Center and vandalized Jaša's paintings; they'd apprehended three minors and a young man of about twenty, he shouted, spraying tiny droplets of saliva on the curves of my ear. Then I saw Jakov Švarc heading over to us, which spurred me to ask Margareta whether she was staying or leaving. I put my hand between us to stop the spray and leaned close to her small, finely shaped ear, with a dot on the lobe. The hair around her ear was moist, and between the slender locks you could see the fragile whiteness of her skin. I had to hold back from pressing my lips on that whiteness and running my tongue along the curving paths of her ear. She merely nodded and pushed her way toward the exit, while I was imagining leaning my ear to her lips. The pushing took time; many people wanted to say hello to her, shooting questioning glances my way, and I stood there, shifting from foot to foot and grinning foolishly. In the end we gave up trying to find Jaša and made it to the front door. Some people stood on the landing by the door, others sat on the stairs, and making our way to the elevator required additional hopping over legs and arms. I pressed the button and the elevator appeared obediently. We got in, shut the metal doors, and started down. When the elevator stopped, it was dark. The wan cabin light left the entrance to the building in shadow, and behind the glass door, we could make out a silhouette. I could feel Margareta tensing. We stepped out of the elevator and slammed the door. The dark grew denser, the silhouette clearer, Margareta's breathing slowed, my heart was pounding hard. If she heard it, Margareta didn't react. The silhouette didn't react either, it turned out to be an acquaintance of Jaša Alkalai's, waiting for a taxi, which, he said, was to take him to New Belgrade. He offered to give us a ride if that suited us, and so Margareta and I found ourselves on the back seat of the cab, while Jaša's acquaintance got in front and immediately struck up a conversation with the driver. We had only gone halfway, and the two had covered the entire political scene, criticizing the government and leading politicians, they had agreed that everything was wildly expensive, that it was a true miracle, the taxi driver said, that people had anything to eat, then moved on to sports, to the value of the American dollar, to the fact that half of Serbia had moved to Canada, and here I stopped listening and dedicated myself to the little finger of my left hand, with which I was lightly touching Margareta's thigh. I didn't move the finger, I didn't steer it, I simply let it follow the jostling of the motor and the darting of the taxi. The Belgrade streets are full of cracks and bumps, and the taxi was lurching in fits and starts, with sudden braking and accelerating, so my finger was shaking and shifting, sometimes resting fully on Margareta's thigh. Meanwhile Margareta was dozing or else meditating, her eyes were closed, and only when the taxi crossed the Sava and my hand crept under her thigh did her eyelids flutter, and she stretched out her right hand and dropped it into my lap. I looked up at the rearview mirror, hoping the taxi driver was too preoccupied with the conversation to notice. Margareta's hand didn't move. It lay in my lap, relaxed, resting gently on the belt buckle. And just as I was wondering whether I should slide my hand under her thigh, Margareta leaned against the backrest, raised her body, and my hand slid deftly into the warm dip. I managed to flip my hand over before her body flopped down on the seat, my eyes anxiously on the rearview mirror. The conversation in the front seat was still in full swing, and they were now discussing delays in the payment of pensions and the scandalously low social welfare disbursements to invalids and other beneficiaries. While the driver was citing examples, Margareta wriggled and squeezed my hand with her buttocks. I moved my fingers, she sat up and spread her thighs, my fingers slipped between her legs. We're almost there, announced the driver, as Margareta increased pressure on my arm. The taxi turned toward the Intercontinental Hotel, then on to the Hyatt, and then it dipped into the web of New Belgrade streets and passageways where I could never find my way. When I first saw a map of New Belgrade, I was impressed by the relatively simple urban layout, the geometric structures of blocks and streets that intersected at right angles. In reality, this simplicity was lost when, on foot or by car, one ventured into the interior of individual blocks or started searching for a house number. Here is fine, said Margareta. The taxi stopped, and after a brief round of thank-yous, Margareta and I got out. I looked to the left, I looked to the right: I had no idea where we were. Zemun is over there, said Margareta, and gestured as if Zemun were somewhere in the sky. I wasn't sure whether this was a hint that I should depart, or whether it was merely information, an orientation of sorts, like the North Star or moss growing on a stump. Once you know where Zemun is, you know where everything else is. Who said that? I couldn't put my finger on it, though there are times when I see, with my inner eye, of course, a shimmering page with those very words inscribed on it. A page, like any page, that could come from any one of a thousand books, and all that is left for me is to hope that at some point in my life a certain detail will turn up that will take me to whoever wrote it. That won't change anything, of course, but why would knowledge always be tied to change? For example, one person might learn the names of the ten Sephirot in order from the largest to the smallest, so: Keter, Binah, Hokhmah, Gevurah, Chesed, Tiferet, Hod, Nezah, Yesod, and Malkhut, and remember them merely as a fact, while someone else, learning about the same ten Sephirot, might ascend higher and higher in his soul, and, ultimately, undergo the desired transformation. I was still standing next to Margareta, indecisive, as she ran her hand through her hair. Then I remembered that I hadn't finished the piece for *Minut* and it got easier. We agreed to meet after I handed in the piece, I wished Margareta a good night, kissed her lightly on the cheek, and set out for Zemun. The triangles are opening, I thought as I walked away, and, suddenly elated, I started whistling an old Beatles tune. The walk to Zemun was not strenuous, but for a body unaccustomed to walking several hundred meters, let alone a few kilometers, it is exhausting. At least, I consoled myself, nothing disgusting awaited me by the door to the apartment. That there might be people waiting never crossed my mind, a consequence of an enjoyable taxi ride and my fine mood, the whistling and occasional singing. I started with the Beatles, then I continued with hits by the Kinks, Manfred Mann, the Dave Clark Five, and Cream, then thought of the song "We Gotta Get Out of This Place" by the Animals. I didn't know all the words and I kept repeating the refrain, until suddenly I stopped and heard the Danube slapping the shore with crystal clarity, though I was still some distance from the promenade. The fear that someday I might flee "outta this place" and not hear the sound of the river didn't last long, and I reverted to whistling and singing, focusing on the songs of Marianne Faithfull, with whom, if anyone even cares, I had once been desperately in love. I went into my apartment, took off my shoes, drank two glasses of water, and attempted to rest in the armchair in front of the television, stared for a while at the dark screen, then went into my study and switched on the computer. I read the piece again, made minor changes, added a paragraph about the opening of the show and the symbolic gesture of the critic who felt it his obligation to join in solidarity with the threatened artist by committing an act of violence against his own text. Maybe we should all follow his example, I wrote, and in solidarity destroy something we have created before someone else destroys it for us. The Danes, the story goes, saved their Jews in World War II by wearing yellow armbands, so perhaps we could save our Jews and ourselves by joining them as victims of violence. That was it. Even if I had wanted to say something more, I wouldn't have been able to, the piece was already too long, and as I printed it, I braced myself for the battle with the editor the following day. At first, when he saw how long it was, he didn't even want to look at it. Cut it, he said, then we can talk. I thought of Feliks the cat but was reluctant to use him again as a means of persuasion. Instead, I urged the editor to read the piece and then decide, and I would abide by his decision. It turned out that I'd done the right thing: the editor's secretary told me that Feliks had disappeared, or was registered as having disappeared, because he hadn't come home for five days, and the editor, she claimed, was in distress, and who knows how he'd have reacted to my inquiries. I sat in her office, on the plastic chair by the coat rack, while behind closed doors the editor read my piece. Then the door opened and he summoned me in. I got up, looked at the secretary, she winked, and I slowly closed the door behind me, like someone saying farewell to the world. The editor didn't offer me a seat, so I stood by the door, my hand on the doorknob in case I had to depart in a hurry. Let me say right away, the editor said, the piece is good. I breathed a sigh of relief: I could let go of the doorknob, and even smile. But, said the editor, you should cut it so it fits the space designed for the column. The smile, of course, vanished from my face. So now what? I asked. Do I roll up my sleeves and cut it down to size? The editor scratched his chin and ran his fingers through his hair. Whether short or long, he said, it is equally dangerous, so dangerous that I am not sure you understand how dangerous it is. He looked at me without blinking. I didn't blink either. The overt naming of names, said the editor, no one likes that, the church especially. The hard line is in fashion these days, he said, which means that reactions are unpredictable. He asked me whether I had all these elements in mind when I wrote the piece. I'd thought of nothing, I said, except the truth. I felt, I confess, like one of the protagonists in the Watergate affair, though what I was doing exposed no political or ethnic plot, brought down no prominent politicians or public figures, revealed no intentions or secrets. It was simply drawing attention to a state of the collective spirit, which could be explained by the historical context and the long isolation of the country from the mainstream of the world, but which becomes a threat, like certain diseases that become chronic and therefore incurable and ultimately a potential source of something far worse. Hatred is a disease, and it occurs when the normal functioning of the individual and the collective spirit is disturbed. To hate another you first need to hate yourself, your own lack of power or ability, we don't seek the culprit in ourselves, where it truly lies, but in someone else, and not in just anyone else, but in a person visible enough and, most important, powerless enough that he can't hide or defend himself. In brief, my intention was not to encapsulate that surge of hatred, though hatred should, no doubt, be branded at all times; what I meant to do was warn of the dangers that threatened if the cracks in the collective spirit were not attended to and if individuals and groups who adeptly use those cracks for promoting their own aims were not stopped. Now I know that I was unsuccessful, or my insights came too late. The spiritual scale was overloaded, the needle was skewed, and this breakdown, if I can call it that, was beyond repair. Besides, who could have thought that only a year later, the country would be deliberately sacrificed, the collective spirit encouraged in its most depraved incarnation —blaming others with a paranoic fervor, denial of the guilt among those who were to blame. I was unaware of that while I stood there with my hand resting again on the doorknob, anticipating the editor's decision. He looked up at me. I felt a drop of sweat forming behind my ear and starting to trickle down my neck. This is a typical no-win situation, said the editor, if I publish this, I'll regret it, and if I don't publish it, I'll regret it. I didn't say a word. I raised my hand and with my index finger brushed away the drop of sweat that had trickled halfway down. We go with it, said the editor, and looked away, as if ashamed of his decision. We go with it, he repeated, come what may. Nothing will come, I said. If nothing comes of it, he glanced over at me, then why are we publishing it? Nothing bad, I answered, that's what I meant. And that was what I meant. Who could have foreseen the storm and everything that followed when the pace of events picked up, getting stronger like soup that has cooked for too long? But if we were to know everything in advance, would life have any meaning at all? Hence the prophecy system, such as that of the Chinese Book of Changes, doesn't speak of the future as a pattern that can be learned, rather, it lays the groundwork for the unpredictable things that will nevertheless crop up. Yin and yang alternate, whole lines break and broken lines heal, after the spring comes the summer and winter follows the autumn, but no one can say with certainty which days will bring rain. So during the rainy season the prudent person carries an umbrella, while the reckless person does not and, of course, gets wet when it rains. Prudence is not precise knowledge, but a willingness to adapt to circumstances in the shortest possible time. I go on and on; I am probably remembering the thrill I felt when the editor announced his decision, and the thrill was the kind that gets one talking, just as I had talked to the editor's secretary on my way out, then to two women and a fat man in the elevator. Don't worry, I told them, it's just that I'm happy. That was when they looked genuinely alarmed. Happy, in this day and age? said their looks. I stopped talking and started whistling. The fat man gaped at me, while the two women crossed their arms over their chests, which was probably meant to signify extreme disapproval. I turned my back on them, there was nothing more I could do, but I went right on whistling, though softer, and through my teeth, first "Yellow Submarine," then "I Want to Hold Your Hand." When the elevator stopped, the door slid open, the women hurried out, the fat man went panting after them, and I, still whistling, thought I should reward myself with a glass of *boza* and a cream puff, and slowly, through the center of town, I set out for the pastry shop on Makedonska Street; Marko called it the last oasis, one of the rare places in Belgrade that had held on to the spirit of the old days. Again I wondered what Marko was up to, why he had vanished, if indeed he had vanished, and then I stopped whistling. When you miss someone it's hard to whistle. Your mouth turns dry, your heart sinks, nothing comes out of your puckered lips. I drank the first glass standing by the counter, then ordered a second and another cream puff, and sat at a table. I saw a face in the mirror that was supposed to be mine, though I wasn't sure. I glanced at the newspaper that the owner was reading at the next table before he got up to serve me. My attention was not drawn to a headline or a photograph, but to a poem at the top of the right-hand column. I assume that the owner didn't read verse but had lingered on the page because of the left-hand column, in which were headlines about traffic accidents and a family tragedy in Zaječar. Though spring was in the air, the title was "Winter Poem." I later bought the paper, cut the poem out, and held on to it until it got lost in one of my moves, if you can use the word *move* to refer to traveling with a suitcase and a backpack in which I kept my most treasured possessions: documents, some photographs, my shaving kit, manuscripts, a small

English-Serbian dictionary, pencils, and a fountain pen that I kept because I was convinced that nothing would happen to me until the pelican spread its wings. I used to know "Winter Poem" by heart because I'd convinced myself that armed with a poem, I would have no fear of winter and cold, wherever I might be. Then forgetfulness began to take its toll, and I only remembered the opening and closing lines of the poem, and since then I have no longer been able to find my way to warmer places. Once I forget the beginning and the end, I'll go so high up north that my entire world will become a curtain of frost. The poem began with the words "Good morning I wish to you, Winter and Cold, you who make ice of the water and the oil viscous," and ends with "the little blaze of wild truth that grows cheerfully" or something like that, "in this beggar who begs not out of need but for others to give." That ending completely undid me, and I nearly began to cry. Luckily, the pastry-shop owner took the paper, and I consoled myself with the drink, then left. I walked toward Terazije. The day was sunny and warm, with lightning speed women stripped down to their summer finery, which exposed more than it concealed. At Hotel Moskva I descended into the underground walkway, crossed over to the other side of the street, and headed for the building of the federal assembly, then across the park and into Palmotićeva Street. This was no random stroll, I was following a route Marko had often taken, and I peered into the small cafés he frequented. No sign of him. I went on to Takovska, where I waited for the bus, got to Zeleni Venac, and after elbowing my way through the teeming throngs of street vendors, got onto the bus to Zemun. Why didn't I go to Marko's apartment that day? Because something inside warned me, though perhaps that isn't quite true, but that is how my memory dictates it to me today, and it is a fact that memory is the greatest liar and that it takes it upon itself to change day by day. Hour by hour, to be more precise, just as it would be more precise to admit that I don't know why I didn't go looking for Marko. Perhaps he was on one of his romantic binges, I thought, which happened with every new girlfriend. For days he would not leave the house, actually his bed, but after two or three days, he'd call to say he was in seventh heaven. Once he called while they were making love, and when I picked up, he put the phone on the pillow and for the next ten minutes or so I listened to their panting, moist kissing, the creaking of the bed, and the slapping of their thighs like the clapping of damp hands. What do you say, he asked as he grabbed the phone again, how did we sound? I wasn't sure what I was supposed to say, how to answer, so I said that it was a catchy refrain. Marko laughed and I heard him repeating it to his girlfriend, she also laughed, said something, and the sounds started again, and gingerly, so as not to disturb them, I hung up. He never told me who the woman was. Memories are a lure for the gullible, how often do I have to say that to myself? At some point in life, however, what had happened becomes more important than what is about to happen, though it should be the other way around, and insignificant details, like the panting in the telephone receiver, begin to look like crucial factors in what life could be. By then I had reached my building, unlocked the front door, stepped into the stairwell awash in the stench of mildew, opened my mailbox, in which I found several fliers, mostly advertising apartments for sale. I crumpled them up and was about to toss them into a cardboard box, which someone had thoughtfully left under the mailboxes, when I noticed on one of the fliers a circle with an intertwined yin and yang. I retrieved it and smoothed it out. Beginner's class in tai chi, the flier announced, Tuesdays and Thursdays from six P.M. to eight P.M. Next was an address that meant nothing to me, which could mean that it was a street in the upper reaches of Zemun or that it was one of the many streets that had changed names over the past few years. Impossible, I thought, that this flier, most likely related to the poster I'd seen two months earlier on the gate at Zmaj Jovina Street, had no significance. Of course, Marko would have said mockingly, had he been standing there next to me, because we read meaning into things that, in and of themselves, mean nothing. I shut the box and went upstairs. Differences were what had drawn us to each other all those years, no reason for it to be otherwise now, though Marko was no longer a real presence. There was nothing nasty waiting outside the door to my apartment, nothing scribbled on the door, the doorbell had not been smeared with excrement, the wall by the door was clean: all in all, I could breathe a sigh of relief. I entered the apartment, full of greenish shadows from the lowered blinds, and tumbled into the armchair, where, eyes shut, I massaged my forehead and the base of my nose. I could have fallen asleep right then, I was so exhausted, and the sleep probably would have done me good, but I didn't dare relax because Margareta had told me the day before that she'd call me in the evening. Did I make it up or had she said that the triangles were starting to open? Pressing lightly with the tips of my fingers, I began to massage my eyes. When I opened them, it was not completely dark in the room, but the green shadows were denser. I looked at the clock: I'd slept for about forty minutes and probably had been snoring with my mouth open, because the left side of my face, part of the chin and cheek, were caked with dried saliva. I went to the bathroom. In the mirror, my face was crumpled like a discarded piece of paper—I splashed it, rubbed it with lotion, smoothed my hair. I thought of Margareta again and felt myself hardening. There was nothing I could do. That creature had a life of its own and the less I get involved, I said to my reflection, the better. I slipped my hand into my pants to free it of the constraints of the fabric, and just then the phone rang. I didn't pick up. It was too early for Margareta to be calling. I stood there holding my rigid penis and waited for the phone to stop jangling. I had not counted, however, on the persistence of the caller, because the ringing didn't stop, my penis went limp, and my legs ached, and a feeling spread through me that the person calling could see me, knew I was here, standing next to the phone, and that he was not calling for the same reason he had called at the start, but because he wanted to fling into my face, or my ear, what a nobody I was, what a horrible soulless man, that it was high time for me to forget that limp organ and reach for the smooth, hard curve of the receiver. Carefully moving through the apartment, crouching behind furniture, I hopped from window to window, watching from behind the curtains the buildings across the way in the hope that I might catch sight of the person who was after me. The roofs were empty, as were the balconies, the windows shut and so distant that I couldn't be sure whether anyone was peering out from behind the curtains or through the slats of the blinds. I cursed myself for not buying a new set of binoculars or a telescope or a camera with a telephoto lens, whatever would have allowed me to see into the distance, while the phone kept ringing furiously behind me. I occasionally turned around and glared at it, as if it would be shocked by my ferocity and stop the noise. Why didn't I instantly yank the cord out of the wall? When I finally did, the silence fell like a balm on my ears. I made the rounds of the windows but spotted no changes. I remembered the man in the treetop by my building. Marko laughed at me at the time, but I myself had found no traces around the poplar later that day, though that didn't completely convince me to the contrary. I am one of those for whom any shred of suspicion, even the tiniest, leaves a permanent scar, and it is enough for me to touch that wrinkled trace with the tip of my finger for the suspicion to come back in full blaze, or in full darkness, which, when I think of it, is actually the more accurate. Suspicion leads to the dark, hope leads to the light, there is no simpler equation. Dragan Mišović would agree, though he might say that I should not associate light and dark with mathematical abstractions, which, despite everything, don't exist anywhere. Numbers are not fruits ripening on a slender or a knobbly tree, they are not berries sprouting on prickly bushes, they are not anything in fact, and just when you think you have numbers the most present, that is when they are the most absent. Now you see them, he'd say, raising two fingers, now you don't, and he'd fold his hand in. I can go on opening and shutting my hand as much as I like, but I have never managed to repeat the magic. I could conjure no magic at all, I should say, though I know that it was a mistake to call anything that happened during those nine weeks magical, for magic, as someone said, is tied to belief in the absolute power of language, and what was happening back then, no matter what language was involved, had to do with the other side of language, where the mystical realm of the ineffable exists in the serenity of silence and the music of the spheres, that which no measure of effort can express in words. Even what I am jotting down now with increasing interruptions, with longer intervals spent by the window, though there are no roofs or balconies here from which my actions or what I've written down in fine print with a ballpoint pen might be observed, wouldn't have changed anything, because all these words, all these tangled sentences, can do nothing more than crack open the narrow door leading to the room wherein dwells the truth, wherein reality is true reality and not a series of multiple reflections, including the one in which our face resides. I leaned over, reached for the cord, and plugged the phone back in. I picked up the receiver and put it to my ear. The line was free, I could breathe and wait for Margareta to call. I put the phone down and went into the bathroom. I almost never look at myself now in the mirror, except when I shave, because I can't bear to see what the years have done to my face, but back then, when all this was happening, I gazed at the mirror like any vain man, I rubbed lotion into my cheeks, slicked back my hair, squeezed the blackheads, snipped the whiskers, brushed my teeth. There was always one more distraction, one more attempt at sidestepping the sequence of events that is key to the story. So be it, but no one can convince me that real life is as orderly as a novel, and that in real life everything is tidy and purposeful, that people appear precisely when their arrival fits into the plot, not a moment too soon or a moment too late, and that everything leads to a climax and a resolution, after which there is nothing left unexplained. Life, to put it mildly, is chaos, a chaos that is not without an order of its own, I agree, but that order is so complex, so tangled, that even with the best of intentions we cannot divine it as order. I note that occasionally I write in the first-person plural, as if I were authorized to speak in the name of a group or a specific segment of the population. There is no one, I am alone, I can barely speak in my own name, and certainly not in the name of anyone else. But enough about me. I am not jotting this down to portray myself in a favorable light or to create an alibi. In fact, I don't know why I am doing it. It's easy to say "I don't know," Marko once said. Not true, was my response, "I don't know" was the hardest thing to say. We quarreled over that, foolishly, of course, but without consequences, as happens between friends. Who are not friends anymore, I must add immediately, a friendship that ended with no pointless words of accusation, like a fine-tuned divorce. Marko went off one way, I another, and we never looked back. I should be saying I never looked back, for how could I tell whether Marko turned around if I wasn't looking back? So I sensed that he didn't look back, just as I sensed that a tear welled in his eye, that he strained his ears to hear the echo of the footsteps receding irrevocably, that he clenched his fists and ground his teeth, and that he battled the inner voice urging him to act in the best possible way, though there were a few times when it seemed his shaking knees would betray him. It sounds like a farewell scene between Romeo and Juliet, I know, but friends are lovers, no quibbling about that here, at least. I hadn't been thinking about any of this, of course, that Wednesday, late in the afternoon, as I waited for Margareta to act on her promise. The only thought that obsessed me was how to continue what had gone on the night before, and this seemed more important than finding answers to the many questions that had been making my life a misery, though when Margareta finally did call I lied shamelessly, saying that I could hardly wait to continue our conversation and finally clear up a few matters. Margareta suggested we meet in her apartment, though not right away, as I'd been hoping, but later that evening. I had little choice: I agreed, and when we hung up, I sat at the desk and began leafing through the manuscript of *The Well*. I opened to the last page from my dream, and as had happened before, I was certain I'd never seen it. The part about Enoch did, admittedly, sound familiar, but the illustration, a square-shaped labyrinth in several colors, almost like a mandala, was entirely unfamiliar. The drawing was centered on the page with the text around it. Enoch, son of Jared, it said, walked one fine day by a stream, listening to the song of a bird, when suddenly the sky darkened, and from a great distance, like vast boats, black-and-white clouds piled in, and from them, with a rumble, appeared the hand of the Lord and a voice was heard mightier than a choir of trumpets, and this mighty voice said to Enoch that it had come for him and that it would raise him to heaven, where he would make Enoch a witness to all the shameful things people did on earth, which sullied God's majestic effort, so that he, Enoch, would comprehend the measure of God's anger and the righteousness of his wish to wipe humankind off the face of the earth, just as Enoch might wipe a tear from his cheek, and having spoken these words, without waiting for Enoch's answer, the hand coiled around him like a swirl of smoke and shot upward so fast that Enoch feared his shoes would come off his feet, but in the blink of an eye he found himself in a marvelous palace, surrounded by inquisitive angels, and here the Lord gradually transformed him into a superhuman being with seventy-two wings and an infinite number of eyes, as large as the whole world, which at the time was lost under the vast waters of the flood, and then he called that being by the name of Metatron, and proclaimed it a prince of divine presence, pure fire, fire that walks, fire that flows, fire that feeds the blaze of the heavens, and from which all springs, and into which all runs, with the condition of finding the right path. The path, I assume, was to be found in the square labyrinth, but for that I needed better lighting and a large magnifying glass. A lamp to bring closer I could find; a magnifying glass, however, I didn't have, just as I had no binoculars and who knows what else. Once and for all I should make a list of all the things I need, then I should go out and look for them and buy them, so that I wouldn't have to fume at wasted opportunities. I could already see the first part of the list: binoculars, magnifying glass, pencil sharpener. I leafed through several more pages of the manuscript, but neither Metatron nor Enoch was mentioned again. Two pages described the proper handling of leeches; one page provided the transcription of a letter in which there was a debate on the opening of a Jewish school in Zemun, which the Slavonian general command definitively denied in January 1814, invoking regulations from 1753, which allowed Jews the right to live only on property they already owned; that same regulation comes up later on, in a letter dated June 12, 1808, with a warning that the Jews in Zemun and Belgrade should be watched closely, as rumor had it that the French consul in Travnik was trying to influence the Serbian rebels through the Jews; on the last page there was a list of Jewish tradesmen in Zemun but with no indication of the year, and below the list a petition of the association of Zemun tradesmen to the effect that the Jewish tradesmen were stealing the bread from their mouths, that without bread they would not last long, which the government should have known without being warned. This reminded me of the fact that, except for that cream puff, I'd had nothing to eat since breakfast. I went into the kitchen, scrambled some eggs, poured myself a glass of milk, spread apricot jam on a slice of bread, and ate it all in a split second. I could have eaten more, but my search around the kitchen turned up nothing; and just like those Zemun tradesmen of two centuries ago, I no longer had any bread, though, unlike them, I had no one to blame. Margareta said I shouldn't get there until after eleven but before midnight, and for some reason, while I waited, time passed more slowly and the second hand needed more than sixty seconds to circle around the entire face of the clock. I remembered Marko's explanation of what happens when cannabis enters our physical and mental system: time, Marko said, passes agonizingly slowly at breakneck speed. And every time I was high, I'd think about how precise that definition was, but now I wasn't high, which could only mean that something else, and it wasn't the eggs, had taken over my consciousness the same way the ingredients of hashish or marijuana do. I wondered whether Margareta smoked, and I couldn't decide. During the seventies and eighties of the last century it seemed as if all younger urban residents consumed cannabis, but this had changed in the early nineties. Drugs got more expensive and less accessible, and alcohol made a big comeback. Hard liquor flowed like rivers, and the end of the century was filled with the consumption of sedatives. All of Belgrade was on valium, their eyes gleaming like car headlights. Margareta, however, didn't have that glassy stare, nor did she have the slightly out-of-focus look or the bloodshot eyes typical for people on hashish. These thoughts made me contemplate having a joint, and I started digging around for the papers, but then gave up. For my encounter with Margareta I needed a clear mind. I looked at my watch: it was time to go. Margareta opened the door, and we stood for a moment, looking at each other, waiting for her breathing to slow. No, she said, she hadn't been racing to the door, she'd been up on a ladder to get hold of some books, then lugged the whole pile, like an armload of firewood, to the table when the doorbell rang. Everything's fine, she said, but she hoped she hadn't pulled a muscle. She lifted both arms and examined them, then lowered them and walked into the apartment. I had only had the chance to catch sight of golden hairs on her lower arms, like those on her thigh, though now I was thinking that I had imagined the hairs on her thigh. Certainly, my vantage point then was better, I didn't need glasses the way I do now, but in that instant I wouldn't have noticed larger markings, such as a mole or a bruise, let alone minute golden hairs. There, I am writing about little hairs as if they were crucial to this story, though many other things, much more serious and full of meaning, wait in some cranny of my mind. This is one more distinction between the real and the recorded: in writing our choice is unlimited, whereas in reality it is a limited selection, and sometimes not even that. Some are disgusted by hairs as much as others are disgusted by leeches, and the fear of a hair in soup may be the same as the fear of a leech latching on to the warm hollow behind the knee. Whatever the case, Margareta was wearing black jeans that evening, so I couldn't expect any proof, at least not any time soon. The apartment looked as it had before, though I couldn't shake off the impression that this time it was in a state of disorder. There's tea in the kitchen, juice in the fridge, there may be a beer, said Margareta, and added that we didn't have much time, though she didn't say for what, and while I poured jasmine tea into a cup I sensed that there wouldn't be time for what I'd had in mind. I went back into the living room, one foot in front of the other, while the cup joggled on the saucer and the tea sloshed over the lip in thin streams. Margareta was sitting at the desk, sifting through papers. I looked around: there was nowhere to sit. I could sit on the floor, but then I wouldn't be able to see Margareta, or I would be looking at her from an odd angle, so I chose to stand. I put the teacup down on the nearest pile of books. Margareta didn't even glance at me, instead she kept flipping from one page of writing to the next, and I chided myself for my naiveté in thinking her invitation implied a continuation of what had gone on the night before. I know what you're thinking, said Margareta, without raising her eyes from the page that was now consuming her attention. No, you don't, I said, trying to keep my voice from quavering. Margareta looked at me, and looking back, I realized her eyes had changed color again. Now they were greenish blue, but I could have sworn that they'd been a gray blue earlier, though at the same time I was certain they'd always been light brown. After what went on in the cab, Margareta continued, you're wondering why we're wasting our time on papers instead of picking up where we left off. I felt my ears burning. Don't feel awkward, said Margareta, and at that moment I thought my ears would grow with shame, the way Pinocchio's nose grew with greed. All in the fullness of time, said Margareta, which is an old turn of phrase but still a good one. She put down one page and took up another. Besides, she said, the Kabbalists thought that the night between Friday and Saturday was ideal for lovemaking, not just ideal, but obligatory, and it was even believed that the best time was Friday after midnight, but before dawn, because if a man and a woman were to do it early in the evening or at dawn they might hear the voices of people, which might encourage the man to think of other women, and that would be a sin. She looked at me, and I nodded, as if I had been expected to give my approval. By that act, Margareta said, consummated on Shabbat, which starts on Friday at sunset, a man and a woman help the Shekhinah unite again with God and so renew his divine substance and restore balance to the world. I had to confess I'd never accorded the act of love so much importance, but I liked the image of the lovers carrying the flagging world on their backs, then sinking into each other to return the exaltation to the world. This made the male sexual organ seem like the lever with which someone, I can't remember who, sought to move the entire planet earth. I couldn't understand, however, why Margareta was telling me all this. If she didn't want, as she put it, to pick up where we'd left off the night before, she could have said so without reciting all the stuff on the role of sexual intercourse in the Kabbalistic notion of the cosmos. In the Talmud, she said, it's written precisely how often men should make love with their wives. Workers should do so twice a week, donkey drivers once a week, camel drivers once a month, and sailors once every six months. More than that, she said, was permissible, but less than that would be grounds for the woman to call for dissolution of the marriage. And writers, I asked, what about them? Margareta shuffled through the papers and said that writers were not mentioned anywhere. Maybe there were no writers then, I said, or maybe they weren't expected to couple with their wives. I'm not sure, said Margareta, but it looks as if a man whose work is less strenuous and who spends no time away from home is supposed to make love with his wife more often. Then a writer, I said, is condemned to sex every night. If you consider that a condemnation, replied Margareta, the answer is affirmative. I laughed. Everything is relative, I said, even sex, so the night between Friday and Saturday is more important than the other nights in the week? Yes, confirmed Margareta. For a while we said nothing, then I spoke up again and asked whether that meant what I thought it meant. Yes, she said, it does. She didn't inquire as to what I had in mind, just as I didn't ask her for any further explanation, but the answer was clear: we would have to wait for Shabbat. The silence settled again between us, a little weightier and longer than before. Margareta went back to her papers while I looked aimlessly at the books on the floor and shelves. I went into the kitchen and poured myself another cup of tea. Why don't you sit down, Margareta advised me when I came over to the desk, because she meant, she said, to tell me a story that was not short. There is nothing I like so much as a long story, I said. The longer the better. I sat down on the floor by heaps of books on which I again set my cup of tea. Don't worry, Margareta smiled, the story won't last until Shabbat. She picked up a sheet of paper and glanced at me almost sternly, with eyes that I was certain were a feline green.

This story, like so many others, said Margareta, begins with a death, in the mid-eighties, when Solomon Alfandari died in Belgrade. He was buried at the Jewish cemetery in Zemun, because, native of Zemun that he was, he was part of the local Jewish community there. Several months later, his widow brought three large boxes to the Jewish Historical Museum containing his books, letters, some documents and photographs, and manuscripts in Serbian and Hebrew. For the next two years the boxes gathered dust in a corner of the museum, then, no longer able to fend off the daily pestering of Alfandari's widow, members of the museum staff inventoried the entire contents of the boxes, and so it happened that a manuscript written in Hebrew finally saw the light of day, actually the neon light of the museum storage room where the inventory was being drawn up. The manuscript had no title page, but since it began with the words *The Well,* the museum staff members listed it under this title in the inventory that was later signed by Alfandari's widow and the director of the museum. But you should know, said Margareta, this is not the same manuscript you have, though it carries the same title as the Hebrew original. As it later transpired, when domestic and foreign Hebrew scholars analyzed the text, *The Well* in Hebrew turned out to be a Kabbalistic text, written some two hundred fifty years ago at the crossroads, as the manuscript said, between two empires, the Habsburg and the Ottoman, and between two worlds, this world here and the one beyond. There was nothing to suggest which worlds those were, said Margareta, and while it was possible that "this world here" refers to the world in which we live, that other world, "the one beyond," could be anywhere. Two years passed but the translation was not completed. The manuscript, the translators said, hadn't been completed either, there were several junctures at which it stopped abruptly and then would start again with sentences that had nothing to do with the passages preceding them. Besides, the manuscript was teeming with quotes from other Kabbalistic sources, sometimes with the source cited, much more often with no citation to indicate where they had been taken from. The same quotes are, for example, copied several times, and sometimes attributed to different editions and authors, which contributed to the theory that the author meant to obscure all traces of himself. The manuscript, one of the translators said, seemed alive, and, in a curious way, was itself dictating how they should proceed with it. During that time, in one of the realities, said Margareta, the war began, and after that the outbreak of hostilities in Slovenia and Croatia, then it was Bosnia's turn. Sensing that where there was the most talk of friendship the worst strife would erupt, the Sarajevo Jews began evacuating. Among the several hundred Jews who arrived in Belgrade was a fellow by the name of Pavle Salom, a distant relative of Solomon Alfandari's. In his suitcase, with a change of clothes, a warm sweater, and slippers, there was room for two more things: a family picture album, now at the museum, and a manuscript in Hebrew, which turned out to be an addendum to the manuscript that the translators had been unable to handle. It took several months for the various parts of the manuscript to be arranged in the proper order, though there were plenty of sentences that couldn't be placed, and which spun around the manuscript like planets. The Belgrade Hebrew scholar Eugen Verber first elaborated on the notion of the manuscript as a living organism, which, as I just said, said Margareta, the interpreters and translators had already ascertained. According to Verber, the author of the manuscript had based the text on the Kabbalistic technique of bringing to life nonliving matter, hence on the technique of creating a golem, which had been modified in such a way that the text itself came alive, was designed to be self-sustaining but not also physically mobile. In other words, the manuscript was not a bizarre ambulatory creature, but it did possess the capability of refashioning itself, as if it were searching for the most apt structure for its meaning. Verber was also the first to note that the manuscript can propel itself forward, Margareta said, like a sort of virus: if a complete fragment of the manuscript were to be introduced to any other text, in any other language, that text too would begin to behave in the same way, in other words, it too would be alive. This is the way the manuscript in my apartment had originated, she told me. Actually, fragments of *The Well* were introduced to the material about the Zemun Jews, and, as I had seen for myself, she said, the manuscript was still seeking its final form. As if made of sand, I said. It makes more sense to say, Margareta continued, that the original manuscript functions like the computer programs of today, and that inside the program is a core, the heart of the program, which can be copied and introduced to any other text, because every text, actually every language, is, in fact, a computer program, which, furnished with the right knowledge, can be programmed any way one wants. Verber, it seems, was well on the way to figuring how the core fragment functioned, but death caught up with him and left us with no answer. The translation of the manuscript, or of one of the versions of the manuscript that was forever in flux, was completed, and then, though this is never spoken of, it has been replaced by a skillfully executed copy, which is without the lifegiving powers, and that copy is being preserved at the Jewish Historical Museum, where they believe they have the complete and unaltered legacy of Solomon Alfandari and Pavle Salom. I stared at her. That explained why in my manuscript I could never find what I'd been reading earlier, and why the pages changed their content, or the content shifted pages, either way, and I understood something else, which I blurted out: You took it, I said. I prefer to say I borrowed it, replied Margareta, and I will certainly put it back when we no longer need it. We? I asked. Who are we? That's the next part of the story, answered Margareta, but there's no point in hurrying, there is a sequence that can't be abbreviated, a path that must be followed, even as it takes detours. I can be impatient, I confess, but I can also be obedient, and though all sorts of questions were seething inside me, I said nothing. If I must be silent, I said, silent I will be. In that case, Margareta told me, she'd read me a part of the translation of the text, which, as she had mentioned, began with the words *The Well,* words that, it bears saying, no matter what changes appeared in the text, always were first. It is not entirely clear to me what they mean, but perhaps, she said, the initial mechanism is concealed in those words, a given sequence of letters or sounds that set in motion what we have described as the program that changes the text. She looked me straight in the eyes, the way a teacher does who wants to be sure that the student is following what he's being told, and tries to catch in his eyes the spark of comprehension or the fog of confusion. Margareta apparently espied the spark because she lifted the page, angling it so that more light fell on it, cleared her throat, and began to read: The Well shines even in the darkest darkness as if it is the most exalted palace in the sky, and mine eyes have seen nothing more beautiful. The year is 5500, the month of Tammuz, and Belgrade is once again in Ottoman hands. Our brothers and our sisters have been crossing the river these last months, leaving behind what could have been carried, let alone what could not have been carried but was for honest resale, and though most of them made their way to Novi Sad or Osijek, there were some who thought that here, in Zemun, was the best possible place to settle, and meanwhile both Ottoman Jews and Habsburg Jews hoped to return to Belgrade, the former because that was where they were from, they were citizens of that empire and believed the troubles would blow over and they would return to their land and property, while the latter, who had spent no more than ten years there, longed to go back, for they had relished the charm of the place of which many said that its position, overlooking the joining of the two broad rivers, made it unique in all the world. Everyone has the right to feel as he wants, I will contest this with no one, but here, in Zemun, on the Danube shores, the serenity is the greater, and besides, as I said, the Well is here. There will be those who will want to know at once how to gain access to the Well, does one descend into it or ascend to it, and although I will elaborate on this later, I will now remark that the path to the Well is long and arduous, much like the Bosnian mountain passes along which it is better not to walk at night, not for fear of robbers, but because of the ravines that beckon with a dark silence or a slippery path. And no matter what the path is like, it is the one and the only path, and whoever sets foot upon it, alone or with others, will find the return difficult, in other words he must be ready for temptation and exertion, for the constant doubt that will assail him like the leeches in marsh water until he arrives at the dark forest and finds the path leading to the Well. Then everything will be returned to him a hundredfold, and both earthly and heavenly treasures will be his to a degree he could never have imagined, nor ever in his dreams could they have been his. I should hasten to add that I know some who will hold this against me, because there are always those who demand a secrecy greater than the one the Lord, may he be blessed, gave us as his legacy, but it seems to me that no secret must remain unuttered in a time of calamity, and so the secret of the Well must be disclosed when I see that once again, as so many times before, our brothers and our sisters trudge down the long dusty road of exile. Even if this exile will never end, the moment has come for us to ready ourselves for far worse things to come, things that even history will fall silent when faced with, and if history falls silent, imagine what people will do, hence we must have our defenses close at hand, and from whom better to learn the skill of defense than from our ancestors and teachers, those who themselves tasted the woes of exile and the insatiable appetites of the executioner. The Well is a marvelous thing, but only the select may penetrate it, a chosen few in each generation, especially those generations that have grown up in wartime and therefore scatter more quickly than in peacetime.

This is why I feel it is important, though it will not be easy, to set forth the skills needed to take up arms of defense at times when our brothers and sisters have no hope of defense from any other quarter, and must act to save their own lives. I long studied this secret skill, I spent many hours both day and night poring over ancient texts, combining letters and numbers, I repeated the name of the Lord, may it be blessed, in a hundred ways, was joined and became separate, became light and became dark, and all with the purpose of leaving the future generations a mast on which they could unfurl the sail of defiance, even as the enemy gloats in the belief that our vessel is sinking. It will never sink, I assure you. I have seen the future, and perhaps it is better not to speak of it, but no matter how far I ventured forward in time, I always found evidence that our brothers and sisters were out there, that we no longer had to tremble in fear that the Lord, may he be blessed, would lose his people. And now, let me set forth the sequence of topics about which I desire to write. I say desire only because I am no longer of sound health, I may fall silent before I say and write it all, so first I will set it out in the most basic of outlines, in the most summary of forms, and afterward, should nothing prevent me from doing so, a detailed explanation will follow, which is in keeping with the instruction given to Rabbi Josef Tajtacak by his teacher, when the teacher told the rabbi that writing in brief, a subject swiftly plumbed, represents the pinnacle of writing, such as what the celestial beings practice, while writing in longer fragments is a trustworthy sign of a text's inferiority. By the way, said Margareta, this summary of his runs on for more than a hundred pages, and who knows, had he ever managed to write out the fuller explanation, how long that book would have been. Besides, she said, many pages in that part are given over to descriptions of the different methods for attaining higher knowledge, and there are all sorts of things here: meditations, exhaustion by fasting and lack of sleep, mathematical exercises, language games and riddles, and it is possible that the translation is not fully accurate, though the substance of it is unquestionably preserved. For instance, said Margareta, and lifted the next sheet of paper, this here describes how he meditated without interruption for several days and nights and practiced permutations of Hebrew letters, until combinations of God's name began to spring from him, entirely of their own accord, and then, he writes, the letters began to resemble strange, dark expanses, like ravines in vile mountains: and suddenly I found myself there among them, alone, and just when I thought that I was lost and that I would never again return to my world, I spied a light in the distance, flickering and mobile like a butterfly, and as a butterfly hovers over a flower, attracted by its sweetness, that was how that light attracted me and hovered over me, over my soul open to a sign of heavenly embrace. I felt as if the light were pouring into me, and when I looked at my body, I saw that it was radiant, and just as that meandering light of a moment before had illumined me, now I shone on all objects, while my hand kept writing out new combinations of the supreme name of its own volition, and my lips moved, enunciating words that appeared before me as in writing on the wall, each word more beautiful than the one before it, though they all possessed a certain terror, from which, later, when it all ended, my teeth chattered. All this showed that, as in any teaching, there must be a certain sequence, just as is written in *The Gateway to Justice,* where it stands that first the body must be purified of the sediment of filth, then the same must be done with the soul, from which all traces of anger and rage must be purged, which is of special importance, so the soul will be freed of all attachment, except to the Lord, may he be blessed, and all knowledge, no matter what learning it stems from, and then, when the body and soul are pure and empty, they should be isolated in an equally pure room, and pray and dedicate themselves to the moving of letters, in order to channel the thoughts in the right direction and to avoid any external interference that would divert them to a wrong path. Then, the Well will no longer be far off, but that does not mean that man dares to relax and neglect caution, for the path within is not the same as the path without, and he who wishes to leave, for whatever reason, must first prepare himself, because once he enters the Well, but is not prepared for the return, he will not be able to achieve that state. When coming back out of the Well a person returns to an impure world, among forces that will rend his garments woven of purity and draw him back into the struggle between good and evil, in which we all suffer for Adam's original sin, and he who comes back from the Well, no matter how long he stayed there, arrives weary and worn from the effort of concentration, and is therefore easy prey for all those demons who, leechlike, attach themselves to him and drain his blood until he collapses utterly and succumbs to their rule, though it is better not to write on that now, lest such horror dissuade those who are still unsure of the teachings and quake at the thought that they are slipping down a narrow path to an impassable gateway guarding the entrance to the Well. He is right, Margareta said, there is no greater obstacle than self-doubt. She looked at me as if she expected me to agree, but I said nothing. No matter how interesting the document that she was presenting to me might be, I could find no explanation in it for the many things I still didn't understand, and I was afraid, if she kept this up, that we'd never get there. Margareta leafed through a few more pages, took one in her left hand and one in her right, and then, after a moment of indecision, decided on the one in her right. The author, she said, used various methods to attain mystical insight, including weeping and fasting, and he noted down the many visions he had, and among them is one that we have taken to be the first and has served as the foundation for all we have built. I held my hand up to stop her and asked if she didn't think that it was high time she told me who the "they" or the "we" she kept invoking were, and could she not explain what this Well was all about. Soon, promised Margareta, although I didn't find this particularly convincing, as she continued to describe the vision. In short, it began with a description of waking up from "chaotic reality" with the help of a "slap with no hand," which, as at the time when I wrote the answer to the advertisement, reminded me of the Zen question about the sound of one hand clapping. I never mentioned this to Margareta, though I meant to, but I only thought of it now, when I can no longer reach her. During most of our lives we try to keep up with ourselves, but we are often no more than observers of what is happening to us, and then, while we sit in the shade of an oak or a pear tree, we regret the chances we have frittered away. I don't know why this is. If someone had asked me, I would have definitely arranged the world we live in differently. It is all so complex, as complex as the vast fabric of conspiracy that slowly emerged from behind what Margareta had said. Perhaps *conspiracy* is not the most apt word, but none other occurs to me. Margareta seemed to be taking her time deliberately with her answers to my questions. We circled around the Well the way a cat, one might say, circles around a dish of milk, except that the cat starts lapping up the milk at some point, while access to the Well, for us, or at least for me, was still a stretch. But I should hold to some sort of sequence, though I'm no longer sure of how valid certain road signs are. After the slap came the story of the migration of souls, in which the author of the document, using complicated proofs and mathematical calculations, claimed that he knew the pathway along which the soul of a famous Kabbalist from Safed, probably Yitzhak Luria, though he never says so explicitly, moved across the centuries, and when the author was penning his text, this soul was dwelling in the body of an ordinary water carrier. Invoking his vision, the author of the document remarked that the soul can always be found, as needed, in someone who recognizes the meaning of the slap. And were it to come to pass that this was needed, Margareta went on reading, then the hour would have come for everything else too, and that would be the time to make use of the weapon to protect our brothers and sisters just as the magnificent golem would protect them, which also implied that the bodies of select people would replace the forms of the letters and become, themselves, language, that the system of the Sephirot coincides with a part of the city, and, most important, there would be a joining of the King and his Queen, actually the Crown would descend into the Kingdom, so that the Lord, may he be blessed, would unite again with the Shekhinah. Then, and only then, will ingress to the Well appear, and they who enter will not regret it. After all this, I thought, I am where I started. I looked to the left, I looked to the right, as if I were getting ready to leave, yet I didn't. Margareta stopped reading and said that now I certainly understood how all the elements were interconnected, and then, feeling my doubts, she enumerated them: he in whom the soul of the ancient Kabbalist now dwelled recognized the slap; that way, others recognize him, and they start preparing incantations for the defense shield in a process by which letters are written out with bodies; the last words are created on the eve of Shabbat, hence on Friday evening, then they mark the system of the Sephirot in the part of the city, which thereby becomes an emanation of divine holiness, making it possible for the celestial King and his Queen to unite; this act then raises the defense shield and opens the door of the Well, which is at the very center of the Sephirot, and as long as the shield remains up, invisible to the ordinary eye, the entrance to the Well, which leads to the other world, remains open. And they who wish to leave, I said, can do so safely? Yes, Margareta said. Even now I wonder whether she really believed in it or whether hers was the gesture of a person who had in fact lost all hope. I could understand that, although I didn't believe that the political and social situation in the country was extreme enough to force members of one ethnic group to such a desperate act. Of course what someone from outside might not feel at all may be horrifying for someone seeing it from within. The horror of identity is that it can't be sloughed off the way a snake sheds its skin, and there is no dungeon worse than an identity that one doubts or that others have proclaimed to be bad or evil. I experienced this myself many times in the years of ethnic strife, facing the prejudices about Serbian identity, and I could only assume how that must have seemed from the perspective of being Jewish or of an identity that had permanently been branded as negative. Even so, it seemed highly unconvincing to me to have faith in Kabbalistic documents at the close of the twentieth century, especially considering the popularity the Kabbalah had gained in fashionable circles. On the other hand, I had to feel respect for those who brought their whole beings to this, investing a vast effort to unite the disparate elements into a whole that made sense. They got the idea for it, Margareta said, in the spring of 1992, when the Jewish refugees from Sarajevo arrived in Belgrade. That was when the younger generations of Jews understood for the first time that exile was in their genes, which led them to speed up their preparations for departure, while at the same time the lack of understanding and overt hostile feelings for the Jewish community began growing. The first letter arrived at that time, warning Jews, in poisonous though surprisingly calm language, to watch what they were doing. There were too many of you among us before, the letter said in closing, and now, with the scum arrived from Bosnia, there are many too many, and this means you should reduce your numbers yourselves, because if you don't, we will do it for you, and anything that upsets Serbian harmony will itself be upset. The letter was signed by the Patriotic Army of Unity and Salvation. No one had ever heard of this organization, no one wanted to believe it existed. Margareta learned of the letter from her father, who was on boards and committees in the Jewish community, and that gave her the impetus to keep going. Meanwhile, the community redoubled its efforts to reduce the number of refugees in Belgrade, organizing their departure for Israel, Canada, and a number of European countries. The Patriotic Army of Unity and Salvation wrote a second letter, in which they hailed the news that Jews were leaving Serbia, promising that those who stayed behind would be allowed to live in an orderly ghetto in Kosovo. The first explicitly anti-Semitic graffiti was scrawled on the walls of Jewish buildings and cemeteries, tombstones were knocked over and desecrated, and soon thereafter the number of writings of that sort mushroomed in the press, as well as in books blaming the Jews for nearly all the evils of the world. She knew I knew most of this already, Margareta said, but she was giving me the full picture, because that way it would be easier to understand the details, even details that had not been mentioned, and I would definitely, she said, be able to understand how awkward this made everything, especially with what was going on: the war, inflation, political chaos, the isolation of the country, the plunge in the standard of living, the pervasive sense of insecurity. Of course I understood, I had no need to say so. Several concerned members of the Jewish community, she continued, were thinking about what the best solutions would be in such a situation, especially since they were disgruntled by the official position of the community, which did not support the current government, but were doing what they could to evade conflicts, believing this to be the best route to peaceful coexistence. The group of malcontents, including her, believed in a more aggressive handling of the issues, though she herself had been torn about choosing the most apt response, until she remembered the translated manuscript. She couldn't recall who it had been, though more likely she preferred not to disclose who was in her group, which was to her credit but a source of additional frustration for me. Margareta did not relent, she went right on talking about how someone, perhaps that same person, she said, or maybe someone else, noticed a series of similarities between one of the manuscript author's visions and the reality in which they found themselves. Seen in that light, the manuscript could suddenly be read as a concrete set of instructions about how to respond to the situation in which the community found itself, against its will. Meanwhile, as if they felt something was stirring, members of the Patriotic Army of Unity and Salvation ratcheted up their campaign: more letters came in, some were published in the press, and the number of incidents that could be described as anti-Semitic also rose, though chances were that the incidents didn't all stem from the same group, which had inspired imitators among the right-wing organizations. The number of crimes leveled against members of the Jewish community soared, said Margareta, and though it was difficult to be sure that all were planned, it was alarming that apartment break-ins, pickpocketing in public transportation, fires in cellars and attics, smashed windows, and threats made over the phone grew radically from one day to the next, especially as all pertained to community members. This was no time for hesitation, said Margareta, and that was the position our group took, because we sensed that sooner or later we'd be facing an open clash. The Patriotic Army of Unity and Salvation split around that time into several factions, just as the political parties had done in Serbia, as the result of inner power struggles and their inability to cobble together broadly acceptable platforms of action. The main branch abbreviated its name to the Army of Unity and Salvation and soon stopped making itself heard; the peace-loving part, called Salvation for All, extended a conciliatory hand, but no one believed that this reconciliation, even if it had been formally embraced, would have prevented the two extreme factions, the Patriots and the Eagle Avengers, from proceeding with their plans. Worst of all, said Margareta, no one was sure what their plans were. They went underground, they made no public statements, but they were recruiting new members. What with the situation in the country, there were more malcontents than one could count, all of them waiting for someone to tell them who was to blame.

About that time, continued Margareta, there were rifts in her group too because some felt that there was no longer any point in waiting and testing fate, that they should strike the first blow without further ado, but the feeling also prevailed that violence was unacceptable and that they should focus on defense. Work accelerated on a definitive translation of the manuscript and preparations for what they called their action plan, not without headaches, because now all elements, including the slap, the mathematical calculations, the linguistic-physical structures, the migration of souls, and the revival of the union of the heavenly King and his Queen, all had to be brought into a harmonious whole, or, most important, into an effective whole, because if the plan were to founder, there would surely be no other chance. And so the entire plan was laid out, to be set in motion by the recognition of the slap, which would reveal the person within whom dwelled the soul of the ancient Kabbalist. And all along, I said, I was thinking it was the soul of the water carrier. Same thing, said Margareta, the water carrier quenches the thirst of the body and the Kabbalist quenches the thirst of the soul, but thirst is thirst, one augments the other, and if both are not quenched, the body and soul will not be in harmony. I had to admit I liked the water carrier more, whatever his name was, but I was there to listen and not to bicker, so I went on following Margareta's story, leaving many questions for later. The only thing I couldn't let lie was the way it had all begun, the slap on the Danube riverbank, that had drawn me into the labyrinth of events from which I still saw no exit. Why me, I asked Margareta, and not someone else, someone Jewish? There are many Kabbalists, she said, who believe that the soul may wander off in different directions, as they believe in India, and dwell in the most varied bodies, and not necessarily human, so it was certainly not impossible that the soul of a Jewish man found shelter, for instance, in the body of a person who was not Jewish. The body, after all, is only a vessel, a transport service for the movement of a soul through time, and the only thing that mattered was that the soul be prevented from venturing into a body where an evil soul already dwelt, because then they would clash, which might destroy the body of the host. I hope, I said, this won't happen to me. Margareta looked at me gravely. She shared that hope, she said, at least until Shabbat was over, after that everything was up for grabs anyway. That set her off again on the right-wing factions of what had been the Patriotic Army of Unity and Salvation, factions that became magnets drawing those who disseminated Nazi and racist ideas, in lockstep with similar organizations in Europe and America. Several times, she said, they clashed, literally. They, said Margareta, meaning the Jewish community, had their own extremist faction, which openly called for physical resistance, even violence, and managed to ferret out the seat of the Eagle Avengers, where a fight broke out, shots were fired, people were injured on both sides. How could, I asked, the public not have noticed? The public was preoccupied with other things, said Margareta, and most people weren't able to absorb differing, especially contradictory, information. She reminded me of how the conflict in Yugoslavia was understood in the early 1990s. Everything was shown as black and white, a way of portraying reality in which one side was the culprit and the criminal, while the other, or several others, were the innocent victims, despite the fact that the Yugoslav reality was more of a color picture, with multiple levels of reality, or better, multiple levels of blame, so all were criminals and victims at once. I wasn't sure I agreed entirely with her interpretation, but I'd had trouble and misunderstandings enough with the current reality so there was no point in burdening myself with a question that too many books would be written about. The world in which we lived was coming to an end with the close of the century, and the apocalypse was, so to speak, around the corner, and perhaps all this was unnecessary. I didn't believe in the apocalypse at that point, and the stories about it sounded to me like the futile groaning of terrified humanity, though now that Serbia was bombed, the World Trade Center destroyed in New York, and Iraq was attacked, I am more inclined to doubt, more ready than I was before, should there be further proof in the offing, to repent and convert. Perhaps I should have expected this, having the reach of Europe in mind, America's self-infatuation, the self-confidence of Islam, Russia's instability, the unpredictability of China, the new nomadic tendencies, but to be frank, none of this interested me. When I think about it, I wouldn't have minded spending my whole life in blessed ignorance, far from the noise and fury of crowds, listening to the music of, say, Bach and Mozart, reading Chekhov's stories and an anthology of love poetry from around the world, with a little garden that I could plant and tend, and when the time came, harvest the fruits of my labor: ruddy tomatoes, sweet peas, potatoes, and carrots. Too late now. All I can do is lament like a failed prophet who bemoans his fate, convinced that it could have been different if only he could have foreseen it. I was also a failed prophet when it came to the evening, or night, I spent with Margareta, and when I left the book-filled apartment on Thursday morning with a throbbing headache, I couldn't decide what to attribute it to: the story that had gone on too long and the overabundance of information, or erotic frustration. The news that the defense plan would unfold over Shabbat, in the course of the evening and night from Friday to Saturday, offered some consolation, but then it was supposed to be part of a ritual and not out of free choice, and, stripped of spontaneity, it all seemed pointless. There was no turning back for me, however, regardless of the fact that the role had been imposed and that I had chosen none of it. Had Marko been there, and had I told him everything, I know he would have first asked me how I could be so sure that everything Margareta said was true, he would have asked for evidence, substantiation, not castles in the air, and only then would he agree to continue. I can't say I had no doubts. I did have doubts. Everything was too tidy, all the elements dovetailed perfectly, led from one to the next, even the mistakes happened when there was the greatest likelihood they would happen, so it was all too much like a Hollywood movie, thick with paranoid plots, and who still believed Hollywood movies? I consoled myself that I wouldn't have long to wait: in a day and a half the whole truth would show its face, and everything would be clear. I wasn't counting on certain other components, on the unpredictable effect of the text that was being typeset and proofed for the next issue of *Minut,* on the power of rumor, on blind hatred, on simple human envy, if envy is as simple as it is human. I must lie down, I thought when I got home, and dropped, fully dressed, into bed. I fell asleep instantly and was woken by the doorbell. I opened my eyes, looked at my watch: I had been sleeping for twenty-five minutes. I had been dreaming, but couldn't remember what. The doorbell kept ringing, longer rings then shorter, and finally I had to relent. I would rather have stayed in bed, trying to remember the dream, but I got up, went to the door, and just as I reached for the key, the ringing stopped. I looked at the key as if it could give me an answer. The key was silent, the doorbell was silent, and, not breathing, I leaned my ear against the door and imagined someone on the other side, also not breathing, who had leaned his ear precisely where mine was, and the ear of that person was listening to the silence of my ear, while my ear carefully listened to the silence that came from that other ear, which reminded me of the dream, or one part of the dream, the part when, as I tried to get out of a large room in which someone had inadvertently locked me, I stopped and put my ear to an opening under a mirror, the function of which I didn't know, the function of the opening, that is, not the mirror, of course, because in my dream the mirror was an ordinary mirror, but the opening was mysterious and I couldn't decide whether it was part of the system of ventilation or of the heating system, or whether there might be a single system for both heating and cooling, it certainly couldn't have heated and cooled at the same time, and in my dream I leaned my ear against the opening in hopes of hearing somebody, because if I heard somebody, somebody could hear me, and I tried to come up with what I might say, and of all words the one I couldn't retrieve was the word for the thing one uses to unlock a door, just as I wasn't sure whether the same word was used for the thing for locking the door, because a locked door, I thought in the dream, is not the same as an unlocked door, and the door you lock is not the same as the door you unlock, which meant that the things that lock or unlock ought to be different too, and at that point a voice reached my ear through the opening under the mirror, an entirely ordinary voice that said, Turn the doorknob, damn it, turn that doorknob, and suddenly I asked myself whether I was dreaming what was happening to me or had the dream reminded me of something that had already happened, and I stretched out my hand, turned the doorknob, and the door opened. It hadn't been locked. Not once since the night I was beaten up in the nursery school yard had I forgotten to lock it. I broke out in a cold sweat, completely absurdly, of course, because it was the response of my body to the possibility that something might have happened, though nothing did happen, but that is the structure of the human soul, or at least the autonomic nervous system, that reacts equally to a real and an imagined threat, to what really occurred and to the prospect of what might have occurred. No matter how paradoxical it may sound, the nervous system is blind and believes itself, or its imaginings, just as much as it believes real stimuli from the outside world. Marko, of course, would have warned me that this could be proof that there was no difference between the outside and the inside worlds, and that the outside world was merely a projection of the inside world, and that we project our own existence in a movie, say, in which we play protagonists directed by insecure, waffling directors who are themselves protagonists. A little complicated, but that's Marko for you. Actually, when the buzzer started to ring, or when I started hearing it ring, my first thought was that Marko was finally back, and even when it stopped ringing and I pressed my ear to the door, I still wondered whether he was standing out there in the hallway, a little impatient, a little irritated, a little unhappy. When I opened the door, it was not Marko, but Dragan Mišović, which exceeded the power of any dream of mine, so I stood there and blinked until he asked if he might come in. I moved over to let him by, adding that I hoped he wasn't expecting me to solve any math problems. This early in the morning, he said, even I can't add two and two. I'd be surprised, said Dragan Mišović, how many people weren't able to do that much later on in the day, even after they'd had a cup of coffee. I brought him into the living room, waited for him to take a seat, then I went into the kitchen to make coffee. If there was someone I was not expecting to see that morning in my apartment it was Dragan Mišović. I wondered what the woman who had often run into him and later moved to Banovo Brdo would have said, or would she simply have refused to believe me? While I waited for the water to boil, I peeked into the living room. It was Dragan Mišović, there was no doubt. I brought in the tray with the coffeepot and two cups. I served the coffee and sat across from him. We said nothing, and it seemed as if we'd never say anything again. Dragan sipped the coffee, a little loudly for my taste but with gusto, so I took that as praise of my culinary talents. I'm not certain, to be frank, that making coffee counts as a culinary talent, but praise is praise, and no one could take that from me. He'd been passing by, he said, and he thought he might drop in. He saw my dubious expression, and laughed. Don't say, he said, you don't believe me. I won't, I said, though that doesn't prevent me from not believing you. Dragan Mišović sighed. It is time for us to take off our masks, he said, and touched his face with the tips of his fingers. For a moment I actually thought he'd peel some sort of mask off his face, but he only scratched himself on the cheek and chin. Margareta has already told you everything, he said, all that's left is the mathematical part, and she was never big on math. I couldn't believe my ears. I might, of course, have picked up something from that evening at the restaurant, when he slipped me the message about the triangles opening, however then, if I'm not mistaken, it seemed like yet another coincidence in the abundance of coincidences, and I realized that so many coincidences were indeed statistically feasible, but that in practice, just another word for life, the number of genuine coincidences is minimal, and that most of the other things could be neatly explained and tied to certain events. She didn't tell me anything, I said hoarsely, about mathematical calculations, and as you know, one could never say of me that I'm at home in that universe. Dragan Mišović undid three buttons on his shirt, slipped his hand inside, and pulled out a thick hardcover notebook. Don't worry, he said, you needn't learn all of this, but it will be useful for you to know at least some of the foundations of mathematical calculations that may come up. I stared, incredulous, at the notebook in his hands. What foundations? I finally asked. And who might bring them up? What I really wanted to ask was what sort of relationship he had with Margareta, I even felt a dagger of jealousy, which slowly, though implacably, pierced my heart. The problem with Margareta, said Dragan Mišović, is that she spreads herself too thin, and I've told her a thousand times to prepare her concept, and, more important, to follow through consistently, but she is never willing to accept this. He shrugged. There are things, he said, we'll never understand, no point in fussing about them. If he keeps on talking about Margareta like this, I thought, the dagger might fly in the opposite direction. I am still astonished today at the thought: Is it possible that I'd succumbed to jealousy like a hot-faced teenager? Why was I so jealous anyway? Because of what I'd imagined might happen, not because of anything real, but something unreal, nonexistent. On the other hand, isn't all jealousy like that? Isn't jealousy always something we're imagining might happen between a person we love and somebody else? So I stood there, or actually sat there facing Dragan Mišović, and while he talked about calculating probabilities, permutations, combinations and variations, or whatever all those mathematical functions are called, I was mending my broken and pierced heart. You never know, Dragan Mišović was saying, how the descent will actually work, whether the guardians of the Well will step forward with questions, or whether they'll only watch, perhaps concealed, through a hole or from behind a corner. The question, therefore, he continued, is how to respond if you are told, for instance, that the person who is entering, or going down, or climbing up, should know all the alphabets, must be familiar with the combinations of all the letters, as well as with the two hundred thirty-one gates of the alphabets, which are inscribed in the ninth sphere and divided into sixty parts? I had no idea what he was saying. That is Abulafi's text on making the golem, said Dragan Mišović, and the bit that comes next is especially important. He cleared his throat as if getting ready to recite: Take pure powder, spin a wheel, start running the permutations until you have done all two hundred thirty-one gates, and then you will receive the influence of wisdom. Afterward take a cup full of pure water and a spoon, and fill the spoon with powder. Sprinkle the powder into the water, and in the process blow gently over the powder. In a breath say God's name until the breath is spent. Start with the head, until you have completed the first eight rows, in order to save the head. And so it goes, in sequence, said Dragan Mišović, bearing in mind that Abulafi warns that the point is not to teach a person to act as God does, but to understand the Lord better, and cleave unto him like a plant in the wind. That means, he said, that if someone asks you to calculate the combinations of God's name of seventy-two letters, you must know the number of combinable letters, and that this number is the same for every place in the name. Listen, I told him, don't you think you are expecting a bit much of me, not even Superman would be able to understand all of this in such a short time. The difficulties are only superficial, answered Dragan Mišović, but, of course, first you must shed your fear of mathematics. No one has ever prepared for a math exam in two days, I shouted, perhaps a little louder than I'd meant to. I was burning with a desire to ask what his role was in all this, which I didn't ask, allowing the number of unknowns I'd brought in with me to be nearly equal to the knowns, and that therefore, at least for me, this complex equation had become insoluble. Dragan Mišović didn't give up. He leafed through his notebook, quoted various sections, wrote out examples, underlined things, then started again at the beginning, so that I had to make yet another pot of coffee, stronger and more bitter than the last, and after Dragan left, I felt the acid rising to my throat, and, standing by the window, ate a crust of dry bread, hoping that, like a sponge, it would sop up the acid in my stomach. Each time, however, when I leafed through the papers on which Dragan had written out the calculations and instructions, the power of the acid revived, and when I had used up all the bread I stopped studying them. I was furious that my knowledge of math wasn't better, which was probably where the stomach pain came from, but what really got me was Dragan Mišović's passing remark that I should be ready to answer in case someone asked me a question. Whom did he have in mind? And did I dare believe this story about a plot within another larger plot, which was probably only part of an even larger plot? In any other situation I would have answered in the negative; I do not know why I hesitated at the time; perhaps because of the manuscript, which had demonstrated its supernatural power and kept reminding me that language, and therefore writing, is a living organism, a sort of benign virus that dwells in a person, and can survive on its own. I flipped the manuscript open the way I used to open the Chinese Book of Changes, without making an effort to cast the sticks or coins and work up the trigrams and hexagrams, leaving it instead to chance, which is just another word for destiny, to answer my question. I opened the manuscript to page 110, and in the left corner read that Eleazar had once been angry at God and told him he had seen through his explanation that it had not been possible to create a perfect world because in doing so he would have been making a copy of himself, in which case there would have been two identical gods, and if there could be two, why not three or four? You are talking in vain, Eleazar upbraided God, you should at least know that the truth cannot be hidden. A perfect world was not created because in a perfect world there would be no need for any god, not for one, nor for a whole multitude, ranted Eleazar, or else the world is perfect, because the evil is as much yours as the good is, just as the night and all its living and not living creatures are as much yours as the day full of radiance and serenity, then in that scheme of things you appear as someone who can offer protection, though in moments of great testing you hide like a bashful bride or a child who has broken a bowl and, fearful of being punished, points at whoever is standing nearest him. There was no indication as to whom Eleazar had in mind, who was bowing down under the weight of God's index finger, because that fragment, as kept happening with the manuscript, turned into a copy of a document of the Royal War Council of November 1781, communicating the emperor's will that the Zemun Jews, like all the Jews in the empire, would be allowed to use their language for religious services, but that within two years' time they'd have to expunge it from their business ledgers and documents, including their wills and contracts drawn up for regulating business. I closed the manuscript and opened it again to page 110. The part about Eleazar was still there, but it was up in the right-hand corner and it melted into another text, a document on the relationship between God and the Shekhinah. The ten Sephirot, it said, are the presence of the being of God, but Adam sinned, and he thought that the tenth, lowest Sephirot, called Malkhut, or Kingdom, was the whole of the divine being. This separated the Shekhinah, the feminine presence of God dwelling in that Sephirot, from the wholeness of the divine being, and it left God and the Shekhinah in a mutual yearning and a desire to reunite. To this day they are sometimes joined and sometimes not, depending on whether people sin, which drives them apart, or perform good deeds, which brings God and the Shekhinah close again. It should be repeated time and time again just how important it is to perform good deeds, for if God is not with the Shekhinah, he is seeking another female companion, and that other female companion will be Lilith, mistress of the demonic hordes, prepared to destroy everything that can be destroyed. So this is the obligation, then, I thought, this union of the male and female elements, which, if done properly, secures the normal functioning of the supreme being. Man must move God, so that God can move man; one influences the other, the one cannot exist without the other. I closed the manuscript and went over to the window. I looked to the left, I looked to the right, then up, then down, but nowhere did I see anyone looking like God. Yes, it was Thursday, a working day, and he prefers to appear on Shabbat, who knows where he was just then. Here Marko would have elbowed his way in, if only he had been there beside me, and he would have said that what I was saying was absurd, for if God was omnipresent, he did not come and go, he was always there and missed nothing. I might have argued that God could shrink, reduce himself to the size of a dot, then there would be things good and bad beyond his ken. I would have hoped that Marko would not ask why God would shrink as if he were cheap fabric, because I had no answer. I knew that he shrank once long ago, when he created the universe, and I knew that he could be no larger than he was, though he could be smaller, but I also knew that my knowledge was shaky and would not serve me. I ought to calm down, I said to myself, my nose glued to the windowpane. The day wore on, it would soon be over, and then it would be Friday, and the beginning of Shabbat, and the obligation I had to Margareta. And not just to her. That too Marko would have loved: that I'm referring to the sexual act as an obligation, and if one thing is not an obligation, and cannot be an obligation, he'd say, it is the moment of union. And I would have had to admit he was right. I stepped back from the window, wandered aimlessly through the apartment, and ended up in the kitchen. The very thought that I should not be nervous as I awaited Friday sundown was making me nervous. Maybe, I thought, I should meditate, erase all from the mirror of my consciousness, but when I tried to imagine myself sitting in a chair, back straight, harmonizing my breathing with the general rhythm of the cosmos, I gave up. I had only one possibility left: to eat something. I remembered how as a boy I liked eating bread spread with lard and sprinkled with sugar, and at the thought my mouth watered, but I had nothing to stop it with. Lard had been replaced with cooking oil, and I could have gone up and down the entire stairwell and rung the doorbells of all my neighbors, and chances were I would not have found anyone who had a spoonful of lard to lend me. I had sugar, true, and I remembered another treat from my childhood: a slice of bread soaked in water and sprinkled with sugar, but I felt like eating lard and the thought of water had no appeal. I noticed a sheet of paper on the table with the yin and yang symbol on it, the one I had crumpled, then smoothed out, with the announcement for the tai chi course, to be held on the street I wasn't familiar with, so I had to look it up on the commercial map of Zemun. It was not in the upper part of town, as I had assumed, but near the city park, and it had indeed changed its name: the earlier Slovenian or Croatian locality had been changed to the name of a Serbian scientist, though my friends still referred to it by its old name. Odd, isn't it: when street names were changed after World War II, many people, possibly out of spite, continued using the prewar names, but once the new government imposed new names after the 1990s war, they preferred, at least for a time, the names from the Communist era. Perhaps it would be best to call the streets by number: governments change, the numbers remain the same. I have a feeling Dragan Mišović wouldn't agree, though I don't see why he wouldn't, but this only goes to show that there's always someone who has an ax to grind, though it also may mean that I'm overly anxious to please, and that, by always making sure I have an exit strategy, I invoke, or rather invent, the ax grinders myself. All in all, this unnecessary suspicion was one more proof that I needed to go out to walk off a little of the tension and edginess, as well as my nervous hunger. I had to hurry, because it was past six, which was the time the class started, so I dashed to the city park, making my way through longer and thicker shadows. The address on the flier took me to spacious rooms on the ground floor of a shabby five-story building, which probably used to house the tenants' building council or a branch office of the civil defense system, and there was a slightly lighter patch on the grimy wall where Tito's portrait used to hang. It felt as if that portrait had had its day a century ago, though only fifteen years have passed since then, and now it seems, maybe because I no longer live there, that its day never happened. Then again, maybe that's the way it is, maybe nothing ever exists, it's only somebody's thought, upon which we stumble accidentally and believe it to be our own. I will never find out, of course, just as I will never find out so many other things before death knocks on my door, or, as things now stand, at my heart, which a doctor here described to me in the past tense, as if it no longer existed. He clenched his fist and said: This is how your heart used to be. Then he opened his hand and said: This is how it burst. He stared into the palm of his hand and said: Goodbye, heart. I too stared at his hand and saw nothing. Goodbye, heart, I repeated after him, just as I am doing now, but back then, in the rooms that, despite the Eastern energy, were utterly gloomy, my mind was not on my heart. I looked at the fifteen people, mostly middle-aged women, doing warm-up exercises, as a young woman who introduced herself as the instructor of the Taoist version of tai chi courteously explained to me. She repeated that this was Taoist tai chi, as if I knew that there were different schools for the study of the martial arts, which, unlike others, is not in the service of attack or defense. The young woman clapped her hands and announced that the class would show me several characteristic postures, and while the group moved smoothly, wavelike, giving me the feeling that I was under water, she called out the names of individual postures, colorful names that were quickly self-explanatory, such as "grasps the bird's tail," "white crane spreads its wings," "arms move like clouds," or "creep low like snake." Maybe I should have joined in to learn how to master my inner energy, maybe then I never would have met that cardiologist for whom the heart is a balloon, though in the end, I admit, it makes no difference. Sooner or later every heart pumps its last, no matter what we call it, or whether we speak of it at all. Silence is a wall around wisdom, but if the wisdom is lacking, the silence can't bring it into being. So I stood there, watched the harmonious movements, and wondered why I was there. Nothing in the room or in the appearance of the people seemed to have anything to do with the rest of what was happening, so I could move on. If I did move on, however, I thought, then I'd be bringing everything into doubt, because if I doubted one of the possible threads, wasn't I questioning all the rest? And what does it mean, to doubt or to believe? What makes these similar and what distinguishes them, and is it possible to believe in doubt while at the same time doubting belief? No, Marko would have said, you don't need a cardiologist. The balloon you've got, he would say, isn't in your heart but in your head. You could do a circus act, he would tell me, with the rest of the freaks, and over your cage there would be a sign: THE HUMAN BALLOON. That's not funny, he would have said to me if

I had started to laugh, though tears would have been more apt. Tears are always apt, I concur with that, though they are never good if you are crying over yourself. Two or three times, alas, I did just that, I was trapped in a dead end and thought tears were my only solution. I'm not ashamed of those tears, even the balloon doctor would have approved, the one Marko was thinking of, or the one I was thinking Marko might have been thinking of, as I thought of our conversation and his presence. The previous sentence just shows the insecurity that possessed me then, the chaos that had become my order, the instability that had replaced my sense of balance. It would have been better if I had, without any thoughts, watched the postures of the introductory tai chi class as they spread waves of calm with their harmony, especially when they leaned sideways, like clouds, as their instructor said, though to me they looked more like sea waves, or better yet, like grain swaying at the lightest breath of wind. I had one more thing to try: I leaned confidentially over to the instructor and asked whether in tai chi there was a movement called "triangles opening." She looked at me, a wisp of doubt flitted across her eyes; in tai chi, she said, as far as she knew, there was nothing mathematical. It was true that the feet had to rest on the ground at a forty-five-degree angle to the axis of movement, but that could be learned without the use of a protractor. She drew my attention to the feet of the class participants, and indeed, they were all at forty-five-degree angles, then all lifted their right leg at the same time, and I saw that row of legs slowly straightening as if dealing a slow-motion blow as a farewell. A moment later I stepped out into the street. From the window of the barracks across the way, a soldier watched me. I recalled my own military service and the loneliness that fed on me like a bedbug, so I waved cheerfully, but he didn't react; instead, if I could trust my eyes from such a distance, he scowled and pursed his lips with scorn. I pictured a company of soldiers doing tai chi early in the morning instead of their routine morning limbering exercises, and that image of the soldiers in their olive drab uniforms moving slowly and mindfully over the concrete surface of the exercise grounds restored my good mood. I loathed the army and was sorry I had spent a year of my life in it, but an army using tai chi would, no doubt, be something different. I remembered our portly sergeant, and when I pictured him trying to stand on one leg like a rooster, I laughed out loud. None of that, however, could alter the fact that there was no connection between the tai chi class and the Well, which I found bewildering, since everything else had been tied in some way, or at least I'd been able to construe something that was convincing enough. For example, I had interpreted the car parked in front of the pharmacy as a lure, to draw me further into a story that I myself had constructed. Had that been the intention of the conspirators, if I can call them that? To persuade me to create a framework of my own, to be the protagonist who invents himself, chooses those elements he finds most convincing, rejects those that have no place in the construct of a reality that, in essence, did not exist? I came to a stop, then moved slowly on. Had I allowed myself to be drawn into a game in which I was by no means in control, as I'd thought I might be not so long ago, but rather an auxiliary piece, a pawn someone was skillfully moving while the pawn was certain that the choice of moves was his alone? I paused again, by the department store, and turned and hurried back to the building near the army barracks. The soldier was still staring through the window, scowling, and when he saw me watching him he winked, or at least so it seemed to me as I walked quickly by. There was no one in the tai chi classroom except that patch on the grimy wall where the picture of Tito had been. Where had they gone? How long had it taken me to leave the building, cross in front of the barracks and walk toward the department store, sidling between parked cars: Five minutes? Ten? I tried to reconstruct everything in the room when I first entered: I remembered a hat stand, on which hung items of clothing, as well as two large boards with diagrams of various postures, sketches showing dance steps, but no one was there. The walls were bare, the floor clean, the window shut. I walked around, knocked on the walls in search of a secret passageway, banged the floor with my foot to detect an echo of emptiness, then opened the window, looking for a ladder or signs left by people who had jumped out. I found nothing. Someone had made an extraordinary effort to clear out all I had seen, that much was obvious, but why? Was it because they hadn't expected me to come back, or was it precisely because they knew I would come back? If the latter, how could they have known? I shuddered at that thought, because if they had known, then they knew everything else, or they were managing my choices and actions with such precision that never for a moment did it occur to me that I was someone other than myself. I'm not thinking here of Enoch the water carrier or Eleazar or an ancient Kabbalist, which I was more prepared to believe, but someone I knew nothing about, someone about whom, clearly, I was not supposed to know. I walked around the room one more time, pausing below the space where Tito's portrait had hung, as if I could learn something from it. I learned nothing, though for a moment I thought perhaps I was overdoing things, the tai chi lesson had simply ended, and the people who had attended it left, taking with them their props. I went out into the street and walked by the barracks. The soldier was in the same place. I asked him if he had seen some women with a hat stand. The soldier tapped his forehead a few times with his index finger, then vanished. Such is my fate, I remember thinking, the closer I get to something, the farther it gets from me, and in the end it will all disappear, just as it had in the past, until I end up alone and disappear myself. I say I remember, but in fact I don't remember whether I remember or not, and I am guessing I say that because I did indeed end up alone and because nothing remained for me except to anticipate that I too would vanish. I don't regret that; everybody, after all, can expect the same fate, and it makes no difference whether a person has made peace with the fact or not, the fact that the only clear meaning of life is death, and all other interpretations, philosophizing about the fullness of life on this earth and the necessity of happiness or the promise of another life as a reward for obedience, are just empty prattle. This has never been as clear to me as it is now, as I stand by the window, alone, owning nothing that anyone could covet except this pen, which is spending its inky heart as I spend mine, torn between fullness and emptiness, between insight and exhaustion. Words, of course, don't count; they're something else, as someone wrote recently, they never say what the speaker means for them to say, but what the listener wants to hear. I'm a little like the soldier whom I asked about the hat rack, except there's no one here to ask me, and the tapping of the index finger on the forehead can refer only to me, or more precisely, to my reflection in the mirror, to whom I sometimes turn even if I am not shaving, with a question requiring an urgent answer. I knew none of this while I stood under the barracks window. The soldier had left, a heavy cloak of grief settled on me, and when I turned to go, I staggered under its weight like a believer bearing a cross in a Christian procession, the difference being that unlike zealous believers, I did not want the cloak. It was smothering me. When I got home, I was barely able to stand, it was even a strain to sit, my only comfort the thought that Thursday would soon be over, and I fell asleep, repeating the word *Friday* as if it were a mantra of the days of the week. I woke up with an erection so hard, it almost hurt. Not yet, I said to my penis, and it sagged obediently. I took a shower, washed my hair and shaved, put the water on for coffee, and went out to get my paper. At the front door I was greeted by a familiar sight: a plastic bag reeking with a heavy stench. I leaned over to pick it up and jumped back horrified: instead of the usual excrement, the severed head of a cat leered from the bag. It was lying in a bloody heap of intestines and innards, undoubtedly from its gut, and heaving with maggots. The cat's eyes were open, the teeth bared, and I could imagine the terrible agony it had gone through. The message was crystal clear, but I would have understood it had it been written on a piece of paper or on the wall of the stairwell, no need for a cat to suffer, and the feeling that filled me was not dread, but fury. I took the bag down to the garbage bin, and for a few moments I stood by it, mutely paying my respects while fat blowflies buzzed around, then I bought my paper, went back to the apartment, and made my coffee. The weather forecast promised a nice day, the only bright news item in the paper; everything else was gloom and doom, even the commentary on the flights reinstated to Sarajevo and trains running again to Zagreb and Ljubljana. There were too many obituaries, with photographs of the deceased who looked as if they had been dead long before they died. It was a horrible beginning to a day that was supposed to change the world, not the entire world, naturally, but the one part that stubbornly defied change. I got up and started pacing nervously around the apartment, staring at the pieces of furniture and various objects as if seeing them for the first time. I looked at the phone in the same way and then it rang. Margareta had promised to call in the morning, to give me the final instructions; the voice coming from the receiver, however, belonged to the editor of *Minut*. He didn't know what was going on, it looked as if I had jangled someone's nerves, he said, maybe more than one person's, and I should watch what I did for the next few days, especially tomorrow, when *Minut* would be distributed. Someone had attempted to break into the editorial offices the night before, but the night watchman had called the police and their arrival, speedy to everyone's surprise, chased the burglars away. If they were burglars, I said. Of course they weren't burglars, agreed the editor. Also, a young man had made an attempt to get into the printing press where *Minut* was typeset and printed. He claimed he had been sent by the editorial office to make some last-minute alterations to the computer type for the issue. He had a pass and a note written on *Minut* letterhead, but the porter insisted on calling the editor, which the man tried to prevent, unsuccessfully, hurling insults at him and threatening to thrash him. Something dangerous is cooking, son, said the editor, and a bit of extra caution would not be a bad idea. He had never called me "son" before, and tears nearly welled in my eyes. I thought of his cat Feliks, and I could hardly speak. My eyes are tearing now too, even though several years have passed since then, and Feliks is probably in cat heaven. If my soul is ever assigned to pass into the body of an animal, I will dispatch it to Feliks, I've decided. I don't know whether the soul chooses its next host or someone else sees to that, someone in charge of the archive of the living and the dead, responsible, so to speak, for the database in the celestial computer. The celestial computer, of course, is God, since he knows everything, including what he doesn't know. The conversation with the editor of *Minut* left me with a bitter taste in my mouth, and I could hardly wait for Margareta to call. I said nothing to her about the conversation with the editor, nor would I have had a chance to, because she didn't let me get a word in edgewise. She recited a long list of my duties, which I assiduously noted on the pad by the phone. I did manage to complain about how many instructions I'd been given by Dragan Mišović, and she consoled me, promising she would be by my side and she would help, if help was needed. She didn't know, or pretended not to know, what was to happen as we went down the Well, or more precisely as we ascended the Well, no matter how preposterous that might sound. One certainly goes down most wells, she said, but in this one you ascend, because it is a path to higher spheres and the Sephirot. Everything else would be synchronized with the beginning of Shabbat: the people writing the prayer with their bodies would be taking their places at 6:22 in the evening, when the sun goes down; the preparation of the mixture for the golem would start immediately thereafter; at the same time another group would be placed in the area of the Well and they would take upon themselves the structure of the Tree of Sephirot; finally, after midnight, the union of the King and his Saturday bride would complete the process, and they would enter the Well, which would be open wide. At that point Margareta stopped and there was no way I could get her to proceed with the details. Should I have given up, or at least felt concerned? Now I'd know the answer, but then, no reason to hide it, I was longing for the possibility of union with Margareta, and that was all I could think of as she elucidated their strategy. Of course, she said, we are making a symbolic golem, not a real one, except it will have real powers. Something like an invisible man, I said, except it's an invisible golem. Margareta laughed, then coughed and said I should be taking this more seriously. A single mistake, one little mistake, she said, and everything will fall apart. I hope I won't make a mistake, I said, and remembering the morning, and the taxi ride, I felt the beginning of a new erection, as if I were talking to one of those women who touch themselves and pretend to come while the phone bill mushrooms with lightning speed. It wouldn't be a bad idea, Margareta recommended, for me to go to a service at the synagogue, because that would help me focus my spirit on all that was happening, and there was no reason to be at the Well before midnight. But I am not a believer, I defended myself weakly, knowing that in fact I wanted to attend the service. When all this was done, she felt I should become a Jew. I thought I was one already, I answered, because of the soul I carry. Yes, said Margareta, but don't forget that there is also the body, and it is necessary to commit the body to God, otherwise it won't work. I imagined a surgical blade on my penis and the blood dripping, there had to be blood involved, and I shuddered. Don't worry, announced Margareta, who seemed able to see me through the phone line, it doesn't hurt at all with a little local anesthetic. The thought of blood reminded me of the severed cat's head, and that reignited the fury in me, which, as is the case in this sort of chain of cause and effect, produced more acid in my stomach, and after the conversation I ended up curled in a ball in the armchair, beset by acid indigestion and gas pains. So undignified for a person who was shortly supposed to play a decisive role in a tangled game of an ethnic group's attempt to secure peace for itself in a place where more and more people had both symbolically and literally been taking potshots at all the ethnic groups living there. Finding an enemy in such places is a favorite pastime, relished in equal measure by ordinary people, the political elite, intellectuals, and artists. There is nothing better than a well-laid-out conspiracy about the existence of conspiracy, for everyone except those singled out as the conspirators, whose repeated denials are seen as proof of the very opposite intentions. Of course it's one thing to practice this as a theoretical discourse and another to be part of it at the crossroads of converging hatreds. But, to come to the point: at six o'clock I was in the courtyard of the Belgrade synagogue. Around the table were seated people, most of whom I had met before, though Dača and his hat were not among them. Three elderly women were there, and that led me to think of the Fates, though the Fates belong to another tradition. Someone must have to snip the threads of life for Jews too, because they do not live forever. True, the women looked nothing like the mythological beings, and one of them was so tiny that she was more likely to have come from the world of dwarves than from Olympus, where the Fates, I'm only guessing here, dwell. I was surprised to see Jaša Alkalaj at the table, though I'd assumed he was involved in some aspect of the conspiracy, as Margareta was his daughter. But maybe it was just as natural for a father to be somewhere other than where his offspring were? Also, more and more often I refer to the plan that Margareta and her friends were devising as a conspiracy, giving credence to Marko and others who mock the notion of conspiracy, at least as rendered in

American movies. This is not a case of conspiracy, but a case of my lack of concentration, my haste to bring this document to a close, if I had the time, I'd carefully peruse all the pages, and wherever the word appeared, I'd replace it with another, but I haven't got the time, because as it is I fear that it will all slip out of my grasp, if it hasn't already done so. This is not a book of sand, after all, that can be read however the reader may wish, but a text the reader's soul should use to climb with the same effort my soul needs to descend the written pages, nearing the inevitable end. Yes, it is terrible that a book has an end, yet life goes on, somehow that fact cheapens every effort at writing, because it means that books are always the measure of something finite, they remind us that we have before us only a limited number of days, weeks, months, and years, that afterward nothing makes any sense anyway, though it is just as possible to claim the opposite: that the finality of the book helps us free ourselves of the illusion of eternal life, whether as a real possibility or as a religious symbol. I don't know if during the service the rabbi said anything about eternal life, I know no Hebrew, but after a while I got bored and started looking around. Maybe the person speaking wasn't the rabbi but his assistant, I didn't understand what Jaša Alkalaj had whispered in my ear as we entered the synagogue, and later I forgot to ask. The service ended, the worshipers started rising and congratulating one another on the beginning of Shabbat, and a line quickly formed in front of the rabbi, which I joined behind Jaša Alkalaj. I don't know what I'd been expecting, but the rabbi merely pressed my hand, saying, Shabbat shalom, then extended his hand to the next person in line, one of the Fates, behind whom waited the other two. He didn't even look me straight in the eyes, I told Jaša as we left the synagogue courtyard. I sounded like a jealous teenager. What were you thinking, answered Jaša, that he'd kiss you on both cheeks and on the forehead too? Besides, he continued, chances are he noticed you weren't listening too closely to the service, and that is unforgivable. He saw my anxious expression and laughed. On his face I recognized features that had been copied into Margareta's face, and I thought that it was absurd to be standing here, talking to a man with whose daughter I was supposed to make love later, though not for pleasure but for a higher purpose. The pleasure would actually be a bonus, because I couldn't imagine a mere mechanical performance of intercourse, though only then, as I spoke with Jaša Alkalaj, did I realize how many subtle and not so subtle levels this entailed. We'd have to make love carefully and in harmony with a ritual that had not been fully explained to me: staying mindful of the obligations that were apparently awaiting as I went down the Well, or ascended it; prepared to answer questions in which there was more math than I cared to know; and finally, ready for consequences that I had not been alerted to, because they were nowhere written down or spelled out. Most mystical texts set out preparations for travel in the finest detail, but very little space is devoted to description of what has been accomplished by following those instructions. I had always assumed that every mystic began from scratch, which may well be true, because to be a mystic is something so personal, something above and beyond a mere set of rules applied to life. No one has achieved illumination by simply going off to a Zen monastery, getting up at dawn, scrubbing the common rooms, eating rice, and going out to beg. For illumination something else is required, something that belongs to that person alone, something that is that person and is activated when they begin the mystical practice. In brief, if I was not mistaken, Margareta and her co-conspirators had not been through a Kabbalistic experience of their own before, which didn't mean that this wasn't available to them. Indeed, sometimes a game—if we can call a game this stab of theirs with no anchor in experience—may produce results more serious than a well-rehearsed scientific approach subverted by technical perfection. All I could do was wait another few hours and test this in practice, but my excitement was mounting and I could no longer concentrate on the conversation with the group of the faithful in the synagogue courtyard. The three Fates walked past and I could have sworn I heard a snipping sound of scissors opening and shutting, despite their smiles. I watched them walk toward the gateway and thought how odd it was that people were so calm, going through their daily and weekly routines, while only a few kilometers away their fellow countrymen were preparing for a decisive battle. The people with whom I was standing, not counting Jaša Alkalaj, obviously had no clue, and I was only guessing that Jaša knew, because in no way did he let on that he knew what was happening, or that I was a part of the story. When I told him I had to leave because of obligations that could not be put off, he merely nodded, which could have meant anything. A body is not a book, just as gestures are not words written down, hence the possibilities for interpretation are all the greater, though a lack of precision is characteristic of both words and gestures, and they both mean several things at once. I didn't want to assume that Jaša Alkalaj was nodding merely to say goodbye, so I told myself that in this movement, just as in some secret Masonic greeting, there was tacit respect and support. One thing I could not understand was why Margareta had insisted I go to the synagogue, yet she herself didn't feel it necessary to do so. For the second time recently I felt I'd been lured onto the wrong path, as if someone deliberately meant for me to be at one place instead of another. When I left the synagogue courtyard, I came across the three elderly ladies standing one right next to the other, whispering as if someone on the street might overhear them. They stopped when they saw me, their gazes were inquisitive while their lips curved in a trace of a smile. For a moment I shifted aimlessly from foot to foot, then walked by them and headed for Zeleni Venac. This time I heard no snipping of scissors. I decided not to take Carica Milica Street but to go down Pop-Lukina and from Pop-Lukina I turned onto a street that ran to a little park, from which narrow, steep stairs led straight down to the bus station for Zemun. A dog took a long time sniffing at my shoes, refusing to obey a woman calling to it from the other end of the park. I looked across the river at the sky over Zemun and saw a ray of light piercing a cluster of clouds. I looked down at the dog, fearing it might pee on my shoes and pants, and when I looked back at Zemun the ray of light had gone and the clouds dispersed, and I wondered whether I'd seen it at all. Sometimes we see what we want to see, I know that, but I didn't want to see anything in particular, just as I wasn't looking in the belief I'd see something. The dog was finally satisfied with the smell that wafted from my shoes and it scampered back to its owner, while I stared for another fifteen minutes in vain at the sky over Zemun. Only later, in the bus, did I realize why the dog had been so taken with my shoes: I had stepped in dog shit somewhere along the way, which was always an unwanted possibility on the streets of Belgrade, and I would have to go home and change my shoes. The first thing I noticed when I got off the bus, before I crossed the street, was that the lights were on in my apartment. Sometimes I leave a light on deliberately, usually a table lamp in the living room, but I would never leave all the lights blazing, and I surely wouldn't do that in broad daylight, because evening had only begun to slink along the sky when I left for the synagogue. Every nerve, every inch of my body shouted: Run! However, I walked slowly, full of caution, one foot after the other, like the pensioners who walk along the Zemun quay, my muscles trembling from the effort of restraint, like a flag in the wind. Why do I compare muscles to flags, perhaps because, walking and trembling, I was visualizing a charge from one of the partisan movies, with banner in hand and a shout on my lips, a machine gun at the ready to spray everything in sight as I entered the apartment, or the bunker, in my thoughts. Instead of stepping into a bunker, I stepped first into the musty hallway of my building. The door to the building was locked, I unlocked it cautiously, as if the enemy was lurking right behind. Then, stair by stair, my back propped against the wall, I went up to my apartment. As I climbed the stairs, the stink of the dog shit on my shoes filled my nostrils and I could barely keep from vomiting. I assume that when the body is tense and the mind focused on possible danger, the senses are sharpened owing to some chemical fusion in the brain. I don't know how else to explain it, though the explanation is moot; I mention it only because I thought I ought to remove the shoes, and with them in my hands, if need be, I could lunge at the people who had broken into my apartment, and the image of me lunging at a band of burglars, brandishing my foul-smelling shoes, flinging myself every which way, made me laugh out loud. I managed to calm down after a few moments, wiped my tearing eyes, went up the remaining four steps, and leaned my ear on the door. Not a sound. If anyone was still in the apartment, they were keeping quiet, waiting for my next move. I conjured that image: me listening at one side of the door, my opponent listening on the other side, so our ears are nearly touching. I pressed my ear against the door until it hurt, then carefully turned the doorknob. The door opened. I went into the front hall, listened, and, spurred on by the silence, stepped into the living room. I took a few steps, then went back to get an umbrella that was hooked over the coat tree; an umbrella is no semiautomatic weapon, but it is a weapon of sorts, and that gave me a measure of security. There was no one in the apartment; I looked behind the wardrobes, under the bed, moved the armchair and the curtain, checked the pantry; the person who had been in the apartment had long since gone. There was nothing that even suggested anyone had been there, nothing had been moved, none of the things on the tables or shelves, none in the cupboards. I'd imagined entering an apartment in which nothing was in its place, but instead of stepping into chaos I walked into an order that had been preserved. This was comforting, but it did nothing to diminish the sense of insecurity, and moreover, the certainty that the apartment was polluted by the very fact that someone had been there. An apartment is part of one's body, and if someone intrudes on it, it is as if they have intruded on one's person. In this case, since everything was untouched, it wasn't like a symbolic rape, though it could be compared to someone pressing up against you, uninvited, in public transportation. But time was passing, I needed to get moving toward the center of the Sephirot, and it was not until I started switching off the lights around the apartment that I noticed what I should have noticed straight away: the manuscript of *The Well* was spread open. And not only that. When I leaned over to look at the page, I thought there might be something wrong. All it took was shutting the manuscript and opening it again to confirm my suspicion: the manuscript on my table was not the same one I'd had in my possession before. My first thought was of Margareta: if she had taken the original copy from the museum, why wouldn't she take the living translation? Hadn't she said she'd return the manuscript when they no longer needed it? True, the planned event had not yet taken place, but she'd sounded confident enough, also she may have just started preparing for the next phase? I could breathe a sigh of relief. Could I really breathe a sigh of relief? I had no proof that the manuscript was in Margareta's hands, and just as she might have been the one to take it, so anyone else might have. It wasn't clear, of course, why anyone else would have made the effort to replace it with the unliving version of the translation; this was also less than clear in the version of the story that had Margareta taking it, but at least I knew that she had access to the other copies and that she would consider the act of exchanging the manuscript a sort of just reward for the effort I'd made. As I stood by the unliving translation, this is what I thought of: payment of debt. I thought of something else: perhaps this was happening so the living manuscript of the translation could be stored in a safe place, or where no one would think of looking for it? Or more precisely, I thought, banging myself on the forehead, where it would serve as a lure, drawing attention away from the original living manuscript, the original book of sand, which could be in only one place: at the entrance to the Well. I looked at my watch, it was nearly eleven, I'd have to hurry, I took off my shoes, put on another pair, glanced at myself in the mirror, flicked a lock of hair aside, turned off the lights in the apartment, locked the door, and rushed down the stairs. I left the building, paused, looked to the left, looked to the right, then went straight to the quay, taking the same route I'd followed three months before. Then it was daytime, now it was night; then the promenade was full of people, now it was deserted; then the rides had been running at the playground, now the horses on the merry-go-round and parts of the train were shrouded under waterproof covers; then I was an apparently uninterested observer, now I was in the middle of something I couldn't properly define. How to describe hatred? How to explain prejudice? How to explain suicidal tendencies at the level of the collective, even of a whole nation? How to find the common denominator for events that belong to different categories, histories, and beliefs? Too many questions. On this last page or two there have been eight, if I count them correctly. I always thought that books began with questions and ended with answers, but in my case it's different, at least as far as questions are concerned, they seem to pile up at the end, while the answers are scattered all over, which is just fine, I believe, because this is not a book, I never meant to write a book, as I may have said before, though I may be mistaken, since no one who writes lengthy works, regardless of the subject matter, remembers every word he or she has written. There are times when I dream of parts of this document that I am sure have never crossed my lips or the tip of my ballpoint pen, but when I leaf through it later, I find them all there. Proof for me once again that every text, every document, every book, all that is composed of words, is made of sand or, better yet, of water. Nothing is less constant than words, yet nothing lasts as long as words do, and in that paradox lie the beginning and the end of all writing, and every human effort, I mused as I walked along the quay. Of course the action defines the man, but the same can be said of words. After all, words are the actions of the mind, aren't they? I turned, as if expecting a precise answer, and in the distance spotted three figures heading my way. It might not mean a thing, of course, and I calmly continued on toward the Venezia, but when I turned again, they were closer, and this prompted me to speed up and veer off from the quay into a street running parallel, where the shadows were denser and the doorways offered temporary shelter. I slipped into one, crouched behind a door with broken glass panes, and decided to wait a few minutes. I counted slowly, as if trying to determine how soon the thunder would follow after a lightning flash, and when I got to three hundred, which might have been about five minutes, I went back out. Nobody was there. The three men had disappeared, or if they had had anything to do with me, they had turned into one of the side streets, tricked by my ruse. I was near the elementary school, which meant I had already entered into the world of the Sephirot contained in the urban plan of the old part of Zemun between Glavna Street and the quay. That quarter is divided, roughly speaking, into nine blocks, which correspond to the Kabbalist Sephirot, though the tenth Sephirot, Malkhut, connected to the Shekhinah, is absent, and that absence, that asymmetry in the order, made it possible, at least as Margareta told it, to realize their plan. By renewing Malkhut, Margareta had said, the entire cosmos would be renewed, the balance of the divine powers would be reinstated, and, most important, the essential energy would be sparked for making the golem or protective shield or whatever it was they wanted to make. The Well was in the middle block, which corresponded to the Sephirah called Tiferet, or Beauty, and which on the human body occupied the navel and the heart. I kept going until I got to the corner of Zmaj Jovina Street. I should have wondered where the people were who were to write the essential prayers with their bodies, but I assumed they had accomplished that task, or, which sounded entirely plausible, they had taken their places in courtyards and apartments, hidden from curious and hostile eyes. I kept going, and the air around me seemed to thicken, slowing down my already cautious movements. On the left was the market, with stalls that had turned into greasy splotches of darkness, threatening, like nests from which wasps might come swarming out at any moment. I tried not to look at them, to pay no attention to the flickering shadows that played at the edge of my vision. When I passed the corner of the building that marked the beginning of the middle block, I stepped, or so it felt, into absolute silence. I looked at my feet, suddenly infinitely far from my body, and saw them as if in a silent movie, undulating and inconstant. They were mine, nonetheless, I thought, while I raised them with effort and steered them toward the goal, the old wooden gate that couldn't be far from here. And sure enough, sooner than I'd expected, I saw the heavy gate flung open, and the rectangular street lamp cast a path across the concrete that led into the inner court-yard. I stopped at the entrance, leaned on one of the wings of the gate, and looked at my shadow. How fitting that image is now, when I am no more than a shadow, slipping over things until it settles on the border between light and dark, in the narrow space between the real and the unreal. At the time, I was hoping for the silence to end so I could hear and recognize sounds and determine my next move. I stepped onto the path, reaching for my shadow, and of course, it fled from me. I took another two or three steps, and when it finally hid in the dark, I saw the familiar scene: the bench, the barberry bushes, the pump with the curving handle, the radiance that emanated from it as if it were coated in silver dust. I wanted to sit down on the bench, I was so drained by the effort of lifting my feet, but the instructions required the bench to remain empty until

Malkhut and the Shekhinah were ready to sit on it together. Fine, I thought, here is the King, so where is the Queen? I sounded arrogant to myself, though I wasn't thinking anything that didn't correspond to reality, or at least the reality we had agreed upon. I played the role assigned me, and I certainly wouldn't be the first actor to identify with a character. Then I noticed that the twigs on the barberry were moving, though there was no breeze. Not a vigorous movement, just a gentle swaying that I spotted only because I was eyeing the rim of the flowerpot as a possible perch for my aching feet. Just then the silver radiance emanating from the pump shimmered, and as it twisted like steam wafting from a kettle in which water is boiling, I realized what was happening: the Well was open, and the vibrating and swaying were caused by a draft coursing between the worlds. What a paradox, I recall thinking, that in a country where drafts are considered one of the most alarming natural phenomena, they are the very signal marking the passageway to parallel space or a new dimension of existence. Let us hope, I thought, that some vitriolic old woman doesn't hasten to block the influence of the draft of air on her fragile health. I had to laugh, and as my laughter bounced off the walls and slowly dissipated, I heard church bells. I didn't have to count, I knew they were tolling midnight, which meant that Margareta was late, and if she didn't turn up before the last chime of the bell, everything would be ruined. Suddenly, like Faulkner's character, I wanted to stop time, or rush off to the church and stop the bells from tolling, but just as his character realized that time would not stop, even if he ripped the hands off his watch, so I had to make my peace with the fact that I'm no superman, and even if I were to make it to the bell tower and wedge myself between the clapper and the lip, nothing would change. I wasn't sure what to do. The ringing of the bells was coming to an end, and once the sound of the last chime had faded and Margareta still hadn't appeared, I could go home. I went over to the bench anyway, and when I was three or four steps away, I felt the gusting of air currents. My trouser legs billowed, my hair fluttered, the chill air brushed my ears and head. The sound of the last clang of the clapper died away, and silence reigned. I thought I heard footsteps, but when I turned, a single drop of water sped downward from the shining pump to the netting covering the mouth of the drainage canal. The drop, I said, sped downward, but in fact it dripped slowly, and it felt as if I was following its drawn-out fall for hours. When it finally landed, I braced for the thud, but it merely slid between the metal interstices, lingering for a moment on one, like a gymnast who at the end of a figure looks as if she will never pull away from the vibrating spindle. I stood there for a moment longer, and then, suddenly assertive, I walked over to the bench and sat down. In the past, when I'd sat there, a powerful stillness had enveloped me accompanied by music, nearly celestial voices, but now there was a quiet rumbling, the muted noise that comes from a transformer that converts one kind of electricity into another. Of course I'm not saying that the Well was a transformer, but something inside it was surely being transformed into something else. I thought maybe I should get up and go, no point staying here any longer, especially if it had all been for naught, and I felt an odd bodilessness, as if I had been emptied out and made into a shell, into something resembling the shell that some insects shed in the process of maturing and transforming. This made me feel so fragile that I dared not move. I sat on the bench as if glued to it, the air streaming around me, a crackling sound filling my ears, and the radiance of the pump and barberries growing brighter and sharper. Then I felt the empty shell of my body gradually filling, and I could see the level of the substance rise from my feet to my belly, chest, and neck. I should hasten to add that *substance* is not the right word, because usually it refers to something material, something tangible, but what was pouring into me wasn't composed of particles but formed an indivisible whole, a compact mass I would like to call the visible manifestation of divine emanation, but I can't because I have no proof that this was indeed divine emanation, or anything else for that matter. As the substance rose to the upper edges of my body, a pleasant warmth spread, a kind of energy that freed me from that sense of fragility and made me at once heavy and light. I felt pressure on my back, an itch by my shoulder, and I thought: I'm becoming an angel. I cringe at the thought now, who was I to become an angel, but at that moment, in the Well, the thought caused no alarm. Feeling the discomfort in my shoulder, I really believed my skin would open and the tips of wings would sprout, moist and still sticky, like the wings of a baby bird clambering out of a cracking egg. I remember I was worried that I hadn't felt the same itch and pressure on the other shoulder, and I thought with horror that I might end up a one-winged angel, a crippled angel, unable to fly, unstable on the ground, a wobbly angel who would long in the end to shed its wing, even if that meant becoming a human again. Better a stable human being, I thought, than an angel tipping to one side. Meanwhile, the substance had risen to my neck and began rising toward my head, and I realized that what was happening was precisely what I'd been anticipating, meaning that the King and Queen were uniting in me, that the radiance of the Shekhinah was filling me, and that the physical union I'd counted on with such certainty had never actually been planned. That's one of the last things I remember. The substance had begun to fill my head, to rise to the crown of my head. I remember that I still had a moment to think, I'll drown! Then everything froze, and when I opened my eyes, I was in my apartment, in the armchair in front of the television set. The TV was off, and it was night outside. My feet were bare, and nowhere, no matter where I looked, could I see my socks and shoes. There was a buzz in my head, my nose was stuffed up, my neck was stiff, as if I had been sitting for a long time in a draft. Then I remembered the Well and the air currents coursing between the worlds, though I still didn't know how I had arrived home, just as I didn't know whether it was the same night outside, or a different one. A glance at the clock, which showed ten minutes to four, told me nothing about whether Sunday was beginning, or Monday, or, why not, Wednesday. It wouldn't have surprised me if it had been Wednesday because I felt exhausted, as if I hadn't slept for three days and three nights. The hole in my memory remained. Something had happened, and I had taken part in it, and now I couldn't recall a thing. I tried to get up, but I simply could not lift my head, not even when I put my hands behind it. The throbbing in my neck and temples was almost palpable: if I were to bend my neck more, the pain would ooze out of me like toothpaste from a squeezed tube. I sank back into the chair, and instantly every fiber of my being went taut: there were sounds of another presence in the apartment. I'm not alone, I'm not alone, I'm not alone, reverberated in my head while I feverishly tried to figure out what to do. Then I heard footsteps and the creaking of the parquet floor; they came closer, right behind me. They stopped. And who first came to mind? Marko, though I couldn't imagine how he'd have got into my apartment. On the other hand, I didn't know how I'd got there, especially barefoot. I thought of the picture of the Beatles marching across the street, and only Paul McCartney is barefoot, and there were rumors that his bare feet announced he was dead. I had never been one to go barefoot and I wondered what my feet symbolized, what the significance was of their bareness, and then I remembered that the Sephirah Malkhut is connected to the feet as much as to the ground we walk on, as with the Shekhinah, and I believed that something had happened in the tunnel. The parquet creaked again and someone's hand touched my cheek. I reached for the hand and brought it to my eyes. Margareta, I said, what are you doing here? She didn't say. I tried to move my head again, and this time I succeeded. I am not sure what I expected or whether I expected anything, but Margareta was the same as before, perhaps a little more pale and a little more tired. I looked at her feet: she was not barefoot. Her eyes were not green, as they had been when I had last looked into them, they were a light gray, though if someone were to ask me now what color that was, I wouldn't be able to pin it down or point to it among the things that surround me. So I held her by the hand and gazed into her gray eyes, she said nothing, I asked nothing. I could wait, and I waited. The blood was pulsing gently in her hand, her eyelids hesitated with every blink, wanting sleep, I heard the air move through her nostrils, her forehead wrinkled, and suddenly I saw it all lucidly, and I knew where my shoes and socks were, and why I was barefoot. I drew Margareta's hand to me, pressed her palm against my forehead, and shut my eyes. I felt the rhythm of her pulse adjusting to the rhythm of the pulse in my veins, and then, as if they had been waiting for this harmony, images began to follow one after the other: I saw the shell of my body filling with something transparent, a substance that was not substance, not part of the material world, and when it reached the crown of my head, it suddenly became so heavy that I collapsed. I'd never experienced anything so unusual: I thought of a person watching himself fall, unable to do anything except try not to imagine the pain that will follow. I collapsed like a half-empty sack, which softened the blow of the body on the ground, though it couldn't prevent my head from hitting the metal leg of the bench. And when I touched the crown of my head, I found a painful bump, though when it happened I hadn't felt a thing. If I may put it that way, the film I then watched was silent; today's version has long since been overdubbed, and, as is always the case with subsequent interventions, it no longer corresponds to reality. Everything that happened was without sound, the rising of a transparent shape from my body, and a broad opening high above me, or above us, because the shape leaned toward me and whispered something in my ear, or at least it seemed to, and the leap of the shape toward the opening, which was both as real and unreal as the transparent shape itself, and which at one moment was high among the clouds and the next moment right above the bench, and when the shape reached the rim of the opening and disappeared inside it, into the tunnel, which, as Margareta had said long ago, was leading upward, it rose to the top of the Sephirot, to the very Crown, and when the shape appeared again at the opening, it was suddenly a fully formed face, with gentle lines and dark eyes, and it soundlessly spoke a word I hadn't recognized then, but now I did, while Margareta's blood and my blood pulsed in tandem, and I said: Eleazar. Yes, said Margareta, Eleazar, though I was sure she didn't know why I had said the name. Several hours earlier, when I was watching the mouth of the shape in perfect silence and the forming of the word I hadn't understood, I thought it wished to give me instruction for my next assignment, perhaps the kind of mathematical puzzle Dragan Mišović had alerted me to, and then I thought with perfect clarity, as if I were reading a prepared text: He must be barefoot. I didn't know to whom the sentence referred: the shape vanished into the tunnel, my body was still lying by the bench, I too was a bodiless shape, and there was no one in the space between the high walls. I approached my body, which is an entirely arbitrary description, because I wasn't sure whether I could move at all, it could be more accurately described as a camera moving, which, when it focuses on a scene, remains in place and the lens turns, and the closer I got, the more clearly I understood that bodiless shapes could not perform physical obligations, nonetheless I continued to approach my feet until they, shod in suede shoes, filled my entire view, and then two hands entered the scene that tenderly, but with confidence, unlaced my shoes, removed them from my feet, stripped off my socks, placed them outside my range of vision, then one hand began to rise toward my gaze and a moment later covered the source of my vision, and the image filled with darkness. I moved Margareta's palm and looked at it, then slowly rested it on my eyes. She knew why I had said the name Eleazar. The palm that had prevented me from seeing had been hers, I was certain, though this further tangled the net. With an open tenderness I thought of Marko, his advice would have done me good, as would have one of his joints. Reality had become so skewed that being high on marijuana now seemed a normal state of mind. I still felt the pulsing of Margareta's blood, but our rhythms were no longer in sync. I released my grip, and she readily withdrew her hand, now our eyes met and I saw that each of her eyes was a different color. Don't ask, said Margareta, just listen. I listened and heard the siren of a fire engine approaching from far away. No, said Margareta, she hadn't meant the siren. She wanted, while there was still time, to offer an explanation. Because things didn't go as they were supposed to? I asked. Oh no, answered Margareta, because they went exactly as they were supposed to. I let her answer slowly sink in. I don't know how long that lasted, that slow sinking, because my mind resisted like a child who refuses to put his pajamas on before bed. Margareta stood patiently by the armchair. She wasn't touching me, she wasn't trying to touch me. She knew she should wait, and she waited, and my first thought was: The King lost his Queen, as if it were a move in a chess game, which ended in an irreparable loss. Margareta sniffled, and I sensed she was crying. Soon after that she left. On her way out, at the door, she stood on tiptoe, touched her lips to my cheek, and whispered in my ear, Go to Jaša's, he'll explain. I watched her go down the stairs, then I heard only the sound of her footsteps, the opening and shutting of the front door, and I never saw her again. Of course I didn't know that at the time; had I known it, perhaps I wouldn't have been so quick to turn the key in the lock, hook up the safety chain, go back to the living room, and sit back down in the armchair in front of the television set. I could have thought of a million things, but I didn't think of anything. Actually, I thought of switching on the TV to see whether at that late hour, on one of the private channels, there were pornographic movies. That would have calmed me, the mindless erotic endeavor and futile spending of semen, the whole farce to demonstrate absent passion. But I didn't turn on the television. I sat there, as the pain spread to my neck and temples again, stronger than before Margareta's arrival. When I asked her, just before she left, how she had got into the apartment and how I had turned up there, she said she'd been helped by friends. Then she left, but I already said that, or wrote it, or whispered it in the dark, bent over my desk. I reach out and switch on the desk lamp. Light is always a comfort, even when the dark doesn't bring fear. And the words I've been jotting down feverishly for days, as if my life depends on them, offer some consolation, though I cannot, when it comes to words, deny the possibility of manipulation, which is not the case with light. Words are like the things left behind after someone close to us dies—do we throw them out or save them, either would have its drawbacks and its advantages, but if we are perfectly frank with ourselves, we will acknowledge that their value is exhausted with the departure of the owner and the only choice is to throw them into a sack or box and deposit them in the garbage bin, which is what we do in the end, though we always hang on to something, something that allegedly means the world to us yet turns useless in the years to come and ends up in the rubbish heap, but as a tribute of sorts to our inability to ignore the customs and habits that shape our lives. I don't know who will be sifting through my things after I die, but that's why I have more or less decided that, when I reach the end of this narrative, not so long from now, there isn't much ink left in my pen, then I'll write in capital letters on page 1, BURN AFTER MY DEATH, but then again I won't, not because I will have given up on the idea, but because that gesture guarantees nothing. The number of manuscripts preserved against the wishes of their authors is not small. If you want something burnt, do it yourself, I told myself, and I prepared a box of matches and a vial of lighter fluid, but then I found myself faced with a conundrum—if I meant to burn the manuscript, why did I write it in the first place? Why not burn it to start with, and save myself the trouble, to say nothing of the paper. The environmentalists would be grateful to me, I'm sure. When once in a while I believed I was a writer, interestingly enough I never asked myself why I was writing a poem or a story, but now that I am writing only for myself, that question obsesses me. Yet I am writing about it anyway, spending the precious heart of my pen. Enough of that. If there is a need for fire, fire there will be. Where did I leave off? I sat in the armchair, staring at the blank television screen, listening to the pain throb in my temples as if it were a disco beat. I closed my eyes, and when I opened them again, it was day. My head was still throbbing, but more slowly, as if the disco beat had changed to truculent, heavy blues. That is how I moved, slowly but steadily, avoiding looking out the window, as the bright sunshine made my head spin. It took me fifteen minutes to walk to the phone, though it was no more than five meters to the front hall where the phone was recharged at night. It was early, but Jaša picked up right away. He knew what I wanted to talk about, and he suggested that I stop by his studio, Isak Levi, he said, would come by, Jakov Švarc too, he had no secrets from them anyway, and it wouldn't be the first time, he said, that he had had to manage things when Margareta's plans fell flat. I decided not to ask questions at that point, and said I'd come by. No sooner did I hang up than the phone rang. Thinking it was Jaša with something more, I said, We're all set, aren't we? An unfamiliar man's voice, making no effort to mask the loathing or scorn, or similar emotion, growled, Your time has come. I heard him hanging up, and I put down the receiver. The phone rang again. Another voice, just as unfamiliar, asked how it felt to be up the ass of the Jews. I heard snickers in the background, the person hung up, the phone rang again, someone informed me that I'd signed my death warrant, and then I yanked the phone line out of the wall. At first I was surprised by this inexplicable flood of loathing, but then through the slowness that besieged my body and soul the simple fact dawned on me: it was Saturday, the new issue of *Minut* had hit the newsstands, and my piece had apparently irritated some readers, as had been the intention, or rather my intention, since texts don't write themselves. I didn't know whether this should gratify or alarm me, perhaps ultimately every piece for the papers is written with this intention, and so I decided to take a shower and attend to the painful throbbing that had taken over my body. They say lukewarm water is the best cure, and after I had toweled down and changed my clothes, some twenty minutes later I felt the pain only in my neck, and I got rid of that with a series of small exercises I learned many years ago when I happened to tune in to a fitness program on channel one. I still remember how the instructor moved his head left-right, demonstrating how to stretch the neck, how far to drop the lower jaw or fling back the head. The only other thing I recall from television are the dance classes, broadcast, if my memory serves me well, from the Ljubljana studio, and a voice that repeated, One step forward, one step back, one-two, cha-cha-cha. I never learned how to dance, just as I never sang in the shower, though when I discovered rock-and-roll in the early 1960s I liked to imagine myself as the front man of a successful band, which I so fittingly dubbed the Invisible Lads. Ah, the comfort that comes from images of childhood and youth! And the misery when one realizes that life has become a series of memories, an album with choice photographs. Why must everything have a reverse side? Why does what caresses you in front, slap you from behind? That's the sort of thing I mused on while I shaved, and dried my hair, clueless as to what was waiting for me out there. The chaos of that day can be put in order now, but it seemed then that order had been irrevocably lost, from the moment I stepped out to buy *Minut* and saw copies of it strewn around the entrance to my building, through my flight across the gardens of Zemun, to the moment when illusions ceased to exist, when all was reduced to a single word: death. When I saw the sea of newspaper pages through the glass entrance doors, I didn't go out. I turned around, went back into the apartment, and plugged the phone in. It rang instantly, and a torrent of curses and threats spewed from the receiver. I hung up, the telephone rang again, and I had to wait for the ringing to end so I could get a connection and call the *Minut* editorial office. The secretary picked up, and her tearful voice turned into a sequence of deep sobs when she realized who was on the line. No, she said, the editor wasn't there, he was on his way to the office, the police had just arrived, the windows had been smashed, black paint smudged everywhere, and she had before her two letters, and here her voice quavered—I had condemned myself to the worst punishment. What punishment did they have in mind, I asked, but she could no longer speak, she squeaked unintelligibly, and all I could do, after reassuring her that I'd be there soon, was hang up. The phone rang again and it kept ringing while I got ready, had some cold coffee, and made my way downstairs. The jangling sound had replaced, in a sense, the painful throbbing in my veins, my blood, with the phone. Someone had picked up the sheets of newspaper by then, but when I stepped out into the street I saw a group of young men clearly waiting for me, because as soon as one of them spotted me, they all turned to face me. We stood that way for an instant, then I took two or three steps to get a better view of the cabs parked at the taxi stand at the next corner, and then moving fast, though not running, I took the first cab and gave the driver the address of the *Minut* editorial office. I kept looking back but didn't notice any cars following us. The taxi driver, to my amazement, paid no attention to my fidgeting and simply asked toward the end of the ride whether it had to do with a woman, was her husband after me. Those men back at the cab stand, he said, they must have been related. By the time I reached the *Minut* offices the editor's secretary had calmed down, and offered me coffee and whispered in confidence that the editor was drinking whiskey, and indeed, when I walked into his office, he was pouring whiskey into a big glass. He raised the bottle in my direction, but I shook my head, and he added a little more to his glass. So what do you say, he asked, should we be drinking to celebrate or to forget? I said I hoped he didn't feel that what had happened was my fault. If anyone was to blame, he said, it was he, because it was my right to write whatever I felt like writing, but the decision to publish was his alone, and anyway, he said, I surely remembered that he'd been of two minds, though as far as he was concerned, this was over and done with, what had happened should not be forgotten, it was now a matter of what to do next and how, the material damage was of the least importance, there were many more delicate issues, he added, and waved a sheet of paper. It was a letter from the church authorities bitterly protesting the insinuations in the piece in which the author (I noticed they spelled my name incorrectly) linked the Orthodox Church to the unacceptable manifestations of anti-Semitism. The church has always made every effort, the letter continued, to stand up to this, and reiterates that it has no history of negative relations with the Jewish people, who have always been received with hospitality in this community. I handed the letter back to the editor. I could write a protest protesting their protest, I said, which made the editor clutch his head. That's all we need, he said, we have enough trouble as it is, I don't need any new headaches, and besides, he grabbed a sheaf of papers, there are plenty of other messages from various parties and concerned individuals, just as, he added, there are open threats directed at me, you, all of us. This one is particularly intriguing, he said, and handed me a leaf torn from a school notebook. For those who do not understand the need to have our nation cleansed of foreign parasites, it declared in letters of unequal size, and who contribute to spreading texts in which our people are accused of various evils, there is only one fitting punishment: impaling on a stake. We will impale you, and display you on Terazije so that everyone can see how our enemies fare. Nor should you expect any mercy. No one among us feels pity for Yid scum and their helpers who drink our blood, and it is the duty of every one among us who has knowledge of the evil deeds of the Yids, from the betrayal of God's lamb and the spilling of the blood of Jesus Christ, to destroy every Yid or other degenerate who stands in our way. I read no further. The secretary appeared at the door, walked to the editor's desk, and deposited another pile of messages. This has been going on since last night, said the editor, since the moment the distribution started. And that was how it was for the next few days: every time I came to the office, the editor showed me the letters and the comments that stood out from the general tone of revulsion and scorn. There were, of course, those who agreed with my piece and called for an investigation, punishment for the guilty, respect for the law, and a public apology. And then, one morning, three or four days later, the editor hugged me and said Feliks had come home. Worn out, thick with fleas and filthy, said the editor, he had lain down in his basket the night before and was lying there still this morning, clearly at the end of his rope. If he hadn't come back last night, said the editor, he wouldn't have lived to morning. I said something about seven lives, or was it nine, I'd forgotten, I was never a big fan of household pets, dogs or cats or canaries, any little animal, for me they were always a sort of elemental disaster, far from stirring in me a sense of serenity, goodness, or any special emotion. A person who gets along with other people, I told the editor's secretary that day, has no need of animals. Feliks is different, said the secretary, her eyes flashing, which led me to conclude that it was better to say no more. There is nothing so easy to promise as silence, and no promise so difficult to make good on, because the more we insist on silence, the stronger the urge to speak, like the story about the shepherd who knew the emperor had the ears of a goat and who, compelled by the urge to speak, tells his secret to a hole in the ground, which he carefully covers up, but the earth speaks through a reed pipe, if I remember it correctly, and the whole world learns what was supposed to be a secret. I thought of this story several days after Feliks's auspicious return, the evening I went to see Jaša Alkalaj. Shabbat was ending; the curses and threats were multiplying; no matter where I turned I was sure to see someone threatening me with a clenched fist or an index finger drawn across the throat; my visit to Jaša's studio felt like entering the garden of primeval serenity. Jakov Švarc was already there. Isak Levi hadn't come, and the glass set out for him was left untouched. Jaša pulled out a bottle of brandy, the time had come for us to make a toast, he said, and before I had the chance to ask what we were toasting, the glasses were full, we clinked and drank up. I asked whether Margareta might join us, and when Jaša gave me a look torn between anguish and relief, I should have known instantly that I would never see her again, but at the time I interpreted it as an expression of parental concern. On the other hand I may have sensed the answer, and for that reason hurried to ask the next question about what had happened to the Well manuscript. Let's say, said Jaša, that it has been returned to its proper owner. So the living version of the manuscript was back at the Jewish Historical Museum, which I still believe, especially after reading a story about a secret transfer of metal chests from the Jewish Community Center to the safe at the National Bank, or some such place, several days after the bombing of Serbia began. I was reading the newspaper that published this news item, or leafing through it rather, because I didn't know the language, in mild spring sunshine, savoring a double espresso, while hundreds of kilometers away bombs were falling in unintelligible patterns on military and civilian buildings. One of the people sitting next to me translated into awkward English the brief article, with a blurred photograph of the Jewish Community

Center, in front of which several people were loading two large chests into a van that resembled a police vehicle. The article speculated that the chests might contain the manuscript of the Sarajevo Haggadah, about which various stories had circulated during the siege of Sarajevo and after, including the claim that the original was no longer in Bosnia. I told my reluctant translator not to bother, because if the story about the transmittal of the chests was true, I knew what the chests contained, along with other museum valuables: the Well manuscript, on which, some day in the future, a researcher will discover my fingerprints that will be duly noted as prints of an unknown person who, judging by their frequency and age, was in possession of the manuscript during the last decade of the twentieth century. This researcher will have to start work soon, because fingerprints don't last forever, they don't fossilize, at least not the ones left on books, especially on books of sand that are constantly shifting, like all deserts. Jaša Alkalaj meanwhile refilled our glasses. If he kept going, I said, I would believe he didn't want to answer my questions. It wasn't that, answered Jaša, he just wanted to encourage me to ask more questions, since I hadn't asked him about anything but the manuscript. In that case, I said, I would like to know what really happened, I mean, did anything happen? Jakov Švarc grinned, as if he concurred with my question, though even today I can't tell whether he had any idea what we were discussing. Why was he even there? Did Jaša Alkalaj ask him to attend because Švarc was an historian, and Jaša saw him as the most objective possible witness or else as the most impartial chronicler of events? If so, then Jaša's error in judgment was odd, in light of his exhibition of paintings, which had originated in a playful mingling of history and art, yet such an error was also understandable in the context of all that was going on in the country, where a distorted image of history was being embraced as the standard and where people of the most varied political views believed that the history of their nation was exceptional and no one but they could understand. After all, why wouldn't Jaša feel and think as they did, even if he wasn't, in fact, a member of that nation? The political conflicts and the struggle for power were based on diverging approaches to issues, such as the economy or the relations to Europe and the world community, but the ideology of the nation was most often considered beyond reproach. All that became far more obvious a year later, during the bombing and in the months after the devastation, but other people should write about that, the real witnesses, and not people like me, who followed the events from a safe distance. Whatever the case, Jakov Švarc and I sat there, sipped brandy, and waited for Jaša's explanation. Hours later, the bottle was empty, Jakov Švarc was asleep on the sofa, and Jaša was still talking. He may not have stopped talking even after I'd risen to go, promising to come back on Tuesday or Wednesday to hear the rest. Most of what Jaša said I already knew, and most of that, perhaps because of Jakov Švarc's presence, referred to what for me was the least interesting part, the history of the idea of Jewish self-defense, which, according to Jaša, sprang from Margareta's dread that the Jews would disappear from the face of the earth. From the start, said Jaša, he felt that this was an idea doomed to failure, not because it seemed so fantastic and unreal, there was nothing that seemed more unreal and fantastic, he said, than our country in the 1990s, but because the Jewish community was too scant for such an undertaking, which just for the unusual form of physical prayer required more than one hundred participants. When Margareta realized this, said Jaša Alkalaj, she got in touch with public and secret organizations that supported calls for political change yet maintained a critical distance from the national euphoria, which had become stronger, and threatened, said Jaša, to destroy the finest minds of my generation, not with drugs, but with the pure evil of ethnic hatred. I didn't know what to be more startled by: Jaša's paraphrase of Gins-berg's "Howl" or his references to secret organizations. Whom did he have in mind? The Masons, members of an assortment of nongovernmental organizations, Theosophists, the Jehovah's Witnesses? All of them, said Jaša, but many more as well. I'd have been surprised, he told me, had I known how many people sought comfort from the madness of everyday life in secret societies, where they renewed their sense of purpose in life by dedicating themselves to charitable works and gestures of goodwill. Now was not the time for that story, but he hoped, he said, that in the future someone would write a real history of Serbian secret societies at the close of the twentieth century, because only then would the picture of the events in this part of the world be complete and it would be made clear that there always was an alternative to nationalism gone berserk. Of course, he went on to say, I shouldn't think he was promoting an interpretation of history in support of Margareta's idea on how to resolve the political and national problems facing our country. Margareta herself would be horrified at the thought, he had no doubts on that score, which, however, did nothing to gainsay the fact that all those issues, like it or not, were connected, and once you started poking around in one of them, you'd find all the rest. Meanwhile Margareta heard of a strange manuscript, rumors about it had circulated in the Jewish community, and when she got hold of the translation, she found she had hit on a pattern that seemed like the ideal key for her plan, but nothing of that would have worked, said Jaša, had not a mathematician shown up who'd shed light on the mathematical elements in the Kabbalistic instructions. I know the man, I said. He knew I would know, said Jaša, though he also knew that I didn't know it was the mathematician who had chosen me, if that is the right word, for the role they felt was vital to seeing the plan through, except that the plan had become so byzantine that Jaša himself, he said, chose to pull out. I stared at him and blinked, trying to remember where I had heard all this before: had I not wondered about it at the very beginning, only later to convince myself to doubt my doubts? How was I chosen? I asked. Did I get more votes than the other candidates? Jaša reached for a new bottle, the brandy gurgled into the emptied glasses, Jakov Švarc's head dropped and his breathing became deeper and more even, and I had difficulties now and then seeing Jaša clearly and following what he was saying. This was a classic feint, Jaša went on, while the front appears to be opening on one side, it actually opens on the other. The mathematician, Jaša explained, read my writing in *Minut* and concluded that I was the perfect solution: I had access to the public, I could transmit information, I could get temperatures to rise. I could provoke the other side while at the same time nudging them to react the way Margareta and her collaborators had planned. Of course, said Jaša, not everything could be predicted, especially when the pieces in *Minut* began to take on a life of their own and provoke a far more tempestuous reaction than had been anticipated. I hoped, I said, that he wasn't suggesting that the break-ins at the Jewish Community Center and the butchering of his paintings were all just a foil, because I couldn't bear that blow. Jaša told me not to worry, those were real, as real as the beating I got at the beginning of the story. I didn't remember telling him about the beating, but it was clear that many people knew far more than I had assumed. All in all, on the basis of Jaša's story, which became more detailed and tangled with every glass, I could conclude that my task had been to stir up the public with my writing, luring various enemy groups to come after me, thereby deflecting attention from the real intentions of the conspirators. That word *conspiracy* again, except this time it had far more credence. Somewhere deep down I saw the flash of Margareta's thigh, which I still blame for everything, I could not believe it had such a hold on me, more powerful than any word. Again I felt discomfort at thinking about Margareta's thigh in front of her father, but his half-closed eyes forgave me in a way. Jakov Švarc snored on the sofa. I looked out the window, wishing I could see the sliver of the new moon. I didn't see anything. I got up; it was time to go. I had, I told Jaša Al-kalaj, just one more question: did something happen that night, and if so, what? I would save all my other questions for my next visit. He looked at me drunkenly, bleary-eyed, and said: Yes. Then: No. Yes or no, I asked, there is a difference between those two words, especially when they are in answer to a question. Yes, Jaša repeated, no. He let his head drop onto the arm of the chair, smacked his lips once or twice, and fell asleep. It occurred to me that I should look for blankets and cover him and Jakov Švarc, but who could ever have found anything in that studio? I gave up, lurched over to the front door, locked it, and put the key back in its place. The elevator was there, and when the cabin began its descent, I went down on my knees and threw up in the corner, careful to keep the sticky liquid from touching my pants. There was no one in front of the building, at least I didn't see anyone, and my walk home progressed more calmly than I had anticipated. Actually, I don't remember the whole walk back, only fragments, a part in which I see myself crossing the highway near the Sava Center as cars zip past, honking, then I remember unlocking the door to my apartment and listening, certain that in the depths of the apartment someone was breathing deeply. There was nobody there, I made sure, turning on all the lights and peering into every room and every wardrobe, I even took a look under the sofa, and then I could lie down, calm, satisfied, though I was hurt too in a way, amusing as that may sound, because I had fully expected to be attacked, physically and symbolically, as the author of the piece in *Minut*. Vanity is strange, I have to admit. I couldn't believe I would wish for any sort of assault on my person, and be disappointed that it had happened to others and not to me. From various sources I learned subsequently why no one had time for me that night: the wall of the Jewish cemetery was scrawled with anti-Semitic slogans; a huge swastika was drawn on the door of the synagogue; the entrance to the Jewish Community Center was buried in heaps of garbage;

a doll dressed in a camp inmate's clothes was left on the monument to the Jewish victims at Dorćol with a yellow star on its left arm and a little black cap on its head; threatening notes were dropped into the mailboxes of many Jewish families; unconfirmed stories circulated about attacks on the elderly, a big fight down by the Sava, knives were drawn and apparently, as the woman I was talking to claimed, even gunshots were heard. When asked how she knew the shots were from guns and not from rifles, or perhaps automatic weapons, she couldn't say, but that was how her neighbor had described it, and her neighbor had been on the front in the early 1990s and knew a thing or two about weapons, and he had been wounded, she said, and still limped with his left leg. It wasn't so visible, she added, but you could hear, since she lived downstairs from him, the sole of his shoe scraping the floor when he moved around his apartment. The first attacks on my piece appeared in the papers that Monday. The church authorities bitterly denied any anti-Jewish sentiment among their leaders, as did several of the political parties, though one party proposed that anyone who didn't like it in this country was free to go elsewhere. No one asked you to come, it said, so no one has to tell you to go. It was announced that an article would run the next day under the title "What? You Haven't Left Yet?" revealing the "truth" about what the Jews of Belgrade controlled, with special emphasis on their role among the Serbian Masons. That Monday I also smelled smoke coming into my apartment from the stairwell, and when I opened the door I saw a small bonfire on which a Jewish star made of yellow cardboard was burning. I called the editorial office of *Minut,* but the editor couldn't or didn't want to speak with me, and the secretary called me later to say that I needn't hurry with a piece for their next issue. Much later, when I was already far away from Belgrade and Zemun, I learned of the lawsuits, the fines, and the confiscation of the property of *Minut,* but all I could do was raise my hands, which I do again now, though this time it has nothing to do with a feeling of helplessness, but because I need to rest my stiff muscles and stretch out my fingers cramped around the pen. The pen is see-through and its heart will soon be gone. The end of its heart will be the end of the story, fitting enough, since when a heart is no longer beating, the story is silent, just as the story is silent when the heart beats too fast and words tumble out, choking one another. That happened to me after the makeshift fire, so much like child's play, and in the evening I went to the quay, convinced that the river would soothe me as it had so many times before. On my way to the promenade I went by the high-rise where the book-filled apartment was; I turned toward the entrance, then decided against it. At the entrance I saw a man who looked familiar, and on the way back toward the promenade I saw two more who looked like him. I turned in another direction: there were more of them, at least six. The distance between them and me was not negligible, but I felt completely surrounded, as if they were standing right next to me. I could have started running, which would have been just as ludicrous as taking them all on at once. Then I noticed another group approaching down the promenade: fifteen elderly people, men and women, moving along at a slow pace but in lively conversation, and I simply slid in among them, striking up a conversation with two short women about the problem of late pension payments and whether mosquitoes should be sprayed the minute they hatch or when they are more mature. The women showed no surprise at all that I had joined their conversation, and based on their accent and what they were saying, I determined that they were from southern Serbia and on their way to Hotel Yugoslavia to attend the opening ceremony of the annual conference of some association that, if I had understood correctly, protected the rights of retired people threatened by what was happening in politics and the economy in the 1990s. I nodded, took one step after another, and kept an eye on what that other group of people was up to. They came closer and closer, until they had surrounded the pensioners, and I found myself in the center of concentric circles. The pensioners then proceeded to a lower walkway, by the river, and the men with the crewcuts followed along on the upper walkway, and I sensed that their patience was ebbing and that they would lose it altogether when the two levels joined at the pier by the entrance to the hotel. I only had one choice, and as we approached the slope that led to the pier, I bent over abruptly, grabbed one of the women, and shouted that she had been taken ill and dashed with her to the entrance of the hotel. The woman was shocked silent for a moment, then wriggled and screamed, and the more she screamed, the louder I shouted that she was suffering from a seizure and needed emergency care and demanded that the way be cleared for me. The men following us halted, uncertain what to do. I galloped toward the hotel, drenched in sweat, because the woman, though short, was plump and wriggling free of my grasp. Some other people rushed over, one man grabbed her legs, another took her under the arms, the woman shrieked, we yelled at her to calm down, that everything would be fine, then we were at the back entrance of the hotel where a largish group had gathered, pushing and cursing, and I took the opportunity to slip into the stairwell and out to the front entrance of the hotel, and from there sprinted across the street and ducked in among the facing apartment buildings. I stopped at a deserted playground. My clothes were drenched with sweat, the shoelaces on my right sneaker untied, my hands trembling, I was panting like a dog in the summer sun. Do dogs pant in the dark? I'll never find that out, like so many other things, from the simple ones, such as how fireflies glow, to the more complicated questions, such as the purpose of color in nature, to say nothing of places I'll never visit or music I'll never hear, and that certainty, the fact that our life, seen through the reflection of human knowledge, is by necessity partial, no matter how we may try to make it complete, always filled me with a greater or lesser degree of despair. It is not a fear of death, it is foolish to fear the inevitable, but the thought that I'll die before I've had the chance to see Bombay and Melbourne, for instance, can bring me to tears more readily than I care to admit. Back then, that evening, in the playground, it was Tokyo and Montevideo I was thinking about, but I didn't cry, mostly because I was gasping with laughter at the thought of the poor woman flailing in my arms and staring at me, eyes swimming with horror. I could no longer stand, I was laughing so hard, and I sat on the nearest swing. The seat was small, I could barely wedge myself onto it, and when I started swinging, I had to lift my knees nearly up to my chin. The chain links creaked, the swing groaned, and when I turned around I saw the moon in the sky. Who knows, it may have been there earlier, I am never sure where to look for it, sometimes it pokes out from the horizon or struts above my head, often it is not there at all, one more thing I will not learn before I depart for the other world: all the trajectories that delineate the movements of the celestial bodies across the cupola that arches over us, resembling graphs indicating economic surges and downturns and, I assume, violent catastrophes resulting in utter destruction. The seat of the swing cut into my buttocks, the moon swung back and forth above me, or maybe it was me swinging back and forth beneath it, who could say, everything is relative in this world, anyway, especially when one is swinging with the head flung back, with the blood rushing to the brain, prompting thoughts one might never otherwise think, or hear, just as I thought I heard a familiar voice ask, What are you doing here? I dropped my feet, touched the ground, stopped swinging. I lifted my head up, shut my eyes, waited for the blood to stop gurgling and go back to where it had come from. The voice that had asked the question belonged to Marko, but when I opened my eyes he wasn't there, just as he hadn't been there for the past few days. And nights, of course. When he left, Marko left for good. I couldn't remember when that happened; I knew, or I sensed, why; in a way, I had had a hand in his leaving, by choosing to believe Margareta's story above all and not trying harder to bring Marko into the game, which, in the end, turned out to be precisely that: a game. Besides, I was relieved that he wasn't here, because his jeering would have been merciless. First he would have ridiculed me, then he would have rolled a joint in honor of my recklessness, then another joint in honor of the joint that, he would have said, had burned for the truth, then another one, in honor of that second one, and so forth. I extracted myself from the tight swing seat, looked to the left, looked to the right, but nowhere did I see the source of the voice that had asked what I was doing there. Had I treated Marko's disappearance too lightly? People don't disappear just like that, or more precisely, people don't disappear for no reason, and then and there in that playground, lit by the moon, I decided to go over to Marko's apartment. The routes that led to my apartment were probably blocked anyway: the men I'd managed to evade were likely to be waiting at my door, and it wouldn't surprise me if one of them was at that very moment straining in the hallway and leaving a semicircle, or perhaps a full circle, of his excrement on the threshold. I set out for the center of New Belgrade, leaving Hotel Yugoslavia behind, and along the way I hailed a cab and asked the driver to take me to a street not far from Marko's. When we got there, I waited for him to drive away, then walked in the thickest shadow, which was not difficult in a city where the system of streetlights had almost completely collapsed, until I came to Marko's street and reached his building. I looked up at his windows and couldn't believe my eyes: a light was on in his bedroom. I crossed the street. His building had an intercom system, but the front door, like so many front doors and entranceways in Belgrade and Zemun, was always unlocked. I pushed it, slipped in, and, without turning on the light, started up the stairs. Something touched my leg, I nearly screamed, however, it turned out to be a cat that arched its back, purred, and rubbed up against my shins. Pssst, I said. Its eyes flashed in the dark and I kept climbing. One floor, the next, and I was in front of the door to his apartment, breathing with difficulty, as if I'd climbed to the top of the Avala television tower. I leaned on the handrail and waited for my breathing to become inaudible. The cat clearly had nothing better to do, I felt it between my legs. I leaned over to pat it and heard the sound of steps in Marko's apartment. I grabbed the cat, and, leaping up two steps at a time, went to the floor above. The cat was purring as if it had an electric motor in its rib cage, and as the minute vibrations of its body were transmitted to my heart, we seemed to be rumbling in unison. There was the sound of a key in the lock, the door opened, someone stepped into the hallway, took a step or two, stopped as if listening, then flicked on the stairwell lights. The cat and I exchanged glances, it meowed, pushed away with its paws, sprang from my embrace, and scampered down the stairs. I inched over to the wooden banister and peered cautiously over it, and right below me saw someone looking up at the cat that had left the stairwell and was winding in and out of the iron balusters supporting the stairwell railing. I stepped back and the voice beneath me said, There's no one out here, it's only the cat. The door closed, the key turned twice in the lock, the chain rattled, and everything went quiet. I waited for the light to go off and walked slowly down the stairs. The cat was not in front of Marko's door or on the lower floors, it must have gone into Marko's apartment, though when it comes to cats, one can never be certain, and I wouldn't be surprised if it were to turn up here, after all these years, as if nothing had happened, as if we were still on the stairs, which to some extent is true, since all the unresolved moments in our lives contain a tiny segment of our being in the constant replay of each, and the more such unresolved moments, the greater the fragmentation of our being, or the less of us left in the reality in which we dwell. Each time the light goes out in the stairwell of Marko's building in my memory, a part of my being disappears, and considering how often I think about it there is not much of me left, just as there isn't much ink left in my pen. I noticed a while ago that I had written out some letters only partially, two vowels and a consonant, which is the most serious warning I have had that the end is inevitable, even as I try every trick to postpone it. Now, for example, I am wondering why I didn't knock at the door of Marko's apartment. What did I have to lose? Nothing I hadn't already lost, or at least had begun losing, though that evening a hope may have still lingered that all of it might yet change and that the loss wouldn't be total, so I slid once more through the front door of his building, this time going out, and found myself in the street. I took a full breath of air into my lungs, looked to the left, looked to the right, and tried to decide where to spend the rest of the night. I didn't come up with anything, or everything I came up with sounded unsafe, especially the thought of spending the night at the home of an acquaintance, which might have exposed them to danger if someone was following me, so I spent the night wandering aimlessly, which wasn't so much aimless as it was a deliberately evasive approach to my apartment. I don't know how far I walked that night, ducking into entranceways and behind shrubs and into the dense shadows whenever I came upon something potentially dangerous, but I know I was staggering by the time I walked into my apartment on Tuesday morning, with the latest editions of the papers under my arm. As before, I was a little disappointed at finding nothing nasty in front of the door and for a moment felt like someone who, against his will, has seen his importance diminished. Vanity is a strange thing, I said that already, it needs no repeating. I fell into my armchair. The soles of my feet were burning, my hands shook, my eyes teared as if my eyelids were lined with sand. The papers were packed with op-ed pieces, rebuttals, and polemics, including an official statement by the Jewish community, condemning every form of hatred and denying, along the way, any tie to me, which was true enough. A letter to the editor signed by fifteen prominent individuals of Jewish background demanded in much harsher terms an investigation to ascertain under whose orders I was working to corrupt the traditionally good relations between Serbian and Jewish people, and expressed unwavering support of the government, which, and I am quoting based on dim recollection, was doing all in its power to secure a dignified place for our country in the merciless ghettoization of the new world order. As a rule, I avoided reading such sycophantic praise, but now my own skin was at stake and it was expedient to offer me in exchange for a promise of peace, therefore I needed to get as detailed a picture as I could about those involved as the only way to ready my defense. Of course anything that would have provided me with evidence—information about the slogans, attacks, the vandalizing of monuments, and the public accusations—was not cited by the newspapers, claiming that this, to quote a television commentator, would have interfered with the investigation. At that point I didn't know everything there was to know, so all I could do was observe with horror the quantity of the attacks and the support they received from certain politicians, church dignitaries, and ordinary citizens. A year later, when Serbia was bombed, the business of forgiving themselves completely overwhelmed all else, allowing the resistance to be focused on the international enemy who in turn could be blamed for everything, for everything that happened and what was going to happen, whatever that was. By then I was somewhere else, not where I am now, but once you leave, all other places are the same, so in a sense it made no difference where I was, and I remember thinking I should write about it, about the magnificent and grandiose yet failed attempt to revive the supernatural in the construct of the world, as well as a deliberate move by a government to play the difference card, to encourage a rift along subtle, often intricate, ethnic and religious lines in an act of self-preservation. Unlike the failed Kabbalistic experiment, this other policy still prevails, but in a reduced form, and was additional inspiration for my resolve, which has meanwhile evolved into desire, then to a feeling of obligation, then to a pledge, and that is where I came to a stop, here by this window, rolled up my sleeves, and got down to work. Yes, writing is work, I repeat that for all those who think of writing as pleasure, and when sometimes, like now, I look up and out the window into the night, I see the face of a tired man. And worried, also, because the ink tube inside the pen is nearly empty. Who knows where all these letters come from, how all the words are born? I asked myself the same question as I leafed through the newspaper, while the soles of my feet burned, my thighs ached, and the phone rang insanely. At one moment I got up, limped to the side table, and picked up the receiver. The voice at the other end delivered a hysterical sequence of curses, threats, and burps. I went into the kitchen, put the kettle on for tea, spread some honey on a slice of bread. If the explanation I got from Jaša Alkalaj was right, and we were all caught up in a double game of sorts, then none of us was what we seemed, which seemed clear enough in the cases of Margareta or Dragan Mišović, but it did nothing to explain Marko. Yet perhaps it does, I thought, except that I don't see it. I should have rung his doorbell, I chided myself, to see who was there, instead of deciding that Marko wasn't there and that the entrance to his apartment was a passage into a trap. After talking with Jaša Alkalaj, at whose studio I was expected again later that evening, I would return, I told myself, to Marko's apartment, nothing would hold me back. I waited for the phone to stop ringing for a moment and called Jaša Alkalaj. I left a message on his answering machine that I would be there around nine o'clock that evening, and then, though the phone kept ringing, I lay down to rest. I woke up late in the afternoon in an apartment where silence reigned. I felt a terrible fatigue, I am one of those for whom sleep during the day brings no rest, and I knew I'd be walking around for the next hour or two with a veil over my eyes and gauze bandages wrapped around my mind. I walked gingerly over to the window, as if I feared sniper fire, and saw rain clouds. Everything else seemed ordinary enough: the passersby were hurrying along, cars and buses moved intermittently across the square, two women stood talking by the door to the pharmacy and gestured as if warding off mosquitoes, a boy was staring at a balcony on which another boy stood throwing paper airplanes, three dogs nosed around the garbage bins, the traffic lights blinked on and off. I could have stood there forever, with my nose pressed against the windowpane, outside the world and yet in it, an observer but not a participant, visible yet unseen. Such a blissful state, however, could not last long and I was jolted by a knock on the door. I pulled away from the window and asked who was there. No one answered, but the knocking repeated. I started toward the door and peered through the spy hole: I couldn't see a thing. Someone was holding a hand over it, and there was nothing to do but step back and hurry to the phone. Kabbalah, magic, Sons of the Revolutionary Light or reactionary dark, it didn't matter which, it was time to call the police. I picked up the receiver, dialed the number, and stood there for a while, not realizing that the phone wasn't working. The line was dead; there was no sound coming from it; I punched the buttons in vain. The knocking, which came again, was now more alarming, though at the same time it made me wonder about the person or the people knocking, because I was certain that a whole horde was crouching in front of my door, so why didn't they just break down the door and do it. I felt like a mouse in a trap, or, more accurately, like a dog the dogcatcher has chased down a dead end, and while the knocking kept up at irregular intervals, I went into the kitchen and out onto the little terrace. The neighbor's terrace, to which I had jumped from the edge of my terrace when I was much younger, now seemed farther away. I would never make a jump like that now, I realized, though a part of my consciousness, still wrapped in gauze, suggested it was better to take the risk, because I would give myself a chance, whereas in my apartment I would meet a certain fate, a certain end. Nonetheless I went back into the apartment. The knocking picked up again as I tiptoed over to the door, and again I asked loudly who it was. No one answered. The knocking stopped. I went to the door and, as I had done so many times, leaned my ear against it. I thought I could hear someone mumbling, the sound of paper being torn, and soft footsteps going down the stairs, but when I leaned my ear to a different spot on the door, everything sounded different: the paper wasn't being torn but crumpled, the footsteps were going up the stairs, and instead of the mumbling I could hear a muffled giggle, and all the while heavy breathing. I no longer recall how much time passed before I realized that it was my own breathing I was hearing. I straightened up and looked through the spy hole. The hallway was empty. I unlocked the door and opened it as far as the chain allowed. I didn't see anybody, I didn't hear anybody, so I unhooked the chain and opened the door cautiously until I could see the entire hallway. No one leaped out at me, no one shoved me, no one brandished a knife, no one pointed a gun. A swastika spread vividly across the door, and under it, in uneven letters: DEATH TO THE TRAITOR. The paint was still fresh, and dribbles of black dripped from the tips of the swastika, hurrying toward the bottom, where they belonged. I thought it was just as well I had not opened the door earlier, because if I'd seen the writing, I'd have wanted to confront the offenders verbally. I could see myself shouting theatrically: How can I be a traitor? Whom have I betrayed? Instead of taking on the scum, you come here to puff out your chests before someone who is trying to rid you of a burden you have been bearing on your shoulders for years! I looked to myself like Lenin speaking from a podium, leaning forward to look more assertive. Nonsense, of course, and I am not thinking of Lenin but of myself, because they would not have waited for me to end, or even to begin, they would have assaulted me straightaway. It was ridiculous to hope for anything else. Death to the traitor, that's the only thing that interested them, and sooner or later, they would do what they had set out to do. I could switch day and night, I could change my hiding places, I could shave my head and grow a mustache, I could wear black-framed glasses, nothing would help. The punishment of a person who thinks differently is always welcome, no matter which side the person doing the punishing is on. The death of one traitor is a lure for hundreds of others, eager to ferret out new traitors and administer new punishments. I should have taken up the bucket, rag, and brush, and washed the swastika off the door, but for the first time I felt I had no strength left: I could no longer wash away as much as they could defile. I also regretted at that point that the Kabbalistic experiment had failed, even if it hadn't been de-signed as a realistic undertaking, because if it had worked, the forces of darkness would have had to retreat before the forces of light and nothing would have been the same. Now it was too late, and the feeling of being driven into a trap flared be-fore me as if fanned by doom. Everything was coming apart at the seams, and it would only get worse. Somewhere it must have been recorded how long all of this would last; fate, in any case, is unchanging. You are rambling on like some washed-up old sage, Marko would have said, and that made me think of going to his apartment again. Although I couldn't prevent gen-eral disintegration, perhaps I could prevent my own further disintegration, preserve some of what was still precious to me. If I didn't do that, I thought, there'd be nothing left of me, and no one, not even I, will be able to look myself in the eye. The evening was fast approaching, dragging night along with it, and who knew what it had in store and whom it would bring in tow, so it would be best, while there was still daylight, for me to head to Jaša Alkalaj's. The swastika, I thought, would have to wait. It may still be there for all I know, on the door where I left it, slightly abstracted by the streams of paint that had dribbled every which way, though recognizable enough.

The rain started as I stepped out into the street, and I didn't have time to look to the left or to the right, or up or down, instead I sprinted over to the bus stop where I leaped onto a bus that was just pulling away. By the time we reached the bridge over the Sava, the rain was pelting with such ferocity that the bus driver had to slow down. Water was coursing in every direction at the Zeleni Venac bus stop, and crowds were huddling in the underground walkway to get out of the downpour, the people waiting for the Zemun and Novi Beograd buses, policemen, peddlers, vendors, shoppers still out and about, even though it was late. I somehow managed to push my way through the crowd, then went on, from doorway to doorway, to Terazije, where I waited for the trolley bus. The trolley bus was a wreck, its windows were smashed, its doors had trouble closing, then suddenly sprang open mid-drive, it stank of damp and vomit. We hadn't got far from the Slavija roundabout when I decided to get off at the first stop, certain that a man was staring at me. I got off, but the man stayed on, so I was left alone at the stop, in the rain, which was coming down in gusts. The next trolley bus arrived after fifteen minutes. Although it was too early for me to go to Jaša Alkalaj's, the persistent rain forced me to head to his studio; even if he wasn't there, I knew where the key was, I could let myself in and wait. He'd given me permission to do so on my first visit, and I certainly wouldn't paint, which was the one thing that was forbidden, he had said. How much time had passed since then? On the calendar, a little more than two months; in terms of experience, a lifetime; it was difficult for me to reconcile these two measures, so different yet the same, and to acknowledge that one of them was inaccurate. And what, I thought as I walked toward the studio, if both are accurate, thereby confirming that we live far longer than the calendar indicates, each person in his or her own time, and that hours, days, months, years are merely a convention that enables us to function more smoothly within the boundaries of the larger world?

One thinks of all sorts of things when rain falls for a long time, especially if he has no umbrella. Although I walked close to the buildings and dashed from doorway to doorway, I was drenched and started to shiver, then ran the rest of the way to Jaša's street. When I got to the corner, I stopped and looked carefully around. I didn't see anything out of the ordinary: there was no one in front of the building entrance, cars were parked along the sidewalk, the garbage bins were open and overflowing with trash, the street lamps shone with a stingy light. I looked at my watch: it wasn't yet nine o'clock. Then I heard the sound of an ignition turning, and a car pulled out of the row of parked cars. A moment later, shouting something I couldn't catch, two young men hurtled out of Jaša's building, both dressed in black hooded sweatshirts. They pulled the hoods up over their heads and their faces were in shadow. The doors of the car swung open, they leaped in, still shouting, and the car careened around and sped off in the opposite direction. I don't know why I didn't turn around and leave. I should have known what I would see in the studio, no point in actually seeing it, but my legs carried me as if heeding somebody's orders, first to the entrance, where I paused and looked back after the fleeing car, then to the elevator, its door ajar, as if it had been waiting for me. The door to Jaša's studio was also ajar. I approached it, and, as if watching from a great distance, from across the river, saw Jaša at his kitchen table. His head was resting on his chest, his right arm dangled by his side, his left lay on the table, palm upward. His legs were out of my range of vision, but I could see droplets of thick liquid dripping from his chin and nose. They were dripping onto his clothes, onto the floor, with such a deafening noise that I had to cover my ears. Oh, Jaša, I said. No, I didn't say anything. Pressing my ears shut, I stepped back, stumbled into the elevator, and groped for the ground-floor button. The noise of the droplets followed me, and the woman who opened the elevator door after it stopped shrieked when she saw me with my hands over my ears and my face in a grimace of pain. I smiled at her, which sent her a step back, and as soon as I moved off, she got swiftly on. I kept walking, feeling I would never get out of the hallway, and when I finally did get out, I walked straight on in the rain, which fell in thick, heavy drops as if this weren't the end. And it wasn't. Some things and events have several beginnings, while others have several ends, they end in stages, as if moving from one sense of finality to another, in slow leaps or spasms. *Spasm* is a better word, because it is reminiscent of deathbed convulsions, and in that ongoing end I was indeed dying, until I became a living corpse of sorts, bait swallowed up in the end by the dark. I don't remember how I got to Zemun: at one point I realized that I was in front of my building, but instead of going home I went on to Marko's apartment. I turned on the light, walked up the stairs, rang the doorbell. I could hear footsteps and laughter. Marko opened the door and squinted, as if trying to make me go away. Behind him, on the coat rack, hung a black hooded sweatshirt. From inside the apartment a man's voice asked who was there. No one, said Marko, and opened his eyes wide. We stared at each other for a few moments, then he slammed the door with all his might. Crumbs of plaster sprayed the floor, the light in the hallway went out, I sprinted down the stairs in the dark and didn't stop until I was back at my apartment. The next day all the papers carried the news about the sudden death of the painter Jaša Alkalaj. No reference to a tragic death, which was probably because the investigation was underway, but I knew it was a matter of time before the news media would broadcast the true story, just as it was a matter of time before the investigation would hear my message on Jaša's answering machine, or the woman from the elevator would remember the man with the hands over his ears. There was a fire that night in the book-filled apartment, and while I watched the smoke billow through the windows and listened to the sirens, I knew I had scant time left. I pulled out a small suitcase, packed up the basics, avoided anything that might resemble a memento, collected my money, passport, and a bag with some valuables that had been left in my possession after the last death in the family, awaited morning, and by noon I was on the minibus shuttling travelers to the Budapest airport. I shook like a leaf, I confess, as we crossed the border, even more so on the Hungarian side, and then, when the ornery Hungarian customs official waved for us to continue on our way, I could finally breathe. Everything that happened after that, all the years between me now and the events I have described, the distance set up between this place and that place, all must go unrecorded. The spot where I am now, by the window in whose panes I occasionally see a figure that is my own reflection, and where I was brought by the kindness of strangers, I will probably never leave. Finality has come at last to my door. It's not death I'm thinking of. I am thinking of how a series of events comes to a definite end and becomes destiny, while at the same time nothing indicates what a new beginning may bring, or whether there will be a new beginning. Perhaps that was why I wanted to tell this story, or write down all that had happened, for a person who talks to himself is considered crazy, while one who records a story is respected, thought creative, as if spoken words are not creation and as if the world was created by the written word, not a voice. As far as I know, God spoke while he created the world, he wasn't reading a document drawn up in advance. The sound of words is the sound of the world, its true face. Reading is an attempt at courting the creator, especially the way people read before they learned to read silently, when they whispered and their lips shaped the letters and words their eyes passed over. But now it is over and done with. When this pen dries up, I will place the last page on top, turn the manuscript over, and start from the beginning. Margareta, whose name I didn't know at the time, stood on the muddy shore waiting for the slap designed to be a trap for me. Don't worry, I will not tell the whole story again. What has been told once can never be repeated. And what happened once, happened once and for all. There is still something, however, that confuses me. Several times over these years, at unpredictable intervals, the image of a blazing gateway at the entrance to a lavish celestial palace comes to me, and I see myself walking along a path of clouds and going from one palace to another larger one, so large that the first palace is inside it, and the larger one is inside yet another, larger still, and so on, until I arrive at the last palace, in which there is a throne so grand that, no matter how far back I stretch my neck, I cannot see its end. If the throne is so vast, I remember thinking, how large is he who sits upon it? At that moment, crystal clear, I hear the trumpets announcing: The Lord is coming any minute now. Then I see myself on the way back and I gape, mouth open, at the arabesques on the walls. Where was I? Is it possible that I did follow Eleazar that evening, that we were on the verge of realizing what had been planned? I am sure I was barefoot, for as I was clambering over the entrance threshold of the last palace, I tripped and scraped the big toe on my right foot. The skin on the toe puckered up like a curly little cloud, exposing a deep wound that did not bleed. I leaned over to look at it, thinking I should urinate into it to disinfect it, then heard a voice within me, which was not mine, saying: Not to worry, in heaven there is no bleeding. Of course not, I thought later, angels aren't warm-blooded animals like us, to say nothing of God. Of course, if he created us in his own image and shape, wouldn't it stand to reason that he too would bleed? I ask that of my reflection in the window, but the reflection is silent, the pane doesn't hum, the night is still. I read once somewhere that our exterior is truly the image of God, but what is inside of us was created by someone else. It didn't say who. Perhaps I should have asked him while I was wandering barefoot around his palaces? More and more often I see our life as essentially consisting of a host of lost chances, with some exceptions. Again my pen records furrows instead of letters, just as life leaves gaps, the difference being that we can change pens, while life is like a blade that, once dull, can no longer be sharpened. A dull knife, that's me. All I can do is groan while I try to carve the sediment of memory into a series of words and sentences. Far away, where it all happened, no one is interested in these words and sentences anyway, and maybe it is best that I go out this very night, before I change my mind, and bury them in the woods, on a slope, under a birch tree, in a box. After that I'll do nothing but keep my silence. There, silent.